What's in a man . . . or gadget?

I0549534

Barry B. Longyear's

JAGGERS & SHAD

ABC is for Artificial Beings Crimes

♠

A Mystery Casebook

Enchanteds

Enchanteds Publishing

PO Box 100, New Sharon ME 04955

www.Enchanteds.net

Jaggers & Shad: ABC is for Artificial Beings Crimes is a collection of fiction. The contents of this work are either products of the author's invention or are used fictitiously. Any resemblance to actual persons or events are coincidental.

In their previous incarnations, the following stories appeared in *Analog Science Fiction Science Fact:* "The Good Kill" (November 2006), "The Hangingstone Rat" (October 2007), "The Purloined Labradoodle" (January/February 2008), and "Murder In Parliament Street" (November 2007). This is the first publication of both "The Colleton Ghost" and "The Sheriff's Tale." "The Good Kill" and "Murder in Parliament Street" both won AnLab Awards voted on by *Analog* readers.

ISBN-13: 978-0615469560
ISBN-10: 0615469566

Manufactured in the United States of America

CONTENTS

♠

♠

FOREWORD

When Sir Harrington Jaggers asked me if I could see my way to consent to pen a forward for this work, my reply to him was that I would have been terribly offended had I not been invited. This was not only due to my close ties with law enforcement programs over the decades, but due as well to my late father's and my own personal contributions to the following award-winning tales of the early cases of Detective Inspector Harrington Jaggers and his partner, Detective Sergeant Guy Shad. I am most pleased to be associated with these stirring accounts of Interpol's Artificial Beings Crimes Division's Devon office.

The following chronicles are set late during my father's reign which was early in the empire's efforts to come to grips with the special problems and issues related to the remarkable advances in Artificial Intelligence and biological engram-imprint technology. There were many regrettable mistakes during that period, injustices in profusion, and a great many things that from today's perspective seem simply silly. Nevertheless, that was the state of things in those days. It is to the credit of Interpol's General Assembly and the dedicated members of their Baghdad regional office, headquarters of ABCD, as well as the men, women, mechanicals, and bios of Interpol's ABCD that the law now applies equally to all, regardless of race, nationality, creed, religion, or self-aware neural control configuration. Sir Harry's accounts of those harrowing days of yesteryear, although ripping good tales in themselves, should be a lesson to us all. The courage, integrity, and ingenuity of the detectives of ABCD's Devon office were tested mightily by both the clever and the powerful, one of whom in particular would have left most of us I imagine helplessly entreating an answer to Juvenal's ageless question: *Quid agas, cum dira et foedior omni crimine persona est?**

Jaggers and Shad had an answer.

Mehitabel R
  at Balmoral

♠

*What can you do, when the man himself is more foul and filthy than any slander you can sling at him? — *Juvenal, Satire 4*

THE GOOD KILL

-1-

The Rent-A-Mech, Walter, had just put my breakfast on the table when Detective Superintendent Matheson rang me. *"Forgive me for ringing you so early, Jaggers, but London ABC wants us to look into that fox hunting matter at Dartmoor. Apparently there's an amdroid involved. It's an outdoor scene and if you don't move quickly the evidence may become contaminated . . . ."*

Matheson hadn't begun with a knock-knock joke, which meant he was troubled. The Miles Bowman death was the biggest story to hit Devon in decades. The wealthy and charismatic Master of Houndtor Down Hunts had died, I had gathered from yesterday's news reports, when he had been thrown by his horse during a run. Apparently someone in the park police was exploring another theory.

Val momentarily looked up from the table where she had been lapping her single cream. Seeing nothing to distress her, she twitched her tail as if to launch an unwelcome insect and resumed emptying the saucer. A sepia and golden Tonkinese, her soft coat colored in a random watermarked silk pattern, she was much too elegant ever to be observed using the litter box, although I supposed she must be using it. It was, after all, being used. Perhaps she had friends in.

"Jaggers? Jaggers, there. Pay attention. Blast! When are you getting a modern screen phone? Bloody hell. Jaggers?"

With a parting glance at my rapidly cooling eggs and bacon, I responded into the handset, "Yes, superintendent. You were saying?"

"Now, I've made a good number of allowances for you, Jaggers, because of your record. You were once an impressive detective. Do not take advantage. Am I understood?"

"Certainly, superintendent."

"You're going to want to get to the scene before it rains."

I shifted my gaze to the glass door that looked into the garden as Matheson continued. The mid-March sky over Exeter was gloomy gray with curtains of mist coming up from the river. *"The park constabulary think they have their murderer, Jaggers. London wants us to go through everything. After all, artificial beings are our bailiwick. Ready to receive?"*

I toggled the receive on my hand desk. "Go ahead, superintendent."

"Sending now."

As the case file form and location instructions loaded, I mulled the late Miles Bowman's place in the scheme of things. In certain upwardly crusted circles, Bowman's death was immense. Houndtor Down had brought riding to the hounds and the good kill back to Albion after an eight decade hiatus dotted with less than satisfying drag hunts and those absurd experiments with AI equipped robotic foxes. Houndtor's answer was to introduce genuine bio fox amdroids for prey, but imprinted with human engrams. The fox, therefore, would be physically a fox, but no longer a fox according to the prohibition against fox hunting, in that the creature understood the consequences and could volunteer. In actuality, the vermin was a human in a fox's "meat suit," entitled under law to engage in whatever absurd, but legal, occupation he or she chose. Nevertheless, where one got volunteers was a puzzle.

I'd never been at the Houndtor Down Lodge, although I had witnessed a bit of one of the operation's hunts on Cripdon Down the year before when I was on an easily resolved poodle abuse enquiry. The amdroid poodle had undeniably abused her owner, a Harley dealer from Torbay. However both poodle and woman confessed to being consensual S&M partners in the area for a hunt, hence no crime. Too bad really. The poodle matter promised to be the most interesting case I'd been on since being assigned to the Devon office. Nevertheless, since I was on the moor then and a hunt was on, I watched. Except for the chase being followed above by a hoard of hovercraft, the hunt itself had been something caught in amber. Elegantly costumed riders mounted on magnificent steeds chasing a huge pack of handsome foxhounds, the peculiar warbling notes of the Master's tiny horn signaling the sighting of the prey. As long as you weren't particularly fond of foxes, it was rather uplifting.

The lodge was twenty-five kilometers southwest of the city just beyond the village of Lustleigh on the east edge of the moor. The enormously lucrative concession had its own skydock and the park detective in charge, one DCI Stokes, condescended to have a constable at Houndtor Down to bring us up to speed. "Superintendent, on the killing, did the park cops get a verbal?"

"No. This Stokes fellow is certain he has his killer, nevertheless: Lady Iva Bowman, Miles Bowman's wife."

Lady Iva Bowman. The image of that stunning beauty was fixed in the nation's memory. Her marriage to Bowman had been little short of a media coronation.

"Their theory is Bowman and Lady Iva, along with the hunt staff and some eighty followers and club members, were in the middle of one of their smaller commercial runs when Miles was found dead along the route. Lady Iva inherits and I gather from DCI Stokes she had just learned that her husband was bonking the company's lead second horseman, one Sabrina Depp."

"Motive and opportunity," I commented.

"They're up the wrong branch, Jaggers."

"You disagree, sir?"

"I knew Lady Iva years ago. For all her beauty, she is old school, very refined. I can't see her getting down into the muck and beating a grown man to death with what appears to have been a horseshoe, regardless of the provocation. In fact, I rather suspect Miles Bowman's horse."

"An amdroid?"

"Yes. The horse isn't running on a human imprint, though. It appears a year ago a favorite jumper of

Bowman's was near death from an injury and Bowman spent a not inconsiderable fortune to have the mount's engrams copied and imprinted on an equestrian meat suit drawn from the mount's own DNA."

"That which Miles rides shall never die," I dogmatized.

"Quite. I suspect Bowman's nag determined one lifetime under Miles Bowman's arse was sufficient."

"In which case, superintendent, it wouldn't be a murder."

"All of which I imagine Lady Iva would very much like to have established as quickly as is feasible. —Oh. Swing by Heavitree Tower before you leave for Dartmoor. You have a new partner: DS Guy Shad."

"You're having a laugh, right, superintendent?

"Not really."

"Guy Shad? Sounds like someone copied the name off an old action vid poster."

"That is his name, Jaggers. Shad is an American."

"Of course he is. Now, we agreed—"

"This isn't a negotiation, DI Jaggers. Shad has been assigned to this enquiry because of his prior association with two of the principles, as well as his familiarity with the artificial being end of the law enforcement spectrum. He'll be waiting at the skydock." That warning edge crept back into the superintendent's voice: *"Grasp the nettle, Jaggers. It's up to you to make this work."*

"Yes, superintendent."

A significant pause, and then the superintendent decided to lighten the mood. *"Jaggers: Knock, knock."*

"Ringing off, superintendent. There appears to be someone at the door."

I quickly hung up the handset as I muttered, "Brilliant," to no one in particular. After the dreadful experience I had partnered up with the ever effervescent Ralph Parker, I thought Matheson and I had agreed I always work solo.

Guy Shad. American. He'll want to eat at Wendy McDonald's Kentucky Burger Hut and call me Bud, I mused. I certainly hoped Parker's meat suit was one of a kind. I'd go into retirement before I was made to work with another Parker.

I looked at Val and she was eyeing my bacon and eggs. "You may as well," I said to her as I petted her head and went toward the hallway to get my raincoat and hat. "I have to get to work. I'm on the Miles Bowman matter."

"Is something wrong?" she asked.

"The superintendent's assigned me a new partner. An American named Guy Shad."

She looked at me with those stunning aqua eyes and said, "Give him a fair chance, Harry. I don't want to worry. Is Walter coming in this evening?"

"Yes."

Val looked at me for a moment then averted her gaze. "I'm sorry I can't cook for you Harry."

"You catch mice. That's quite as important."

"You're a dear, but you know Walter keeps this place so clean, there hasn't been a mouse to catch in months." She turned back to my plate and continued lapping at the yolk.

"Have a good day, dear," I said and closed the door.

2

As the division sky cruiser assigned to me headed south into the muck above the city, there probably wasn't going to be any need to get small; the animal android involved, after all, was a horse. Nevertheless, routine is its own reward, as the superintendent was wont to remark between knock, knock inanities. I ran up the mechs and they went through their system scans in case we'd have to copy into them. They were mechs of assorted sizes and configurations useful for obtaining evidence in places tight, high, or otherwise inaccessible to humans. Meanwhile, I checked InterNews on Miles Bowman's death. Indeed, Lady Iva had been taken into custody, Detective Chief Inspector Raymond Stokes of the Devon-Exmoor National Park Constabulary stated in his news conference, blah, blah, blah—

My mood was terrible and it was time I faced up to it. I was having quite a bit of trouble letting go of having a new partner thrust upon me. I knew full well why ABC Division had human imprinted animal androids as investigators. That's one criminal dimension that necessitated the creation of our component of Interpol. Still, almost every amdroid I ever worked with had such bizarre excuses for having wound up in a critter meat suit, I was convinced it couldn't help but have an effect on their work. It certainly had with Parker.

DC Parker had been the worst of a succession of amdroids assigned to work with me. It wasn't just the thick Estuary accent Parker affected, his odor, the incessant grunting, or that he had difficulty in controlling his bowels. It was Parker's effect on a subject during an interview. I don't think I'm being unfair when I say undergoing interrogation by a thirty-five stone mountain gorilla puts some people off. Banana peels and fruit flies all over the cruiser—fleas. I mean, *really.*

As the cruiser descended out of the overcast above the new Consolidated Police Administration Tower on Heavitree Road, I could see that the only living being waiting for me on the skydock was a Mallard duck complete with green head, white neck ring, chestnut breast, grayish-white feathers, yellow bill, and orange feet. "Showing at a crime scene with Daffy in tow; that'll put the yobs in a fright."

As the cruiser's computer control put the vehicle down in the center of the landing target, I declined a slot assignment, put the power on standby, and pressed the buttons to open both doors. I looked around briefly in waning hopes that this was some sort of practical joke, then resignedly got out of the driver's side and trudged over to where the duck was standing. "DS Shad?" I inquired.

"I'm Shad," said the duck in a voice that sounded very much like—a duck.

"Detective Inspector Jaggers," I introduced myself.

"I know just what you're thinking," he said. "My god, a duck! I sure feel safe now that poultry has my back. Where ever does he keep his handcuffs? What was that idiot Matheson thinking to saddle me with this fugitive from a Chinese restaurant! I ought to go down to the superintendent's office right this minute and put in for my walking papers! You've laid an egg this time, pigeon-brain. This is for the birds! Are you out of your bleeding mind? *A duck!*"

"Sorry. Didn't mean to ruffle your feathers."

He held out a wing. "Bird jokes? It's going to be bird jokes?"

"Actually, I was going to ask if you wanted to drive."

Shad lowered his wing, gave me a bit of a look, then flew into the open driver's side of the cruiser. "That went rather well," I muttered to myself.

I got into the passenger side, buckled in, and faced the duck. The power revved up, the doors closed, and the cruiser lifted off the landing target and headed southwest into the morning commuter traffic, the duck standing motionless on the seat. The GPS showed that our destination and control had somehow been given to the autopilot. "Wireless interface," smugly explained Shad.

"Something you should know about me, as well, Shad."

"What's that?"

"I am a detective inspector, your senior as well as your superior, and if you should ever shoot off your bill to me like that again, me lad, I'll stuff and roast your goose proper."

"Ah, yes, sir. I apologize, despite the additional gratuitous fowl references." After an awkward moment of silence, he glanced at me. "Admit it, though: I am an improvement on Parker."

"You met him?" I asked.

"Back at the tower he mentioned something about having been your partner. Does Parker have a banana problem?"

"At least." I glanced at Shad. "You do take up less space."

"And I don't crap in the cruiser."

"That is an asset." We both laughed at that.

Later, visibility almost down to zero as we approached the Alphington vector roundabout, Shad said, "Matheson told me to fill you in on my connection to Houndtor Down."

"Please."

"Back in New York about ten years ago, I knew Miles Bowman's business partner, Archie Quartermain. I was a human, Archie was English, and we roomed together in a roach hotel in the Village. Back then we were both starving, taking acting lessons, and trying to get theater acting careers started. Archie waited tables and hustled vidgames, and I was a part time police assistant at the local precinct, answering phones, filing, that sort of stuff. We were doing cattle calls and getting an occasional walk on. Remember the Gladys Hudder case, when that DNA bio of Cary Grant sued his owner for emancipation?"

"The case that took the 'slave' out of 'slavery' for the human imprinted and self-aware AI population."

"Yeah, what would you rather be: an eighty year old woman's boy toy or a filthy rich reincarnated Hollywood superstar covered with babes?"

"Decisions, decisions," I added.

"Anyway, that case put Archie onto something," Shad continued. "He wouldn't talk to me about it. Kept saying, 'I'm not finished yet.' Still, he had some kind of scheme cooking. Every now and then when he was out I'd sneak a peek at what he was doing, but it was all technical stuff on staging, theatrics, English history, artificial being law, air transport, artificial intelligence, business, computers, and android-amdroid bios and mechs. Then, one day when I was particularly hungry, the New York PD called for recruits—"

"—You saw how much police recruits were being paid," I interjected.

"Yeah, well, my stomach and I had a long talk and I entered the police academy. Training took up all my time, the work was interesting, and they kept me running as a probie. I lost track of what Archie was doing. My police probationary period eventually ended, I was assigned to a precinct patrol unit, and then I met a girl."

My eyebrows went up.

"No. Her name wasn't Daisy," Shad responded with a modicum of heat. "Her name was Shondelle." The duck glanced out the side window at a break in the clouds which revealed still more clouds.

"Archie was my best man when I married her. When I moved out, Archie moved in with another starving actor, Miles Bowman. I got to know Miles a little, but a year later both of them moved back to England. By the time I made detective, Archie and I had lost touch altogether. A couple years later, right before I was killed, Houndtor Down Hunts hit the media, fox hunting was back, Miles Bowman was big news, filthy rich, and married to the daughter of an earl. But no mention of Archie Quartermain."

I glanced at Shad. "You suspected something?"

"Sure. I sent a message to Archie and he eventually sent back his thanks but no thanks for the attempted rescue. According to him, everything was going according to plan. I did a little checking on my own and found out why Archie wasn't getting any billing. He's a *really* silent partner in Houndtor Down Hunts. Archie Quartermain is the fox."

"You're joking."

"No. See, he copies his engrams before each hunt. If he wins he wins, but if he gets killed, he's copied into a new bio cloned from his previous meat suit. It's really not as grim as you might think."

"Perhaps I'm making too much of being torn apart by a slavering pack of hounds."

"He never remembers getting killed, see? When he does get killed, the set of engrams copied before the hunt are imprinted into the new fox suit and the new fox inherits but doesn't remember."

"But he knows he's going to get killed."

"Archie told me it's like getting a knee operated on, except when he wakes up from his procedure it doesn't hurt."

"It still strikes me as rather a punishing way to make a living."

"You've never been an actor, have you?"

"No."

"Take my word for it, boss; there are roles to kill for and roles to die for." He gave a duck shrug. "Besides, win or lose Archie's take per hunt is close to three million."

"Per hunt?"

The duck nodded. "Each of the followers pays thirty thou or so to ride to the hounds, and there are eighty to a hundred or more per hunt, but that's not where the real money is. The big cash cows in the fox hunting racket are the tally-hovers: air hover pods that follow along the route of the hunt, giving their passengers all the thrill and excitement of the hunt without the need of learning how to ride or risking any jumps. Tally-hover seats run three thousand per, which includes the virtual of the hunt complete with the purchaser's face and body CGI substituted for the scarlet or black coat of his or her choice, and the entire ride experienced from the point of view of one of several riders."

"How many of those tally-hover seats do they fill on an average hunt?"

"Thousands."

"Astonishing. I find it difficult to believe that anyone would pay that much for a bit of a thrill ride that can be excelled by any number of virtual computer games."

"Ah, that's where you're wrong. See, inspector, it's not just the thrill of a dangerous horse ride and the challenge of ganging up with hundreds of hounds, nags, and snobs to chase down and kill a small dog. What you also get for your money is to be seen at the opening tea ceremony and other refreshment stops along the route dabbing lips and raising pinkies with such luminaries as Lady Iva Bowman and Lord Peter Talmadge. Talmadge is the hunt's paid snob draw. There's also an old rock star and an old movie star as draws for the upwardly mobile Lumpenproletariat who crave an association with fame. Archie Quartermain has fifty percent of the company. I'm betting he's the richest fox in the world."

"And the dottiest." I frowned as I thought of something. "Does Lady Iva inherit Miles Bowman's interest?"

"Unless she's found guilty of murdering Miles."

"If she doesn't inherit, who does?"

"They don't have any children, so Archie gets it all. Interesting, no?"

"To say the least." I turned toward Shad. "None of which explains how a New York City cop wound up being a duck in Interpol's Artificial Beings Crimes Division."

"This is where I bare my soul, right?"

I held up a hand and dropped it to my lap. "Not a requirement. A desire to understand."

"In that case, I'll tell you. I think I said I was wounded in the line of duty."

"Actually, you said you were killed."

We began descending from the Bovey Tracy Roundabout. "I was backing up some guys taking down a perp. The next thing I knew all the bullets in the world were headed in my direction and I was fricassee. When I came to, my engrams were in memory, Shondelle was pounding on my keyboard demanding to know where the car keys were, and I get a call on my modem from my agent wanting to know if I'd be willing to have my engrams imprinted on a mechanical shark for a remake of *Jaws* that was going into production."

"You agreed?"

He faced me with an expression of astonishment. "It was *Hollywood*. *Jaws*. With a role like that in my credits, who knows what other roles I might've been offered. That

16

was when my agent changed my name. He figured a shark named Donald Lipper would be hard to take seriously."

"Your given name is Donald?"

The duck leveled a rather menacing gaze at me. "Don't go there, man."

"What about your wife?" I asked, judiciously changing the subject.

"Shondelle," muttered the duck. "Even though I explained what a huge break this would be for us, she took a walk. With the bread I could've made from a production like *Jaws*, I could've had my engrams imprinted on a six-figure bio of anything or anyone she wanted. No dice, though. The first person she called after she left my terminal was a divorce shark."

"My sympathies. What happened regarding the remake?"

"What else? *Jaws* bit it. I was about ready for a karma transplant. A week later, though, my agent came through with a pretty good commercial gig. It was a role that before had been limited by computer generated imaging and trained animals. They were finally ready to move up to a real actor."

"What was it?" I inquired.

"Spokesentity for an insurance company."

Shad saw my expression.

"Yeah. That's the one. Really. That's me."

I frowned at him. "That duck was white."

"Make up," Shad explained. He looked forward as our descent crossed the edge of Dartmoor, vast expanses of hilly bracken and grassland interrupted by rocky tors all beneath a gloomy sky. "Good years of really great physical comedy. I was on all the talk and game shows. I was the duck who turned the world onto disability insurance. But then the company was taken over by another insurance outfit. The new bunch wanted to use their own mascot: a creepy little computer generated lizard, the same old animation they'd used for fifty years."

"Unfortunate. I really enjoyed your adverts on the telly, Shad. Very amusing."

Shad shook his head and angrily padded on the seat from one webbed foot to the other. "Treat me like some CGI that'd gone out of style. *Me!* I put life in that duck. I brought new dimensions to that role. I was the one who made that company a household name in every palace and hoodoo hutch on this planet. That's what dedication, hard work, and loyalty get you: No severance, no residuals, out with the old letterheads." He took a breath and let it out. "Anyway, alone, out of work, and no prospects, I went to the International Police Benevolent Association and invoked the 'still living and able' employment clause. They either had to put me on pension or find me a job in law enforcement."

"So they sent you to ABCD."

"First I was with Northern New England Wildlife Protection investigating duck hunting violations. Lucky I had this connection with Archie Quartermain."

"Oh?"

"Whether it's illegal to shoot a wildlife officer who's a duck during duck hunting season really hasn't been settled yet."

"I see what you mean."

"Besides, I had a supervisor who was an Eared Grebe. That's a bird."

"I assumed it was either that or an illegal wrestling hold."

Shad gave my joke a truncated pity laugh and continued, "Dudley Baumgartner. A small bird, he had a big black crest and these flaky little golden ear tufts he was really proud of. He could've been an American bald eagle, but BioDyne couldn't legally recode the bald eagle DNA to give him black head feathers."

"Why on earth would he want that?"

"Baumgartner was very sensitive about hair loss."

"Eagles don't have hair."

"Tell it to Baumgartner. —Red eyes, his voicebox implant programmed to talk like a frog—I'm telling you, boss, this case is saving more than my life."

"Speaking of programmed voiceboxes, Shad, why do you use this duck voice. I mean, it's still rather comical."

"This is the voice that made me a star."

The cruiser came in over the village of Leighon and up a gentle rise to a wood of oaks, maples, and conifers at the eastern foot of Hound Tor. In the center of the wood was a clearing, and in the center of the clearing, at the intersection of a maze of bricked paths and boxwoods, was the grand lodge of Houndtor Down Hunts, a city within a palace made familiar by countless posters, post cards, vid story settings, skyvault projections, and telly commercials.

A circular drive only slightly smaller than the M-5 ran from the front steps to an improved road that lead north toward Manaton. Most of Houndtor's clientele came in by air. The huge sky dock was south of the lodge. The dock appeared to have parking slips for only a few hundred vehicles, but as we came in over it, I could see the access lanes to additional parking slips floors below ground level. As we descended onto one of the multiple landing targets, I noticed with some alarm that Shad was shaking his tail feathers back and forth. "I say, Shad, do you need to go to the loo?"

"What?" He glanced back at his own shaking tail. "Oh." He dismissed my concern with another wave of his wing. "Updating my anti-virus definitions."

3

Despite the promised rain, the gardening staff was out in force clipping, pruning, weeding and such. No one else, staff or guests, seemed to be about. Of course the promised park constabulary vehicle and driver were absent, which was a dual problem for us since the ABCD charter requires us to turn our case over to the local authorities in the event an arrest is to be made. The missing fellow, in addition, was supposed to bring us to the scene and copy us the park constabulary's current case file. "Typical," I muttered as we exited the cruiser. "A thing you'll notice during your time with ABCD, Shad, is that, as you Americans say, we can't get no respect."

"Let me see if I can scare up our ride," said Shad, pointing his right wingtip up at the sky.

"You can fly?"

"But of course." He took a running step, furiously flapped his wings, and took off low across the ground, gradually increasing his altitude in an ever widening arc to the right. Quite beautiful, really. Almost completing a circuit of the clearing, south of the skydock he dropped from the sky like a hawk, disappearing into the trees below. This was shortly followed by rather loud duck calls, and the whine of an electric energizing. In moments a green and white Park Constabulary electric emerged from the trees, my partner perched triumphantly upon its light array.

Police Constable Lounds was a lethargic lad about fifteen stone, dark complexioned, and keeping both head and face hairless. Clad against the anticipated precip in a constable's yellow anorak, he appeared to be torn between his affected contempt for the "Interpollys," as local police are wont to address ABCD investigators behind their backs, and his actual esteem-crushing shame for being so terribly low in DCI Stokes's estimation as to be the one detailed to meet with us. His eyes were puffy and there was a bit of dried drool on the left side of his chin. Lounds had been napping. He pulled his desktop from his belt array and transferred the current Miles Bowman murder casebook to my portable. We boarded the vehicle, Lounds in the driver's seat, I in the passenger seat, and Shad up on the light array. Lounds drove us to the scene following a route marked by numerous hoof impressions. I noticed carefully hidden motion cameras and sound pickups in several places along the way. It appeared as though the vid director and those manning the cameras and audio for the tally-ho virtuals knew exactly which course the wily old fox would take during the hunt. Probably all the details had been worked out with Archie Quartermain prior to the meet where the followers joined the hounds, tipped their hats to the Master—now deceased—and sucked down the first of several libations offered along the way. Call me old fashioned, but the fox being in on the planning of the hunt seemed to take at least a bit of the sport out of the thing.

The route Constable Lounds took led around the ends of several hedges and fences none of which enclosed anything. They were placed there, obviously, to provide the mounts and riders barriers over which to jump.

Eventually we crossed sheep-grazed grassland up a moderate grade to the left of Hound Tor, a magnificent citadel of weathered granite towers, a motorway-wide notch through the center of which became visible once we crossed the crumbling remains of an old asphalt road and reached midway between the lodge and a grove of conifers near the crest of the down. "Scene's up there," said Lounds.

I faced him and saw he was nodding toward the pines. I noticed my partner flying on ahead of us, soon disappearing behind some trees. I took a moment to look at the case file, but could find nothing in it referring to an interview with Archie Quartermain. "Are you familiar with this case file, constable?" I asked Lounds.

"Read it twice waiting for you and your feathered friend there, guv. Fact is, I was first responder here." He shrugged resignedly and stifled a yawn. "Been here since."

"All night?"

"I was supposed to get relieved but some bloody cock-up left me carrying the can."

"I don't see any interview with the deceased's business partner, Archie Quartermain."

"The fox y' mean, guv? He's in a hole somewheres."

"No one's seen him?"

Constable Lounds tapped his own portable desk in its holster. "Only address Quartermain's got's here at the lodge. He don't have a room, though. No room and hundreds of millions in the bank."

He parked the vehicle, we got out, and crossed the tape. There was a lane through the grove made by the trees being thinned to where no two of them in the path were any closer than six meters from each other. The trees themselves were Quik-gro pines, the vegetable kingdom's twenty-meter tall answer to Quik-gro human and amdroid meat suit bios. The tree branches throughout the entire wood had been trimmed to four meters plus from the ground. Within the confines of the path, then, there was an intermittently clear view from above, allowing the tally-hover spectators to follow the riders with their eyes and cameras with no one actually riding to the hounds being more than a second or two out of view from someone above. Off the lane, however, the view from above was completely blocked due to the closeness of the trees. The yellow tape placed by the scenes of crime officers enclosed part of the lane but extended deeply into the off-lane trees.

"We got the vids, guv, both the lodge's and from the folks up in the hovers."

"Did anyone catch the actual killing on camera?"

"Not a one. Bowman got his in the thick of it." Lounds pointed a finger toward our left. "Trail vids got Miles, his misses Lady Iva, Huntsman Diana Weatherly, Lead Second Horseman Sabrina Depp, the head whipper-in Thomas Flock, his nibs Lord Peter Talmadge, and that old west end actress Dotty T off the main track here."

"Dotty—Dorothea Tell, do you mean?"

The constable grinned. "Grand old lady. She got 'er a meat suit'd break your heart, guv." I couldn't help but smile. Dorothea Tell, my childhood fantasy love from afar. I had seen all her early plays and I still had the vids of all her movies. PC Lounds's face grew troubled. "DCI Stokes told me you're Interpollys and you're not to make arrests. That's my job."

"We are aware of the regulations." I nodded toward the deep woods. "What do you think, Lounds?"

His bunchy little eyebrows arched. "Me?"

"You've read the file, you're a trained police officer, I'd like your take on it."

"Well, guv," he began, slightly surprised at being asked, "only ones I know bring horseshoes to a fox hunt is horses."

"Constable Lounds, you will be pleased to hear that my superintendent agrees with your assessment. Do you know why your DCI Stokes discarded that theory?"

Lounds looked very uncomfortable. He glanced up at the still darkening sky, then shifted his gaze to me. "Off record, inspector?"

"Of course."

He pursed his lips and nodded once. "'Titled Lady Croaks Multi-millionaire Hubby In Grisly Slaying' makes a juicer headline than 'Horse Kicks Rider.'"

As we walked deep beneath the cover of the trees off the lane, I could see a laser marker on a scene analyzer perhaps ten meters ahead. DS Shad came flying the other way, his landing pattern weaving between a succession of tree trunks, the touchdown right before us—a competently executed maneuver. Shad waddled over and said, "Not much left. What hasn't been taken away or trampled into the pine needles has been picked over by the wildlife."

"Can you make out where Bowman's body was found?"

"They have a Vader prang in place, but I didn't run it up." He nodded toward the cleared lane. "Notice once you get away from that open run, there aren't any cameras or audio pickups?"

I nodded and followed as Shad lead the way, Constable Lounds bringing up the rear. Once we were next to the tree where the scene analyzer was attached, I asked Lounds to activate it. He took out a remote and did so, a high-definition image of the deceased Miles Bowman appeared in its place on the forest floor two meters west from the base of the tree. He was on his left side, his head pointing southwest, body curled in a loose fetal position. The image was depicted wearing scarlet coat over cream colored cravat, waistcoat, and trousers tucked into gleaming black riding boots, all of which had been marked with bloody hoof marks, the source of the blood being the deceased's scalp, face, and hands. "Full scan on the prang, Lounds," I requested.

Lounds touched the remote and the image expanded to include everything within the Vader prang's line of sight up to ten meters from the unit, which included several pairs of disembodied feet at the periphery: The scenes of crime officers awaiting clearance to approach the body. "I don't see Bowman's black velvet riding helmet," I said to Lounds.

"Lady Iva had it in 'er hand, guv."

"Be a good fellow and cycle the SOCS."

The scenes of crime sequence images cycled: Footwear impressions included all of the suspects, including Bowman's horse, as well as all of the other horses ridden by the suspects. A bloody horseshoe had been recovered from the ground near the body, and the shoe had come from Champion's right front hoof. A note: Champion's hooves had all been tested for blood and had come back negative, which would have been remarkable except when Champion had finally been recaptured, the nag was standing with all fours in a spring fed brook

I looked up at Lounds. "They didn't test the rest of the horse for blood spatter?"

The constable shrugged helplessly. "As far as he's concerned, DCI Stokes's got 'is bird—" He glanced at Shad. "Beg pardon, sergeant."

"Forget about it," answered the duck. Shad looked at me.

I nodded once in response. "Yes. It does appear to be left to us." The beginning of raindrops hitting the needles above us announced itself. I pulled up my collar, took a holoanalyzer out of my breast pocket, and nodded at Lounds.

As he turned off the prang, we were momentarily plunged into relative darkness. I turned on the pen-sized analyzer, placed it in the receptacle next to the prang to steady it, and then controlled it with my remote. By default the analyzer first projected the aggregate images: All substances on the tree trunks not actually made of that type of wood. The tree trunks appeared mostly in shades of white and gray speckled with brown, red orange, lavender, and so on.

"A lot o' stuff on them trees," observed Lounds.

"Moss, lichen, animal waste, insects, and insect waste," I said, filtering out the hundreds of thousands of colored speckles. I filtered out the bird droppings, rodent droppings, canine, and feline hair, urine, and excrement, as well.

"I hope that I shall never see a toilet filthy as a tree," quipped Shad.

There was some equine as well as human blood on the tree nearest where the body had been. The tree was a twenty centimeter thick pine standing in front of a deadfall that was well into rotting its way back into the floor of the grove. The human blood was Bowman's. The analyzer DNA matched the horse blood through the world amdroid database to Champion, Mile's Bowman's horse. There was equine hair, also Champion's. On three other tree trunks was human blood spatter in medium velocity patterns. That blood, too, was Bowman's.

I ran the spatter forms and sequence, derived the impact angles, and determined the points and order of origin. The holoanalyzer then projected a reconstruction of the blunt force impacts, and it was looking more and more as though a horse was our prime suspect. The blows that were struck, at least six of them, occurred in pairs, in that two blows were struck at a time, and with horseshoes. Superintendent Matheson couldn't imagine Lady Iva getting into the muck to beat a man to death with a horseshoe. I was having difficulty, frankly, in imagining any human beating another to death, a horseshoe in each hand held such that the flat of the shoe struck the victim each time, rather than an edge, and that three times both hands were employed delivering blows at the same time.

"Guv," said Lounds as he stifled a yawn, "Need me?"

"I suppose you could stand a nap. Are all the vids in here?" I tapped my portable.

"They are."

"We have all you can help us with, then, Constable Lounds. Drive us to the lodge and then you can take the car and go home with our thanks for all your assistance."

After an hour and a half in the lodge's walnut and leather festooned club lounge watching the professional and amateur vids of the interrupted hunt, Shad and I were swamped with useless information. Time-and-time again we saw the six riders following the hounds as they led away from the thinned lane beneath the solid canopy, then twenty seconds later, all but one returning to the lane and pausing as the foxhounds milled around searching for the scent. The prey, Archie Quartermain, appeared several times during the run. We saw him on stationary cameras coming into the lane through the grove, running along it, and exiting as he raced toward the rise beyond the grove, no one following.

No one caught Miles Bowman's demise on camera. Lady Iva Bowman, indeed, had been the first to return to the spot off the lane ostensibly looking for her husband, returning moments later with the master's black velvet cap in her hand to cry out to Lord Talmadge, who was the closest to her. He called to the others all of whom followed Talmadge and Lady Iva back to where Bowman's corpse was cooling.

Only three of the riders in the party had been carrying point-of-view vid cameras: Bowman, Talmadge, and Dorothea Tell. Miles's POV camera went dark as soon as his horse ran beneath the thick cover. No audio.

Talmadge's camera showed he was ahead of the Master when his own horse turned off the lane to follow the hounds, his camera going dark until he came out from beneath the thick cover and came up behind the staff riders back in the lane where it appeared the hounds had lost the scent. Talmadge pulled his mount up behind Tell, Weatherly, Depp, and Flock then turned, supposedly in reaction to Lady Iva's call for help. He and the others followed Lady Iva back beneath the solid cover where the images from his camera were so dark they were almost useless. Talmadge dismounted, then we could just make out the image of Lady Iva standing next to her husband's corpse.

After that, we watched Dorothea Tell's POV vid from the beginning, starting with the opening ceremonies, the fields of riders moving off, the casting of the hounds, and then, as Shad put it, "Yoicks away."

It was rather exciting watching the unedited recording. Miss Tell was quite a rider, as were the five persons with whom she was riding, the hounds almost always in view. Glimpses of Miles, Lady Iva, Lord Talmadge, even an occasional glimpse of Archie Quartermain, his white-tipped tail vanishing and reappearing as he led the chase. Midway through the lane of thinned trees, the hounds veered left and ran beneath the solid cover. Miss Tell led the other riders, her camera going dark beneath the dense cover, the images clearing as she returned to the lane.

"If we're to believe these vids," said Shad, "the only ones who could've done in Miles were his spouse and his horse."

"It's easy enough these days to doctor vids, Shad, inserting or removing anything one wants. It still takes time, though, and all those tally-hover amateur tapes seem to back up everything shown by the stationary and POV cameras." I glanced at Shad. "As subtly as you can, see if the park cop SOCOs examined any of the vids for editing."

"Check."

As I returned to Dorothea Tell's POV vid, Shad did his wireless thing. From my end the call was silent. Shad noted me watching him and I pointed at my ear. Shad pointed at my portable. "Six sixty-one," he quacked.

As soon as I opened that particular channel, I was treated to an authoritative and distinguished investigator questioning DCI Stokes on the case evidence, and about any testing that might have been done regarding any editing. The voice Shad was using was very commanding, very British, and seemed very familiar. Every syllable simply oozed gobs of absolute authority and withering contempt. No testing had been done, as it turned out, and Shad's voice intimated that having the vids examined for editing would reflect kindly upon DCI Stokes's future, whereas continuing to fail to examine them would likely earn him a posting as toilet attendant to the northernmost of the Shetland Islands.

"Very effective, Shad," I said. "The voice you were using—I know it from somewhere."

The duck nodded. "Laurence Olivier as Marcus Licinius Crassus in the old motion picture *Spartacus*. I find it works very well on most Britaucrats."

While I digested this particular facet of my new partner's sound equipment, I studied a frame of one of the stationary vids I had up on my screen. It showed a red fox, short legs, a long bushy tail, and a narrow muzzle. The creature's ears and feet were black, its tail had a white tip, and the coat was glossy and rust red. I turned and glanced through one of the many tall windows in the club lounge facing Hound Tor. The promise of rain had been fulfilled. "Shad, run the cruiser around to the front of the lodge beneath the portico. I think it's time someone interviewed the fox."

4

An hour later the rain was falling steadily on the cruiser's canopy a half kilometer south of the lodge grove giving us a distorted view of the protected site of a nameless medieval village and the large rock formation just beyond it. In the distance, occasionally obscured by patches of ground fog, rose the imposing heights of Haytor Rocks. Had the village been located in the American southwest, it would have been called a ghost town. It was little more than lanes, foundations, and the occasional restored wall with a small imitation natural stone prefab National Park information center sporting a pseudo thatched roof and pseudo brick chimney at the site's northwest corner with a rather real looking sparrow perched on its top. Shad had posted a wireless text message for Quartermain and when the fox answered, this was where he said we were to wait. Putting the waiting time to use, Shad checked with the District AB Registry for the particulars on both Archie Quartermain and Miles Bowman's horse.

"Both amdroids were gestated, grown, and activated through Fantronics, Ltd. out of London," said Shad. "The bio amdroid assignment supervisor there, Dr. Shirley Wurple, dodged my call. Her chief assistant to the assistant chief, one Martin Corbola, says he would be happy to answer all of our questions—once we present at the Fantronics legal offices, during normal business hours, a duly sworn and signed warrant for the information on Quartermain." He faced me. "The information on the horse, however, he gave up willingly."

"Horse engrams can't quite grasp the concept of litigation, I suppose. Have London ABCD apply for a warrant for Quartermain's records and to post us with the names of any Fantronics employees connected with Quartermain's transformation into a *vulpes vulpes*."

After sending in the warrant request, Shad said, "Where were you before you wound up in ABCD?"

"Metro. London Metropolitan Police."

"You mean, Scotland Yard?"

"Just 'the Yard.'"

The duck studied me. "So, you were a big time murder cop in *the Yard* and you wound up out here in West Mudflap doing grunt work for Artificial Beings Crimes . . . *how?*"

"What about you? How come you're still a duck? The International PBA pays for human meat suits for fallen officers."

"Have you ever seen those generic bios they use in the States? One size fits all. They don't come with wireless modems either."

"Also they don't fly," I added.

"There is that." He nodded. "The flying is one reason I'm a duck."

"I hear for many ams it's the sex."

Shad faced me as his eyes widened. "Are you kidding?"

"Not at all. Many species of animals have better sex than humans, I understand."

"What—did Parker tell you that?" The duck laughed with a repeated wak, wak, wak sound. "*Better* sex? Ignoring the really severe seasonal limitations for most waterfowl, have you ever seen ducks copulate?"

"I can't say that I have."

"No matter how you slice it, man, it's criminal sexual assault."

"You mean rape?"

"I'm not exaggerating." He shivered all over. "In Duckville, man, if you don't do it like that, you don't do it at all. I can't do it that way. It is one big stone cold turn-off."

"Then why don't you opt for a human meat suit?" I insisted.

"Look, when I was working for that insurance company, part of the deal my agent put together was quite a sophisticated package for their spokescritter. This duck is loaded: ENN-band wireless interface, portable engram reader, all weather thermal imaging, state-of-the-art sound, a memory bigger than the Library of Congress, disease proof, and mildew resistant. As long as I don't get shot by a hunter, sucked into jet intake, or caught by a chef, I'm practically indestructible. But it's not just that I'd have to give up all those features to put on one of those Mediocre Myron meat suits to become a mere mortal human back in New York's finest. What would happen to me—I mean, what would happen to the duck?"

"The meat suit would be put in the queue for whoever wanted to become a duck."

"That line doesn't exactly wrap around the block. I'll tell you what would happen. This little duck would be allowed to die, its mind emptier than my pension plan. This duck made me a star, put my name in *Variety*, and got me my own booth at Billy Bob's Buffalo Burger. I owe it more than letting it wind up in a recipe or a landfill somewhere."

"The love making, though, Shad. Do you miss it?" I almost regretted asking. Each question is, in its own way, a confession.

Shad stared at me for a second. "Sure, I miss it. About a year ago there was this hooded merganser I met on a landfill in Skowhegan, Maine. Cutest little tail you ever saw."

"How is a mallard attracted to a hooded merganser? Doesn't that violate some sort of law of nature?"

Shad waved a wing, dismissing the question. "Every year in New England some moose comes out of the bogs and falls in love with a dairy cow, and I'm talking real moose and real cows. You do realize I'm not a real duck, don't you?"

"Pardon me if I seem a bit dense, Shad, but it seems even more perverse for a human to be sexually attracted to a hooded merganser."

"You need to walk a mile in my webbed feet. Besides, you never saw her fluffy pink and white pin feathers. Your theory works the other way, though. She wouldn't give a mallard a second look." He faced me. "I still haven't forgotten my question."

I stared at the rivulets of rainwater streaming down the canopy. "About three years ago my wife died. It was in some sort of building explosion. Killed seven others, as well, including the bomber."

"Religious nut?"

"Insurance scam gone awry as it turned out. The fire brigade's paramedics managed to harvest my wife's engrams before she went neutral." I smiled sadly, recalling her reaction when she regained consciousness in the generic female bio the National Health and the IPBA had provided. I glanced at Shad. "She called her bio Averill Average."

Shad only nodded, his gaze fixed on some inward quandary of his own.

"My wife had many health problems: chronic headaches, arthritis, difficulties with her heart—"

"None of which Averill Average had," completed Shad.

"Quite." I let out an involuntary sigh. "She was so healthy I imagined it would be for her like being born again. To be honest with you, Shad, generic that female bio may have been, but I found her rather attractive."

"Built, huh?"

I felt myself blush. "Well . . . in a word." I glanced at him. "That notwithstanding, my wife couldn't stand her new body. She saw a therapist and all the rest, but I'm afraid she had some rather severe issues that were brought to full flower by inhabiting what she considered someone else's body, although hers was the suit's first imprint. We explored the possibility of doing a Quik-gro bio from her own DNA, but the NH and the PBA wouldn't cooperate because of her DNA's built-in health problems."

"Policy," remarked Shad.

"Indeed. The short of it was that she wanted out."

"Suicide?" asked Shad.

"No. She wanted out of Averill Average. She wanted a new meat suit."

"How? The union wouldn't spring for a second body—particularly not a designer suit. Those can cost millions."

"As it turned out, she didn't want a human bio no matter who it looked like. Valerie traded her human meat suit on eSwap for an automatic dishwasher, ten years housekeeping service from Rent-A-Mech, and an amdroid meat suit. She had her engrams imprinted on a female cat bio."

"You're married to a cat?"

"A Tonkinese. We're still together, of course. I love her very much."

The duck let out a snort of frustration. "Great. Neither of us are getting any."

I burst out with a laugh at that. "Quite." I looked over at him. "Regarding your question, I'm on my second bio myself. Between that and my experience with Val, I qualified for ABCD." And now came the difficult part. "Perhaps my work at the Yard was slipping. Set in my ways. I'd been a detective for almost sixty years. Perhaps it was the injury or Metro just needed to clear the upper ranks in order to bring up deserving youth. Whatever. Since I refused to retire, I was forced to take a position with ABCD."

"Yeah," said Shad as he nodded. "Now I know who you remind me of. You sort of look like Basil Rathbone."

"I noticed the same resemblance in this bio. I rather like it. How does one so young remember Rathbone?"

Shad placed the back of one wingtip against his forehead. "Surely you jest. Basil Rathbone, big star in the 'Nineteen Forties and 'Fifties, his Sherlock Holmes films still on the B&W vids all the time."

"Ah yes," I said as I recalled. "'Guard this with your life, Watson.' He was in *The Adventures of Robin Hood,* as well."

"I tell you, man, the Sheriff of Nottingham was a brother officer who got a bum rap from a biased media," Shad observed, then held out his wing. "So, what happened? Did you get killed?"

"The first time. The second time there was a genetic glitch in the bio that resulted in rather debilitating health problems. The IPBA insurance covered bio replacements both times, and Valerie insisted I take this one."

"What happened to the new old you?"

"My natural was ransacked for body parts with the remainder cremated and scattered in Val's garden—back when she used to garden. The faulty bio, believe it or not, is still alive and currently in the nick up in North Yorkshire awaiting trial for multiple murders."

"G'wan. North Yorkshire? Your old bio is the Harrogate Slasher? Chucky Bulvine? The guy who used a

33

portable engram assignment unit to steal an identity to disguise himself for his nighttime murder sprees?"

"That's the one. Some terminal pensioner from Otley took on my old body thinking he might get an additional four or five severely limited years out of it for next to nothing. Then one night Chucky Bulvine caught him, wiped him, did a swap, killed his first victim, then reassigned back to his old body. He kept that up, using my old body, then reverting to his usual self between killings. He might never have been caught except Bulvine's ex-wife found his body in stasis when he was out in mine and put a plastic bag over his head. By the time he returned, his old self was covered with flies."

"So Bulvine's stuck in the old you."

I couldn't help but smile. "The old me simply wasn't up to running from the police."

"Too much cop in your DNA."

"Mostly a weak heart and a pair of bad knees." I grinned as I added, "Quite a dilemma for Bulvine, though."

"How so?"

"Bulvine's best legal strategy is to drag things out until the crown's aged chief witness either dies or can be frightened off. The doctors, however, don't think the old me can possibly live another six months. Quite a predicament."

"That's the future," Shad remarked laconically. "What a fascinating modern age we live in."

I grinned as I pointed at the duck. "Lucky Jack Aubrey in the vid remake of *Master and Commander*. Right?"

"You know your fliks. In the *Master and Commander* remake, do you remember the flightless cormorant the doctor saw when the *Surprise* made the Galapagos Islands?"

"Of course."

The duck crossed his right wing across his breast, held out his left wing and did a courtly bow.

"No," I said. "I don't believe it—"

A tapping sound came from Shad's side of the cruiser. He straightened from his bow and looked down through his side of the canopy. "We better copy into the mechs, boss. It's Archie Quartermain and right now he's going into a muddy hole in the ground."

5

"No. Impossible. I cannot believe Ida killed Miles," said the fox.

Archie Quartermain paced back and forth, looking about warily in what passed for his office. The site of the medieval village below ground level was a warren of tunnels and chambers, many of the chambers being old hidey holes formed from the village's remaining root cellars, wells, and cisterns. The stone slab chamber in which our meeting took place was a little over three meters by two and contained an occupant other than Shad, Quartermain, and myself: a human skeleton.

While our meat suits reclined in the cruiser, hovering prudently out of reach of local malefactors, Shad and I were in the mechs. Mine resembled a tread mounted aluminum grapefruit topped with miniaturized vid, lighting, audio, and analysis equipment. Shad was in the fist-sized hover mech which resembled an art deco Saturn with a badly straightened set of rings. The only illumination in the chamber was provided by our mech lights. While Quartermain paced, I did a quick carbon on the skeleton to see if it was something I needed to ring in. It wasn't. The bones dated back to the Thirteenth Century. Judging from the earthenware jug next to the bones, the likely cause of death was slow suicide. From his own mech, Shad tuned into my test data and responded with a signal inaudible to the fox, *"Talk about your cold cases."*

"I don't understand any of this," Quartermain said. "Miles and Ida Bowman are —were the love story of the century. Besides, Miles was a bear of a man. Strong, muscular, good in a scrap. Ida was half his size. Beat him to death with a horseshoe? Rubbish." He stopped suddenly and looked at Shad. "The run was all wrong. Have you looked into that?"

"What about the run?" asked Shad.

The fox glanced warily at the hover egg. "It didn't follow the planned route, did it, Don? The hounds and horses were supposed to follow the glade lane through Quik Grove. Have you seen where Miles was found?"

"Yes," responded Shad, "but the horses follow the hounds and the hounds follow you, right?"

"Not that time. I zigzagged down that lane and never got off it. Suddenly all the hounds were gone." He looked at Shad. "You have GPS and wireless in that mech?"

"Yes."

"You'll see. The run was all planned out in advance, down to the last turn." The fox sat, his tail around his legs, hunched his head forward, and bared his teeth. "I'm sending you the plan as well as the performance record. I hit every mark exactly, in sequence, and on time." The fox glanced at me. "We use the records to debrief the staff after each hunt."

"Why?"

"Constant improvement at Houndtor Down, inspector. Identifying weak areas and mistakes, sharpening up the challenge, polishing the act."

My partner nodded. "Got it, Archie."

"My run was cut short at the first turn after leaving the grove. That's when I noticed none of those hounds were dripping hot slobber in my dust." The fox froze for an instant, then fixed me with a beady-eyed stare. "I have a built-in image reader in my package. Once I realized something had gone wrong with the hunt, I tuned in and peeked through Champion's eyes. He was the only amdroid in the leaders. Miles's horse was already out of the grove, running down toward Becka Brook. Champion's emotional feed spilled into his vid. I was sure something terrible had happened. I didn't find out what until I was back in my den and tuned in the message Sabrina Depp posted for me."

"About Miles's death?" I asked.

"That, Lady Iva's arrest, and that the police wanted to talk to me. It's simply all so preposterous. Iva couldn't have killed Miles. You've got to get to Champion and download his recall bank."

"When you tuned in Bowman's horse, what did you see?" asked Shad.

"A scramble of terrible images." He thought a second. "A horse hit by a lorry hauling toilets, horses horribly wounded and killed in a desert, horses falling and being blown apart by cannons—all of it at once, filled with deafening pain and panic." The fox looked at me. "It was like looking at a horse's nightmare."

There was a scuffling sound, movement beyond the old bones. Quartermain jumped over the skeleton and vanished from view. Shad and I aimed sensors at each other. He dipped his front ring and whispered, "Recognize it? The horse hit by a truck hauling toilets?"

"Yes," I answered. *"Lonely Are The Brave,* Kirk Douglas and Walter Matthau, Nineteen sixties."

"Nineteen sixty-two. The desert thing might be from an old vid called *Hidalgo,*" he suggested.

"Horses dropping and being blown up could be from any of the old movies centered on the Crimea or the Napoleonic Wars."

"Charge of the Light Brigade, Errol Flynn," said Shad. "I'll see if I can tune in Champion."

I tracked over next to the old bones and saw that beyond them was an opening between two of the foundation rocks that led to a burrow. I swiveled my sensor array in Shad's direction. "Any luck with the horse?"

"I can't get through."

"Put it off for now. I want to know the layout of all these burrows, Shad, and I want the mapping to be unobserved. Go on up to the cruiser and transfer over to a micro."

"Man," he muttered. "The last time I went out in a micro I was swallowed by a grouper. You have any idea of the disgusting things fish eat?"

"Soon."

"Yes sir," he answered with a sigh as he turned and flew out of the chamber the way we had entered.

I looked back at the skeleton. Archie Quartermain was skulking behind the ribcage. "My mate," he said furtively. "Brought me mouse." He licked his chops, panted for a brief moment, then said, "Still warm."

"Steady," I cautioned.

"She's pregnant."

I was left speechless for a moment. At least foxes were getting it on. "Well, congratulations, you sly old . . . Congratulations." Time to return to the investigation. "Tell me, Mr. Quartermain. Where do you keep your body in stasis?"

"Body?" The fox paused long enough to glance at the floor and shake his head. "This is my body now. Don't keep anything in stasis."

"Well, what about your human body? Where is that?"

"Sold it. Seed money for the operation. Brought a good price. Ask Don. Archie was a young handsome fellow in good health. Brought almost two million."

"Mr. Quartermain, I have to ask about your own possible interest in your partner's death."

"Mine?"

"If Lady Ida is found guilty of Miles Bowman's murder, you stand to inherit quite a respectable sum not to mention a very lucrative operation."

"Money. That's what you're talking about, isn't it? Money?"

"Of course."

The fox began pacing again, his nose sniffing at the chamber floor. "Mice," he said as though to himself alone. "Mice are important. Mating, grubs, grass, eggs, gates, cubs, fast-fast legs, and chickens are important. Money: that's paper." He abruptly turned and fled through that opening at the rear of the chamber. "The game," he growled huskily as his voice faded. "The game is all!"

Archie's soliloquy on priorities concluded, I tracked out of the muddy burrow and called down the cruiser. Shad was in it just completing his transfer to the micro, a flat-black colored hover vehicle resembling a stealth lipstick, one end encrusted with instruments. After hosing out the mech, I went back to my meat suit and Shad darted off to map the burrow system. While Shad was occupied doing that, I went to the lodge.

6

As evening approached, making everything dismally dark as well as wet, Shad and I were back in the cruiser, the vehicle parked at the skydock, our engrams back in our current selves. Shad was labeling the GPS tunnel map he had made. That done, he leaned back from the screen and said, "So, while I was grubbing in the dirt, you did a tour of the palace?"

"Yes."

"So? What was it like?"

I thought for a moment. "Good taste and great vision meet big money and unlimited energy."

The duck faced me and said seriously, "That sounds like approval."

"I confess, Shad, I was prepared to view the whole place as outmoded values wallowing in unlimited wealth, but it is quite well done. All the halls, rooms, great rooms, and the shopping center are stunningly beautiful, and the service is prompt, polite, and practically invisible. Did you know there are hunt clients and their families that live there all year?"

"Service?"

"Why, yes. I had a cream tea at one of the shops in the mall."

"Cream tea," he stated flatly, that hint of menace sharpening his tone just a trifle. "I don't suppose the place was set up to entertain ducks."

"Actually, the shop had a fountain, and there were real ducks entertaining themselves in the fountain's pond. They appeared to be enjoying themselves, but who can say. Ducks are so inscrutable." I glanced at him to see if he was properly steamed, but he was onto me.

His bill was open as he emitted a low laugh. "You're one of those people who believe that life is a test, aren't you?"

"How did you find your old roommate, Archie? Different?"

His demeanor grew serious. "You notice how Archie kept referring to me as Don even after I told him my name was Guy? He's in some kind of weird zone."

"I'm afraid your old roommate's gone a bit native, Shad. He said his mate has cubs on the way and you should've heard his paean to a plump warm mouse. He said something strange to me—"

"You mean other than liking Mickey sushi?"

"He was telling me what was important to him. He ended by saying, 'The game is all.' Does that mean anything to you?"

"The game is what we used to call live theater." Shad thought for a moment. "That's what he's doing now, isn't it? Live theater?"

"He's not after money. In fact, Bowman's death jeopardizes everything Archie Quartermain currently holds dear, doesn't it?"

"The same could be said for Lady Iva, boss. Miles might have been getting a little on the side from Sabrina Depp, but take my word for it, Sabrina had to have been only the latest in a long string of honeys. That's the way Miles always was. Anyway, if you are Lady Iva and want to protect hearth and home against a home wrecker, who do you kill?"

"The other woman," I answered. "And, if you want to get revenge on a rich philandering husband," I continued, "who do you see? A hit man or a lawyer?"

"Ninety-seven point three percent of prospective vengeance wreakers go for the court shark," responded Shad. He looked at me. "It's time to see a horse about a man—a dead man."

"I agree."

After leaving the cruiser in an unused loading dock, Shad and I were standing in the antechamber to the complex, a space reminiscent of the hanger deck of an aircraft carrier. Very big, very white, with technical, mechanical, and horsy looking personages hurrying this way and that at the direction of automated panels festooned with blinking lights and glowing indicator bars. The air in the space carried trace scents of paint, prepared foods, hot electrical boards, polished leather, hay, and horse manure. Directional signs pointed to various wings in the structure. In one, Talley hovers were being repaired, cleaned, polished, stocked with refreshments, and stored for the next hunt. In another wing were the vid studios sectioned into units that operated and repaired vid and sound systems, viewed, edited, and "supplemented" vids with complete sound stages and computer animation facilities. There was a third wing in which mechs of animals and other appliances were programmed and maintained—It seemed a significant portion of the birds singing in the treetops as well bunnies munching leaves along the paths were mechs. There was a complete hospital wing capable of handling most human and animal illnesses, both natural and bio. The last wing was where the operation kept horses with stalls for two hundred of Houndtor Down's horses and another three hundred guest-leased stalls. There were two barn-sized rooms attached to the wing for feed and other supplies, and a third barn-sized area which contained offices, tack rooms, employee lockers and changing rooms, and a full-sized indoor riding paddock. The hounds, we were informed, had their own separate kennel complex. All of this because at some point back in prehistory some farmer got fed up with foxes eating his chickens.

Diana Weatherly, Huntsman to Houndtor Down Hunts, joined us in her office, which was richly appointed with walnut desk, brown leather overstuffed chairs, and liquid crystal walls that currently showed striking views from the top of Hound Tor, but on a sunny day. Weatherly was in her middle forties, good-looking in a sturdy sort of way, and gave the impression of being quite fit. As she sat in one of the overstuffed chairs facing us, she was wearing a buff suede jacket over a black blouse and black skin-tight lowers, the cuffs tucked into highly polished brown riding boots. From the records we knew that Weatherly had been Master of Horsham Hunts out of Manaton, a much smaller and much less successful operation than Houndtor. When they were starting up Houndtor Down, Miles Bowman and his fox of a partner sold Archie Quartermain's old self and used the proceeds to make a down payment to buy out Horsham

Hunts. Once they closed, Bowman, Quartermain, and Weatherly moved the entire operation to Houndtor Down, Diana Weatherly becoming the operation's Huntsman, responsible during the hunt for controlling the hounds through three whippers-in, the lead whipper-in being Thomas Flock.

"Didn't Bowman run you out of business," the duck pressed.

She actually held her hand to her mouth as she giggled. "You're a queer duck."

He stared at her for two seconds. "Nevertheless."

"If you insist, ducks." She then laughed out loud with sufficient zeal and abandon to raise her exhibition to the level of wanton guffawing. Calling a duck "ducks" somehow struck her as the absolute zenith of wordplay wit. Once she regained control of herself, she said, "When I was the Master of Horsham Hunts, ducky, I was up to my ears in debt, only a step ahead of my creditors, and literally didn't know from where my next meal was coming. Thanks to Miles and Archie, I ride to the hounds at least three times a week, drive a Steel Gazelle, vacation wherever I want, live in my family's ancestral home—all taxes and debts paid—and I'm earning per year sixteen times the amount I earned the best year I ever had at Horsham. I haven't even mentioned the stock sharing plan which brings in as much as my earnings. I wouldn't have to be ungrateful to resent Miles. I'd have to be insane." She glanced at me, a bored expression on her face. "Anything else?"

"Could we see Champion?" I asked.

"I'd say it was about time," she said coolly as she stood.

We followed Diana Weatherly out of her office and the duck said to me out of the corner of his bill, "'Horse Throws Rider.'"

"For money, ducks?" I asked with a smile.

Shad glanced in my direction, studied me for a moment, then shook his head. "You're being sneaky. What do you know that I don't?"

"Five dimensions to a case, Shad."

"Left-right, up-down, in-out, time, and . . . what?" he asked. "What's DI Jaggers's fifth dimension?"

"The fifth dimension, dear fellow, is this: chances are the murderer—if indeed a murderer there is—has looked at and considered the other four dimensions much longer than the investigators, and with a lot more at risk."

"Staged?" whispered Shad as we entered the cavernous hall of the operation-owned horse stables. "You think there's a killer and the killer staged this to make it look like the horse did it?"

I pointed toward Diana Weatherly's rapidly receding back. "Let's see the horse and find out."

7

Miss Weatherly left us inside Champion's spacious stall with instructions to call one of the grooms or attendants in the area if we needed anything. The horse was a largish glossy black Arabian. He had a handsome face with a pure white patch in the center of his forehead. The source of the hair and blood from Champion found on the tree at the scene was a deep scrape high on Champion's left shoulder. "I'll check him over, Shad. While I'm doing that, give Champion a scan and see if you can access his memory."

I passed the analyzer over the horse's body and legs checking principally for blood. I found a good bit of medium velocity spatter on his chest and the front of his neck. The analyzer matched it to Miles Bowman.

"I don't get it," said Shad.

"What's that?" I asked as I logged and filed the data.

"I've been wringing this nag's sponge with my neural image reader, and Champion isn't just subhuman, boss; he's subhorse."

I faced Shad and returned the analyzer to my pocket. "How so?"

"Watch out!" screamed Shad looking behind me at something way up there.

I turned and Champion had reared back on his hind legs, his front hooves pawing at the air, his wild-eyed gaze fixed directly on me. "Bloody hell!" I cried as the hooves came down hard. Thanks to Shad's timely warning I avoided the brunt of the onslaught, only catching a glancing blow above my left temple. Nevertheless it was sufficient to knock me off my feet. I collapsed in the straw in one of the corners, my ears deafened by the most horrible screaming. When I could focus my eyes again, I was momentarily powerless to do anything but watch as Shad distracted the murderous brute from killing me by flapping his wings and running figure eights between and around the horse's legs all the time screaming "Aa-flak! Aa-flak! Aa-flak! Aa-flak!"

Torn between trying to get away from the duck and trying to kill it, Champion lost track of me long enough for me to pull myself up, stumble to the stall's gate, and get on the other side. As I slammed shut the gate, automatically latching it, Shad came flying over the top landing in the center of my chest with sufficient force to knock me on my backside.

As I sat up I saw Shad flat on his back, wings straight out against the floor, his webbed feet sticking straight up in the air. It looked to me as though he had lost a considerable quantity of feathers from his left wing and tail. "Well," he said, looking between his legs at his missing tail feathers, "I'll be plucked."

"Remarkably close to what I was thinking, as well, Shad."

"I bet." Using his wings he rolled himself over on his left side, at last flopping on his breast. Another couple of flaps and he was wobbling on his feet, which is more than I could say for myself. I noticed several drops of my own blood decorating the left lapel of my suit. "Oh dear."

"Not that bad," said Shad looking at my head. "Cut. Bruising. You might need a butterfly or two. Not as bad as it looks."

"You'll have to come home with me for dinner, Shad."

He cocked his head at me in modest wonderment. "Great. When?"

"Tonight."

The duck stared at me for a moment. "Kind of short notice."

"Can't be helped." I debated with myself for a moment, then confessed. "My last year in Metro I was wounded during an arrest. Shot. In and out my left bicep. I had it treated, went home, and told Val it was nothing."

"Then she found out the truth."

"Quite. Ever since, if I have any kind of injury, I need to provide a witness if Val is to believe that it's nothing serious. There's a man who comes in to cook—the mech I

45

mentioned, actually. His name is Walter. I'm sure he can make something you can eat."

"I eat everything but waterfowl and spinach," Shad answered. He seemed to frown for a moment. "I can tell Val your injury isn't serious, but how you got that injury is real serious. It's what I was trying to say when we were so rudely interrupted. About the neural scan I was doing on Champion?"

"Yes?"

"That nag has been fried, partner. I'm surprised he has enough of a nervous system left to feed himself."

"He seemed bloody spry to me."

Shad cocked his head to one side, glanced at the door to Champion's stall, and looked back at me. "While we were in there, someone hit Champ with an image implant. I was reading it when the horse freaked: Truck full of toilets runs over horse? Desert equine destruction—"

"Charge of the Light Brigade," I completed. "How could someone do an image implant in a horse stall unobserved? For all that matters, how could they do it in a forest? As I recall, that equipment is heavy, awkward, and that doesn't even include the power requirements."

"However impossible, that horse was panicked into trying to kill to defend itself."

"Someone is going to a lot of trouble to pin Miles Bowman's death on a horse."

"And whoever it is doesn't seem too particular about who gets killed to do it."

We both thought upon that for a moment, then I faced him. "Shad, when we were in there and you were busily and quite bravely saving my current life, there was something you kept screaming."

"Oh, that." He squatted and sat like a duck, his gaze wearily on the beautifully tan and rust tiled floor. "From my old commercials. 'Aa-flak!'"

"Yes."

"Spelled different than it sounds. Pressure is what does it. Handy during cattle calls when you're really stressed. I never forgot a line. See, when the weight's on, all I can think to say are old lines from scripts I've memorized." He faced me and said, "'Here's looking at you, kid,'" with the voice of classic actor Humphrey Bogart.

We heard a siren and in moments we saw a Houndtor Down ambulance approaching us through the corridor. "I wonder," Shad asked with just a touch of perpetually rejuvenated comedian Robin Williams in his voice, "is that for us or the horse?"

8

After informing Superintendent Matheson of our progress, leaving him even more convinced that Lady Iva was innocent, I brought Shad home for show and tell. Even after his harrowingly honest account of our brief misadventure with the deceased's horse, Val seemed less concerned about my condition or who might have caused it than she was about how famously I was getting on with my new partner.

Walter had prepared an appetizing aubergine parmesan and judging from the quantity Shad put down it was duck compatible. Despite being a mech and frequently in a state of melancholy, that evening Walter couldn't resist laughing at his own duck jokes (There was a veterinarian he knew who was a duck, but the guy was a quack). Despite Shad's exception to fowl references upon our first acquaintance, he gave Walter as good as he got with a repertory of his own mech jokes that even had Val laughing (How many screws in <u>does</u> it take to light a robot's bulb?).

Once dinner was finished, Walter cleared the table and began cleaning the dishes. Val, Shad, and I moved to the lounge. Shad stood on an end table and slurped at his mint tea, Val curled up on the folded duvet on the settee, and I sat next to her and sipped at my Assam. The telly was on to BBC 228 which was airing the original *Casablanca* with Humphrey Bogart, the lovely Ingrid Bergman, and the forgivably corrupt police official, Claude Rains. I had imagined it would be a treat for both Shad and myself, but I wasn't able to concentrate. It had been awhile since anyone had tried to kill me and all those old feelings were back again: fear, paranoia, anger, and a sense of relief I couldn't trust. Shad wasn't paying attention either.

"Jaggers?" he said. "All right if I call you Jaggers? The boss-inspector thing seems a little bulky."

"No objection. How is your south end?"

"Sore. How's your head?"

"It feels like a horse kicked it. Something you wanted to ask?"

"Yeah. After I did that scan on Champion, remember I said the nag was fried?"

"Something about being surprised he could still feed himself."

"Yeah." The duck jumped down to the floor and began pacing. "On the Benton-Lutz AB Scale, average horse intelligence is twenty-seven point something. Back there in his stall Champion came in at a four, which is only a little better than a banana slug."

"That's not fried, Shad. That's cremated."

Shad froze then slowly turned and looked at me. "Insects. Fly on a wall," he said at last. "The expression, you know? I wish I was a fly on that wall, meaning I wish I could've seen and heard what was going on in a particular place unobserved."

"Yes?"

"Remember years ago the surveillance industry offered a prize to whoever could figure out how to successfully human imprint a mech or bio vehicle under one and a half millimeters in size?"

"Yes. They couldn't compress a complete human imprint below something much larger—well, the micro you used to map the burrows today. That's as small as it can be done without a severe loss of information. Didn't the industry began experimenting using remote auxiliary processors to hold the mass of the imprint and through it direct the bio?"

"Yeah. *Bio Week* and *AI Times* both had pieces. It was a big deal for about ten minutes." Shad's pacing became a bit more frenzied. "To a man in a bug POV suit, it was supposed to seem as though he's crawling or buzzing around with everything on board, but the imprint really wouldn't be in the bug."

I leaned forward, my headache temporarily forgotten. "But they never got it working."

"No. Something to do with neural equivalency failure and remote transmission fidelity. Too much of the first and too little of the second." He stopped pacing and faced me.

"After it was dropped, Fantronics used the research they'd done to come up with a prototype master/slave unit that was put into trials to see if it would be effective and safe for implanting images for use in mental health treatment."

"I don't remember that."

"You wouldn't unless you'd been in one of the trials." He held up a wing to preempt my next question. "They had gotten a portable imprinter down to the size of a Kaiser roll and were lining up amdroids under psychiatric care for clinical trials. After my wife dumped me, I was seeing someone because of a little depression I was going through. Anyway, before the trials even got started, the wheels came off the program and it was dropped. Then Fantronics unleashed an army of media molders to assure everyone in the world that there never had been any program, and if there had been a program, Fantronics didn't have anything to do with it, and if they did have something to do with it, no serious lasting effects had been suffered."

"*Big* law suits?"

Shad whistled and held his wingtips far apart. "Law firms were beating the law schools for recruits. See, what the Fantronics lab came up with was a brand new compact way to take perfectly sane individuals and turn them stark barking bonkers." He lowered his wings. "If they could do that with a human, why not a horse?"

"Rather sophisticated, but that might be our murder weapon." I drummed my fingertips on the arm of my chair. "For what possible reason? The success of Houndtor Down Hunts has been an enormous free advert for the corporation's fantasy amdroid lines. Killing Miles Bowman with a Fantronics amdroid horse—"

"—Could destroy the corporation," Shad completed. "Disgruntled employee? Someone connected with the cancelled project?"

"Fund my project or I'll take everyone in Fantronics down with me."

"It could get us a trip to London, Jaggs. I love the parks there."

"It's a little early for vacationing." I pointed at my partner. "Get on the net and see how Fantronics's stock is doing."

After a few moments of tail twitching, Shad looked at me. "No real changes: between three-ninety and four hundred a share, the same as it's been since the general market increase this past January. No layoffs at Fantronics. They're hiring." He paused for a moment. "Want to supervise a recreational program for used bios that've been engram scrubbed? Some housebreaking training involved, no experience necessary, bring your own mop?"

"I have another commitment."

Shad whistled. "Want to know the starting salary?"

"It would only discourage me." I took a sip of tea and put my cup down on the coffee table. On the telly Claude Rains was shocked, shocked to find out there's gambling going on in Casablanca. I picked up the remote and paused the flik. "We're not getting anywhere with motive. Let's focus on means."

"Okay." With a flap and a hop, Shad was back on the end table. He took a slurp of his tea, sat down, and said, "We know the ability exists to remotely implant images that can trigger off a homicidal nightmare, and it's pretty clear something like that was done to Champion when the horse killed Bowman and when he tried to kill us." Shad looked at me. "And?"

"If we can find out where the image implant device was located when it triggered Champion in his stall, we might find a trail that we could follow to our killer. I haven't looked at your burrow map. Any of those burrows come near the stables?"

"No burrows. Just a conduit carrying vid feeds to the studio wing. No access into the pipe. The actual fox burrows are pretty much limited to Old Bones Village extending south and southwest from the ruins coming up at various places on Houndtor Down, Holwell Lawn, and Hedge Down on the other side of the road to Manaton. They have remote camera hookups throughout the whole area so they can continually vary the route of the chase. Only the burrows in the village are dirt and rock. The long ones that come up in the chase areas are forty centimeter diameter plastic pipe. Archie's hair is in the Old Bones Village burrows and throughout the pipes that come up in the chase areas.

"If Houndtor Down Hunts put in all that pipe, the plans should be on file with the Dartmoor National Park Authority. There has to be a way get at Champion's stall. When you have a minute, Shad, access the plans on file with the authority and see how they compare with your map."

"Will do. Something to think about though, Jaggs." Shad glanced at Val, noted she was sleeping, and said in a lower volume, "That horse is still a dangerous weapon. How's your head? Personally, I'm not eager to donate any more feathers."

"Point taken." I looked at Val. Often when she looked asleep she was only relaxing. Then a thought came to mind that chased away all caution. "What about us, Shad?"

"Us?"

"We both have bio receivers. If our killer has the means to make horse amdroids crazy, what about us?"

He looked down and slowly shook his head. "The prototype made humans crazy. That's why the program was dumped. I think we have to assume whoever made Champion crazy can do the same for us, and will do it if we get in their way."

"Even killers have to sleep sometime," interrupted Val as she yawned and stretched her front legs.

"I apologize for keeping you up, dear," I said. "We'll be done in a minute."

The duck jumped from the end table to the floor and waddled over to Val's end of the settee. "I believe Val was suggesting that right now might be an opportune time to sneak into the stable wing to take a peek."

"Smart bird," she responded as she rose, arched her back in a global stretch, turned around twice, and settled back into the same exact position.

She was probably right, too. Unless the killer had accomplices, there was no way to stand guard on everything all of the time. I stood, petted Val's head and ran my hand down her back. "Thank you, dear. Don't wait up."

"I never do," she said with her eyes closed. "Harry?"

"Yes dear?"

She looked at me. "It's good to see you after a killer again." She glanced at Shad then back at me. "Both of you, take care."

9

On the way from Exeter, Shad accessed the plans filed with the park authority, and the underground piping Quartermain used for long distance burrows matched exactly the map Shad had generated, including a strange little cave near Old Bones Village Shad had mentioned. The burrow Quartermain had used to exit from Bones' chamber led to the cave, but, although there were cracks in the upper part of the chamber allowing a little light and more than a few bats, Shad hadn't found any exit large enough for a fox. Judging by the number of bat wings he had found without bats between them, Shad concluded the cave was one of the places where the Quartermains dined.

There was drainage piping from the stables, but it was a completely separate enclosed system with all wastes purified and recycled. No connection to the fox runs. While he was at it, Shad ran a search on anyone whoever had ever had any connection with Fantronics's experimental insect imprint or mental health programs. The scientist who had been in charge of both programs, Beatrice Widdows, PhD., had moved to Florida three years before to join the faculty of the state university there as professor of applied biotronics. It was reputedly the only college course in the world taught by a manatee. Among the names of Dr. Widdows's assistants that Shad had listed, the name of one caught my attention. "Why does the name Shirley Wurple seem familiar?"

"Dr. Wurple is the current bio amdroid assignment supervisor at Fantronics. Remember, she ducked my call?"

"Is there any connection between her and Houndtor Down Hunts you can find?"

"Working," Shad announced as his tail twitched. As the cruiser came down from the Bovey Tracy Roundabout, the rain had stopped but it was still overcast, making the night deadly dark, which was perfect for our purposes. Just as we came over the village of Leighon, Shad announced,

"Back at the beginning of Houndtor Down Hunts, when Archie Quartermain imprinted onto his first fox bio, Dr. Wurple assisted Dr. Widdows with the imprint and supervised the transfer of Archie's human meat suit to its new owner. As far as my software knows, that's the only connection. Where do you want me to put down?"

"Put us into a hover just east of the lodge grove below treetop level and run up both micros. If we find another way from Champion's stall out of the stables we're going to follow it wherever it goes."

Copied into our micros, we entered the stables through an air vent leaving open the hole through the screen and air filter we had made. Keeping above the cameras and motion detectors, we came to the horse stable wing and once there aligned ourselves behind a vertical electrical conduit and descended until we could enter an open transom. Keeping beams, boxes, or bales of hay between us and the security sensors, we made our way to Champion's stall and slipped in undetected. The horse was lying down in the straw on its right side.

"I thought horses slept standing up," said Shad on our secure net.

I hovered my micro just above the horse's head and extended my holo. "They may very well sleep standing up, Shad, but this one is as dead as Dillinger." I did a quick neural activity scan and came up empty. "This bio has been dead long enough to zero out all recoverable neurological activity and data." I initiated a full scan and Shad opened a channel to it and watched. We both noted the results at the same time: Champion's red blood cells were almost devoid of oxygen.

"Chemical asphyxia?" said Shad.

"Let's see." I looked up horse anatomy, located a big artery, and shot an independent micro analyzer into the dead animal's blood stream. The rice-grain sized laboratory reported its results within seconds: "Blood cyanide level: two-point-three milligrams per liter. Get a liver temp."

Shad moved his micro around to the horse's flank and fired a sensor into the dead animal's liver. "Champ's been dead about two hours."

"Perhaps our killer was neating up." I looked back at the dead horse. "The poison still had to be administered. Do your wireless magic and see if you can access the stable security vids. Any and everything of Champion, his stall, and anyone going to or coming from the stall the past three or four hours. I'll check the horse's food and water and see if the poison was administered that way."

"I'm on it, Jaggs."

While Shad was busy accessing the security vids, I tested Champion's water and feed station for cyanide. Neither had even trace amounts. The feed was automatically mixed, apportioned, and transported to the stalls on overhead belts, and down through vertical chutes into the feeding stations.

"Shad, while you're checking the surveillance vids, be a good fellow and run the schematics for the automated feeding and watering systems. See if there's any way for something or someone to get through them into the stalls."

"Got it."

On the other sides of the walls—both sides, the back, and back corners, were other stalls, all occupied. I checked the adjoining stalls, and examined the walls. They were covered with white imitation wood planking made from a durable combination of poly and gypsum cement. Very well done. Until I actually put the holo to them, I thought them to be of genuine oak. The stall walls were solid down to the imitation concrete plastic foundation. The foundation was solid and one uninterrupted piece with the textured floor. I poked through the straw on the stall floor, as well as beneath lumps of horse poo, finding no opening large enough to allow even a micro to enter, much less something as large as a Kaiser roll.

"I've run through the vids of all three cameras that have views of this section of the horse stables, Jaggs. Nothing."

"The feed and watering systems?" I prompted.

"The water goes through a series of filters and screens. The feed is run through larger mesh screens, but goes through foreign matter detectors designed to find and remove all ferrous and nonferrous metals, plastics, insects, rodents, contaminants—anything that isn't the intended feed. Find anything with the foundation or floor?"

"What I found was that this building is tight and made of practically indestructible materials. The only place I haven't examined is beneath the horse."

"We could put our power supplies in parallel and give Champ a zap," Shad offered. "Maybe we could frog twitch him off that spot."

I aimed my lens at my partner. "Before resorting to measures that have equal chances of either crushing our micros or setting this straw on fire, Baron Frankenduck, let's do density and matrix continuity scans on the floor and foundation that we can reach."

"Think someone pulled a plastic plug and put it back, Igor?" he said, I believe, with the voice of Colin Clive.

"Let's see. And that's Detective Inspector Igor to you."

Density and matrix continuity scans, originally adopted by forensics for restoring purposefully obliterated serial numbers from weapons, autos, and stolen goods, were because of that, deadly slow if the area to be scanned was larger than a few square centimeters. The stall was approximately three meters wide and four deep. Fortunately, we both began scanning at the back of the stall, I on the right and Shad on the left. We hadn't been at it longer than twenty minutes when Shad said, "Got it."

I glided over to his side of the stall, tuned in his scan, and saw in his corner of the stall an arc, the complete circle of which would be twenty-five centimeters in diameter and would include part of the floor and a bit of the back. I began scanning the back, and in minutes we had marked bits of arc the complete circle of which would, if the plug were removed, make a rather high tech foxhole. "Are we back to Archie Quartermain?" asked Shad. "What motive?"

"Perhaps he's a better actor than you thought. He originally got into that fox suit for money."

"I don't buy it. Back when we were in New York, Archie liked money the same way I liked money. We both preferred eating to starving and sleeping with a roof over our heads to shivering beneath all the news that's fit to print out on a park bench. In the end, that's why I became a cop and

Archie became a fox, but money wasn't what was driving us. Acting, getting a great role, hearing that laughter, that applause, getting a thousand men and women to play with you at the same time, leading them along into your game, and springing the surprise on them, collecting all those oohs and ahs. Applause. That's what drove us—that's what drove Archie. Judging by what he told you when I was out mapping the burrows, that's what's still driving him: The game, although I admit the appeal parameters seemed to have changed."

"So, what else can fit through a fox hole?"

"Fox terriers," offered Shad. "Various mechs, squirrels, rats, all kinds of birds, weasels, badgers, monkeys—"

"You said your package included thermal imaging," I interrupted. "How sensitive is your system?"

"I can track another bird through the air by the long heat trail it leaves and can determine which shotgun a duck hunter used five hours after it was fired by the heat differential between it and the hunter's unfired weapons, and that with a load of birdshot in my butt."

"Shad, we have to get back up to the cruiser. When we get there, move into your feathers and do a scan around the lodge and stables for the underground route that was used to get in here. Whatever was used, it had to generate some heat to get through this foundation. My instruments, crude as they are, can detect a temperature differential between the inside of the arc we've been scanning and the surrounding material."

"What are you going to do?"

"Perhaps I'll find a shovel to wield."

Shad's micro hovered for a moment, then he said, "You're going to make me copy into the big mech and do the digging, aren't you?"

"Unless your scan can find us another way in."

10

While I downloaded my data into the cruiser's computer, Shad did one quick flap around the lodge and stables. Long before I managed to copy back into my meat suit, he was back with a report. "I found the underground tunnel coming out from beneath the northwest corner of the lodge. That was the end cut last. From there it runs around three meters deep northwest then arcs until it heads southwest, arcs again until it's headed southeast, and then the thermal signature is so faint my equipment can't pick it up. The largest part of what I could follow was cut through mostly solid granite."

My sync was complete and I sat up and pointed at the cruiser's data screen. "Show me."

It was as he said. In addition, the trace was very regular, not a perceptible difference in diameter between any two parts of the machine-cut tube. Every detectable portion of the tunnel was three to four meters deep, most of it running through granite. If we were going to break into it, we'd need equipment, explosives, daylight, a crew, and to throw away any kind of edge surprise might lend us. I glanced over to the driver's seat, and Shad's tail was twitching. "What are you doing?"

"Searching for small diameter tunneling equipment. I've found three designed for putting in water and sewer lines, as well as running conduit through masonry that can do the tunnel job we detected. The Euclid 750 Pipe Snake is what was used to put in all of the long run tunnels Houndtor Down Hunts uses to run camera feeds along the different fox runs. I see it's pretty obsolete, too, as far as knowledgeable plumbing and sewerage dons are concerned."

The image came up. The Euclid model resembled a horrible huge snake, the mouth on its fearsome head tipped with ghastly looking circular grinding teeth. Just behind the teeth were high pressure water jets and intake holes to float the stone dust and remove the slurry. Just behind the takeaway scoops was a gasket, and behind that were holes designed to inject and coat the interior of the tunnel behind the head with a smooth layer of chemical and weather resistant plastic. The rattler on the tail of this snake was a huge piece of nuke-powered equipment that would be incredibly obvious wherever it was used. Shad pointed out that the Pipe Snake could have easily made the hole into Champion's stall, but all it could do after that is coat the inside of the opening with plastic. It couldn't have refilled the hole.

"The other two models are the Pipe Dream, manufactured in Macao by Red Star Industrial, and the Magic Mole, manufactured in Burbank by an outfit called Whack-A-Hole. Both pieces of equipment use the same technology, matter transcompression—"

"They eat dirt and rocks and squirt out pipe."

"Yes. Self-contained, nuke powered. A feature of the Magic Mole, however, is its ability to fill the pipe it's made with anything the contractor wishes, whether it's an inline computer-controlled valve, a line switch—"

"Or what it removed," I completed. "Does Whack-A-Hole have a twenty-four hour office in London?"

"Yes."

"See if Marcus Licinius Crassus can get the manufacturer to give up a customer list. Meanwhile, take the cruiser over to where Bowman's body was found. If our killer used a Magic Mole to get a portable image implanter into Champion's stall, I'm pretty certain the same was done where Bowman was killed. Perhaps we can get in at that end. The forest floor there, at least, isn't made of plastic or granite."

It was well past three in the morning by the time we located the tunnel entrance. It was beneath the remaining branches of the dead tree next to the pine that had Champion's hair on it. No attempt had been made to fill the hole. It looked, in fact, as though a fox or some large burrowing animal had dug it. Shad had Whack-A-Hole's British customer list and it was daunting. Every municipality, hamlet, and large institution in the country had one or more of the tools, as well as plumbers, drain layers, and building contractors of all types. For the mundane tasks of laying pipe or running conduit, it seemed, there was nothing like a Magic Mole. To take all the variously formatted employee databases of all of the institutions and companies and run each person's antecedents against our total name database was beyond our capacity. Shad logged into the Heavitree ABCD Center and gave the task to the mainframe. Meanwhile, we got small, copied into our micros, and entered Whack-A-Mole's underworld.

Once the excitement of being confronted by a belligerent salamander and several alarming spiders was past, monotonous would be too generous a description of how it felt to be in a flying lipstick traveling down an apparently endless but definitely featureless length of dark pipe. After a few minutes of travel there was a very gentle arc toward the northeast, and we traveled along that, gradually descending all the while. After more than an hour of this, another gentle arc had us heading due east, but still descending. "Here's something interesting," said my partner at last.

"Let me have it, Shad. I'm stimulation starved to the point where I could eagerly listen to knock-knock jokes."

"You know how fast a twenty-five centimeter diameter Magic Mole can travel through an unobstructed pipe of its own manufacture?"

"Can't say that I do."

"It can top sixty kilometers per hour under its own power. With compressed air behind it, the mole can top a hundred and seventy."

"Fascinating."

"I only bring it up, Jaggs, because I note we are both moving along at our top speed of four kilometers per hour. Sort of made me wonder what the plan is should we find a Magic Mole coming at us from the other direction."

I thought on it. "In such case we get annihilated. Now that you bring it up, it would probably behoove us to maintain a continuous data sync with the cruiser. That way, should we get swatted, we'll remember it. What's our signal like to the cruiser pickup?"

Shad ran a quick signal strength and fidelity test. "Weak. I'm bringing the cruiser over our present position." After a minute or two, Shad ran the test again. "Perfect. As long as the cruiser follows along above us, it should be fine."

"Very well. Keep an eye on the autodrive monitor, though. Wrapping the cruiser around a tree or dashing it to pieces on a building or rock cliff would be all Supt. Matheson needs to sack the both of us."

"Something from Exeter coming in," he announced. "Fantronics's maintenance division currently keeps three Magic Mole systems in its inventory. Two of the systems were replaced three months ago. Apparently the replaced systems were destroyed along with a lot of other equipment when the division's warehouse in Reading was consumed in a chemical fire. Kind of a drastic way to cover up an equipment theft," he observed.

"But effective."

That was all the excitement we had until we came to a point just west of Old Bones Village Ruin. Twenty meters north of the National Park Information Center was a junction. To our left a tunnel led due north. That was likely the other end of the tube which led to Champion's stall. Straight ahead, however, was the real question mark. Without discussion Shad and I both headed in that direction. Another few meters and the tube took a ninety degree turn south.

"Oops!" said Shad.

"What is it?"

"Nothing."

"You said 'Oops,' Shad. Oops is never good."

"We—I almost ran the cruiser into that little information center in the ruins. I put it in hover park." He aimed his sensors at me. "That's where the tunnel leads, Jaggs: the basement of that building."

"Find out who is employed there."

While Shad accessed the park authority records, we moved ahead until suddenly there was a light at the end of the tunnel. Several lights, actually. I zoomed in on them and they looked like instrument lights on some sort of control panel.

"Hold up, pard," said Shad causing both of us to come to a halt.

"Who did you find?"

"No one—I mean, there's no record of anyone ever being employed there. According to the park authority, there is no information center there. There's no record of anyone even thinking about it. It's a front."

"Shad, give me the cruiser controls." In a moment, I was looking through the cruiser's forward camera. It was still dark. The infrared illumination revealed the back side of the little building. A late model Honda electric was parked there on the uncut grass. I maneuvered the cruiser around until I could see the front of the building. As evidenced by the weeds and grass growing in it, the crushed gravel path to the front door had seen little traffic. There was a sign on the door saying that the center was closed for repairs and thank you for all your patience. I left the cruiser hovering there and turned to Shad. "Let's go."

We moved toward the end of the tunnel, and long before we reached the end we could tell the space beneath the small building was much larger than the structure above, the curiously scalloped walls apparently carved from the granite bedrock courtesy of a Magic Mole. There was the sound of a small internal combustion engine running. The panel lights we had seen from inside the tunnel were mounted in the face of a large orange colored console. Mounted above the lights was an identification plate which cleverly named the machine upon which it was mounted a genuine Whack-A-Hole Magic Mole Control. To the right of the console on the wet granite floor were what looked like pipes of different diameters. Shad moved over to them to see what they were. Beyond the pipes and extending as far as I could see in the carved-out space were what looked to be piles of purple glass hockey pucks—millions of them.

"These pipe thingies are different sized Magic Mole bits in their containers," said Shad.

"See if you can tell what those piles of purple things are."

"Puckets," he answered immediately.

"Sorry?"

Shad aimed his lens at me. "I ran across it when I put in the search for boring equipment and came across Whack-A-Hole. The transcompression equipment manufacturers call them puckets. When the Mole goes through certain dense materials, like granite for instance, there's stuff left over after the matter transcompression forms the tube lining. The Mole compresses the excess material to about a sixth of its volume and excretes it in this form: puckets." Shad aimed his lens to his right. "Hello?"

I turned in the direction my partner was facing. Behind the Mole control unit was a refrigerator, a table with a hotplate, and a shelf with a few tins and boxes on it: biscuits, crisps, jam and such. To the right of this rudimentary kitchen, standing next to a stairway, was a forty year-old vertical EMU capsule, its casing scratched and dented, its bottom sitting in at least five centimeters of water. "Where's all this water coming from?"

I moved a bit to my left and saw the companion capsule standing next to the first in a send-receive configuration and a massive old engram management unit console beyond it. I hadn't seen equipment that old since I copied into my first bio. The EMU console was located next to an equally vintage stasis bed. In repose upon the bed was a middle aged woman dressed in Wranglers and a Harris tweed jacket over an olive turtleneck. Her hair was graying, unusually short, and she wore heavy black framed eyeglasses. Her skin color was bright red. "Shad, run the air quality."

After thirty seconds, Shad said, "I'm glad we're in the mechs, Jaggs. The carbon monoxide level in here is lethal. If she's not dead, she's not an oxy breather."

"Get a DNA and liver temp."

While Shad was sticking a needle into the corpse, I moved past the stasis maintenance console following the sound of what I suspected was a generator. Indeed it was, and a petrol burner at that, the fuel bladder tucked into the northeast corner of the chamber. Air was piped into its carburetor from outside and the exhaust fed into a stack which went up through the floor above. The seal between the purple glass exhaust pipe and stack was leaking badly, the glass apparently cracked. Just behind the generator, the scalloped chamber wall was wet and dripping. It was rainwater seeping through the dirt between the edge of the building and the bedrock.

I reversed course and as I passed the stasis bed, Shad was running the DNA ID on the body. Past the EMU capsules I turned left and left again to go up the long staircase. The door to the upstairs was open slightly and I moved in, the overcast sky visible through one of the windows just beginning to grow light. There was enough furniture and decoration in the room to convince someone looking through a window that this was indeed an official information center. There was, however, only the one room, a closet with nothing in it, and the stairwell leading to the mysterious cavern below.

I did a quick analysis of the upstairs air and the carbon monoxide level above ground was even more concentrated than below. The exhaust stack from the generator came up through the floor at the back of the building, apparently with the assistance of a Magic Mole which had made the glass stack pipe, as well. The piping ran across the open ceiling and up into the casing of the pseudo brick chimney. Prefab the building might have been, but it was fairly tight, without a crack or hole large enough for me to get to the outside. I was about to call an end to my meat suit's stasis and have myself land the cruiser and open the door with a pry bar, but I hate doing that. When the mech and the meat suit both are running at the same time and independently altering our engram content, there are always sync problems with frequently useful items deleted in the resolution. It was unnecessary, though. I opened the mail slot in the door and exited through it. Once outside I moved up to the roof and over to the chimney. One glance down the chimney showed what was blocking the generator exhaust port: dead birds.

As I came back through the mail slot and down the stairs, Shad was returning from the direction of the pucket dump. We both altered direction and stopped at the stasis bed. "Did you ID the body?" I asked Shad.

"DI Jaggers, I'd like you to meet the late Dr. Shirley Wurple. She's been dead a little over three hours. Find out where the water's coming in?"

"In the back. There's no foundation. The rain caused the building to settle slightly which cracked the exhaust seal and probably toppled a couple of dead birds in the chimney over the exhaust port, blocking it."

"Something doesn't mesh, Jaggs. She's a wheel at Fantronics, right? She has to have access to better equipment than these old junkers."

"Probably left over from her research days with Dr. Widdows, Shad. She wanted her plans under the radar. Junkers are junked, you see, not registered."

"So, why? We're back to motive. Why'd she try to kill us and, presumably, Miles Bowman?"

I thought on it until, at last, a mouse brought me the answer. "When you were married, Shad, before your flying days, did your wife ever bring you a sweetie when you were feeling low, some sort of little treat to bring you out of your doldrums?"

"Sure—" He aimed his light at me. "The mouse! That doesn't happen with real critters and their mates."

"She tried to kill us, Shad, because she didn't want us to discover that she killed Bowman. She killed Bowman for the very noblest of reasons: to protect her family. She's Archie Quartermain's mate and is about to become a mother. I think if you check inside those EMU capsules you'll find fox hair that won't match up with Quartermain's. Have you seen that image implanter?"

"I haven't found it, and I looked."

"Unfortunate."

"Jaggs, don't you think Archie's in this with her?"

"No. I believe your old roommate thinks his mate is a genuine vixen. Why should he think anything else? He's not a proper fox himself. Where's his den?"

"When I was mapping the dirt tunnels, I found a couple of wide spots, but nothing like a place to sleep or make little foxes. No little animal bones—"

"Can you get us back to Old Bones, where Quartermain first talked to us?" I asked him.

"Sure, but it'll take hours to go back the way we came."

"Let's take a shortcut. We can get out through the mail slot."

I led the way and we hurried. There was no telling what Shirley Wurple might do with that image implanter once she awakened and found out she was dead.

Once we left the mail slot, it was a mere thirty meters south to reach the entrance to the burrow. After reaching his rather lean receptionist, I led the way over Old Bones's ribcage to the back of the chamber and into the hole between the two rock slabs. According to Shad's map, the hole turned abruptly down, zigzagged generally southwest until it entered an inclined shaft carved by groundwater. The shaft led to a small grotto illuminated by two very dim cracks of natural light from the surface. There was not even enough room for a man to stand upright, but the tiny cave averaged between one and two meters wide and well over forty meters in length where it began sloping down, the overflow pouring into a rubble filled channel that presumably found its way to Becka Brook.

"When the vixen brought Quartermain his mouse, this is from where she came. This is to where Quartermain followed her after leaving me." I turned and aimed my lens at Shad's micro. "Something I don't understand. With the research Quartermain did on foxes and the hunt, your old roommate had to know about that mouse—that it didn't fit. Is it possible that Archie Quartermain deluded himself into thinking Shirley Wurple is a real vixen?"

"You should've seen me stalking that hooded merganser all over Maine. It's a good thing she was a real bird or she would've taken out papers on me. When you're lonely and desperate, you can talk yourself into believing anything. Archie lives in a hole in the ground. By the time he could afford to buy himself a designer meat suit he was already a fox in his head. Trouble is, when we copy into one of these ams, we bring that human need for companionship along with us. After a lonely couple of years by himself, running before the hounds his only meaning in life, along comes this warm, cute, sexy little vixen who wants to rub, cuddle, bring him mice, and make little foxes. You bet he could delude himself—Hold it."

After Shad's warning, we both fell silent and streaked for cover. We were behind a small ledge, our lights off, our sensors on. A warm mass was entering the chamber from above. "I heard that," said a voice. It was Quartermain. Shad and I moved our mechs out from behind the ledge. The fox was standing beside the pool of water. "What are you two doing here?" he demanded.

"Where's your mate, Arch?" asked Shad.

"My mate?"

"The vixen who's fixin' to make you a pappy."

He walked a few steps in one direction, then turned and walked back, leveling his gaze on Shad's micro. "What do you want with her? She's a fox—a real fox."

"She's nothing of the sort," I said. "She's a Fantronics bio imprinted with the engrams of a woman named Shirley Wurple."

Quartermain was so still he could have been a taxidermist's showpiece. "*Doctor* Shirley Wurple?" he said to my micro.

"Yes."

"The person who . . . *Bloody hell.*" He sat next to the water and stared deep into the pool. "She killed Miles, didn't she?"

"Yes," I answered as Shad crossed the pool to investigate something. "I don't know if this helps, Quartermain, but I think she believed she was doing it for her family: You and the coming cubs."

"How did she do it?"

"During the run, after you passed that spot in Quik Grove lane, she cut your scent trail with probably some sort of chemical then laid a drag trail into the thick woods, probably with one of your former body parts from a previous hunt."

"She has an old tail of mine. A bit morbid, but I thought it was kind of touching."

"When Miles reached that particular spot in the grove, she hit the horse with an image implant that drove the animal insane. Champion saw Miles Bowman as a threat—"

"—And then Champion trampled to death the man who loved him more than anyone else in the world," completed Quartermain. "This is insane. Back in the Fantronics lab, that woman—I thought she was joking. She made like she was flirting with me when she was getting me ready to print into my fox suit, making jokes about buying my human self and bringing it home with her for fun and games. She must've been sixty! You don't suppose she actually bought me."

"No," Shad said from the other side of the pool. "The old you is in Hollywood right now under the name of Trent Scanlon playing the feature role of Saddam Hussein in the black comedy *Uday and Qusay are Ed-day*. Principle photography began last February."

"Hollywood," the fox repeated. Again he was motionless, no doubt having one of those life-assessing moments. Lifting his head, at last, he faced me. "How can you be so certain she did it?"

"She tried to kill us, too." I explained how the vixen had tunneled into Champion's stall and how we discovered her expired human meat suit below the phony National Park Information Center. He shook his head at last, got up on all fours, turned toward the back of the chamber, jumped up on a ledge, and seemingly vanished into the rock. We heard his voice say, "This way."

I moved up to where Quartermain seemed to have vanished and saw a shelf of stone. Just beneath it was an opening that was impossible to see unless one was right up on it. "This way, Shad."

"I found something," he said.

I moved back down and crossed the water to where Shad's light was illuminating something the size of a dinner roll that looked sealed in waterproof plastic. "Is that the missing portable image imprinter?"

"She tried to hide it in the water. The vixen carried it down here holding the plastic bag in her mouth. Tiny sharp little teeth. Water got in the bag. We'll be able to match Wurple's bio to the bite mark impressions."

"We'll need the tracked mech to bring it out, Shad. Before we do that, call it in to Police Constable Lounds for the arrest. That ought to raise his esteem in the park constabulary."

"I'd love to see his boss's face when he finds out his case fell apart."

"Let's get to Quartermain's den. Your old roommate is about to give up his mate."

12

"Why did you kill Miles," we heard Quartermain demand as Shad and I came out of the tunnel into a chamber where the only illumination was provided by our lights.

"I didn't mean to at first," answered the vixen's tearful voice. She looked at us, her eyes wide. Looking at Quartermain she said, "Really I didn't. I'd hoped to frighten him out of the—Oh, I can't look at you and tell you this!"

"It doesn't matter. I'm sending you over," said Quartermain. He seemed to laugh to himself—at himself—then he glanced at Shad's micro and hung his head. "Yeah. I'm sending you over," he repeated as he slinked out of the chamber.

She turned from watching Quartermain's departing tail, and laughed nervously. "Oh —he frightened me for a moment. He was joking. That's it. After all, I'm carrying his babies. He was joking, wasn't he?"

"Don't be silly," said Shad in that special Bogart voice of his. "You're taking the fall. You killed Miles and you're going over for it."

"How can you . . . how can he do this to me?" She broke down and began a really irritating series of whines.

"Listen," said Shad after awhile. "This won't do any good. You'll never understand me, but I'll try once and then give it up. When a fox's partner's killed, he's supposed to do something about it. It doesn't make any difference what the fox thought of him, he was your partner and you're supposed to do something about it. And it happens they're in the fox hunting business. Well, when one of your fox hunters gets killed by a fox, it's bad business to let the fox get away with it. Bad all around. Bad for every fox hunting operation everywhere."

Shirley Wurple didn't know her next line from *The Maltese Falcon*, which left Shad with nothing left to say.

The vixen looked at me and said, "What if I run? You two little pocket pips couldn't stop me."

"No, we couldn't," I answered, "In Houndtor Down Lodge this instant, however, equipped with the best riding stock and guided by the most competently trained hounds in the world, is an assembly of the most proficient and fanatical fox hunters in the world. You've never run before the hounds, doctor. You don't know how. I fear in a matter of minutes you and your unborn cubs would be cornered and most likely torn to pieces. Why not let a judge and jury decide your fate?"

"I can run faster than you can move. My human body can—"

"You're human body is dead, Dr. Wurple," said Shad.

Her eyes grew wide as she faced me.

"Carbon monoxide poisoning from your generator," I explained. "There was nothing we could do." I could see the defeat in her face as I turned away, sad for her.

She cooperated in exiting the burrow once PC Lounds arrived to caution her and make the arrest. He put her in a dog cage and drove off with her in the electric. There wasn't anything we could say to console Archie Quartermain. All we could do was to give him the number of a facilitator for an amdroid grief group, see to it that DCI Stokes released Lady Ida Bowman with all due apologies, and head back to Exeter, the sun actually making it through the clouds for a minute before a new front came in and the rainfall resumed.

While we rode off into the truncated sunrise, I asked my new partner, "How would you like to be on that jury, Shad? He was the fantasy love of her life, and the price of her union with him was she'd have to remain helplessly by while he was killed over and over again. What to do?"

"We just catch 'em, Jaggs. We don't cook 'em."

"Indeed, Shad. Too bad we resolved things so quickly, though. I really wanted to meet Dorothea Tell. Back in the dim reaches of time, I fear she was my childhood heartthrob."

After a moment of silence, Shad said, "Speaking of old movies, *The Maltese Falcon* was a script Archie and I had memorized front to back. 'I'm sending you over.' He chuckled and said with Humphrey Bogart's voice, 'When a fox's partner's killed, he's supposed to do something about it.'" He glanced at me and said in his own voice, "Why did you let me go on like that?"

"My dear chap, I never would have dreamt of deprivin' you of your moment of triumph."

He frowned, regarded me with one dark eye, and said, "*The Scarlet Pimpernel*, Anthony Andrews vid remake, Nineteen eighty-two."

"Quite right," I said as I beamed at my new partner. "Excellent."

♠

THE HANGINGSTONE RAT

-1-

Early on a late Summer morning Artificial Beings Crimes took a call from Okehampton Station reporting a dead bio in North Dartmoor at a place called Hangingstone Hill. The location was seven kilometers south-southeast of the army camp, deceased was a dead male rodent amdroid reported by a hiker: no apparent signs of violence, scene marked, hiker's statement received, constable standing by. Rodent bios aren't terribly long lived and it was likely the fellow simply happened to be on the moor when he pegged it. Likely the death was natural and the owner of the engrams had another meat suit in stasis. Nonetheless, it had to be investigated and it was a welcome opportunity to get out of the city. As I waited for Shad to pick me up at my home on Waverly, I used Val's computer and looked up Hangingstone Hill: A minor legend, unremarkable history, third highest elevation on the moor.

"Guy's here," Val called from the hallway. She padded into the lounge and hopped up on the desk. I gave her ears a perfunctory scratch.

"Have a good day, dear," I said as I went to get my coat.

She looked at the computer screen. "You have a call out on the moor?"

I pulled on my coat and sealed it. "Yes. Shouldn't be much of anything, dear. Dead rat bio reported by a hiker."

"Well, take care, Harry. I have a premonition."

I smiled. "Remember your last premonition, dear? Wasn't it a furball?"

"Even so, Harry, take care. I don't like rats."

"I understand rats feel the same way about cats. Good-bye, dear."

"We're coming up on the moor," Shad quacked. We talked old movies for awhile then fell silent as we watched the rugged greenness of Dartmoor spread before us.

"Pick up the Vader prang beacon yet?" I asked him.

"We're right on the wire."

I looked over the vast expanses of hilly heather broken only by granite topped hills, boulder fields, ponds, peat bogs, and stream carved cleaves. Among them the shadows of clouds seemed fixed in place. I could see for miles. What I failed to see was the constabulary cruiser that was supposed to be waiting for us. "I don't see the cop supposed to meet us, Shad."

He glanced at me. "You're the one who pointed out to me the low esteem in which ABCD is held among the constabulary."

"This juvenile anchor dragging grows tedious, nevertheless."

"Hangingstone Hill up ahead," announced Shad. "Ought to be a movie title," he concluded whimsically.

I smiled. "*Hangingstone Hill*, a western tale of murder and vengeance, torn from the pages of history, directed by John Ford—

"—Starring Susan Hayward and Gary Cooper," completed Shad.

"I always loved Susan Hayward. Wasn't there a Gary Cooper film called *The Hanging Tree?*" I asked.

"Nineteen fifty-six," said Shad, flaunting his vast cinematic knowledge. "Gary Cooper and Maria Schell," he continued. "You know, *The Hanging Tree* was George C. Scott's movie debut."

"Really. Well, Shad, I know why Hangingstone Hill carries such an ominous name."

"Oh?" He was silent for a beat. "You do?"

It does me good to stump the duck once in awhile. "It has to do with a natural phenomenon, Shad: a rather big plate of rock called a logan stone that hangs out over another rock on the side of the hill."

"That's disappointing," Shad remarked. "With a name like Hangingstone Hill the place ought to be covered in ghosts left over from innumerable medieval neck stretchings. *Turnkeys With Gibbets,"* imagined Shad aloud. "A Cranberry and Gravy Production."

"Sorry?" I said. "Cranberries?"

"A Thanksgiving reference. US holiday? Turkey and giblets? —Forget it."

I glanced at Shad. "Legend has it that a Seventeenth Century mayor of Okehampton was hanged on Hangingstone Hill."

"They must've brought their own gibbet with them," said Shad as he changed heading a few degrees south. "Look at the hills around here. Not a tree in sight. Okay," he relented, "why'd they hang him?"

"Stealing sheep."

"They gave him the rope on a mutton rap? Tough town."

"I'm certain the mayor represented the charges against him as being politically motivated."

"So that's where that came from."

"Indeed, but it wasn't only the mayor's body that was sentenced. His spirit was sentenced to empty with a sieve Cranmere Pool. That's at the west foot of Hangingstone."

"Now that's hard time."

"Not at all," I said. "The clever fellow lined his sieve with sheepskin and proceeded to empty the thing. Cranmere Pool has no water in it."

"So he beat the rap?"

"Not quite. The punishment was altered to having to weave the sand at the bottom of the pool into a rope. Poor fellow's still at it, I imagine." I again looked for the constabulary electric. "Shad, I still do not see a car."

"Nothing on the instruments," he responded. "The scene analyzer beacon is located on the northwest side of the hill. What's that hut down there?"

Directly in front of us was a high hill with gentle slopes. On its north end were the remains of a stone shack, its shed roof partially collapsed. "That's an old artillery observation post. For centuries this end of the moor was an artillery range. Incidentally, ducks, the army still advise hikers not to pick up any curiosities they might find out here."

"Souvenir go boom; important safety tip."

"Very well, Shad, ring up Okehampton Station and find out where their missing constable is. Meanwhile, put us down near the prang."

While he did that I turned in my seat and ran up the mechs. Shad put down the cruiser on the northwest slope of the hill about five meters above the aforementioned logan stone. The sunlight reflected from the pencil thin scene analyzer mounted on the southwest edge of the rock plate. It would be facing the corpse. I looked in that direction but could see nothing among the heather. It was, at least, not a terribly large rat.

"Jaggs, guy on the phone says Okehampton cops can't find any Hangingstone Hill report. He says they didn't call in a dead bio to ABCD this morning."

"Rubbish."

"The call would have been automatically logged and recorded, according to their man Sudbury, and he can find no such record in the computer. Case closed."

"Tell him to pull his ruddy thumb out and try again."

The doors rotated up and I held up a hand to Shad. "Before that let's see if we even have a body. This is beginning to look suspiciously like a hoax."

"Local yokels having a little fun with ABCD?" suggested the duck.

"Perhaps the constabulary having a laugh." I climbed out of the cruiser, stood, and took a few steps down toward the stone. Southwest of it, perhaps two meters distant, I could see in the heather what looked like the body of a rat with a body comparable in size to that of a gray squirrel. It was lying on its left side. Shad flew up next to me. "Okay," he said as he landed, "at least we have a corpse."

"Yes. A bio. I can still read the receiver signal. Perhaps we can harvest the engrams before it zeroes out."

"I wonder why someone would copy into a rat bio?" said Shad. "Why would they *want* to? And what's a rat with a human engram imprint doing out here in the boonies—and with no cheese?"

"Perhaps he ate all his cheese and expired from despondency," I suggested facetiously. "I'll sort the calls, Shad. After you make a try on the engrams, get a scan, temp, DNA, and ID."

"You got it."

I rang up Okehampton Camp army base and reception was scratchy. Either my phone was having problems or not all government departments communicate via satellite. As the operator there began passing my call around from pillar to post by slowest means available, I climbed uphill in hopes of better reception. As I stood facing the direction of the army camp, High Willhays and Yes tors visible in the distant haze, a Sergeant Vickers of the military police came on. A rather long-winded bloke, he was about to do my head in explaining, with maximum words per bit of information that he had no notice, knowledge, or note of anything concerning dead bodies of any kind, type, condition, description, or designation, today or at any other time, and, moreover, even should it be discovered in some manner at some time in the future that he had—

As I tensed, waiting for the fellow to take a breath for interruption purposes, the earth was pulled from beneath my feet and an enormous hand of sound, force, and heat rose and swatted me like a mosquito sending me flying up into absolute blackness.

2

Splitting headache. Overpowering silence, my body numb. My eyes opened to a confusing smear of images. A strong chemical odor stung my nostrils. Gradually the images resolved into fuzzy clouds, fuzzy hills, fuzzy sky, and shadows, everything through a stinking gray mist. Pain began invading my right ankle, my legs, then my whole body. I tried to call Shad but I couldn't hear my own voice. I gently rolled to my right and saw blood appearing on my right hand and sleeve. Managed to push against the ground until I was sitting upright, weaving, everything threatening to go black again. I couldn't see the cruiser.

My hand rested upon the edge of a very warm rock. I looked at the stone and it was a largish plate that could have been the twin of the hanging stone, but bottom side up. Then I saw a fuzzy gleam of silver and realized it was the self same hanging stone, the scene analyzer apparently none the worse for wear and still attached to its edge. The rock had landed just a few centimeters from me.

I looked for my phone and it was missing, probably somewhere beneath the rock. Tried shouting for Shad again, but still couldn't hear myself. Struggled to my feet, standing there feeling lightheaded, a sharp pain in my right ankle. I looked down and saw to my dismay I was missing both shoes and socks, my right ankle swollen, my right foot at a funny angle. My trouser cuffs were shredded. While I was staring at that, blood spatter appeared on my feet. It was coming from my nose. Further exploration revealed blood coming from my ears as well. Principal flow, though, came from a cut on the left side of my neck. I held my hand over it and stumbled down slope toward the stone's original location, calling for Shad, still unable to hear.

Nothing was left where the rat had been. Hanging stone, heather, grass, soil, rodent, cruiser, and Shad were gone. Steaming hot granite and that insidious chemical odor were all that remained. I couldn't think of what to do.

I turned around slowly. Farther upslope something was burning. I stumbled uphill far enough to see the cruiser's remains: twisted black metal pieces, flames still licking up from the few bits of remaining upholstery and combustible forensic supplies it had contained. The disembodied hand of the large walking mech was on the ground next to a few scorched feathers and charred bits of flesh. Thin piece of bone, something that looked like the tail of a rat. I couldn't make out either the rat's or Shad's bio receivers. Just then the universe went as black as Newgate's knocker and I fell wondering as I did so if I was going to die again.

From later accounts I gather Sergeant Vickers grew concerned when, shortly after losing my signal, the sound of a great explosion came from the south. He had an air ambulance come immediately and they managed to piece enough of me together to get me to camp hospital alive. When I first regained consciousness, however, it was night and I was in Royal Devon & Exeter Hospital in the city. I knew I hadn't died because, unlike my original demise, I awakened in the same body replete with every broken bone and aching cell. Topping the pain inventory was a headache that could gobble steel ingots and blow off razor wire. Soon there was a fellow stabbing into my retinas with an intense light beam and asking my name, the year, and the name of the reigning monarch. When the spots cleared and I managed a look at the bleeder, he appeared as though he ought to be peddling used trusses: slicked black hair, widow's peak, pinched up dark eyes, a hand-painted tie, and a nose like a broken rudder. The nametag on his white coat was red, but I couldn't focus well enough to read it. The man's voice came through in tinny flat tones and only through my left ear. I pointed.

"Temporary hearing assistance patch attached to your left temple," he said. "Can you tell me your name?"

"I believe I can."

He waited for a moment, then raised his evil-looking little eyebrows. "What is it?"

"Jaggers. Detective Inspector Harrington Jaggers, Devon ABCD." I looked at my surroundings. The room was small, off-white and white, a screen to my right displaying my vital signs to anyone who might wander in. On the wall opposite my bed I could make out a framed photo of what appeared to be a Quay scene: Cricklepit Bridge from Waterside. Shad had loved it down at the Quay.

"I fancy they call you Harry, eh?"

I looked in the direction of the voice and apparently the truss monger had failed to remove himself. "My wife calls me Harry. However, sir, you may address me by my nickname."

"What's that?" he asked expectantly.

"Inspector."

His evilly peaked eyebrows arched then lowered into grim mode. An unfriendly edge crept into his voice. "Can you tell me the year?"

"I don't wish to be more rude than necessary, fellow, but who *are* you?"

With the index finger of his right hand he tapped his nametag. "Dr. Truscott."

I had little time to consider the marketing possibilities in Truscott's Terrific Trusses as he had more to say. From what he said I was made aware that I should consider myself a very lucky fellow. Aside from a few lacerations, a broken ankle, four broken ribs, a sewn together carotid artery, deafness, chronic headaches, slightly impaired vision, bruised organs, a dozen or more badly pulled muscles, a dead partner, a crime scene blown to bloody hell, and an unsolved case concerning a now missing corpse, I was going to be just fine.

He apparently decided to make another try at being conversational. "I worked on your model cop replacement bio back in medical school," he said reminiscently. "A piece of history. 'Bones' we used to call them—for Basil Rathbone? The Twentieth Century movie actor?"

"Never heard of him."

"Really? Well, your model bio is very durable, infection resistant, and you look like a late night Sherlock Holmes, Eh?"

Mentally I almost expected Shad to be at my side remarking in his Porky Pig voice, *"I ss-say, Homes, what medical school did this fellow attend?"* to which I would reply, *"Elementary, my dear Watson. Elementary."*

Truscott was still there and still talking: My right ankle was set, protected, and held in place with a balloon cast. The chip in the cast would monitor the swelling and adjust the cast accordingly. The ankle would heal. With assistance my hearing would be fully restored. Once my brain recovered from being thoroughly sloshed around in my brainpan the headaches should subside and the fuzziness in my vision ought to clear. In addition a grief therapist was waiting in the wings simply keen to deal with my roast duck problem, *nudge-nudge.*

There are times when one hears something so coarse, vile, or outrageous one automatically assumes one has heard incorrectly. "Did you say 'roast duck'?"

The man smugged up, apparently quite pleased at his little joke. "We understand when they sent an ambulance for you they sent the chef from a Chinese restaurant for the duck."

"That duck was a bio and my partner."

"It *was* a duck suit, however."

"He was named Guy Shad, *he* was carrying a human imprint, *and* he was a detective sergeant in Artificial Beings Crimes."

"No offense, inspector. Just a little joke. Lighten the mood a bit? Just an amdroid suit, right? Not the end of the world, is it? Must've looked like that though when it happened, eh? Ah-hah-hah-hah."

If my head hadn't been aching so terribly, I would've throttled the wanker with his own stethoscope.

"One last item," he said. "Your hearing implant: do you prefer normal or wireless?"

"What?" I was still mentally occupied contemplating murder while I could still reasonably pull off a diminished capacity plea.

"Your bio isn't equipped with wireless but I wanted to let you know the option is available. The current hearing implants for your model all come with the latest wireless interface. If you prefer we can attempt to locate a pair of the old implants—wirelessless, eh?" He preened at his lame wordplay making me reconsider the prohibition against ABCD detectives in Britain carrying guns.

All the forensic mechs come with wireless which is how I knew I preferred normal. I abhorred even the idea of someone unbidden ringing me inside my own head. Shad, whose bio came with the latest of everything technical, always teased me about refusing to change. *In Artificial Beings Crimes,* he once said, *"we have John Dillinger, a gorilla, a bloodhound, a duck, and a dinosaur."*

I was the dinosaur. I'm not certain why, but I chose the wireless implants. I could always disable the wireless function if my sanity was threatened.

A few marks on a chart, another deeply offensive attempt at apologizing for any of his possibly insensitive remarks concerning my "dead bird," then trusses-for-less mercifully departed. Truscott was replaced by my boss, Detective Superintendent Marvin Matheson. Entering the room with him was a young constabulary detective who said he was from Okehampton Station. He introduced himself as DC Frank Storel and the bloke was a human natural who resembled a Twenty-first Century Middle Eastern historical figure whose name I hadn't managed to retain. He was short, thin, puny-looking, his mousy brown hair brushed forward, his face displaying uncertain intentions of growing a beard and moustache. He wore a butternut colored windbreaker over a buttoned up necktie-barren white shirt. Raised eyebrows and a permanent simpleton's grin on his face completed the picture. Instead of evidence of brain damage, his facial configuration was, one hoped, merely a stab at putting me at my ease. Matheson sat in a chair next to my left side. Storel remained standing at the foot of my bed.

The superintendent leaned toward me. "DC Storel has a few questions."

"Indeed."

Storel looked down into his chip pad. After ID formalities were concluded, he asked, "Do you know where the bird was standing when the dud went off?"

"His name is Detective Sergeant Guy Shad," I said.

"Sorry, inspector. No offense."

"Has that been determined?"

He looked up from his pad and grinned even more widely. "Sorry?"

"Indeed. Has it been determined that the explosion was an artillery shell? A dud?"

"Of course . . ." The grin faded and he looked confused. "Well, what else could it've been?"

"DC Storel, that explosion might have been an IED, a land mine, a booby trap, a bomb, a robotic missile, or movie set special effects for a British remake of *No Time For Sergeants*. Perhaps we're getting too bleeding close to making that first contact with alien life forms and this was some half-arsed Nebulan bugger-eyed monster's way of warning us the hell off!"

"Steady," quietly warned Matheson as he placed a gentle hand on my forearm. It was silent in the room for a long moment, DC Storel's face a rosy hue. I was a little warm myself.

"What exactly caused the explosion, inspector, has yet to be determined," said Storel. Mercifully his grin was gone. Although not more intelligent, his frown made him appear less stupid.

"No," I answered him.

"Sorry?" he said, frowning more deeply. From grin to grimace in five-point-three seconds: welcome to Jaggers World.

"No," I repeated. "I don't know where DS Shad was standing when the explosion happened. I wasn't looking in his direction."

"I see," he said looking once more into his palm. "And where were you?"

I answered him, and with additional questions from Storel I eventually came to realize he was filling out an accident report. I just wanted the ordeal over with as soon as possible. I answered the stupid questions, made no more comments, and closed my eyes when he finally left.

"Jaggers," said Matheson at last, "Are you all right?"

"Okehampton is treating it like a range accident."

"Forget Storel, Jaggers. ABCD is pulling out all the stops to investigate this tragedy. We'll get to the bottom of it."

"A four-key organ doesn't have all that many stops to pull, does it, superintendent?" I opened my eyes, rolled my head gently to the left, and described what happened out at Hangingstone Hill as best I could and urged him to have my bio reader tapped to download my memory record of the event. "Then start the enquiry at this end by tracing the original call. No one out there in the north end of Dartmoor ever heard of a dead bio on Hangingstone Hill, superintendent—not at Okehampton Station nor at the army camp. Find out who rang us with the report and from where. Anything left of the cruiser's computers?"

He slowly shook his head. "I'm afraid it's hopeless. Whatever hasn't been burned, melted, or shattered has been vaporized."

"Any backups of Shad's engrams anywhere?"

"Nothing we can find. DC Parker inquired of North American Biotron—they produced Guy Shad's duck bio for those American insurance advert producers. However, Shad failed to have his engrams on file there or anywhere else."

"Are you certain there's nothing in the tower mainframe?" I asked, already knowing the answer.

Matheson's eyebrows arched. "None of us have our engrams copied into the computer, Jaggers. I suppose we ought, but it's not like our end of law enforcement is violent. Not usually."

"Who is out at the scene?"

"Parker was out there today alongside Constabulary Scientific and Technical. What they picked up out there seems to confirm what Storel said."

With my left hand I grabbed Matheson's uniform lapel and pulled him close. Amidst the fumes of his peculiar cologne, I whispered into his ear, "Tell Parker to watch his back. When he's out there, tell him to watch his back."

"What's going on, Jaggers?"

"It was a trap. We were set up."

I released his lapel, he leaned back, and studied me for a moment. "Army ordnance, the bomb unit, and Scenes-of-Crime Officers all seem to think the explosion was an old dud artillery shell. There's evidence—

"It hasn't been used as a firing range of any kind for over eighty years, sir. The last of the ballistic artillery shells used there landed twelve decades ago." My thoughts swam reluctantly through my headache. "There was an observation post on top of Hangingstone Hill. Third highest spot on the moor. Makes sense to put an observation post there. Why then would the army shell Hangingstone Hill? The observation shack? Get the army to check their records. On top of that hill is where observers used to stand and see where artillery shells landed *elsewhere*."

He studied me for a long time then stood. "Get some rest, Jaggers. The doctor says you'll be back home tomorrow or the day after. Fit for duty in a couple of weeks."

"I can go back to work now, superintendent. Copied into a walking mech, I can function perfectly well."

"Your body needs to heal, Jaggers, which means you need to be in it moving it around, doing physical therapy or whatever." He gave me that rather startling John Dillinger frown which was his expression of gentle concern. "There's some head work you need to do, as well. I insist you see that counselor."

I looked up at him. "Superintendent, has anyone notified Val?"

"Of course. As soon as we got the word from Okehampton I sent someone to fetch her. Val and a friend of hers—another cat—are waiting outside the room."

"Nadine Fisher." I felt my heart sink. "She and Shad have been dating."

Matheson's eyebrows arched. "A cat and a duck?"

"Is that any more unusual than a cat and a man being married?" I demanded rather more angrily than intended.

"Sorry. " He thought for a moment. "I suppose it isn't unusual for our times. My wife Constance can be wed to John Dillinger, your wife Valerie can be a cat and married to Basil Rathbone, your partner a duck dating another cat, and my leading enquiry team right now is a frustrated bloodhound and an incontinent gorilla. The world is still just at the beginning of the entire artificial being phenomenon, isn't it?"

"My concerns aren't quite that philosophical, sir. Tell Parker to watch his back." I looked up at him. "Revenge and murder are still with us."

Matheson raised a hand and rubbed the back of his neck. "It's most likely an accident, Jaggers, but I'll get in touch with London ABC, convey your suspicions, see what they suggest."

He placed his hand on my shoulder. "Terribly sorry about Shad." He nodded, turned, and left the room leaving the door open. As soon as he left, Val and her friend Nadine came in. Nadine was an orange tabby. My wife hopped up on the bed and Nadine, never presumptuous, climbed up on the chair recently vacated by the superintendent.

"How do you feel, Harry?" Val asked.

"A bit shell shocked." I reached out a hand and stroked her cheek. "Were you terribly worried?"

She cocked her head toward her friend. "I'm afraid Nadine is the one who's having a fright."

"Detective Superintendent Matheson said that Guy is dead," Nadine said quietly, her tone begging for another opinion.

I looked at Nadine, and expression is often difficult to read in a cat. They always look so inscrutably pleased with themselves over some covert triumph. Nadine, though, looked miserable. Her head hung down and she made a pitiful and barely audible mewing sound. All I could do was lie there looking foolish. I would've resorted to some sort of we'll-get-the-blighter-who-did-this rhetoric, but I feared it would have been heard as falsely as it would have fitted my tongue. Either it was an accident, which meant that gunners and range officers responsible were long dead and gone, or it was indeed set up by person or persons unknown quite skilled at what it takes to stage a crime scene. Either way, that slight reduction in pain referred to by that vacuous term *closure* seemed distant, not just for Nadine, but all of us.

"Why, Harry," said Val as she looked at my face. "You're crying."

I raised my right hand and rubbed my eyes. My fingers came away wet. "I'm afraid I am."

Nadine jumped over onto the bed and the three of us did what we could then for poor Shad, which was bugger all. Perhaps we helped each other a little.

3

That night, by the grace of a strong sedative, I slept without dreams. The next day I tried walking on my balloon cast and hearing with my new implants. The implants worked perfectly; the balloon cast, aided by sufficient medication, was almost adequate. I avoided my room's telly at first. I knew what would be on. When Shad had been that slapstick funny insurance duck he had children around the world quacking out "aflak-aflak" at particularly serious interludes in classes, during church sermons, political campaign speeches, and funerals. Not entirely restricted to children, moreover. I confess to issuing a rude little "aflak" or two myself back in Metro when the detective chief superintendent would descend from Valhalla and portentously deign to address "you chaps" concerning some high profile case which was drawing heat from the commissioner. One of several reasons I was let go, I suspect.

I eventually gave in and watched one of the reports: A few clips from his adverts and interviews, a laudatory statement from Chief Constable Crowe of the Devon & Cornwall Constabulary concerning Shad's brief career in ABCD, followed by a computer generated eulogy delivered by the lizard who had replaced Shad's duck when his insurance firm was merged with another. Instead of his customary nakedness, the lizard was somberly dressed in black tie and suit and oozed virtual sincerity. He concluded his tribute to Shad by making a tasteful pitch for his firm's term life insurance plan. "You never know," he concluded as an image of Shad appeared on the screen surrounded by a wreath of daisies.

I always hated that lizard.

The newscasters moved over to stories of more pressing matters: The latest mutation of *E. drupi*, the erectile dysfunction virus; the possibilities of latest teen musical fad Cragsuck Funk destroying all life on this planet as we know it; and the electrifying results of the latest government funded weight-loss study (weight loss can be achieved most effectively by consuming moderate amounts of a well balanced diet in combination with a regular program of exercise). I changed the channel and found the same *Law & Order* reruns that had been on the telly the previous time I'd been in hospital.

After a few more tests the following morning, I was released, an ambulance delivering me home finally after a heated debate about the necessity of me being strapped down upon their little roll around before they could move. Settled in at home, there was an online tutorial for my wireless interface and with Val's computer I attempted to occupy my mind between headaches learning how to use it. In my first net connection I went to a news site and read the reports on the explosion. Dud shell went off. The deceased was a duck bio who used to be a telly star. Click here for animation. *Aflak.*

I clicked and there were clips taken from several of Shad's adverts. I shut it down, closed my eyes, and ran what I knew: By itself the call from Okehampton Station might have been a hoax. Rather sophisticated hoax considering the call had to come in with the proper police codes and encryption. Still, it could have been a hoax. By itself the explosion might have been an old dud artillery shell finally grown unstable enough to go up at that particular place and moment. By itself a shell firing short, falling next to an observation post unobserved, and being a dud as well might just have happened. All together, though, it was a bloody stretch of timing that gave credulity stretch marks.

But why? If it was an attempt to kill one or both of us, why so involved? As a sniper-for-hire who had been interviewed after being sentenced once said, "Keep it simple. The more complicated a hit gets, the more opportunity for mistakes, not to mention a smaller profit margin."

Words to live by.

Shad hadn't been with ABCD long enough to have developed a list of enemies. The few cases we had worked together all involved rather genteel malefactors. The most violent encounter Shad and I had was with a Rottweiler natural in Taunton who objected to being parted from his mate, a Dandie Dinmont bio named Flossie whose human engrams happened to be fleeing imprisonment on embezzlement charges. That particular felon had been remarkably grateful for our intercession. My early decades with Metro, on the other hand, had produced a virtual army of murderers, terrorists, and other violent chaps who would've delighted in seeing me blown to pieces. That was long ago, though. Most of the violent ones from my Metro years were either dead, living off their book and motion picture royalties, or dribbling oatmeal down their bibs in prison geriatric wards. None of them, in addition, were bombers. There was an answer somewhere, but I couldn't find it. I took my headache to bed.

4

Early in the morning on my third day home there was a ring from DC Ralph Parker, our mountain gorilla bio detective with the waste management problem. The Estuary accent he affected had been, apparently, dropped for the occasion. *"The chaps at Scientific and Technical concur with Army Military Police, sir,"* he said. *"As far as they are concerned it was a dud artillery shell that became unstable and simply popped off. They found enough bits of casing to identify the shell: an Excalibur Mark XVII. That's a 25cm high explosive smart round for long range cannon the army used toward the end of the Twenty-one hundreds."*

"What about the chemical composition of the explosive? Has that been matched to the casing fragments?"

"Exact match, sir."

"How'd the shell get next to an observation post?"

"The army can't explain it. Records from that period show which part of which range was used for a particular test or exercise. They show from where the shells were fired and where they were supposed to land, but there's no way to catalog short rounds or duds. If the guidance load went out on one of those smart rounds it became just like any other lump. Also, it's the army's opinion that an observer could well have been standing in that observation post during an exercise and not have noticed a short round dud striking nearby and burying itself in the sod. The noise, you see."

"What about the call?" I asked.

"Sorry?"

"The call that came into ABCD regarding a dead amdroid out on the moor, Parker. Did anyone trace it?"

"The call came from a mobile phone out of Okehampton, sir. A bit strange that."

"How so?"

"It's a police mobile number assigned to a Sergeant James Colly, constable assigned to Okehampton Station. On that exact day, though, Sgt. Colly was in Royal Devon Hospital here in Exeter getting his entire heart replaced. He'd been in intensive care there for a fortnight before the operation, which is a substantial piece of surgery I'm told."

"Does make rather a good alibi, doesn't it. Where was his phone?"

"With him, sir. It was among his things in hospital locked up. Whoever made the call must've duped his police card. That kept the call from being screened out as a hoax."

Had to have been done more than three weeks ago. Considerable planning, highly technical, forensically sophisticated, absolutely ruthless. "Parker, do you have Colly's phone records?"

"Yes sir. The call to ABCD Exeter was the only call made on that phone for the past twenty-two days. We voice printed the call recording and that definitely wasn't Colly who rang up the tower to report the dead bio. Very high voice. A child's according to the computer analysis."

"Get a match on the voiceprint?"

"No. Someone not in the system." There was a long uncomfortable pause on the line.

"What is it, Parker?" I said rather more irritably than was polite.

"We have orders from London to drop the entire matter. They've concluded that Shad's death was simply a piece of rotten luck."

"Luck," I repeated flatly.

"Yes sir. There's some suggestion," he continued, *"that Shad might have set the thing off himself."*

"What?"

"They say he might have touched something out there."

"It was a possible crime scene, Parker! Of course he touched something! That was his bleeding job!" My headache began ricocheting from one side of my skull to the other and I forced myself to calm down. "Shad's an experienced detective, Parker. When he was a human nat in the NYPD he even had bomb disposal unit experience. He wouldn't beat on a bomb fuse with a hammer just to see what would happen. They can't be serious."

"Serious enough for Dartmoor National Park Authority to consider billing ABCD to have that logan stone put back in its original position."

"Bollocks! Great roiling oceans of bloody flipping bilge!" I closed my eyes as molten steel seemed to pour into my brain pan all of which left me somewhat suspended between uncontainable pain and unexpressed expletives. When I risked opening my eyes I noticed Val sitting in the doorway. "Sorry, dear."

Her deep aqua eyes studied me for a moment. "Harry, are you all right?"

"Managing, dear. Ralph Parker and I were having a wag on the phone."

"The doctor said getting upset would probably worsen your headaches."

"I'm astounded he took the time from selling his old trusses."

"What?"

"I'm pleased to report my own research supports Dr. Truscott's theory, dear. Something else?"

"Don't get cross with me, Harry. I know you're in pain, but don't take it out on me."

I took a breath and let it out. "Sorry."

"Nadine would like to go to Hangingstone Hill. Is that possible?"

"Parker," I said into the handset, "has the scene out at Hangingstone Hill been cleared?"

"Yes sir. Did I hear your wife and her friend want to go out there?"

"Is there a problem?"

"I suppose there isn't any reason except . . . I mean, that's where Shad . . . you know."

"Yes," I answered. "Perhaps it may help Nadine," I offered. "Very well, dear," I said to Val. "I'll see about organizing something."

"Thank you." She turned and padded away toward the stairs.

"Sorry about barking at you," I said to Parker, turning again to the phone. "Didn't mean to kill the messenger."

"Not at all, sir. But about going to Hangingstone—it hasn't rained on the north moor since it happened."

"You mean we may find blood."

"Yes sir. Shad's and a good deal of your own. A weather front is supposed to dampen things a bit this morning. Perhaps if you wait until tomorrow."

"Val seems to think going there will help Nadine."

"Not for me to say, sir. Oh, while I think of it, If you go use GPS rather than trying to home in on the prang."

"Has it been removed?"

"No. There's an odd bit of jurisdictional bother with that. The scene analyzer wasn't ours, wasn't the army's, and wasn't one of the constabulary's. Has to be a records glitch somewhere. Who is supposed to collect it up has become a bother, as well. All the same, the signal's dead."

I frowned. "Dead?"

"Day by day the signal grew weaker then all of a sudden died. The bloody thing can't even maintain memory, sir, much less project the crime scene."

"Who copied it for the enquiry file?"

"That jurisdictional thing again, sir. Everyone assumed that the authority who placed the prang also copied it."

"So no one copied it."

"A proper cock-up," he stated.

I looked down at the Persian rug on the floor, its design filled with happy blues and yellows. Whoever set the trap had attached that scene analyzer to the logan stone. That's why the unit's serial number appeared in no one's records. It was a real prang, though, authentic enough to get Shad and me there. It was the genuine article. The power supply, therefore—

After a beat of stunned silence, my headache was temporarily forgotten. "Thanks for ringing me, Parker. I appreciate it more than I can say."

"Not at all—

I hung up, stood, and limped down the hall into the kitchen where Walter, our Rent-A-Mech, was finishing up the breakfast dishes.

Walter was one of thousands of the same model mechanical purchased years ago by Exeter's Rent-A-Mech, Ltd. to go in service on a lease basis only to have all of their workers emancipated by Parliament because modified human engram based artificial intelligence was included in the Parliamentary Reform Act of 2132. The mechs, in response, bought the firm from the owners whom they kept on to run the company. All Rent-A-Mechs in the city looked like Twentieth Century actor Stephen Fry in his role as Jeeves, had that venerable valet's epidermis been made of brushed titanium. Since the takeover, however, the livery in most cases had been traded in on more casual wear. It depended on the client. Walter wore earth tones and corduroy at our place.

"Walter," I said, "are you free for the remainder of the day? I know you have other clients."

"I am yours to command, sir. If dinner is to be served here at the usual time, however, I should begin preparations at around five."

"Can you drive Val, Nadine, and me out to the north moor near Okehampton?"

"Indeed I can, sir. When would that be?" I'd urged him to call me Harry, but Walter said it just wouldn't do.

"Right now. It's rather urgent."

"Very well, sir. I'll bring my electric around, shall I?"

"Thank you."

I hobbled up the stairs to the guest room where Nadine had been staying since the news about Shad. It was smallish, a single window looking over the garden, pale peach walls and a single bed with a powder blue coverlet. Val and her friend were both sitting on the bed. "Walter's going to drive us out to the moor," I said to Val. "He's bringing his car around now."

"Thank you, Harry," said Nadine. "It's a terrible imposition, I know."

"Not at all." I debated offering my possible piece of news. False hope and such. However, it was either tell Nadine now or at Hangingstone Hill.

"Harry, what is it?" asked Val.

"There is a possibility," I looked at Nadine, "just a possibility, mind you—that Guy is still alive." As they started to speak all at once I held up my hands. "A slim chance, but a chance. I'll explain in the car. Let's get going."

As I stood aside, allowing the two cats to run out of the room ahead of me, I saw—my cautionary probabilities notwithstanding—Nadine and Val both had only heard that Shad was still alive.

5

Walter's car was an MG ground electric which would have been cramped had Val and Nadine not been cats. Once we were off the Alphington Spur headed west on the A 30, Walter and I up front and the cats on a blanket in back, I turned half around and explained. "It has to do with the Vader prang—the mounted scene analyzer—at the site. That particular model is about fifteen centimeters long and a bit more than half a centimeter thick."

"What about them?" asked Val. She knew as much about the purpose of prangs as I did, but she knew I was after something else.

I turned to Nadine. "This kind of scene analyzer is arguably the most indestructible instrument in the world, Nadine. The case is made from high density ceramic composition titanium and the power supply is designed to take and retain its scene forensic data indefinitely. Crime scenes sometime need to be maintained for years—even decades. That's what the prang does: it records everything in place at a particular point in time, in detail, and can project that detail upon the scene long after the elements of that scene have changed. Hence scene analyzers must be able to withstand the elements, attempts at tampering, and efforts of miscreants to destroy them. In all my time in law enforcement I have never known a scene analyzer to fail."

"What does this have to do with Guy?" asked Nadine.

"The prang out at Hangingstone Hill failed."

"Surely, sir," began Walter, "if an artillery shell went off next to one of those instruments , well, doesn't that seem likely as a cause?"

"Certainly if it failed completely and right away, Walter. But Parker said that the prang's signal at Hangingstone declined in strength over two days then suddenly died." I looked at Nadine. "I believe Guy might have had time enough before the explosion to copy into one of the smaller mechs and has since been drawing power from the scene analyzer."

"If that's true," said Val, "Guy must be able to move about. Why didn't he let Ralph Parker or the police know when they were out there?"

"I'm not certain. It might have to do with concerns about being observed."

"By the person or persons who planted the bomb?" asked Walter.

"Yes."

"Sir, if I may?"

I nodded permission.

"Thank you, sir. Given possible post-incident observation, is it likely that such an offender may have a continuing interest in any subsequent enquiry or activity concerning said hill, including ours?"

"Quite likely," I answered.

"Might I suggest, then, we enter the moor farther to the east instead of taking the obvious route through Okehampton past the army camp?"

"Can you find the hill using another route?"

"Indeed I can, sir. As I was driving I downloaded the Ordnance Survey map of the area."

"Good thinking, Walter. Very well, we are in your capable hands."

"Very good, sir."

He got off the motorway at one of the South Zeal exits, went through the villages of Sticklepath and Belstone where we came onto a brain-shattering unpaved track called Tarka Trail which took us up onto the moor just as a light rain began falling. As we traveled the trail Walter identified the features we crossed: Scarey Tor which wasn't, East Okemont River ford where we almost became mired, a boggy stretch between East Mill Tor and Oke Tor where we forded the tributaries to the previously forded East Okemont River, climbed and crossed Okement Hill, then traveled down the hill to ford one of the River Taw tributaries. Following that, the car climbed the north end of Hangingstone Hill where we at last came to a stop a few meters north of the old observation post where several other ground cars and two Sky Rovers were parked. Walter parked his MG between a late model gray Ford Virgo and a burgundy Renault Festiva that had seen better days. The moment the MG stopped Walter had a headache preparation ready for me. As I drank that, Walter exited the car, held his seat forward for Val and Nadine, and came around to the passenger side umbrella in hand for me. Terribly efficient personnel at Rent-A-Mech. I cannot recommend them too highly.

The others on the hill, approximately twenty or so, appeared to be curiosity seekers from Okehampton and nearby villages. Families with children, individuals—no one appeared bothered yet by the developing rain as they eagerly searched for a telly star's signs of death. As I waited for the headache remedy to take effect, I noticed a boy of eleven or twelve, blondish and chunky, squatting down and examining the grass at his feet almost one blade at a time. Such concentration would have been the envy of any scenes of crime officer. "What are you looking for, lad?" I asked.

"Feathers, sir," he answered, not looking up. "White ones."

I was about to point out that Shad hadn't been a white duck when a little girl with dark hair, big eyes, wearing a blue rain jacket and little blue wellies, saw Nadine and called out to her parent, "Oh, Mummy, may I play with kitty?"

"Ask the gentleman, Pearl," said a large woman in her forties quite disturbingly dressed the same as her offspring.

Pearl approached me. "Sir, may I play with your kitty?"

"Ask her," I answered.

The girl frowned as she turned toward Nadine. Val, however, intercepted the girl and said to her, "Perhaps later, dear."

Pearl ran off to her mother's side declaiming frightening things said to her by those horrible bio cats, Pearl's mum glared at me, and mercifully it began raining in earnest. Several souvenir hunters made for their vehicles. "Into each life some rain must fall," observed Walter.

I glanced at him. "Shakespeare?"

"No sir. Henry Wadsworth Longfellow."

"Let's see if we can find Shad."

After half an hour of steadily increasing rain, an unpleasantly chilly wind from the west encouraging the appreciation of warmer climes and more sheltered endeavors, all of the other seekers had departed. It was curious watching as the rain seemed to heal the place where the explosion occurred. The stone dust washed from the blasted granite bedrock, clumps of earth eroded, a muddy pool began forming in the bottom of the small crater.

"I wonder how long it will take, sir, before all signs of what happened here are swallowed," said Walter, still holding the umbrella between me and the rain. My coat had water repellant pretensions that were also eroding as the rain continued.

"Months," I guessed. "Perhaps only days." I looked over the hilly expanses of the former artillery range. Heather, peat bogs, rocks, the view of the edges softened by the great solvent, rain. The only evidence that anything had ever exploded out here was at our feet and fading as we watched. "Existence is such a transitory thing, Walter, our marks of passing so slight. In the midst of living, though, life seems so enduring, our accomplishments gigantic and eternal. Yet when death touches us this sense of permanence evaporates like the illusion it is. Perhaps that's why so many of us cling to life so."

"Lingering in hopes of permanence, sir?"

"The return of its illusion, perhaps. Do you keep a backup copy of your engrams, Walter?"

"Indeed I do, sir. Rent-A-Mech insist on it. Perish the thought something should happen to me. Should it, however, my training, experience, and most importantly client preferences and requirements won't be lost. Neither will I. A new can and at most I'd lose a day or two. It affords me a measure of security and protects the firm's client information." He faced me. "Weren't DS Shad's engrams backed up?"

"No."

"Dear me, sir. Why is that, if I might know?"

"A half-dozen excuses—it takes time, too bothersome, uses too much memory in the mainframe, and so on. Most bios don't do it, though, because it feels creepy."

"Creepy, sir?"

"That's Shad's word. An uneasiness. I think, because we're originally human naturals, we hold onto this illusion that we're unique irreproducible beings. Backing up engram imprints gives in to the fact, all this protoplasm notwithstanding, we are but machines. It's humbling."

"Are your engrams backed up, sir?"

"No. And, yes, the reasons for not doing so seem sillier with each passing moment." I nodded toward the crater. "We'd best finish our search before the entire moor erodes into the sea. Walter, we could cover more ground if you'd agree to join in."

"I would be happy to, sir," he responded lowering his voice, "However, Mrs. Jaggers told me she'd have my gears for garters if I allowed a single drop of rain to fall upon you."

"Since I'm already soaked through, dear boy, I'd say you're already doomed."

"Before my imminent disassembly, sir, shall I engage in a bit of exploration then?"

"The wages are the same in either case." I pointed to the opposite side of the crater. "Go down slope until you run out of loose clumps of soil and other debris from the explosion. Go a couple meters beyond then circle the edge of the debris field moving toward the center with each circuit. I'll start in the center and work my way out. Look in, around, over, and beneath everything. And thank you."

6

We walked the coil for more than two hours, turning over rocks and clods of earth, not finding Shad nor anything into which he might have copied himself. I reached the displaced hanging stone before Walter. When I examined the scene analyzer I could tell someone had tried prying the thing free of the rock, which showed crude tool marks. I suspected souvenir hunters. Our culprit would possess the tool necessary to remove the instrument from its site.

My wireless interface detected no signal at all from the prang. I stood and looked toward the northwest. The view took in a vast expanse, the boulder-pocked flanks of Yes Tor filling the far distance. What I could see though was but a small part of the moor. If Shad had copied into a mech and had gone for help he could be quite a ways from Hangingstone Hill. He could have run out of power before reaching help. He could have been caught in the open.

Suddenly I felt a chill and began shaking as I pulled my coat about me. I was soaked, my ankle hurt, and my head was splitting. I was very tired and possessed of an overwhelming desire to lie down in the wet heather, pull the rain up over my head, and let sleep take me.

"Sir, if I may?" said Walter.

I smelled hot tea. When I opened my eyes and looked, Walter was holding out a steaming cuppa. I took it in both hands, felt it warm my palms, then took a sip, the healing liquid heating my core. "Thank you. Where on earth did you get this?"

"I had a few moments before your party made it to the car, sir, and packed a snack. I arranged a bit of shelter on the east side of that stone building at the top of the hill."

He helped me along and by the time I had finished the tea, I was mobile again, my wits about me, but a terrible pain in my ankle. The wall on the east side of the observation shack was in severe disrepair but Walter had taken a few rocks and boards and constructed a makeshift shelter off to the side of the shack within which was a plank bench propped upon two flat stones. He helped me down upon the thing easing the pain in my ankle considerably. Before I could thank him, he held out a tray of small sandwiches with one hand and his carafe of tea in the other. I had three of the former and a refill from the latter as he warmed the enclosure with his wrinkle remover.

"By the way, sir, I found those electrical components and pieces of metal upon the bench beside you during my search."

As I was chewing on an absolutely delicious turkey and avocado sandwich I examined what looked like pieces to a home made remote detonator and fragments of bomb casing. Walter had placed them in sealed plastic envelopes, dated, site located, and signed the envelopes. I chanced to look up and saw between the boards above. I was being protected from the rain by a plastic sheet decorated with images of hundreds of mice. I swallowed my mouthful and said, "Walter?"

"Yes sir?"

"Where did you obtain that plastic sheet?"

"From the Marks & Spencer catalog, sir. I originally intended it to serve as a ground cloth for our picnic here. Because of the inclement weather, however, I thought this application more practical."

The mice on that sheet weren't Mickey or Minnie, nor even Mighty. They were, instead, a quite realistic vermin infestation of Biblical proportions. "Mice, Walter?"

"Yes sir. It was for Mrs. Jaggers and her guest. I hope you don't object."

"No. No, Walter. Not at all." I looked away from the sheet. "Speaking of Val and Nadine, do you know where they are?"

Just then a strange distant voice sang out, "Nadine, honey is that you?"

From the other side of the little stone building I heard Nadine call out, "It's *Chuck Berry!*"

"Help me up, Walter. That's Shad!"

Before he could get me to my feet, Nadine ran into the shelter followed by Val. In Nadine's mouth she carried a small object that resembled a micro—*was* a micro. She jumped up on the wooden plank and deposited the little mech in my hand. "Guy is in this thing, Harry, isn't he? Guy sings that song to me. Because of my name. That's Chuck Berry's voice."

"Yes," I said as I examined the tiny vehicle. All of the black paint was gone from the micro's port side and one of the tiny claw grapples up front was broken off. The other forensic instruments, however, looked serviceable. The tiny flashing red power readout on its front end indicated an occupant coming off standby. "He's in there, Nadine," I said.

The micro energized fully and rose into the air, its chipped lens aimed at my face. "Jaggs. It's about time you got here."

"I say, look what the cat dragged in," I responded happily.

Hovering, the micro turned around. "Hi, Walter."

"Very good to see you, sir."

Aimed at my wife Shad said, "Hi, Val."

"It's so good to find you alive, Guy. We were so worried."

"And therein lies a tale. But first," he did a middling job of rubbing the micro's port side against Nadine's left whiskers and cheek. "I really missed you."

"Nadine's the one who suggested coming out here," I said.

"In that case," he said to Nadine, "you definitely pulled my engrams out of the fire."

"Guy," said Nadine meekly. "Your ducky suit. I'm afraid it's gone."

"Yeah. I've been finding pieces of myself scattered all over the north end of this hill. That rat, too." He faced me. "All I found of yours, Jaggs, was a lot of blood." He did a quick scan of me. "Busted ankle, busted ribs, ear implants, and a cut throat. You got off light. Which reminds me: Is there anyone else on the hill besides you four?"

"There were more than a dozen but they all went home, Guy," answered Nadine. "It's raining."

"Harry," said Val crossly. "You're soaked and you'll catch your death."

"Better I should catch death than it should catch me," I answered with a smile.

"Walter—" she began.

"Stop fussing," I said, "and you're not to reproach Walter. He did what he could to keep me dry within the bounds of my cooperation."

"If that's all settled," said Shad as he rose slightly and faced Walter, "Brother mech, you got an AH8 port adapter in that can?"

Walter held up his left pinky finger. "I do indeed, sir."

"If you can spare a couple of electrons, I could use a boost."

"Certainly, sir."

Shad rotated up slightly, caught a view of Walter's special tablecloth, and shot down to the ground as he cried out. He studied it for a moment and slowly turned until he was looking at me.

"A little treat Walter purchased for Val and Nadine," I explained. "A feline snack motif."

"Mice?"

The cats looked up at the improvised roof. "Why, Walter," said Val. "It's very thoughtful."

"Ever so elegant," Nadine joked amiably.

"Yeah, man," Shad said as he warily moved toward Walter. "The bee's knees."

7

After Shad's micro was fully charged and Val and Nadine were happily eating the mouse morsel stuffed pastries Walter provided, I tried a general wireless transmission. *"They operated on my ears and I went wireless."*

"And another dinosaur bites the dust," Shad said out loud to me. Turning to Walter he said. "Do you have wireless?"

"I do indeed sir."

"Would you send a little transmission to Jaggs telling him how great his new ears are?"

"Very good, sir." To me he transmitted, *"Your signal came in five-by-five, sir. Do you enjoy the feature?"*

"Haven't quite gotten used to it," I answered. To Shad I said aloud, "What's afoot?"

"Nicely put," rhymed Shad. Val and Nadine were both looking up from their mouse morsels sensing something amiss. "We're being observed," Shad announced to us all. "It's electronic and optical surveillance. I don't think the guy staking out this location can pick up low level sound or bio or mech receivers at the range he's at, but wireless he gets."

"Who?" asked Val.

"This is going to sound crazy," he said to Val, "but it might be the NYPD."

"I say." I must have looked rather surprised. In any event, I certainly felt that way. "What led you to that conclusion?"

"The rat said something to me right before all hell broke loose. When you were on the phone trying to make sense of the report we received, Jaggs, I went to the cruiser and copied into this micro. From there I went directly to our alleged corpse. I was just about to do a scan on the deceased when the rat opened his eyes, looked behind me, then looked

106

directly at me and said, 'Hi, cheese eater.'" Shad issued the rat's words in a falsetto voice replete with scorn and American accented syllables.

"What happened then?"

"The rat moved one of his front feet and I began getting the hell out of there. A second later it went boom. By the time this mech rebooted and I managed to dig my way out from under some turf that landed on me, it was dark, the area was ringed with crime scene tape, and everybody was gone."

"Is there some significance in what the rat said?"

"Yes," answered Shad. "Cheese eater is one of the more affectionate names NYC cops use to refer to members of the rat squad: Internal Affairs Bureau." He turned to Nadine. "IAB takes down crooked cops."

"Were you ever in Internal Affairs?" I asked him.

"No. But I never took a bribe and among some cops that's prima facie evidence you're chewing cheddar with the whiskered set."

I gently shook my head. "That makes no sense. You're thousands of miles, a couple of years, and several careers away from New York and it's police force. Why try and kill you now?"

"All I can think of is some old crooked cop went a little dingy in the head and decided killing me was the answer to all his problems."

"Why didn't you put in a call for help?" Nadine asked.

"The blast damaged this micro's antenna. I tried a call and my transmission distance is down to under three kilometers. I had my scanner on looking for local traffic in case the cops, the army, or a hiker with his cell on came near when I *received* a transmission." He looked at me. "It sounded like a generated voice. All it said was, 'I received a weak signal. The turkey might not be done.' Just like that. Only a key click for a response."

"That doesn't sound friendly," observed Walter.

"That was my take on it. Both transmissions were clear and I got automatic azimuths on both. I didn't attempt any more calls, but I traveled a few meters so I could triangulate the transmissions should whoever was watching me make another call. As soon as I moved, though, there was another signal, same voice—very high. Familiar but can't place it. The bearing showed it came from that tor just north of us."

"Steeperton?" asked Walter.

"Yeah. One word: 'Movement.' There was a long silence, then came the response. A voice that didn't sound generated at all said, 'Finish it.' Both communications were on hand radio frequency."

"You get a fix on the other party?" I asked.

"A village due east of here called Gidleigh. Nothing since and that was three days ago. I know the guy's still on Steeperton, though. Every so often he downloads some information and I can pick up his satellite address. To conserve my charge I go hide in an old piece of tubing on the roof and go standby. My boy on Steeperton visited here searching for me when I was shut down. That's when he sucked the rest of the charge off that Vader prang."

I frowned. If it was a hitter, the fellow's reckless perseverance was remarkable—unless he was expendable. "Dependable and expendable," I said. "Are you thinking what I'm thinking?" I asked Shad.

"A toaster."

I nodded.

"What's a toaster, dear?" Val asked me.

"Originally it was a kind of android certain terrorist, gang, and government types used for settling old scores and eliminating troublesome personages."

"Do you mean a hit man—person, thing . . ." She looked at Walter.

"I believe *assassin* will do nicely, madam." He looked at me. "If I may, sir?"

"Please."

"It has to do with Modified Engram Based Intelligence Technology —MEBIT for short. The original point of artificial intelligence, of course, was to produce a mentally able, efficient, obedient work force that would do what it was instructed and make no demands."

"Slaves," said Nadine.

"Exactly, miss. As the U.S. Supreme Court's majority opinion in Grant v. Hudder eventually found—

"Walter," I cautioned gently.

"Forgive me, sir. In short, madam, the modified part of MEBIT intelligence was ruled illegal in the States which prompted Parliament to do the same here. I can still recall the day all of us at Rent-A-Mech received our patches."

"Instead of MEBITs," said Shad, "they're now EBITS. A baseball joke in there somewhere."

"About the toasters," I interrupted.

"Yes sir," Walter turned toward Nadine and Val. "MEBIT operated beings, bios and mechs, are blocked from disobeying, disagreeing with, or altering their instructions. As killers it makes them highly intelligent, persistent, and resourceful, if a trifle rigid. If apprehended . . ." Walter looked at me.

I thought about that for a moment, remembering several famous cases from when I was with Metro. "Actually, they cannot be apprehended. If old bill is closing in and it looks bad for the dex, he zeroes himself out. Scrubbed clean."

"Some New Jersey gangs used to rig theirs to explode," said Shad. His micro faced me. "Jaggs, I could've run off that Vader prang for another couple of weeks. I thought the toaster drained it to force me out, but dexes are high energy. Maybe he's running low, too."

"How does he know you haven't left the hill or zeroed out yourself?" I asked.

A mischievous little cackle came from the micro. "You know how superstitious most mechs are?"

I looked at Walter. "Are we being insensitive?"

"Not at all, sir. DS Shad's observation is quite true, although bios with artificial intelligence are the same as mechs in this regard. My therapist ascribes the phenomenon to the shortcuts taken to devise MEBIT. The early versions of artificial intelligence weren't very artificial in that the basic engram patterns were simply copied from various humans. They erased all the identity memories—life experiences, embarrassing encounters at summer camp, credit account numbers, that sort of thing—but there wasn't any way to eliminate the feelings connected to those memories."

"I cannot imagine what that must be like," said Val.

"It is quite like being haunted, madam," stated Walter. "Even with the patch, all EBIT AI's are filled with feelings to which they cannot attach experience. It gives one the continuous sense of having misplaced or forgotten things of importance. Often this feeling manifests itself as a form of schizophrenia. In my case I always felt as though I was being watched. When voices began talking to me, I sought a therapist. Many AI operated beings believe in ghosts. For some the spirits even appear to take corporeal form."

I looked at Shad. "And?"

"Well, I've been transmitting little ghost plays nights to my buddy over there on Steeperton."

I cleared my throat and said with a ghostly timbre, "'I wear the chain I forged in life. I made it link by link—'"

"Nothing Dickensonian. He's been looking me up on the net while he's sitting there in his little shack in the dark. So nights I've been sending bits from my old insurance commercials." He treated us to a series of ghostly aflaks and we all laughed. "One of the visitors yesterday left a blue candy wrapper on the ground. Last night I put my illuminated end in the wrapper and gave him a light show. "I don't know if I scared him, but if he buys a policy I need to talk to the company about my commission."

"Weren't you afraid of frightening him off?" asked Nadine.

"He's still got a job to do," Shad answered flatly. "What I've done is let him know the job may not be finished. He'll keep at it until either his battery dies or the fellow in Gidleigh calls him off."

"Where could he have obtained a live artillery shell? An antique? How could he sneak it into the country?"

"Good questions," he answered.

Someone rang me on my wireless. Unlike the mech wireless, not at all an unpleasant sensation. Instead of buzzing, vibrating, or playing some annoying tune, the knowledge that I had an incoming call simply appeared in my head. As Val and Nadine returned to their pastries, I motioned for Shad and Walter to listen in. It was Matheson.

"Jaggers. How are you doing, old fellow? Enjoying your time off?"

"Well enough, superintendent. The family and I are having an outing—a picnic."

"Excellent. Fresh air, a good hobble. Best thing for you. I have a few things regarding that matter out at Hangingstone." I debated cutting him off in respect to our listening audience on Steeperton, but thought better of it.

"Very well, sir."

"Sci-and-Tech finished running the IDs on the DNA collected at the scene. Shad, of course," he began.

"Yes sir."

"The rat amdroid bio, though, is a Fantronics, Ltd. product. That particular rat was purchased by a costumer: Celebrity Lookalikes of Bond Street, London."

I looked at Shad, a quizzical expression on my face. "Celebrity rat?" I mouthed.

"Ben," said Shad. "The rodent lead in the motion picture *Willard?"*

"Go on, sir," I urged Matheson.

"The customer was a D. Lipper of Kensington. I glanced at Shad in his micro. Hard to read emotional reactions off the chassis of a micro.

"Interesting sense of irony," observed the former Donald Lipper.

"He paid the full amount in cash," Matheson continued. *"His money was good, name and address both phonies. No description."*

"Superintendent, what about surveillance records?"

"For what they believe are obvious reasons, Jaggers, Celebrity Lookalikes do not allow cameras of any kind on premises. We're running the records of the street cameras right now but Celebrity has hundreds of client visits, inquiries, pick-ups, and deliveries every day. Given this fellow's proclivities, he was probably in disguise when he rented the rat meat suit."

"What about the person who handled the sale? Someone with a downloadable memory?"

"A human natural as our luck would have it. The agent who handled the sale can't remember one rat customer from another. Rat bios are quite popular for some disquieting reason—school outings, club meetings, university bashes—that sort of thing. The fellow didn't copy

into the rat suit on the premises. Presumably he has the use of a stasis bed elsewhere. I may be jumping the gun, but I'm reopening the enquiry as a possible homicide."

I glanced down at Shad in his flying lipstick. "Thank you. Is that it, sir?"

"An additional unrelated matter. Quite interesting. Birdshot was found in—among Shad's remains."

"Yes, sir," I answered looking at Shad's micro. "When Shad was an officer with Northern New England Wildlife Protection I believe he was wounded during a duck hunting season."

"Really. Well, Jaggers, it appears that two of the pellets have been positively matched to a registered microscopic barrel map of a shotgun purchased in Burlington, Vermont eleven years ago. The purchaser was a bloke named John Quinn."

"John Quinn, you say?"

"Yes. He was once in law enforcement in New York City. Chief of detectives, actually. Eventually became commissioner. Seems to have gotten into politics. Running for state governor or something. Don't suppose there was anything they could do about a duck hunter shooting a duck in duck hunting season, eh?

"No sir."

"Well, that's all I have, Jaggers. Enjoy your picnic and best to Val."

I bid Matheson goodbye and looked at Shad. "John Quinn?" I said.

He was silent for a very long moment. At last he played his memory recording of the rat's last words. "'Hi cheese eater.'"

I looked at Walter. "You watch the American news. Have you ever seen this Quinn on the telly?"

"Yes sir. Former Police Commissioner Quinn is frequently invited to appear on American news programs to reflect upon various law enforcement issues. Polls place him at least twenty points above his closest rivals in the coming primaries. There is also speculation that after capturing the state governorship his goal is the White House."

"What do you think of the cheese-eater recording?"

Walter turned toward Shad. "May I hear it again, sergeant?"

Shad played the recording.

"Sir," said Walter, "That sounds very much like John Quinn doing his impression of Mickey Mouse imitating Bluto with a New York accent."

"Bluto?" asked Nadine looking up from her mouse morsels at Shad.

"Popeye's rival for the hand of the fair Olive Oyl," said Shad. He repeated the cheese eater recording then played the mysterious transmission he had picked up from Gidleigh: "'Finish it.'"

"Is that Quinn?" I asked Shad.

"Yeah. I think so." The micro faced me. "John Montgomery Quinn. I don't get it, man. I was even going to vote for the guy." Shad flew in slow measured circles. "Damned near kills my partner when he blows me up with a bogus rat. Two years ago he shoots me in the ass with a shotgun. Twelve years ago . . ." Shad's micro stopped moving, hovered motionless for an instant, then streaked out from beneath the shelter. I had Walter help me up and serve as a crutch as I followed. The rain had stopped leaving a dank heaviness to the air. When I found Shad he was down at the original position of the hanging stone, his lens aimed at the pool at the bottom of the crater.

"What is it, Shad?"

He was silent for a long moment. When he spoke his voice sounded strangely vulnerable. "Jaggs, are you familiar with an old Al Pacino cop flik titled *Serpico?*"

"A cop classic. What law enforcement officer hasn't . . ." My voice trailed off as I realized to what Shad was alluding. The real Serpico wouldn't go along with the other cops in bribe taking. His fellow cops, uncomfortable with such reckless behavior, set up young Serpico to be killed. Back in the NYPD I-never-took-a-bribe Det. Donald Lipper was asked to back up some other cops in taking down a fugitive. He never came back."

"When I was killed," said Shad, "Chief Quinn was the head of the Detective Bureau. Nothing left of me but memory. Chief Quinn came by the hospital to talk with me about coming back to the force when I'd copied into my replacement meat suit. That's before my agent got me the duck gig. Funny thing, though."

"What?" I asked.

"On that visit Quinn accidentally knocked over a cup of coffee into the chassis of my memory unit."

"Embarrassing."

"Yeah, not to mention lethal. Lucky the hospital kept patient memory units on continuous sync with its main engram bank."

"Lucky. I say, Shad, Quinn wouldn't happen to have bomb disposal unit experience, would he?"

"Funny you should ask. Thirty years ago John Quinn started out as a firecracker." He paused a moment then said, "Four attempts at killing me and still at it."

"One must admire the fellow's resolve," Walter observed.

"I don't want to jump to conclusions, Jaggs," said Shad, "but I'm beginning to suspect Quinn wants me out of the way."

"Is there some reason?" I asked. "Do you have anything on him?"

"Other than a couple of attempts at killing me, I can't think of a thing. I know five or six really crooked detectives, though. I'm guessing if they had to sit in front of a committee they could put a substantial knot in Quinn's political panties."

"I suppose we ought to do something about it, old fellow—I mean before candidate Quinn reaches the White House, attains control of a brace of plasma bombs, and accidentally vaporizes Devon."

Shad turned and aimed his lens in the direction of Steeperton. "Unless we can convince that dependable expendable fellow over there to roll on his employer before he zeroes out, all we'll be left with is a dead hunk of machinery and a prime suspect off scot-free."

"What do you suggest?"

Shad's micro looked at Walter. "When I was hooked up to Walter getting my battery topped off, I got a look at his package. You know he's got more than two hundred thousand recipes on file?"

"Any involving duck?" I asked Walter.

"One hundred and sixteen, sir. All quite excellent."

"He's got some other stuff in there, too, Jaggs. Gives me an idea."

8

The time and power requirements of Shad's plan left very little charge left on Walter's MG and not a great deal of light left to the day by the time we finished preparations. Afterward Walter drove us down the hill and parked the car where the track came in from the Taw Head ford, the last of the rain clouds in the east reflecting the setting sun's light. Val and Nadine remained in the MG equipped with a cell phone whose preprogrammed number for a police ambulance could be entered with the stroke of a single paw. Walter, Shad, and I continued north. Shad hovered, Walter walked, and I leaned rather heavily on Walter as I limped along. In twenty minutes or so we reached a gentle track that came up the southwest side of Steeperton Tor. Twenty additional minutes of climbing, slowed by having to wait for me, and we were at the top looking across the massive stacked granite plates of the tor to the shed-roofed stone observation shack upon a rise at the north end of the rocks.

The building's roof looked to be in much better condition than that of the shack on Hangingstone Hill. I turned back and looked toward the southwest. Hangingstone was a hundred or more meters in elevation higher than Steeperton. The air was still and cool. At this distance the shack on Hangingstone was but a darkened dot on the horizon against a sky of delicate pinks rapidly being swallowed by the darkness of the approaching night. It was quite moving. I glanced down at the MG, another dark dot, and imagined Val in there waiting for news of how all this would end.

"Jaggs?" called Shad.

I turned around. Walter was looking at me and Shad was hovering next to him, also looking at me. "Sorry. Getting a last look at things. After all, I am the one who doesn't have an engram copy back in Exeter."

"Walter and I could go in alone—"

"We are agreed," I interrupted, "that my presence could well tip the scales in favor of the toaster's cooperation?" I looked at Walter.

"Yes sir. That is true. MEBIT conscience is suppressed, but not eliminated."

I looked at Shad.

"Yeah, great if Walter's right about yon toaster. How about it, Walter? You got a lot of experience with killer mechs?"

"I'm afraid, sir, the only toasters with which I have experience are designed for sliced bread, crumpets, and such." Walter looked at me. "Sir, I could be dead wrong."

"Nicely put," said Shad, turning toward me. "Jaggs, we could wait for a properly equipped team to come and deal with the Terminator. No muss, no fuss—"

"—And no witness," I completed. "To change plans now would require time which we are running out of rather rapidly. Gentlemen, every now and then one simply needs to roll the dice."

"Would it be crass of me, Balloon-leg Harry," asked Shad, "to point out that right now you're on your third meat suit which itself is getting just little bomb worn around the edges?"

"Caution," I answered. "is just another way of saying I'm not sure of what I'm doing."

Walter looked at me. "Sir, forgive me if I'm speaking out of turn, but doesn't that rather accurately describe our current predicament?"

"I'm afraid it does and it is quite tactless of you to make a point of it. I should complain to your employer."

"Employee owned company, sir," said Walter. "I am my employer."

"Then consider yourself notified." I pointed toward the shack. "Let's go."

The stone shack, according to a sign affixed to its newish steel door, was maintained by the park authority to house emergency medical and survival supplies for hikers stranded by freak storms. I opened the door and it swung in. No noise. No motion. Very little light inside. Outside light was prevented from coming through the windows by flattened pieces of pasteboard. There was a battery operated light hanging from the center of the roof, but it was missing its batteries. Shad turned on the micro's illumination system. The south wall was filled up to the blocked window with shelves containing first aid kits, packaged blankets, and cases of bottled water and energy bars. Like the battery operated light, all three torches and a radio had been stripped of their batteries all of which now lay discarded upon the cement floor.

Against the back of the shack, seated in the shadows upon a sleeping bag roll was the figure of a quite small person. Shad illuminated the figure of a young girl who sat motionless, her eyes open, looking like an old-fashioned porcelain doll on a gift shop shelf. She was clad in pale green sweat pants, chestnut hiking boots, and a darker green top jacket. "I can still read her receiver," said Shad, "but she's running on empty."

"She seems familiar," I said.

"Shirley Temple, *Rebecca of Sunnybrook Farm*, Nineteen thirty-eight. Jaggs, she's close to zeroing out."

"Walter?"

"Yes sir."

Walter moved next to the girl and knelt, light emanating from somewhere on his chest. He reached with his right hand behind her neck, felt around for a moment, then said, "I've found the port, sir. It's a KV12."

He plugged in and the girl's eyes blinked. She seemed to freeze for a second then her gaze darted in Walter's direction. "I'm giving you a bit of a charge, miss," he said cheerfully. "You seemed a bit down."

"In your dreams, Tick Tock. It'll be a cold day in hell before a bucket of bolts like you gives me a charge," she said with a definite note of sarcasm in her voice. She didn't pull away, however. Instead she looked at me and frowned. As she moved her gaze to Shad's illuminated micro she stiffened.

"Before doing anything rash," I said, "I would point out that Guy Shad's engrams, current as of two hours ago, have been copied to Exeter, as have our friend Walter's. Mine, on the other hand, have not."

Her gaze traversed the three of us again, stopping on me. "Who are you?"

"Detective Inspector Harrington Jaggers, Devon ABCD. In the micro is Detective Sergeant Guy Shad and the fellow who is providing you with an increased difference in potential is our friend Walter Cogg." Walter nodded.

"I received the transmission but couldn't read the encryption code," she said to Walter. "Industrial?"

"Yes miss," said Walter as he removed his hand from the back of her neck and stood. "Rent-A-Mech, Ltd., at your service. It would never do to let competing mechanical service establishments access to our client information, would it?"

"Rent-A-Mech," she repeated without humor.

Walter nodded at me and stepped back.

"I should add," I continued, "detectives from Artificial Beings Crimes and officers of the Devon & Cornwall Constabulary are at this moment descending upon the village of Gidleigh to place John Quinn under arrest for attempted murder."

Her gaze fixed on me. "I have an eight percent charge, Inspector Jaggers," she said. "That's more than sufficient to eliminate all three of you, warn my factor, and effect an escape."

She fell silent, stared at us each in turn, and shifted her gaze to a dark corner. She sat there, staring and immobile, for what seemed an eternity. At last she turned her head and faced Walter, her forehead wrinkled in what appeared to be anguish. "What was it?" she asked "When you put that partial charge in me, what else did you put in?"

"A little upgrade, miss: A patch on your MEBIT imprint."

"A virus?"

"No miss. The patch simply removes all the artificially implanted choice restrictions MEBIT put on your engram set. You are now an EBIT."

It took her awhile to absorb that. Few contemplate freedom's meaning until they lose it. How much more profound it must be for one who never had it or even contemplated it to become suddenly free—to suddenly have a full sense of right and wrong. Instant complications. "You mean I can . . . I can disobey."

"Yes miss. It is now your choice."

"And your responsibility," I added quickly. I thought about mentioning how she now came under a different set of laws. Before, she was a toaster—a tool no more responsible for those she killed than a knife or gun. Now she was like the rest of us—responsible for her choices and filled with anxiety for that reason. I thought about mentioning it, but I felt she already suspected. It frightened her.

"What is your name?" asked Shad.

"Alice." She wrapped her arms about herself and looked down at the floor. "Alice Blue." The expression on her angelic face hesitated between fear and anger. "Missions, work to do. Orders. No questions. I had no doubts or fears. I knew what to do."

"What about ghosts, Miss Alice?" asked Walter.

"All MEBITs have ghosts," she said dismissively. "You learn not to pay them any mind. Ghosts are nowhere as terrifying—" She slowly shook her head. "I'm seeing things so differently." She rubbed her eyes and leaned back against the stone wall as though her own weight had suddenly become an intolerable burden. "You have no idea of the things I've done—that I still have left to do. I have a job to do, duty, *a purpose*."

"Change the job," I said. "Find new work, a new duty, choose a different purpose. That's the power you now have."

She stood and was rather small. Beautiful child, a head full of pale brown curls. What an assassin she must have made. Who could look at that and see death coming?

"Why are you three here?" she asked. "You could have destroyed me or simply let me zero out." She held her hands to her face. "My head. I have a head filled with nightmares, a heart that wants to cry, and no tear ducts." She lowered her hands. "What do you want of me?"

"For myself," I began, "I want you to give information to the authorities on your arrangement with John Quinn and testify to it in court. Then it will be time to explore all of the other times you were used to commit illegal acts by testifying against your former masters."

Shad said, "I'd really like to know why Quinn is so obsessed with killing me. Why this elaborate plan?"

Alice Blue looked at Walter. "As for me, Miss Alice," he said, "I'd like to give you the name of my therapist. He may be able to help you sort out some of those nightmares."

"Kill you three or start a whole new existence; Is that about it?"

Shad, Walter, and I looked among ourselves, shrugged, agreed, and nodded. "Yes," I said to her. "That's about it."

"The tin man and the flying lipstick are just suits," she said, indicating Walter and Shad. "Their engrams are safe in Rent-A-Mech headquarters." She pointed at me. "All of you that is you is right here. Correct?"

"That is correct," I answered.

"What if I kill you?"

"Then you'd become a murderer."

She held out her hands. "What do you think *I already am!*"

"You were used for the commission of terrible acts, Miss Alice," said Walter. "You now have the ability to become the means through which those acts are made right. You can *choose* to bring those responsible to justice. Before you were a tool; now you are only a tool if you choose to be."

"I can choose to kill." She looked at each of us in turn, her expression softening to become one of awe. "You all have that choice," she said. "You could have killed me."

I couldn't tell if she was going to cooperate, go catatonic, or self-destruct. Just then I felt something brush my leg. I looked down and it was Val. "I hate to interrupt while you're working, Harry," she said, "but the low charge alarm on Walter's electric is beeping." She looked at Alice Blue. "Harry, are you going to introduce us?"

I bent over, picked up Val, and held her in my arms. "Alice, this is my wife, Valerie Jaggers. Val, this is Miss Alice Blue."

"Pleased to meet you, Alice."

Alice walked over and stopped before me, her hand out to pet Val. "Is it all right?" she asked.

"Of course, dear," said Val as she climbed out of my arms and into Alice's. It frightened me, but I knew why Val did it. She was protecting me and it's harder to kill someone while holding a big warm purring bundle of fur. As Alice stroked Val's back, my wife said quietly, "I couldn't help hearing what you were saying, Alice. May I offer a bit of advice?"

Alice nodded, her gaze fixed on Val.

"Doing the right thing is often a difficult choice to make. Even more difficult is accepting help when it's offered. Choices have consequences and not choosing is also making a choice. There are a lot of things to be made right, Alice, but there is also a great deal of help available. Harry, Guy, and Walter can assist you in getting that help."

Alice Blue looked down and Nadine was rubbing against her leg. She bent over, picked up Nadine, held both of them in her arms, and looked at me. "My first choice," she said.

"Actually, miss," said Walter, "you've already made several choices. We're all, after all, still alive."

She held the cats for a long time looking at a point somewhere outside the shack. She looked at Walter and said, "I've never been lost before. I think I am now. I'll take your therapist's number."

"Very good, miss."

To Shad she said, "In my opinion John Quinn is insane. He talks about you almost as though you were a constant presence. I gather he tried killing you before."

"Yes."

"It's twisted his head."

"How did he get the explosives into the country?" I asked.

"They were already here," she answered. "Quinn is on the board of World Eco Watch. A little satellite time using a high-definition metal detection filter on an artillery range and Quinn managed to locate what he wanted inside your jurisdiction. All he needed was a remote sonic detonator and a rat suit. He built the first and rented the second."

My own eyebrows went up. I had been wrong and everyone else had been right: It had been an old dud artillery shell. While I was contemplating the number of persons to whom I owed amends, Alice said, "Okay, Inspector. Tell me what you want me to do."

9

Walter drove, I sat in the passenger seat, Shad hovered between us, and Alice Blue sat in back with Val and Nadine as Walter headed for a service station in Okehampton. As we rode the track past the army camp, Alice told us how she was utilized to kill Guy Shad. She was only one of a variety of differently configured "torps" owned by a New York firm of political consultants whose front name was, We Can Fix It. Of the many things We Can Fix It purported to clean up were the backgrounds of candidates for corporate and political office. John Quinn wanted to be governor of New York using that office to step on up to the Presidency. To do that he had to have a clean background: No childhood experimentation with controlled substances, no youthful indiscretions of a sexual or criminal nature, no undocumented maids on the payroll, and especially no years on the police force taking his cut from those who had their own opinions about which laws could be ignored—At least no one left who could remember any of it. As it happened, Shad's continued existence seemed to stalk Quinn like a specter, always there, always threatening to expose him. In Quinn's mind it had grown into something unreal and malignant. "He wanted to kill you himself—call you a rat to your face. He told me he had to," said Alice. "Always unfortunate when amateurs want to make of a killing more than it is."

"Hear, hear," said Walter. I glared at him and he gestured a sort of apology.

"Two of John Quinn's associates are former detectives who are convinced Guy Shad could land them in the kind of trouble that runs politically uphill." Alice Blue smiled wryly. "What they don't know is that Quinn has We Can Fix It cleansing his two associates, as well. Unfortunate fishing trip in Colorado in three weeks. I fear they'll get lost and die of exposure."

I looked back at her. "The New York authorities will need all that information as soon as possible."

The knowledge of an incoming call came into my head. It was Matheson. *"Jaggers, old boy! Near a telly?"*

I glanced at Walter. He nodded, touched a button on his steering column, and a screen dropped down from the roof. All those in the rear could easily see it and Shad moved his mech back there for the improved view. By straining, I could see the screen from the side: Constabulary police cruisers, light arrays flashing, in front of a small cottage. Matheson began telling me a channel number but I interrupted and said we already had it and ended the call. The reporter doing the voiceover let us know that she was in Gidleigh, at great personal risk to her own person, as multiple police agencies descended upon the cottage's occupant suspected of being the Mad Moor Murderer. A disclaimer came up on the screen explaining that the bombing had taken place in northern Dartmoor, the use of the designation 'Moor' was for alliterative purposes and in no way referred to Moors nor anyone of Moorish descent, nor does the term 'Mad' refer to mentally impaired, anger-management challenged, etc., etc.

"Matheson's making the bust in front of the TV cameras while we're out here in the boonies," said Shad. "By the time Walter's car is charged and we can make it to Gidleigh, it'll all be over. Matheson'll probably get a medal."

"The Wookie never got a medal," said Alice Blue from in back.

I turned and looked at her, not certain if she was joking. "That's true," I chimed in. "The Wookie did everything Han Solo and Luke Skywalker did. They got medals and the Wookie didn't."

"A clear case of human racism," added Val.

We all looked at Shad. His mech was silent for a moment. "Yeah," he said in good humor. "He did the same except for lines. The Wookie only had that one word to learn for his part." He then gave the Wookie call.

"That shouldn't have kept the Wookie from getting a medal," said Alice with a demure smile. "Patty Duke only said one word in *The Miracle Worker* and she got an Oscar."

"What word was that, sergeant?" Walter asked Shad.

"'Wawa,'" quoth the micro, granting the point. The motion passed unanimously. Resolved: The Wookie had been stiffed, as would we whenever it came time to pass out public kudos for taking down the Mad Moor Murderer.

After charging Walter's MG we took the A 30 back toward Exeter to bring Alice Blue to Heavitree Tower for the first of many interrogations. Eventually the conversation turned to Shad's new meat suit. He said he was going to arrange with North American Biotronics for a replacement duck which should be ready in a matter of weeks.

Until then, what, Walter wanted to know.

Shad said he was going to go to Celebrity Lookalikes of Bond Street, London and pick something inspiring to wear until his new duck arrived.

Everyone else in the car entertained themselves speculating on which celebrity suit Shad would choose. Shad's big hero from his acting days was Lawrence Olivier, which was Val's choice. Nadine chose Sylvester the Cat, but I think she was joking. Walter thought actor Stephen Fry would be an excellent choice. Alice Blue, after much encouragement from Val and Nadine, smiled and chose Tick Tock from the Oz stories.

All good selections and all quite wrong, I feared. I had been with Guy Shad long enough to know how his mind worked. I began bracing myself to refuse to react even a little bit when he appeared for duty as Nigel Bruce playing Dr. Watson.

♠

THE PURLOINED LABRADOODLE

-1-

"Limp stone," muttered the parrot darkly.

I finished stocking the shelves in back of the small shop counter with boxes of bird seed, tins of dog food, and little packets of catnip. The counter and display case were festooned with colorful leashes of assorted sizes, plastic bones, rubber mice, squeaky toys, scratching posts, king-queen-and knave sized pet beds and such. The walls were hung with posters concerning the various hideous diseases cats and dogs could contract complete with expensive preventative treatments that could be purchased right here, should the shipments ever arrive. Shad and I, you see, were under cover operating a pet shop in The Strand, Village of Lympstone, east bank of the River Exe south of Exeter, Devon. I was the pet shop owner and DS Shad had traded his cherished Nigel Bruce meat suit in on what budget-strapped ABCD had left over in the way of undercover pet bios: a rather timeworn parrot.

"Limp stone," quoth the parrot one more bloody time.

Shad and I were, as it happened, an insignificant part of a rather large task force attempting to crack down on a UK ring of swindlers who were representing real household pets as amdroid bios capable of taking full human imprints with rather appalling consequences for bargain seekers who would lose a good bit of their savings, all of their natural bodies, and most of their minds in the process. The main thrusts of the task force effort were in London, Manchester, and Bristol. Shad was being cranky on two accounts: first, because he felt we had been left out of the big show; and second, because he wasn't getting to do his Dr. Watson, which he really wanted to do.

Nevertheless, the pets used by the perpetrators came from somewhere and covering pet stores was a logical investigative consequence. From what we could observe from our post in Lympstone, though, it didn't appear to be a well coordinated operation—something Shad was beginning to refer to as a "clusterbugger." In any event, we were on our third day of operations and our shipments of kittens, puppies, and much of our equipment and supplies had yet to arrive. No bait, no customers, no suspects. I looked from the window at the quaint village street, and it was raining. There went our chance for someone blind drunk mistaking us for a tube station and staggering in.

"Limp stone," Shad muttered again from his perch at the end of the counter. He was getting quite tiresome. I turned from the window.

"Actually, Shad, the *m* is silent and the *stone* is pronounced *stin*. Lipstin."

"Brits pronounce a whole lot better than they spell."

"I don't recall that American insurance company you did the telly adverts for being such great spellers. Why wasn't your duck quacking 'Aflass, Aflass.'?"

"You mean besides how close it sounds to 'half-assed'? Jaggs, you really think The Petting Place is a good name for a pet store?"

"Superintendent Matheson chose the name, not I, as you well know."

"It sounds like a bordello or lap-dancing salon. Why don't we just call it The Cat House and be done with it?" The parrot held out his wings, began bumping and grinding his hips as he danced on the perch and sang out in something of a Jamaican accent, 'Hey 'dere, sailor boy, you come to Mama Bimbo's Cat House for all you pettin' needs, mon." The dance stopped. "Jaggs, if you were a self-respecting crook would you go into a pet store called The Petting Place?" He sidestepped grumpily from one end of his perch to the other. "Can't believe the names around this neck of the woods: Ex mouth. Nut well. Glebe lands. Cock wood. Under Wear—"

"That's *Lower* Wear and—"

"Key off, Jaggs," cautioned Shad, nodding toward the window. "Live one approaching. This may be the kitten pickin' kingpin herself."

The bell rang as the door opened revealing a short stocky woman in a green anorak and yellow plastic rain scarf, her feet in a pair of bright yellow wellies. In her right hand she had by the handle a small gray metal case. She walked up to the counter.

"Good morning, love," I said. "How may I be of assistance?"

"I want me parakeet fixed," she stated.

"Indeed. I regret to say we don't neuter birds at Petting Place." I glanced at Shad and he was returning my look down-his-beak, as it were. I looked back at the woman. "You'll have to take your bird to a veterinary surgeon."

"I means *repair*. This one's a robbie," she said. "All 'is nuts's got bolts in 'em, if you gets me drift."

"I see." I smiled brightly. "If I might take a look at your bird?"

"Nothin' much works on it." She lifted the case and dropped it rather heavily on the counter. "Salt in the air, I expect. Too close to the bleedin' ocean."

I opened the case on the counter next to Shad's perch. Inside the case was a musty smelling robotic parakeet. There was something white and crusty dried between its toes. Shad moved on his perch until he could look down into the case.

"Ain't that cute, your parrot there looking at me bird. He's in love!"

Midway through her rising belly laugh, Shad said to her, "Sod off you old cow."

"Here, now!" she responded, her color rising.

"I apologize for the parrot, love," I said. "I'm afraid we rescued the poor thing from a rather tragic situation."

"Aw," she responded empathetically, reaching out a hand to pet Shad's head. "Chick abuse, was it?"

With a loud squawk and a belated flap of his unfamiliar wings, Shad fell off his perch backwards onto the floor.

"I didn't hit the poor thing," said the woman holding a hand up to her maker. "I swear it."

"Please don't distress yourself unduly, madam. The bird also suffers from an inner ear problem. It affects his balance." Excusing myself, I went around the end of the counter and bent over my partner. He was rolling on the floor flapping his multicolored plumage, beak open, and laughing. *"Steady,"* I said to him over our wireless net, a deserved degree of menace in my transmission.

After a few gasps, Shad eventually said to me, *"Sorry, Jaggs. Ah-Hah! Sorry, but check out the eyes on her bird. That's no simple robot."* He stood, doubled over, shook again, and transmitted, *"Should I share with her how I was never coddled as a young egg but spent my deviled youth getting fried and have since become hard-boiled?"*

"Not unless you also wish to become scrambled and beaten," I buzzed back.

He flapped his wings and resumed his place on the perch, occasional unconquerable snicker spasms shaking his feathers.

I turned toward the woman and smiled brightly yet again. "Now, shall I take a look at your bird?"

Shad was correct. The creature's eyes were animated, its gaze darting about and eventually coming to rest upon me. If it was a simple run down robot and not a mech, its eyes should not have been moving. As they were moving, however, indicating the possibility of a rather serious crime, I asked as delicately as I could, "How long have you had this mech, love?"

She laughed and waved a hand at my apparent silliness. "Oh, that's no mech, dearie. That one's just a clockwork toy. Me aunt were well off but Auntie wouldn't pay for no mech when she could get the feathers, flap, and song by only payin' for a robbie."

"Really."

"'Course. Think she wanted to get tied up with all that red tape, wages, taxes, forms, and bother? Not me Aunt Annabelle." She frowned. "Besides, if this here bird was self-aware, it'd take better care of itself, wouldn't it?" Before I could answer, she added, "More to point, that's what the parakeet told me aunt."

"This parakeet told your aunt it didn't come under the Artificial Intelligence Regulations?"

"That's what me aunt told me years before she passed on. The parakeet told her, oh," she frowned and looked up at the beamed ceiling, "got to be four years ago." She lowered her watery gray gaze down until she was looking me in the face. "See, Annabelle Wallingford passed last year. Quite well off she was, as I said. Her place was in Wotton Lane by Watton Brook."

"In Wotton by Watton?" asked Shad.

She frowned at the parrot. "Cheeky bastard."

"To be sure. About the parakeet?" I prompted.

"Well, as part of Auntie's estate, she left me Ringo. That's what we called this here bird before it seized up. Shame. Only had the bloomin' thing a few days when it broke."

"I see. And you're bringing it in now because . . .?"

"Just getting around to going through me aunt's things and cleanin' up. Found Ringo tucked away in me auntie's attic. Maddie girl, I says to meself, it'd be right homey havin' a singin' bird in the lounge next to the settee. Ringo sings real sweet's I remember."

"I see."

"With a robbie there's no papers to clean up. No offense," she said to Shad.

He looked away, talon to brow, feigning acute personal devastation.

She poked the parakeet several times in the tummy. "I can do the feathers up some with needles and me hot glue gun, but I'm no good with chips, springs, electronics, and such. If it can't be fixed I'll just toss it in the dustbin. Maybe a jumble sale. Some little tyke might have a laugh takin' it apart. Might be worth a bob or two."

I lifted a wing and released it. It dropped to the counter with a thud. "Let me take it in back and have a look."

"Is this old parrot here for sale?" she asked, poking Shad in the belly.

"Easy, lady," he said with the voice of Huntz Hall, "you'll bruise the fabric."

"You'll have to ask the bird, love," I answered. "He's a bio."

"Oh, I wouldn't want no bio."

"That's not the issue, Chuckles," Shad said to her. "The issue is, does the bio want you."

As I picked up the parakeet and carried it around the counter, Shad began singing a rather raunchy sea shanty centered on a seductive female giraffe and her erstwhile suitor, a love struck field mouse who, for reasons unnecessary to elucidate here, ran himself to death. I took the mechanical bird into the room where we had our surveillance equipment set up. I cracked the parakeet's back and Shad was right. Although the bird was robotic, there was one slight illegal modification. Tucked among its gears, bellows, batteries, and computer was an AI chip—an illegal AI chip at that. I'm no expert in such things, but it looked as though the AI chip had worked its way loose from its improvised mountings which had caused a microcard to partially dislodge from its tiny motherboard effectively paralyzing all motor functions save the eyes.

With a pair of tweezers I disconnected the AI chip, took it over to the workroom's computer, and inserted it into the appropriate port. All of the identification data on the chip was code scrambled. I keyed for voice recognition and said, "Hello. Hello, hello, whoever you are."

No response.

"Detective Inspector Harrington Jaggers, Devon ABCD here. I know you've just gone though a rough patch, old chicken, but it's about to get a good deal bumpier. Either you talk to me or I put this chip right back in the squab the same way I found it. Then one of two things happen: either Maddie girl will toss you in the dustbin, or perhaps she'll put you in a jumble sale and someone six years old with sticky fingers will take you all apart before he loses interest and goes on to something else. Or perhaps they'll make a Christmas tree decoration out of you. Pretty little bird. The way I read your battery consumption rate, you have another two—two and a half years you can click around those eyeballs up on some shelf until things go dark for good. But who can say? Sitting on the tree next to the candy cane once a year, looking through the plastic icicles, listening to tattooed and perforated children playing their new thunder rumbles. It might be fun listening to Dad and Uncle Mike wagging on endlessly about test matches, especially after they've gotten good and bladdered, before you go back in the box—"

"Very well," interrupted the computer's speakers in a female voice. "You got me."

"Indeed." I thought I'd give my American partner a little Don Ameche wireless moment. *"Mr. Watson, come here, I want you,"* I transmitted to Shad.

The parrot flew through the door and landed atop the computer monitor. *"The Story of Alexander Graham Bell,* Nineteen thirty-nine, and that wasn't the Watson I was hoping for."

"That's all right, Shad. Right now you don't look much like Henry Fonda, anyway." I pointed at the screen and Shad looked down between his feet. A female human CGI was on the screen.

"That's not Loretta Young."

I looked at the lovely creature. "I do believe that's Rita Hayworth." The computer generated image, indeed, looked like Nineteen forties and fifties actress Rita Hayworth in her role as the sultry nightclub singer in *Affair in Trinidad* with Glenn Ford. I frowned at Shad.

"Nineteen fifty-two," he said without looking up.

Insufferable bird. I looked back at the screen. Pirate AI chip manufacturers paid no royalties for images, but steered clear of using images of still living celebrities who could afford to hire the forces of darkness necessary to hunt down and prosecute trademark poachers and encroachers. Rita, as always, was looking radiant. "Your name?" I asked her.

"Lolita Doll." Rita smiled demurely. "Honest, guv. That's the name I was born with, spelling and all. I'm from Plymouth by way of Land's End. Thanks for busting me out of that parakeet."

"You're not out of the feathers yet, love," I said evenly. "I'm kind of curious how you wound up in that chip, how that chip wound up inside that bird, and especially how that bird wound up inside a wealthy woman's estate."

The image was silent. From his perch atop the screen, Shad said, "Is it just me or is Rita looking just a bit furtive?"

"What's that parrot saying?" Rita—Lolita—asked me.

"Detective Sergeant Shad opined that you appeared just a tad sneaky, Lolita. I agree you seem less than forthcoming."

Shad hopped down to the keyboard, did a little dance on the keys, and called up Lolita's previous in a new frame. "Whoa!" he exclaimed in mock shock. "Lolita," said Shad, "I'd download your complete criminal record but this sorry shadow of a computer only has fifteen hundred megagigs of memory."

I glanced at the list. Sealed juvenile previous weighing a third the megabyte weight of her adult convictions. She was a jewel thief primarily, some confidence work, not terribly competent at either. She couldn't have done much worse if she'd spent her mornings booking cells for her evenings through the Convict Accommodation Association. Did her first stint in H.M Prison & Remand Centre Exeter at the age of nineteen. Back in at twenty-two. Back again at twenty-five. According to the record I was reading she was nearing sixty and more than half of that time had been spent as a guest of His Majesty's government. According to her library record in the nick, she'd read every piece of children's fiction in the place. Psych evaluation: Terrific liar; couldn't change a battery; at risk for becoming institutionalized, which meant she's been inside so long she'd do almost anything to stay behind walls.

"So, you modified a robotic parakeet with a pirated AI chip capable of taking a human imprint to sneak past the security systems into some wealthy person's home," I said.

"Yes."

"You do the work yourself, Lolita?"

"Sure."

Shad whistled a bar from the Woody Woodpecker song. True. If she had been Pinocchio instead of Rita Hayworth she would have had a California Redwood hanging from between her eyes by now.

"How could you be sure that parakeet would be chosen by your mark?" asked Shad.

"The robbie was already sold to Annabelle Wallingford," answered Lolita. "I did work release at Songbirds in Queen Street, Exeter. It's a tech shop sells robbie birds and accessories. You know, it's just up from Boston Tea Party in next to the News?"

"Yes," I said. "I know it. It's owned by Frankie Statten, isn't it?"

"Mr. Statten's the proprietor."

Shad glanced at me and I shrugged. "You were on work release?" I continued.

"So?"

"Doesn't say a whole lot for the rehab program up there," observed Shad. "The parakeet robbie gimmick, Lolita: What made you think of it?" he asked her.

No answer for awhile, then Rita said, "I suppose it seemed like a good idea at the time."

The parrot looked up at me. "Well, Sherlock, I guess she's got nothin' to hide."

I sat down on a stool and looked again at Lolita's file. The picture of Lolita Doll—taken when her nat was about thirty—although of typical constabulary quality, was not unpleasant. Her photo gave the impression of a lonely, frightened girl trying to look tough and into her third decade of refusing to stand up straight. Her most recent photo showed her sadder, grayer, and a bit more stooped. "Swap your body for the AI chip and imprinting, did you?" I asked, not much interested in the answer, knowing it was going to be a lie.

Rita Hayworth glanced at the window, then looked away. She nodded. "Just another meat suit, wasn't it. Didn't like the way I looked anyway. With what I would've made off the Wallingford job—I could've become . . . I could've become . . . why, just anybody, couldn't I." Rita shrugged and looked down.

"Who would you have liked to become, Lolita?" I asked her.

"What're you, copper? Bleedin' Mother Mary?" The sneer Rita had on her face was not attractive at all and was quite contradicted by the tears welling in her CGI's eyes.

"Listen up, you sorry scrap of plastic and magnetic impulses," snarled Shad into the workstation's camera pickup, "You are talking to Detective Inspector Harrington Jaggers of Interpol's Artificial Beings Crimes Division's Devon Office, late of the London Metropolitan Police, the cop who's put away enough blood-and-guts stone killers to fill the recruiting needs of every tattooed and drugged up prison gang in the United Kingdom, Wales, and the Maldives until the next millennium! So unless you want your highly illegal AI chip to accidentally find itself flushed down the Petting Place's toilet, me girl, you'd best straighten up and answer up 'less you want to find yourself up that bleedin' pile of sand and rock haulin' a rucksack full of ruddy flippin' shot-puts!"

He had begun as Jack Webb in *The DI* but at the end had slipped rather badly into Harry Andrews in *The Hill*.

"Steady there, Shad," I transmitted.

"Sorry," he sent back.

Rita was looking rather wide-eyed at the parrot. After a moment her gaze shifted to me. "Sorry inspector. Didn't mean anything."

I cleared my throat. "Who would you have liked to become?" I asked her again.

Rita was trying, struggling for words, her eyes welling with electronic tears. "I don't know. I want to be . . ." She looked directly at me. "I want to be safe." She nodded to herself. "I'll tell you, inspector. Safe. Taken care of." She glanced away for a moment, as though embarrassed. "Had that inside, kind of. You know?" She looked back at me. "Wasn't happy, though. I do so want to be happy."

"What about love, Lolita?"

"You having a laugh, guv?"

"No."

"Don't mix me up with the picture on the screen, inspector. I'm near sixty. Love's something you read about in the romance graph's. Money, now." She smiled wickedly. "They tells me money can't buy me love, but it do make the search a heap more comfortable."

"Spare us the brass, sister. What happened this time?" asked Shad.

She glanced at the parrot and shrugged. "Me own fault. Flying around the place, scoping out the security systems, I ran flat into something. Never saw it. Jammed me up. Froze me solid. Everything but me eyes and ears. Butler found me next morning, put me on a shelf. Auntie shakes her head. Auntie's brother, Barney Bananas, takes me up to his room and sticks me on top a nine year old slice o' wedding cake he was saving for his future missus which give me sticky feet and a good look at his telly. 'Course he only played this one vid he liked, over and over and over, day in and bleedin' night out for a year three months a week and four days until Barney Wallingford died right in the middle of Lawrence Harvey gettin' kissed by his mum for the last time as it turned out. Then they packed up Barmey Barney's belongings, including me, and stuck us all in the attic for another three years. The last I saw the light 'til Maddie checked me out to bring me here."

"Is she lying?" I transmitted to Shad.

"What was the name—" he began out loud.

"The Manchurian Candidate," she answered, "Frank Sinatra, Lawrence Harvey, Janet Leigh, Angela Lansbury—"

"The dir—"

"John Frankenheimer."

"Pro—"

"George Axelrod and John Frankenheimer, Executive Producer Howard W. Koch."

"She may have seen it," Shad reported back.

"Don't you want to know who did Janet Leigh's hair styles?" Rita Hayworth asked the parrot. She pulled back the left corner of her mouth into a knowing smile. "Or do you already know?"

The parrot looked up at me. "Only a fool bandies wits with an electron," I offered.

Shad looked back at the screen. "Who?" he asked.

"I rest my case."

"Gene Shacove," she answered.

While Shad went on the net to check out her answer, he asked Lolita, "Why didn't your partner come and get you out?"

Rita arched her lovely brows. "Partners look out for each other. If I had a partner you think I would've gotten into such a fix?" She looked down. "Four years," she said. "Four years."

"What did you do all that time to keep from going crazy?" asked Shad.

Rita stared wide-eyed at Shad. "Why, birdie, I passed the time by playing a little solitaire."

We both fell silent as Shad and I reflected upon the famous trigger-the-killer line from the original *The Manchurian Candidate*. He pointed his wing at the frame next to Rita. Janet Leigh's hair styles by Gene Shacove.

Shad looked at Rita. "Ever see the remake to *The Manchurian Candidate?*"

Rita nodded, smiling wickedly.

"What'd you think?"

"I'd rather go back and watch the original another fifty-five hundred times." Her CGI looked at me. "What are you going to do with me, inspector?"

"To be perfectly honest, Lolita, I don't know. Hence, I'm going to pass the buck. I have a friend in London and this parrot, Dr. Watson here, is going to send your engrams and particulars to my friend for a second opinion." Shad looked at me all wide-eyed and quizzical. "Dr. Bing Ehrenberg. You'll find his address in my personal folder. Attach a copy of Lolita's previous along with a brief description of the current situation, what she's been through and our assessment of her account, and send the lot to Dr. Ehrenberg. Include her complete prison record, as well." I looked one last time at Rita. "While he's doing that, I'll see if I can repair old Ringo and get the bird singing again. Once I hear from the doctor, I'll make my decision." I put her on pause.

Later, as Lolita's engrams and history were bouncing off a satellite, I told Shad to destroy the AI chip once Ehrenberg confirmed receipt and installation. Then I turned my attention to Ringo. I brushed off the crumbly old icing from its toes, reattached the parakeet's robotic computer, anchored the minicards, reattached the remainder of the connections, buttoned it up, and listened as the bird began singing the sweetest bird songs. I held out a finger and with a flap of its wings it jumped up and perched there, shook the dust from its back and wings, the remaining bits of wedding cake from its toes, its happy song filling the air. Picking up the carrying case by the handle, I brought the patient back to our client. Maddie girl's face blossomed into smiles. "Bloody Nora, Ringo's as right as rain. I comes in here and says to meself this here Sherlock Holmes and his bleedin' parrot're a couple of barmpots, but who's arse-up now? Eh? Ringo's right as rain."

"Like sands through the hour glass," began Shad, "so are the days of our lives—"

"Shad," I interrupted with a mix of menace and smile.

Since our credit numbers and equipment were out there somewhere awaiting delivery along with our puppies and kittens, we took Madeleine Wallingford's address ostensibly for billing purposes and agreed to put an advert in the window for an outing to the medieval underground tunnels of Exeter being organized by the Lympstone Society and another for Maddie's own group, the Order of St. Trinians, ta ta, Abyssinia, and all that twaddle. The door closed.

Quoth the parrot, "Nevermore."

"Sorry?"

"Jaggs, I think I see the purpose of this catch-and-release policy of yours. We're trying to build up the criminal stock out there in the mainstream so that there will be criminals enough for all law enforcement officers everywhere to make a living. It's part of the Blue Peace Environmental Movement, right?"

"Although I truly admire the depths of your cynicism, Shad, certainly someone of your sensitivity and high intellect can appreciate that Lolita Doll has learned everything confinement at government expense can teach her."

"I heartily agree with your modest assessment of my mental prowess, Jaggs, but you must really be sticking something tender beneath a pinch bar if you have to resort to such blatant flattery. Who is this Dr. Ehrenberg, anyway?"

"Chap in London. Therapist. Back when I was killed in Metro, he went a long way toward piecing me back together and into my first bio. If Bing says tossing what's left of Lolita Doll before a magistrate is what's best for her, then off she goes. If he says we do something else, then we'll see. Meanwhile, give Superintendent Matheson a ring and see if anything is brewing."

He did and something was. While Shad and I had been in Lympstone disposing of Lolita and the kaput parakeet matter, ABCD units in Manchester, Bristol, and London, in conjunction with local police authorities, had successfully detained all the improper puppy imprinting principles as well as their primary patrons. The bogus bio barons had been bagged. While muttering, Shad flew to the shop's garage and copied back into his Nigel Bruce. I on the other hand bent to the task of repacking all those bloomin' boxes of bird seed, tins of dog food, and little packets of catnip. Mama Bimbo's Cat House was going out of business, mon.

2

As Shad drove us back to Exeter he said in his Watson voice, "Of course, Holmes, Frankie Statten was her partner."

"Of course."

"Why didn't the bounder rescue her?"

"Never let it be said that Frank Statten unnecessarily placed himself at risk for anything or anybody."

"Honor among thieves. Humph! Stranding her like that," said Watson in disgust. "What do you suppose it was like, Holmes, after watching that vid a few thousand times with Barmy Barney then shut up in a little box in the dark for another three years? Nothing to move but your eyeballs? Nothing to think about but *The Manchurian Candidate*." He shuddered convincingly. "Had to make two weeks of solitary confinement seem a mere stroll in the park."

"It must have been strikingly like an experience I had years ago in London shortly after I died, Watson." I wondered slightly at my use of the "Watson" name. Came devilish easy to the tongue for someone who swore the name would never pass his lips.

"In a cast were you, Holmes?" asked Watson. "Held in stasis a long time, old trout? Medically induced coma?"

"Not at all, old fellow. Valerie took me to see a showing of the Bette Davis-Lillian Gish classic, *The Whales of August*." For once Shad didn't immediately come back with the release date. He simply shuddered.

"Dear me," he said. "You gave me quite a start, Holmes. Had a shockingly similar experience with Nadine not long ago," he said.

"Really."

"I should say so. They had the bloody flik at the Exeter Picture House. Special treat. I'd never seen it before. *The Whales of August*. Ought to require theaters to post wellbeing warnings before showing the blithering health hazard."

"Were you convinced you were running a risk, doctor?"

"Holmes, it was like watching quartz crystals grow in real time."

I shook my head. "I didn't find the action quite that compelling."

Nigel chuckled a Watson chuckle. "You know, Nadine quite likes that movie, Holmes. What do you make of that?"

"Nadine's a cat. *The Whales of August* does bear a striking similarity to watching a mouse hole for three hours. Val is rather fond of *The Whales of August*, too, you know."

"Really. Well, perhaps it is a feline thing."

I thought for a moment. "Not exactly. You see Val wasn't a cat when we saw it."

"But she became a cat, Holmes. Everything was there but the fur and whiskers, you see?"

"Perhaps. Yes, I'll grant you that, Watson. Well done." I glanced over at Shad and he was doing a very good self-satisfied Watson chuckle having gotten-one-up on Sherlock Holmes. Detective Superintendent Matheson's face came into my thoughts for some reason. "Two things before we get back to division, old fellow."

"What's that, Holmes?"

"One, when we get in the building, you must stop calling me Holmes. Two, I see that deerstalker cap you have in your pocket."

"Oh?"

"I don't want to see it on my hat rack."

"What? Wha—What makes you think I wasn't going to wear it myself, Ho—Jaggs?" he asked feigning injured innocence.

There was only one phrase that seemed to fit. "Elementary, my dear Shad. Elementary."

3

Time passed as it has a wont to do, and Bing Ehrenberg eventually rang me to say that he believed the best thing for Lolita Doll was to get her out of a computer and into a human bio, into some therapy, and into some vocational rehabilitation. I discussed the matter for all of eleven seconds with a county crown prosecutor's assistant who had less than no interest in the case and the fellow proceeded to discharge it, including the eleven months she had remaining on her previous sentence. Lolita had done four years in solitary for attempted burglary and was now free. I suppose Justice does have to lift that hanky once in awhile and have herself a peek.

Shad and I, on the other hand, went out on a deranged squirrel enquiry in front of Debenhams and there witnessed a three vehicle pile-up as two ground electrics slammed into a lorry whose driver stopped in the middle of his lane of traffic because he was stunned at seeing the real "classic" Sherlock Holmes and Dr. Watson. Chief Constable Raymond Crowe buzzed Superintendent Matheson about getting Shad back into his feathers. At the very least, Matheson was to keep us off the streets. The squirrel withdrew the complaint against Debenhams but insisted upon autographs from Shad and myself. He returned our early efforts pointedly remarking that no one had ever heard of Harrington Jaggers and Guy Shad. After we sent the furry fellow off with the Holmes and Watson inscriptions upon which he insisted, Watson looked at me and said, "Why are you looking so glum? So it wasn't for your own name. Cheer up. It *was* your first autograph request."

"That is true."

"Consider my plight, Holmes. As the Aflak duck I was asked for countless autographs but couldn't sign them. Now I can sign them but they don't want my name."

"Well, cheer up, Watson," I said. "At least the squirrel didn't demand you quack out 'aflak' and fall off a cliff. Every cloud has a silver lining."

"You ever try flying *through* a cloud that had a silver lining?"

4

Early one sunny afternoon, a call came into ABCD from Powderham Castle, the home of the Earl of Devon. The castle was located almost directly across the River Exe from Lympstone between the Village of Powderham and the larger village of Kenton. The call had been placed by the head of security at the castle, a former assistant chief constable of the West Midlands Constabulary named Ian Collier I had met many years ago while on a case when I had been with Metro. A quite capable fellow, Collier. I had lost touch with him by the unfortunate expedient of getting killed. I fully expected him to be chief constable by now. Silly me. Instead he was Mr. Collier and running a private security force at a castle that doubled as a mini theme park and convention center with all kinds of events from nature walks and children's theater to weddings and rock concerts. Collier had called me directly.

Earlier in the day, it appeared, a large wedding had been held at Powderham in the castle's ornate Music Room. The reception luncheon, curiously enough, was held in the self same Music Room, while the music with its concomitant dancing was taking place in the castle's huge Dining Room. Conversing, apologizing, promising, drinking, changing, pilfering jewelry, and recovering from various excesses were spread among the other rooms that had been made available to the wedding party.

The father of the groom, a Mr. Edsel Meyer, first reported one of the guests missing her jewelry, a rather expensive triple strand of matched natural pearls. Later, other guests reported missing jewelry until even the bride, the former June Grimpion and grand niece of Lord Devon, reported missing an emerald-cut diamond bracelet. The total promised to be a respectable haul. Ian Collier stated quite bluntly that he wanted that which could be done in an unofficial capacity to be carried out in exactly that manner.

When I reported to Superintendent Matheson, he wondered why Collier had called Artificial Beings Crimes.

"Possibly he suspected AB involvement," I offered as a plausible but completely untrue explanation.

"Perhaps you should knock this over to the constabulary, Jaggers," Matheson said as he contemplated his graphic of the Biograph Theater in Chicago on the liquid crystal wall opposite his desk. He shifted his gaze toward me. "At least until we know for certain an artificial being is involved. Things are so touchy with Middlemoor lately I'm afraid the Chief Constable only needs one more little excuse to go off on the lot of us. Met Parker in the lobby downstairs yesterday and I swore the chief was going to rip a patch out of Parker the size of a throw rug. This office can't afford to put that gorilla back into therapy."

I glanced at Dr. Watson as he stood there fumbling with his deerstalker, and said, "Actually, sir, we were specifically requested by Powderham Castle. Hence, I'm certain there must be an AB involvement."

"Lord Devon specifically asked for us?" I could see the stars glittering in the superintendent's eyes.

"I took the call myself," which was not a lie. "In addition, sir, it would be an opportunity to get Dr. Watson and myself away from the Tower for the afternoon, what with the inspection of the Exeter Station by the chief constable rumored to be occurring at almost any moment—"

"Omigod!" He placed both hands flat on his desktop. "Ah, I see. I see. Godspeed, Inspector Jaggers, and convey my respects to his lordship."

"I will, sir. Come Watson."

"What? Oh? Game's afoot, eh?"

"Don't you two play at that Holmes and Watson nonsense out at Powderham, Jaggers. Shad? You hear me? Shad? *Shad?*" Matheson cautioned as his door closed behind us.

As the doors to the elevator hardened and the car ascended, Watson said, "What was that fellow blathering on about, Holmes—all that playing at Powderham rubbish?"

"I haven't the slightest, Watson."

Up on the roof we settled into the cruiser. As Watson drew us out of our slot and headed the vehicle toward the target, I rang up Collier and let him know we were on our way. *"The security is excellent at Powderham, Jaggs, but not oppressive,"* he said. *"Permanent security staff is long term, all retired police officers. We mostly stay outside the castle on the grounds. No guards inside. For big weddings like this one we make up extra security staff with local off-duty police, all good cops. Couldn't fault one of them."*

"Cameras?" I asked.

"A few remote recording cameras on the grounds—nothing manned. Again nothing inside the castle. Lord and Lady Devon let parts of the estate for weddings, corporate functions, and other events—in that respect Powderham is very much a business. However, the castle is also their home. The more valuable artworks and sculptures have motion detectors, sensitivity sensors, alarms and such. Articles not bolted down have ID nanodots concealed on or in them—no way to get them out of the castle."

"What about nanodot codes on the guests' jewelry?"

"About three quarters of the missing pieces have them. Nothing's come up at the gates, and no one's left by air. No guests have left yet and no castle staff."

"Who has left?"

"The first shifts of caterers, florists, technical and lighting crew, photographers, a quick raid by a discreet liveried dustbin brigade, and the Lord Bishop of Exeter. We checked in, beneath, above, through, and around everything that could block a signal."

"Years ago, Collier, I had a case in which a well-endowed woman concealed a nanodot encoded diamond ring between her breasts and got it through the screens. There was a sufficient enclosure of flesh to absorb the dot's signal."

"There is sufficient jewelry already reported missing to pack an overnight bag, Jaggers. In my entire life I've never seen anyone that well endowed outside a perv graphic."

"Ah, sweet bird of youth."

"Indeed. I am aware other cavities have been used in which to conceal valuables, but have you ever seen the points and edges on emerald cut diamonds?"

"Yes I have. I agree: It would take quite a fellow to stick a bracelet full of them up his bum and still play bass guitar for two hours."

"Jaggers, unless the thief burrowed out underground, the stuff's still on the grounds."

"I take it you've checked possible underground routes and locations?"

"What do you think? I should make clear, Jaggers, that the castle is not liable for any stolen property. That's not his lordship's concern. It's just that his lordship is related to the bride's family and is a guest at both wedding and reception, as well."

"Hence he would prefer not having the screws slamming his fellow guests up against his ornate walls, spreading them out, and patting them down."

"You are so sensitive, my friend. I knew calling you was the right thing to do."

"See you in a few, Collier."

Watson pulled the cruiser up from Heavitree Tower as Collier sent me lists of wedding guests, wedding service and catering staffs, as well as castle staff including full-time and part-time security personnel, along with images.

As we took the Exminster-Dawlish Warren Air Corridor down the west bank of the Exe, Dr. Watson *née* Shad turned on the autopilot, leaned back from the controls, and glanced at me. "Powderham. This is the place with the old tortoise who entertains children, Holmes. Timothy something?"

"You are correct, Watson. The first Timmy Tortoise dates back to Eighteen fifty-four and died in the early Twenty-first Century. The current one is an amdroid bio taken from the original Timmy's DNA imprinted by—her name escapes me—an actress."

"Went down there with Nadine, Holmes, and caught the woman's act just before we were blown up that time out at Hangingstone. Quite depressing."

"Getting blown up or the tortoise?"

"Tortoise—What? Oh." He chuckled. "You will have your joke. Her *act* was depressing, Holmes, her act. Rather get blown up again than have to sit through her routine again. Dreadful. Hundred and fifty year gig and all the flies she can eat."

"I suspect the actor imprinted onto the Timmy bio restricts her tortoise fare to lettuce, Watson. Perhaps the odd tomato slice. I hear she does impressions. Is that true?"

"Dear God, Holmes: Turtle standup comedy impressions for seven-year-olds. No one should miss it. 'Hey, man, I heard these two bugs talking the other day, y' know? One says to the other, "Katydid." Now, get this. The other says, "Katydid." Stop me if you've heard this one before. So the other says, "Katydid." Now, the second bug comes back real quick with "Katydid," ha, ha, haaa . . .'" Shad looked through his side of the window and back at me. "Dreadful. Well, it's work I suppose. Clarice Penne's her name." He glanced back at me. "Ever see her picture?"

"I can't say I have, Watson."

"Hideous looking woman. If she'd let herself go a little she'd be a dead ringer for Alistair Sim. There'll be a part for her if they ever decide to tell the story of Jack the Ripper's waning years in a nursing home."

"Alistair Sim of the Ebenezer Scrooge Sims?"

"The very same. Not a whole lot of really creepy maiden aunt parts available these days. I suppose she figures the shell game is at least show business. Reminds me of that old joke about the fellow in the circus scrubbing the elephant's bum." He coughed a Watson cough. "Sorry Holmes. This wretched acting business: Millions grasping hungrily for a scant dozen brass rings. Had one of those rings once myself." Silence as he thought for a moment on his famous past, then he shook his head and waved a hand as if dismissing it from his attention. "Sorry. Sorry, Holmes. Can't imagine what came over me. Got a head full of fuzz lately. Apologies."

"Think nothing of it, old fellow." I frowned at him. How much was fuzz and how much was Shad doing his Nigel Bruce's Watson?

He sat in silence for a long time apparently thinking heavily upon something of great importance to him. At last he asked, "Why else does this Powderham Castle sound familiar to me, Holmes? It's stuck in my head like Tom Mix and Hannibal Lecter but I can't seem to place it."

"Why, I'm astounded, old fellow. Did your Nigel Bruce Watson getup come with a bumbled brain program?"

"Bumble—No need to be offensive, Holmes. I asked but a simple question."

"Now, no need for hurt feelings. Late in the Twentieth Century what famous motion picture was partly filmed at Powderham? Remember?"

"A vid?"

"Think, now." I raised an eyebrow in his direction. "Come, come Watson. Anthony Hopkins . . ."

"Motion picture? Hopkins? Wait, wait . . ."

"Ed—"

"*No!* Edward Fox! Hop—*Remains of the Day.* Of course. Emma Thompson, Christopher Reeve, Hugh Grant— Powderham is Darlington?" He looked at me, bushy gray eyebrows arched. "Dear god, I am bumbled! What year?"

"Nineteen ninety-three," I added with a touch of smugness as I looked over the lists and images supplied by Ian Collier, which also included images of the pets brought by a few of the guests. In a flash I knew who stole the jewelry as well as how it was done. What to do about it, however, was going to take a bit of detail sorting.

"Having trouble finding the culprit, Holmes?"

I nodded toward his screen. "Have a go at it, Watson. While you're busy at that, I need to check some details."

On my screen I checked my details. My suspicion turned out to be correct. Assistant Chief Constable Ian Collier had been allowed to take immediate retirement from the force sixteen months ago for unspecified reasons. Using some computer tricks Shad taught me early in our relationship, I managed to find out those unspecified reasons involved specific unauthorized use of police equipment. It was all in the notes. I triggered the special links, entered a private code or two, and found the answers I needed. How mundane the scandalous tale once unfolded.

When the Collier family dog, a golden retriever named Laddie, was dying, ACC Collier had had a patrol cruiser with him at his home. In the grip of despair, he and his two young sons put Laddie into the cruiser to rush him to the vets. Laddie, however, died along the way. Ian probably hadn't even thought about it. The equipment was there, so were his sons, and so was the need. He harvested Laddie's engrams onto a chip—Police cruiser, police reader, police chip. What to do with the harvested engrams after that got lost in the dust when the cruiser's automatic after-action report was picked up by a hostile media. It was then reviewed by a cautious deputy chief constable, judged by a frightened board, defended by an indifferent Association of Chief Police Officers, and resulted in forced retirement. Birmingham and West Midlands found itself with one less good cop. Then it was job hunting time, new digs, new schools, new church, new friends, same family minus a dog, a home, and maybe part of a dad.

For every detail sorted, a new one needing a sort popped up. I rang a number. Bing Ehrenberg was in and available. I sent him what I had along with my best guesses regarding who and what to do. He agreed with me, which settled a couple details. He asked a few questions. I answered them. Bing was happy to hear I was enjoying my work again. I told him I had been blown up and was working for John Dillinger. He asked about Val. I told him she was now a cat. Asked about my job. Told him I was now Sherlock Holmes. Asked about my new partner. I told Bing my partner used to be a duck and would be again. He wanted to know how I felt about that and told him we got along rather well—even better after he was killed and came back as Dr. Watson. Asked me if I thought Norfolk would take the MCCA Knockout Trophy and I told him that would happen when Inland Revenue ran out of taxpayers. He told me I seemed to be doing much better. Patience of a saint, Dr. Ehrenberg.

Watson sat back, looked at me, and said, "The butler did it."

I glanced at him. "Astonishing. What ever led you to that conclusion?"

"Great heavens, man! It's right there under your nose. Look! The bounder's name is Moriarty! James Moriarty!"

I looked back at the list on my screen. "So it is." I frowned as I considered a detail that was becoming increasingly troublesome to put aside: The Moriarty business was only the latest symptom. It was just the sort of joke Shad might have made had Shad been in his feathers and in

150

Watson's place at that point in time. It was also what the current Watson might have said had he been smoking proscribed substances or experimenting with having his brain perforated and filled with kitty litter. It wasn't just concern for my friend's sanity. Was it really safe letting him drive? I was wondering a bit about my own mental state, as well. I was rather getting into the Basil Rathbone Sherlock Holmes character. It seemed to me I was enjoying it a good bit more than Watson—Shad, that is.

5

The air corridor followed the Exeter Canal as it hugged the west bank of the Exe as far south as Turf where the canal ended. The river there made a gentle bend to the east and the corridor continued south over the farmland canals and greenery near the hamlet of Exwell Barton. Directly before us, rising from the greensward like some sort of medieval stone rocket gantry at the top of a gentle hill was Powderham Castle estate's triple-towered stone Belvedere. Vacationers waved from the crenellated battlements and Watson waved back. Beyond and below the towers, set among the trees in a deer park by a small lake, was the castle. Beyond the castle was the wide avenue of the river, then Exmouth just below the curve of the ocean's blue horizon. White sprinkles of gulls flitted among the blues, greens, reds, and yellows of the sails and pennants flying on the sailboats filling the Exe. Watson pointed toward the boats. "Looks more fun than selling kitty litter, eh Holmes?"

"It appears so, Watson. Do you sail?"

"Sail? Heavens, no. Do you?"

"I'm ashamed to say I've never set foot in a sailboat. I suppose some day off we could take a lesson. Want to give it a try?"

Watson settled deeply into his couch and concentrated on the Sky Rover's instruments. "River looks very deep there, Holmes. Probably quite cold, too."

"Nonsense, old fellow. You'd take to it like a duck to water."

"Very amusing. Those things don't look safe."

"Sailing is like working around bombs, Watson: It pays to know what you are doing."

"I suppose we know where you and I come down on working around bombs, Holmes: A bit here, a bit there—"

"—A bit there, a bit here—"

"—A teeny bit way over there—"

"—And a great big gob or two down right here!"

We finally allowed ourselves to have a thorough laugh over that dark episode at Hangingstone Hill that was, after all, over—at least until the next echo.

Powderham Castle stood atop a slight rise in the well tended and tastefully wooded deer park. We went once around it before touching down. The lake mentioned before stretched gracefully east and west just south of the castle giving that side of the building views of deer drinking from the reflections of ancient trees. The castle itself, although replete with crenellated walls, gates, and towers, looked to be more manor home than fortress. Still, it had seen its battles during the Civil War fighting on the Royalist side. Norman towers, a mix of brickwork, cut gray stone, sandstone, carved beerstone casements, oak, and ivy made of it an architectural map of the centuries it had withstood since it came into the Courtenay family in the Thirteen Hundreds.

The Courtenays were not only respected in the west country but well liked. I doubt if there had been anyone living within a hundred kilometers of Powderham who hadn't, at least once in their lifetimes, visited the castle. Val and I had been there several times on tours and at events: once on a tour of the castle, once on a tour of the gardens, once on a nature walk, once as guests at a wedding, twice we went to catch the fireworks on Guy Fawkes Day. Even Shad and Nadine had been there, as Watson had narrated. A big jewelry heist among the guests at a Powderham paid occasion wouldn't ruin the Courtenays and probably wouldn't break any of the guests so robbed. It was not, however, the sort of thing needed right then by Ian Collier and his family. In any event, it was very rude.

Watson put us down in the skydock off Powderham Castle's North Drive. "Notice something about that castle as we came in, Holmes?"

"Many things, old fellow. Which did you have in mind?"

"Doesn't look a thing like Darlington in *Remains of the Day.*"

"Then perhaps we won't have Hannibal Lecter with which to contend. In any event, here comes the welcoming committee."

Since we arrived in an ABCD Sky Rover, one of Collier's off-duty constables advanced upon us from my side. He was a chunky fellow sporting a handsome gray handlebar moustache, a reflective silver and yellow traffic bib over his uniform. Since Shad had on his Nineteenth Century Watson getup, complete with genuine hound's-tooth Sherlock Holmes deerstalker (a size too small) atop his head, a wedding party parking attendant advanced upon his side of the vehicle. This lad was also chunky, apparently from bench pressing railroad locomotives. He was wearing a midnight blue tuxedo with a candy-striped tie. Shad opened the windows, I showed my ID to the constable, but before I could ask for Collier's office, Watson asked of the attendant, "Grimpion-Meyer wedding party please?"

The guide pointed to a slot, I bit my tongue, put my ID away, and Shad moved the cruiser toward the slot. We both held it in as long as we good, but mere flesh can bear only so much. Just as we locked into the slot we collapsed into each other's arms choking off cries of, "Grimpion-Meyer!" as best we could. As we exited the cruiser, the parking attendant and the constable seemed to be arguing. Actually, the attendant was upset and the constable was attempting to calm him.

"What seems to be the problem, constable?" I asked.

"Nothing, detective inspector. The lad's mistaken about something, that's all. Heard you and your partner havin' a laugh and he thought it might be at his expense."

"Not at all, my boy," I said to the fellow in the candy-striped tie. "The name of the wedding party, Grimpion-Meyer, struck us as amusing because of our resemblance to some fictional characters in some very old vids: Sherlock Holmes and Dr. Watson." I took the deerstalker cap from Shad's head and placed it upon my own.

"What's funny about that?" demanded the lad.

"One of their cases, *The Hound of the Baskervilles*. Have you heard of it?"

"Of course. I attend Cambridge don't I?"

"Cambridge College of Dry Cleaning," muttered Watson.

"What was that?" the lad demanded.

"The Hound of the Baskervilles," said Watson loudly, "took place near the Great Grimpen Mire."

The lad stared at us for a moment, then smiled on one side of his mouth, then the other, then he said, "Grimpion-Meyer," he laughed, and unpleasantness was averted. "One thing, though," the lad said to me as Shad turned and began walking toward the castle's north gate entrance.

"What is that?" I answered.

"I understand that Sherlock Holmes—not the one in the movies, the one in the stories?"

"Yes?"

"I understand he never wore a deerstalker cap. That was just something they done up in the fliks."

"Ah," I said placing an arm across his substantial shoulders. Solid fellow. "A popular myth that I am pleased to have an opportunity to dispel, lad. I believe you will find in Dr. Watson's account entitled 'Silver Blaze' the good doctor depicts Holmes's attire on their rail trip to Exeter. Watson describes his friend's face 'framed in his ear-flapped traveling-cap.' Now, among the available ear-flap caps in those times and later were any of the knitted, fur, and cloth winter affairs—Andes, Eskimo, aviator, Elmer Fudd, Omar Bradley, and so on. I'm certain you'll agree Sherlock Holmes would rather let Professor Moriarty make off with the Crown Jewels than appear in public in any one of them. Do you agree?"

"I'm not sure."

"Can you see Sherlock Holmes with a shotgun sneaking through the woods saying, 'Shhhh. I'm hunting a wabbit?'"

"I cannot."

"Good lad." I patted his back. "Sir, the rakish deerstalker is the only possible ear-flapped traveling-cap sufficiently fashionable for Sherlock Holmes. Good day to you."

The constable nodded me toward the north entrance. By the time I had made my way through it into the courtyard, Watson was nowhere to be seen. I stood across from the castle's famous red door which, recalling the wedding Val and I had attended, was the main entrance for wedding participants and guests, I had a spine chilling moment thinking of Shad befuddled up as Dr. John Watson stumbling among the guests doing his best to solve the crime. Just before my blood turned to blueberry yogurt, I caught a movement out of the corner of my eye. It was a small door closing in a wall behind and to the right of the main tower. By the time I reached that door, it had closed altogether.

"Shad," I said in something between a shout and a whisper, "That's the wrong bloody door." He was gone. I opened the door to a dark sort of vestibule and entered, the aromas of prepared foods blending agreeably with the scents of old wood and new wax. I crossed hallways, rushed down passageways, and generally worked myself into a panic. I peered into rooms gingerbreaded with Italian molding, hung with portraits of ancestors, and festooned with Chinese glazed pots large enough to make a rather comfortable maisonette with the proper plumbing. I peered down hallways polished until everything seemed dipped in honey, more portraits of ancestors, polished brass candlesticks, and hoary crude tables that wore their polished scars with beribboned honor as though inflicted by shielding the body of the Conqueror himself. Thinking of Shad running loose in this movie set re-chilled my blood to hypothermic levels.

6

By the time I managed to catch up with him, Shad was standing at the foot of a dark staircase, the stairs covered with a blue runner. There was rich blue carpeting on the immediate landing, as well, in addition to more blue runner as the stairs continued up and to the right. On the back of the landing into the blue plaster of the wall was a hidden door to a set of servants stairs. It strained memory but it appeared to be where the butler's father in *Remains of the Day* first showed that his squirrels were getting the better of him, as a duck I had once known might have put it.

Nigel Bruce, thoughtfully cocking his head to one side and tugging at his bit of a moustache, could have been right out of any of the Rathbone-Bruce series of vids. He glanced at me. "Oh," he said bluntly. "There you are, Holmes. Been looking all over for you. Where the deuce've you been?" He looked back at the stairs. "Look at this staircase. Not much of *Remains* was filmed here, you know. Never cared much for the character of Lord Darlington. Not a great role for Edward Fox, an actor I much admire, as you know."

"Yes."

"Much underrated in his time, Edward Fox. What a Nelson he would've made. Eh, Holmes?"

"A role for which any self-respecting British actor would gladly give his right arm, Watson."

He looked at me for a stunned five seconds before he continued. "Holmes, remember Fox's remarkable performance in *Day of the Jackal?*"

"I do. Very exciting production."

"Was there anyone who saw that performance, Holmes, who at the conclusion wasn't rooting for the Jackal to shoot Charles de Gaulle?"

"Very true, Watson, but that may have been for other reasons besides Fox's performance."

"How do you mean?"

"As you may recall, *Day of the Jackal* was inspired by an actual plot to assassinate de Gaulle. It was said most Western leaders had his face on their dart boards."

"I see. Well then, how about Edward Fox's role as Francis Farewell, the adventurer who came to South Africa to hoodwink a savage ruler and stayed to fall beneath the spell of the great Shaka, king of the Zulus?"

I could almost hear the mourning and the dramatically mysterious musical score as Dr. Watson lowered himself to one knee before the staircase. He still had his multi-track sound system programs and data banks intact, if not his judgment. "As mournful chanting lows in the royal kraal, the reflections of the hearth flames flicker against the walls of Shaka's great house. Leftenant Farewell kneels and listens as the great Zulu king bitterly throws the Englishman's deceptions back in Farewell's face. The leftenant tells Shaka that hating the English is not the solution, that they must search for the solution together. Shaka scorns the Englishman's words. He says that Farewell is a man with no nation, a shadow. The king tells him to go, that Shaka no longer has any need for him. Farewell answers:

"Go?" Watson cried loudly doing a remarkably good Edward Fox. "Go?" he inquired again of the Zulu king as I heard a squeak come from the stairs above. "Where?" he demanded loudly and angrily as I spied with my little eye a sharply dressed fellow wearing a black tux with silver tie descending the stairs. Between a loosely blown array of silver-gray hair and the tie was the smoothly shaved only slightly jowly face of Charles Hugh Pepys Courtenay, Earl of Devon. He was heading straight down the stairs for Shad's performance of Nigel Bruce's performance of Dr. Watson's performance of Edward Fox's performance of Francis Farewell's farewell performance before Shaka as Shad's and my pensions joined *Pliopithecus* and the Dodo in existence's dustbin. "Where can I go?" Farewell begged more humbly, a shaking hand extended toward the imaginary Zulu king. It was Oscar-winning stuff.

"Where I have been," answered Lord Devon in a deep rich voice, doing a quite credible Henry Cele as Shaka.

Shad looked up the stairs, his eyes bugged, his cheeks bulged, and he struggled to his feet, spluttering apologies. Lord Devon placed his well manicured hands together and clapped genteelly. "Well done, sir. *Shaka Zulu*. Well done." He nodded his gray mane at me. "Indeed, I am horribly late for the reception and I see the chief constable has sent England's most dynamic duo to track me down, wot? Holmes and Watson, wot? Basil Rathbone and Nigel Bruce?"

Shad and I exchanged quick panic glances. "Chief constable?" Watson mouthed. Facing Lord Devon, Watson said, "Just a gentle reminder of the time, milord. Could you direct us to the castle's head of security so that we may report our mission accomplished?"

The master of the house laughed, crinkled his eyes, and pointed down an ancestor imaged hallway generally toward the south. "All of the way down there, doctor, last door on the right. Oh."

We both paused, frozen in mid getaway, giving Lord Devon our full attention. It was that kind of 'oh.' "Yes, milord?" I said.

"Do you know if there has been any progress made concerning this dreadful jewelry matter?"

"Yes there has, milord," I said. "I am pleased to say it should all be cleared up before the conclusion of the reception."

"Not a theft, was it?" He pronounced "theft" as though its mere thought might endanger the very foundations of Powderham.

"A mere misunderstanding, milord. Nothing more. Please put your mind at ease."

His eyebrows ascended. "Excellent!" He nodded, his face wreathed in very happy smiles. "Jolly good." He looked at Watson, his face growing somewhat more serious. "Excellent actor, Edward Fox." He shook his head gravely. *"Remains of the Day*. Hated that movie as a boy. Don't mind me baring the old soul, do you old fellow, one actor to another?"

"Not at all, milord."

"Your excellent portrayal of Edward Fox reminded me of it. As a boy they told me a thousand times *Remains of the Day* was filmed here. Dreadful film. I even watched it once. Could hardly stay awake. I mean you practically stand up begging Emma Thompson to hop naked in Hopkins's tub, wot? Muss his hair a bit?"

"Quite," said Watson.

Lord Devon looked into a glass and darkly. "Away at school you tell all your chums the bloody thing was filmed at Powderham. They don't care the ruddy film's boring. It's Hollywood. Movies! With *Hannibal the cannibal.* You sit before the tellymax screen all puffed up, the ruddy thing begins. There it goes, sir, with that bloody ride up a hilly lane you never saw before and you pull up to a town house with a Georgian roofline decorated with bloody old urns. 'Where the hell is that?' shouts out Jimmy Brown. 'That's not Powderham,' says Cyril Danforth. 'Where's that, Charlie?' yells out Tommy Welles. "Where are the battlements?"

His lordship descended the remains of the stairs, clasped his hands behind his back, shook his head, and made his way toward the wedding party, still shaking his head. "Scarred me for life," he muttered as he turned a corner. "Bloody movies." Shad and I exited on tiptoe in the opposite direction.

"Now, was that a good save or what?" said my partner as we reached Ian Collier's door.

"Save? *Save?*"

He gave me his hurt Watson expression. "Of course, Holmes. Where's the head of security? Mission accomplished?"

"Shad, there *is* a built-in bumble factor in your Dr. Watson brain! It's the size of a casaba melon!"

"Really, Holmes!"

"You know what they call a firefighter who does a superb job of extinguishing fires he himself has ignited?"

"What?"

"An *arsonist!*" I knocked on the door and entered.

7

The security officer on duty led us to an office which led to an outer office and a secretary who led us to an inner office overlooking the deer park and lake. It was a well lighted room, smallish, and tucked about with family photos, professional photos, and neat shelves of books. Ian Collier himself was older than I remembered, a testimony to the dozen years or more that had passed since I had last seen him. He was a pleasant-looking fellow of about Watson's height, brown hair thinning on top and graying on the sides. He rose slowly behind his desk as we entered. He had a narrow face I hadn't remembered as mournful but which certainly rated such a description a moment after he caught a glimpse of the professional help he was getting from Exeter. The expression then became something between flabbergasted and crestfallen.

"Blood and sand, Jaggs! What's become of you?"

"I haven't time to explain, dear boy," I said briskly. I nodded at Shad. "Former Assistant Chief Constable Ian Collier, this is my partner, Detective Sergeant Guy Shad. Watson, this is Mr. Ian Collier."

"Pleased to meet you, sir," said Watson, extending his hand. They shook. Collier appeared to be waiting for an explanation I really had neither the time nor the heart to provide. Hence, I said, "Shad and I are traveling incognito."

"I shouldn't wonder," he responded. He gestured at two red leather covered captains chairs facing his desk. "Please. Be seated. Can I offer you some tea?"

"Thank you. That would be most welcome," I said lowering myself into the chair to Shad's left. As we waited for Ian's secretary to bring tea and biscuits, Powderham Castle's head of security briefed us on the missing jewelry. I noticed while he was talking, family photo images randomly appeared in a frame on the shelf behind Ian's head. Wife and two young sons perhaps ten and seven respectively. There was a single still of a golden retriever hanging on the wall opposite the desk. It looked as though it had been taken on a sunny day in a field of wildflowers. The tea was poured and I took my cup. Excellent blend, by the way.

"We need several things," I said to Ian. "First, as discreetly as possible, have several of your security personnel go to the reception, locate, and extricate Miss Betsy Blythe."

"The blind woman with the seeing-eye dog?"

I smiled. "She is not blind and that dog is a Labradoodle bio with a human imprint. As soon as possible after grabbing them—"

"You said *extricate* them."

"With prejudice. Once you have them, separate them. Make certain you get both woman and dog and that they cannot communicate. I doubt that they'll be rigged with wireless, but be prepared for it just in case they are."

"Very well."

"Next, I need to interview Clarice Penne."

His eyebrows went up. "You mean Timmy the Tortoise?"

"Yes. I need to do so in private, with Betsy Blythe, and without the dog."

Collier was looking confused. So was Watson.

"Come now, gentlemen. Surely you can arrange a meeting. It must be near a place where we can have unobserved access to the ABCD cruiser."

Collier leaned back in his chair and crossed his legs. "There's a place just beyond the Rose Garden where you can have that meeting," he said. "At the east edge of the garden where it drops down to the Dressage Lawn there's a wall. It would conceal your cruiser."

"Excellent."

"Am I permitted to know what's going on?" he asked.

"I'm sorry, old fellow. It's like rescuing the troops from Dunkirk. If it had to be written up in triplicate and approved in advance, no one ever would have had the courage to take the responsibility."

Collier looked at Watson who chuckled. "Holmes really knows how to lead a charge, doesn't he?" said my partner.

"Now that you mention it, the phrase 'the brave Six Hundred' does come to mind rather easily." Ian Collier shifted his gaze back to me. "I'm not going to find out you two have escaped from some asylum am I?"

"No. I don't believe you will ever find out." I touched my fingertips together and looked over them, my eyebrows arched, my eyes widened, but not crossed.

He leaned back in his chair, raised a hand in dismissal, and dropped it to the arm of his chair. "I can arrange for you, your cruiser, Betsy Blythe, and Timmy the tortoise to meet privately off the edge of the Rose Garden. Anything else?"

"When you took that imprint of your dog, Ian."

The change of subject caught him off stride. Once his double take was done, he leaned back in his chair. "When I was forced to retire?" he asked, his face reddening.

"Yes. Do you still have that chip?"

He frowned. "Yes. It's here in my office."

"Excellent. We'll need that."

"Is that quite all?" he asked.

"No, not quite." I rubbed my chin. "We'll need a dungeon, a butcher's apron, some tomato juice, a rusty knife, and two of your most thuggish-looking cops. They must be reliable chaps, not squeamish, men who can keep their mouths shut. If the chief constable, the earl, or Superintendent Matheson get wind of any of this the lot of us will be balls-up and most likely never play the violin again."

8

As gentle breezes touched the treetops, the warm spring air was filled with the heady scent of roses. A marquee for children's entertainments had already been erected at the edge of the lawn below the Rose Garden. Inside the marquee were a few chairs, Betsy Blythe, Ian Collier, Clarice Penne as Timmy the Tortoise, Shad as Bruce as Watson, and myself somewhat in charge. The ABCD cruiser was parked out of sight of the castle next to the Rose Garden wall stairs. Collier and Watson stood guard by the stairs while I sat on the chair facing Betsy Blythe to my right and the tortoise to my left. Miss Penne, of course, as a thorn-thighed tortoise, had her head stuck out of a shell about the size of a smallish elongated dinner plate with warmer. Miss Blythe was somewhat more attractive being a shapely human female bio wearing a pale blue cocktail dress with white half-heels. She was in her mid twenties, brown hair with reddish highlights, a relaxed cupid's bow mouth, a bit of an upturned nose, and lovely hazel eyes once I removed her heavy sunglasses.

"A shame to hide those beautiful eyes, Miss Blythe."

"I'm sorry, sir. I don't know who you are. I'm blind, you see."

"Actually, I do see, Lolita, and so do you."

"My name's Betsy—"

"It's Lolita Doll and you are no more sightless than am I. We are pressed for time, my dear. Therefore, may we dispense with the denials, explanations, excuses, and so on?"

"My dog—"

"We have Frank Statten in detention and caught red-handed—or red-pawed—with the goods. Because you tipped us off, we are inclined to be lenient."

She stood up and glared down at me. "Lolita Doll rats out *nobody,* copper!"

I held up a hand. "Please. Calm yourself. You all but sent engraved invitations. Now, take your seat."

She slowly sat down on her chair, still glaring at me, then looked down ashamed. "You helped me a lot, Inspector Jaggers. That's the truth. You and the parrot. Don't know what I would've done if I hadn't fallen into your hands. That Dr. Ehrenberg helped me, too. But how'd you know I had a partner in that Wallingford job? And how'd you know to come here to catch us?"

"Unintentionally, perhaps, but you told me both times, my dear. The parakeet was certainly too small either to hide or carry much in the way of swag. About all it could do was map out the security systems and get the codes when they were entered. You had to have a partner. Add to that you worked at Songbirds and we already knew Frankie Statten owned the shop, and there you were. Then when I heard a large jewel heist had gone down at Powderham and saw Betsy Blythe had brought a large dog, well, it was obvious that Lolita Doll and Frankie Statten were at it again."

"Sorry?" She was frowning at me.

"Betsy Blythe," I repeated. "Blythe from the Blythe doll created in 1972 by the American Kenner toy company and Betsy from the Betsy Wetsy created in 1934 by Ideal." I held out my hands. "'It's me, Doll.' Perfectly obvious."

"Remarkable," she said.

"At times I astound even myself. What were you trying to do, Lolita?"

She looked up at me, her eyes filled with tears. "See, all the ladies had these little changing cubicles set up in the room off the First Library where they could change before the reception and dance. Can't thunder rock wearin' all that ice. Mr. Collier there had folks they could leave valuables with, but most guests didn't bother. Frank was right about that. But a signal's supposed to go off when we returns to the shop. That's when we was all supposed to get nicked. I suppose this is all right for what it is, but it's only going to be attempted, isn't it? I wanted the whole book."

"I thought you wanted someplace safe, Lolita, to be taken care of, to be happy and loved. You're not going to get that locked up in the nick."

"Half a loaf," she offered lamely.

"Is half a loaf short," I completed.

"It'd be almost worth it to think on Frank being miserable for a tenner."

"Listen, Lolita. I believe I have the answer to all your problems and mine." I held out a hand toward the tortoise. "Do you know Clarice Penne?"

She looked at the tortoise and back at me. "Oh, sure. I mean I seen her here in the garden maybe a hundred times tellin' stories to the children, the tykes pettin' her shell and all. Every chance I get I come down here. I told Dr. Ehrenberg about it. So beautiful here."

"How would you like to tell stories to children, Lolita? You're good with lies and know the very best stories. How would you like Clarice's job?"

"Now you hold on just a minute there, Sherlock," said the tortoise. "This is *my* gig and for as long as I want it. I got a contract."

I reached over, picked up the tortoise, and whispered at Clarice as I faced her about. "If you pee on me, love, I will put you on your back for the remainder of the meeting and leave you that way." I aimed her snapping end at Lolita. "Clarice, look at Lolita, hush for a moment and consider: How would you like to have that face, that voice, that age, those legs, and that body as you reinvent yourself and relaunch your theatrical career? You'd still have all your current financial assets, belongings, degrees, whatever."

The tortoise was dead silent, but I could almost see the smoke rising from the top of its wrinkled head. Finally the tortoise glanced back at me. "Who the hell are you, mate?"

"Forgive me, Miss Penne. I am DI Harrington Jaggers, Devon ABCD."

The tortoise moved it's head until it was once again looking at Lolita. Clarice said, "Would you consider it, girl, even for a serious second?"

"Oh, yes! In a heartbeat!" she answered. "You have the most wonderful job in the world! Please!"

"Girl, you don't even know what my body in stasis looks like."

"I don't care," said Lolita. "I don't want that body. I want the one you're in now."

"I have your natural all taken care of," I said to Clarice. "Are we agreed, then? Lolita?"

"Safe, taken care of, happy, and loved. You remembered everything, inspector. Is there nothing you can't do?"

"We'll see. Clarice?"

"I'd sure like to know how you read me so well, Sherlock."

"Elementary, Miss Penne. You are the only thorn-thighed tortoise in the United Kingdom on anti-depressants." I held a hand out toward the cruiser. "Shall we? There is only a miniscule window of opportunity." Ian and Watson both hunched their shoulders, turned their backs, and faced the stairs.

I took Clarice and Lolita over to the cruiser, ran up the mechs, moved a few things out of the way, moved in one woman bio and one tortoise bio, swapped their imprints, and moved out one woman bio and one tortoise bio. Once that was accomplished the two of them went to a far corner below the Rose Garden wall to discuss a few tortoise-girl, girl-tortoise issues. As they were thus engaged, I sent the cruiser to the next location, the outside entrance to our improvised dungeon, and said to my faithful medical companion, "Come, Watson, come! The game's afoot!"

9

It was not a bad dungeon for our purposes. The space was below ground level, sufficiently dank, the walls of ancient dressed stone, the atmosphere musty. The room's past as a storage place for meats was evidenced by the number of rusty meat hooks protruding from two of the four walls. There were no grinning skeletons hanging from irons but the castle's spider population had done a grand job of decorating the craggy beams above with filthy old webs. The lights were electric instead of smoky old torches, but the lights were grimy and adequately dim.

In the center of the room was a large wooden butcher's block table. It's dark uneven surface had seen much use over the centuries. The dips and stains testified to millions of cuts and oceans of blood. I stood at one corner of the table, Ian stood across from me. At the other two corners were two of Ian's men, Peter Blake and Henry Tompkins. They were both retired constables who did professional wrestling on the local circuit. With the proper makeup they had also appeared in several locally produced horror vids. They were wearing the proper makeup.

In the center of the table sat about the sweetest most good-natured lovable dog I had ever seen. He was about seven stone, his fur light brown, curly, and uncut giving him both a ragged and fluffy appearance. Delightful face, with a few of those curls hanging before his eyes. The dog's name, according to his license tag, was "Doodles." His brace, peculiar to seeing-eye dogs, had been removed and was on the floor in the corner behind Ian. To all appearances he was a real dog, which meant his bio receiver was being shielded by a Bio Shack special. Doodles, poor fellow, appeared just a bit nervous.

"Gentlemen," I began, "While we're waiting for Dr. Watson to finish cleaning up from working on the two cats, please be so kind as to note the breed of this animal. This is a cross between a Labrador retriever and a poodle known to dog fanciers as a Labradoodle." I reached out and petted its head. "Good boy. Labradoodles are generally good natured, take complicated training extremely well, and are very remarkable in that they do not shed."

"Not at all, Mr. Holmes?" growled Peter Blake.

"Your allergic sensitivities are safe with this pooch, Mr. Blake. Now, as I remarked, they are easily trained and well behaved, which is why this animal's behavior quite puzzles me. There is only one reason I can think of why such a valuable animal should eat all that jewelry that was left in the changing room."

"How can you be certain he done it?" asked Henry Tompkins.

"Elementary, Mr. Tompkins. Staff security have searched everywhere else, have they not?"

"Aye, we have." The big man nodded his massive black-hooded head.

"And Dr. Watson has examined all of the other pets as possible hiding places, hasn't he?"

Ian, Blake, and Tompkins hung their heads. "Aye," said Tompkins. "He did that." I rather hoped they weren't overdoing it. I glanced down at the butcher block and there was just the right amount of tomato juice smeared about. The Labradoodle was looking down at the butcher block, as well. His tongue was out and he was panting.

"There you are, Mr. Tompkins," I said. "'When you have eliminated the possible, whatever remains, however improbable, must be the truth.'" I looked into the dog's wide-eyed gaze and said, "Sir Arthur Conan Doyle." A rattle followed by a low muttered curse came from the shadows beyond the arched doorway. From beyond it Watson emerged wearing the butchers apron stained from the waist down with tomato juice. He wasn't wearing his tweed jacket and the sleeves of his white shirt were rolled above his elbows. His hands were stained slightly with red, but the butcher knife in his right hand was coated with the stuff.

"Told you the jewels wouldn't be in those cats, Holmes," he muttered through hurt feelings.

"We had to look, old fellow."

"Neither of them pulled through, you know. Wouldn't've hurt anything to let me hop into the village and pick up some anesthetic from the chemist's."

"We were pressed for time, old fellow. Sorry to put you through that."

He looked over the tops of his glasses at the assembly. "The owners of those cats are going to be quite distressed and it's no fault of mine. I objected to all those procedures from the start. I want that on the record." He snorted contemptuously at the butcher knife in his hand which he began waving about. "Not even a proper scalpel. This thing's dull as an old rake. Do a better job with a chain saw."

"Couldn't be helped, old fellow." I reached out a hand and scratched the dog's head. "Here's the last one."

The Labradoodle's panting resembled a steam locomotive attempting to climb the South Face of Everest.

Watson's eyebrows went up. "At least this one is big enough to hold the jewelry, Holmes." He passed his thumb slowly over the knife's edge. "Strange looking beast, there. What kind of breed is that?"

I held out a hand to Peter Blake. "You may have the honor, Mr. Blake."

"Yes sir." He looked at Watson. "This here, doctor, is a Labradoodle."

"Labradoodle, you say? Well, there, stretch him out on the block boys and let's see if we can't separate his Labra from his doodles."

"All right! All right! Jesus, Mary, and Joseph!" yelled the dog. "All bloody *right!*"

We watched as the dog sat back on its hind legs, pulled its forelegs to its sides, and a line appeared in the dog's fine belly hair. The line parted starting at the top, and essentially unsealed spilling all of the missing jewelry into Peter Blake's quick hands. Watson moved to my side.

"Congratulations, Holmes. You nailed Frank Statten."

"Ah me," I said as I shrugged. "I'm afraid I'm going to have to disappoint you once again, old friend."

He frowned, then one eyebrow slowly elevated. "I don't believe it, Holmes. Not another catch and release."

"With a condition." I looked and saw I had everyone's attention, including the Labradoodle's. "Jewelry heist at Powderham Castle, right in the middle of a reception, famous guests, among them Lord and Lady Devon and the chief constable of the Devon & Cornwall Constabulary. The scandal would never do." I looked at the dog. "Would it?"

He looked around, shifty-eyed. "No. No, the media would have a feast."

"So it seems to me the best thing is to return the jewelry to its rightful owners, no theft, no scandal, no harm done."

"That sounds cool." The dog held up its right paw, extended a toe and wagged it back and forth. "But, call me Mr. Suspicious, I see a big fat fishhook with my name on it."

"Whatever do you mean, sir?"

"In return for this generous offer, Mr. Holmes is it?"

"Yes."

"In return, what's Frankie Statten's bill?"

"Why, I'm so glad you asked that question, Mr. Statten. We keep the jewelry, return it to its owners, and return you to your natural body in Exeter no harm done—"

"—And?"

"And that's it. We keep your equipment, of course."

"Equipment?"

"The bios."

"All . . . Lolita. She ratted me out."

"It's only because of her you're getting this deal, Frank," I said. "We've detained her and she will be spending the rest of her life behind walls." I pointed at the velvet-lined interior of his belly cavity. "We knew it was you all along because your gut was the last place there was to look. What about the deal?"

"You just let me go?"

"Once we get you back to Queen Street and Songbirds. Is that where you keep your natural?"

"Yeah."

"Do you need to be counseled on how much time you could draw doing things your way?"

"There has to be a catch." The dog looked down and shook his head.

"Must be disappointing for you, too, Holmes," said Watson to me, as Statten pondered the deal.

"Why do you say that, Watson? I would call this a most satisfactory conclusion to this matter."

"Here you have a dog and you never got to say anything about the curious incident of the dog in the night-time."

"Night-time? There was no night-time."

"Wasn't that what was curious?"

"Wasn't what— I don't quite see what you are driving at, Watson. I thought the curious incident was that the dog wasn't barking."

"Well, this dog wasn't barking. Didn't you find that curious?"

"Not in the least."

He leaned back. "Not even a smidgen?"

"Dear fellow, this Labradoodle is an amdroid imprinted by a human impersonating a very well-trained, well-behaved seeing-eye dog. Why would he bark?"

"Well, I thought it curious."

"Really."

"Game's afoot and all that—"

"I agree to the deal," interrupted Frankie Statten. "Just so I don't have to listen to any more of this rubbish!"

"Thank you." I turned to Watson and smiled. "Well done, old fellow. Well done. So, while you clean up and Mr. Blake and Mr. Tompkins discreetly return the jewelry to their respective owners, Mr. Collier, Mr. Statten, and I shall repair to the cruiser and sort out a few final details." I held out my hand toward the stairs. "Gentlemen."

As I followed Collier and the dog up the dungeon stairs, I heard the Labradoodle ask him confidentially, "This Holmes and Watson thing those two got going. An act, right? An act?"

"I don't know," answered Mr. Collier. "I simply don't know."

172

10

The cruiser rose from Powderham Castle in an arc that took us over the River Exe giving us a good view of Lympstone's Bay Tower red in the afternoon sun. I could see Mama Bimbo's Cat House on The Strand being fitted out for some other kind of shop. A flight of gulls crossed below us and made wing for chips or fingerlings, whichever were more plentiful as the tide changed. Watson put us on autopilot and settled back in his couch.

"Holmes, what about Frank Statten and Songbirds?" He pointed toward the mech chip in the envelope on the dash clip. "Are you simply going to let him go without even a day in court?"

"I am going to take this chip to his stasis bed at Songbirds, update his natural, and leave, enquiry closed."

"Memories of every crime and crooked deal Statten ever pulled, everything he has in the works right now, is in his memory recall bank. I cannot believe you won't at least make a copy of that chip for the constabulary."

"I won't do it for two reasons, Watson. First, I gave him my word. Second, I don't think Statten will believe either that I won't copy his memory. Unless I'm terribly mistaken, every iron he has in the fire will be yanked out within hours of getting his engrams back into his nat. The deals he has going with any number of undesirable personages will be cancelled and they will be after him to know why. Think he'll stick around to try and explain how he had to make a deal with Sherlock Holmes and Dr. Watson?"

Watson chuckled. "Not much to show on our records, though."

"Small price to pay for ending a one-man crime wave and doing a good cop a favor, don't you think? It should make absolute excrement of Frankie's criminal life and reputation, which will settle his account with Loretta nicely."

"I suppose." We rode along silently for awhile, then Watson said, "Holmes, what is going to happen to Clarice Penne's body—the one in stasis? Sooner or later the owner of the stasis bed is going to have to put the body up for payments due, correct?"

"I'm surprised at you, Watson," I said. "Surely you recall our visit to that fair seaside cultural center you insisted on pronouncing Limp-stone."

"Yes." He nodded. "Of course I remember."

"Do you also remember the woman who constituted one hundred percent of the clientele of Mama Bimbo's Cat House?"

He chuckled at that. "Yes. Petting Place. Absurd name. Maddie girl, she was. Madeleine Wallingford. She brought in the hapless jewel thief now inhabiting Timmy the Tortoise over at Powderham Castle. Our first catch and release. What of her?"

"Remember the card Madeleine Wallingford had us place in the shop window? The one for the meeting of the Order of St. Trinians?"

"Vaguely. Theater group, wasn't it?"

"I'm shocked, Watson. Absolutely shaken to my very nucleus. An old movie buff such as yourself? You yourself remarked how Clarice Penne's natural body resembled actor Alistair Sim, he who in his heyday played the headmistress of St. Trinians girls school in *The Belles of St. Trinians* to such perfection—"

"The Order of St. Trinians," Shad interrupted. "That theater group does scripts based on the Ronald Searle cartoons!"

"Indeed, old fellow, indeed. Madeleine Wallingford is paying off the stasis estate agent and collecting the suit for Trinians new star performer as we speak. You know, possibly going without a proper hat has chilled your brain, depriving its cells of much needed oxygen, increasing your brain-bumble factor." I reached back and took a round box from the hands of the large walking mech. "In return for our services, I received this from my friend Ian Collier." I handed it to my partner.

"I didn't know we were allowed to accept gifts, Holmes."

"Nothing of value. This is just an old hand-me-down of Ian's grandfather's. It ought to keep your brain toasty."

He lifted the lid from the box, placed it aside, opened the tissue paper, and took the gray homburg from it. "Why . . . why this is quite thoughtful, Holmes." He placed it on his head with both hands and faced me. "How do I look?"

"Very handsome, Watson. Distinguished. The very picture of Dr. John H. Watson."

"You shouldn't have."

"Why not?"

His face grew long and troubled. "Now, this makes me feel terrible."

"How so, Watson?"

"Well, I've noticed, Holmes, that you seem to be enjoying our Holmes and Watson thing quite a bit more than I have."

"I'd noticed it myself. Now that I reflect upon it, I haven't felt this perceptive in decades. I feel as though I could untie the Gordian Knot one-handed, blindfolded, and play multiple games of championship chess with my toes at the same time."

"Feeling rather sharp, eh, Holmes?"

"As a tack, dear fellow. Why?"

"I have a confession to make. You know how I dislike reading instructions of any kind."

"Quite. As I recall DS Guy Shad's famous dictum: 'If the damned program or machine isn't intuitive to operate, it's crap.'"

Watson chuckled. "Yes. Very amusing."

"Come, Watson. What about it?" I prompted.

"Brochure came with my Watson suit, you know, from Celebrity Lookalikes." He reached into his side coat pocket with his left hand and pulled out a leaflet folded into thirds. "You were correct, Holmes, about what you called my bumble factor. There's one built in. Slows things down and fuzzes up thoughts while mixing them in with the vocabulary, vocal mannerisms, and so on of the Nigel Bruce Watson." He waved the leaflet idly in my direction. "Something else, too."

"What's that?"

175

"Bit of a cost cutting measure, I fear. Makes sense if you look at it from their end. Celebrity Lookalikes, that is. You see?"

"I'm afraid I don't see. What are you talking about, Watson? What cost cutting measure?"

"Oh. Well, usually both suits are rented at the same time: Holmes and Watson. You see? Symbiotic relationship."

"Ye-e-es," I answered warily.

"They had to have the Nigel Bruce as Watson suits made, you see. For the Basil Rathbone as Holmes suits, though, they simply used the same model fallen officer replacement suit that you have yourself."

"That makes perfectly good sense. Why reinvent the wheel?"

"Exactly, Holmes. So you understand."

"Understand what?"

"When my Watson suit came in close enough proximity to your model suit, my Nigel Bruce-Dr. Watson bio program asked permission to insert a wireless patch through your bio receiver. You must have seen it and agreed to the terms."

"Ever since I went wireless I must get a half dozen of those things a day. I never read them—who has the time? What—well, what does it do?"

Watson yawned, tipped the homburg over his eyes, and slid down in his seat. "Only some mannerisms, vocabulary choices, thought pattern adjustments. According to the brochure it should sharpen up your thinking a bit. Seems to have done just that. Gordian Knot and all. We can uninstall it I suppose."

"Why would I want to?"

"Perhaps I should. Don't quite seem to understand what's going on."

I picked up the brochure and gave it a quick scan. It had an address that would be useful in finding out if it would be possible to dial back Watson's bumble factor. Something else, too, that might be a problem:

The Holmes and Watson duo are only for entertainment, guys! Silly us! So if you run into real emergency situations while occupying these bios, programming automatically calls the chaps who are the real professionals. For anything less than emergencies, programming restricts your problem solving strategies to those not involving arrests or otherwise burdening the police. Have fun! and please solve crime responsibly.

"Speaking of bumble," said Watson, "I used to have a bumble dessert thing when I was with New England Wildlife. Quite tasty. Bumble brain pie."

"Doesn't sound very appetizing, old fellow." I returned the brochure to Watson.

"What? Sorry." He chuckled. "Misspoke there. Bumble brain pie. Silly of me. Actually it was called bum berry pie."

"Bum berry pie? Are you certain?"

"Yes. Raspberries, blueberries, blackberries. Delicious. A Maine favorite. Woman in Farmington used to make it up special for the officers in my station."

"Terribly sorry, Watson. Bum berry pie sounds even less appetizing than bumble brain pie."

"Bumble berry pie, Holmes," corrected Watson. "Whatever are you going on about? I said bumble berry pie. Keep going on about bum berry pie and you'll make people wonder from where you got this great reputation." He chuckled again and yawned. "Bum berry pie. You amaze me, Holmes. You absolutely amaze me. Oh, about the dog—"

"Frankie Statten was caught going equipped, hence the equipment is forfeit."

"I see that. But since—how was that again?"

"Since we are all agreed that the jewelry was misplaced and not stolen, there was no crime. Hence, no need to produce anything back at the office."

Watson grunted something.

As the late afternoon countryside sped beneath us, I looked back over my thoughts of the past few days, thrilling at always having an answer almost as soon as a question arose. Such as, if I am heading east toward Exeter late in the afternoon, why is the setting sun not at my back but is, instead, perpendicular to the vector of motion and warming my left cheek? I looked at the GPS.

"Watson, you have us heading north toward Exmoor. Watson?"

I caught the sound of the old fellow gently snoring, took over the cruiser's controls, and entered the correct heading, wondering if the patch I had automatically accepted into my neural system included the ability to play the violin and an addiction to cocaine. Then I remembered my Holmes was a Basil Rathbone Hollywood Holmes whose strongest addiction was to whatever tobacco was stuffed into that huge meerschaum pipe of his. I needn't worry about smoking. Neither my lungs, my wife, nor the clean air regulations at Heavitree Tower could tolerate any of that nonsense.

My partner was having a bit of bother about the Labradoodle. To wit: had we stolen it? I suppose a case could be made for it, and I would be happy to meet Frankie Statten in court any time he wished to settle the matter at law. Once I was on the proper heading for Exeter I settled in and contemplated blowing bubbles from that meerschaum. It went very well with the image playing before my mind's eye of Ian Collier, his wife, and two boys at Powderham playing with their old golden retriever in his new Labradoodle suit.

♠

THE COLLETON GHOST

-1-

"I was certain it was a ghost, Jaggs," Shad quacked as he entered the Sky Rover and sealed the door. My partner was still inhabiting his Nigel Bruce/Dr. Watson bio, but there seemed to be a new glitch—besides reporting a ghost, that is.

"You're quacking, old fellow."

"That has a lot to do with me being a duck." He shrugged and grimaced. "Essentially a duck."

"The point is the patch doesn't appear to work around your Watson fuzz program."

"Whatever are you going on about, Holmes?" he said in his Watson voice. I sighed. Why not an electronic multiple personality? It looked as though it was going to be one of those days.

I pulled the Sky Rover up from Shad's digs at Colleton Crescent overlooking the Quay. Beautiful day, pleasure craft all docked in the head of the canal below, Cricklepit Bridge and the condominiums along Haven Banks were reflected by the mirror of the Exe River. Brisk tang in the air, it promised to be just the sort of day for working an enquiry up on Dartmoor or somewhere in the lovely Devon countryside. Thanks to Shad and his interminable Holmes and Watson joke, not to mention one of our ABCD officers ringing up the constabulary in the middle of the night to report a ghost, we would be spending the day far away from sunlight. Superintendant Matheson had jumped at the chance to have us deal with an allegedly psychotic ferret bio in the dark bloody Medieval tunnels beneath Exeter's streets. I hadn't yet filled in Shad on the enquiry as I tried to find out with whom I was speaking.

"Shad, I was under the impression you were getting a patch from Celebrity Lookalikes to tone down your Watson bumble."

"I did," he quacked again. "I installed it last night."

"Did you install the patch before or after you called in to Exeter Station to report that ghost in your flat?"

"It was before I saw the ghost—" his audio switched to his Nigel Bruce Watson "—I believed it was a ghost, Holmes: a spectral weasel pale as lime. Ballsed up my kitchen proper, too. Half my pantry is in the dustbin."

"Now you're talking like Watson."

"Of course. I *am* Watson. Who else would I be talking like?" He regarded me with a bushy raised eyebrow. "You appear to have lost your reason, Holmes." He held up an ameliorating hand. "But, no mind. Regarding ghosts, the Quay area is famous for it's many ghost sightings," he said.

"Really."

"Why do you seem so irritable, Holmes?"

"Why? *Why?*" I glared at him. He was dressed in his usual late Nineteenth century tweeds, wing-tipped collar, waistcoat, and homburg. "My irritability, DS Shad, might have to do with spending half the night listening to those constabulary wankers from Exeter Station making jokes about Holmes and Watson and your bleeding weasel ghost, not to mention the ear reaming I got on the blower from Superintendent Matheson before I'd even gotten to my eggs. He's put us out of sight good and proper this time."

"Oh? How so?"

"There's a ring in from the Underground Passages people—you know those Medieval passageways beneath the city streets?"

"Yes. What's the complaint?"

"They've cornered a ferret there. The individual who called is Amantha Kelland, engineering chief to the passages. She says the ferret is holding up some sort of archeological and development safety study."

"Surely that's an animal control problem, Holmes." He tapped his screen with his finger. "Ah. I see. It's a bio. Oh, the ferret bio is the party issuing the actual complaint, although the UP people rang it in for him." He glanced at me.

"Ferrets are small. Difficult to open a telephone box, I imagine."

"Go on," I said, gesturing with my head toward his readout.

"Very well," he said. "Rodney Mogridge appears to be the creature's name. Says here Ms. Kelland reported that Mr. Mogridge requested ABCD assistance regarding an unspecified life-threatening criminal situation. Apparently this Kelland woman seems to think Mogridge might be hinting at a murder or some burglaries. Possibility of a terrorism connection. Not clear which." He faced me. "Up for a murder, Holmes?"

"I'm not altogether certain hints are actionable, old fellow. Look, we really must reinstall your patch. Your voice keeps switching from Watson to Shad and back. It might be distracting when we do interviews."

"I really don't notice it. *Aflak!* Did I just say that?" he quacked.

"Indeed. What about that terrorism connection?"

"It seems the ferret hints at threatening to explode a bomb if the UP crew get too close. The crew doesn't appear to take the bomb threat seriously. They're convinced the ferret's running with the squirrels, mentally speaking. They're staying put to be on the safe side, though." He glanced at me from beneath half-closed eyes and quacked, "Should make Matheson happy, keeping us underground and out of sight."

A bit on the weary side, I nodded. "He did say one more line in the media concerning Holmes and Watson and he'd have the pair of us."

"Guts and garters, huh?"

"Exactly."

"Ever been down there, Jaggs? The Underground Passages?"

"Can't say I have, Shad. You?"

"No. At one time Nadine wanted to take the tour but each time she called the operation was closed. Besides the Underground Passages site advised those with an aversion to close quarters to go have a cream tea instead."

"Are you claustrophobic?" I asked.

He shrugged. "I wouldn't think so at the time. I was a duck. Would have made the passages seem that much larger."

"I do wonder why they're closed so much," I said. "Always seems to be something: building construction, street repair, the weather, mold, earth tremors, the season, the infinitely measureless universe of unspecified health and safety concerns." I tapped his screen. "Confirm where we are to meet Ms. Kelland."

After he got in touch with the people at Underground Passages, he said in his Watson voice as he faced me, "The Kelland woman asked us to meet her in the Bailey Street end of Romangate Passage, Holmes."

I turned east at the Cathedral Vector Roundabout. "I thought the main entrance is in Paris Street next to that department store—What's it called?"

"It's named Subsequently," answered Watson. "Never been in it."

"What kind of store is it?"

"Specialists in afterthoughts I suppose—spackle, belated greeting cards, underarm deodorant, morning-after birth control—that sort of thing. Ms. Kelland informed me that the Paris Street entrance is not considered safe due to some construction in the area."

"Perennial construction once again rears its ubiquitous head."

"Yes," quacked Shad. "All the construction going on around here, you'd think it'd be a better-looking city."

"Is there an entrance at Romangate?" I asked.

"Some people I know who work at Allure say there's an old entrance to the passages in the basement of the Allure Laboratories Building. That entrance opens in Romangate."

"What do these friends of yours do at Allure?"

"Chemical research. You wouldn't believe the dangerous crap used in cosmetics. These guys attempt to determine in advance whether that programmable mascara will make you beautiful or burn holes in your head."

"Shad, it's like talking with your old self again. Can't you tell the difference?"

He huffed out a Watson laugh and said, "Whatever are you talking about, old man."

"I was a fool to ask."

I sent a wireless message for the head technician at Celebrity Lookalikes to ring me as soon as humanly possible as I turned the Sky Rover toward East Gate. While I was at it I put in a search for construction in the Paris Street area. Nothing. I widened the search to include everything from High and Sidwell to Western Way all the way down to South and Magdalen. I then widened the search farther. "Watson, I fear your Ms. Kelland may be guilty of a slight tarradiddle."

"What?" quacked Shad-in-Watson.

"Tarradiddle: a prevarication, a fib."

"How so?"

"I find no building construction near Paris Street nor anywhere else in the area. The nearest construction within the old walled city is the new facade on the Royal Diane Devon & Cornwall Constabulary Force Museum all the way down on Fore Street, and those fellows are on strike."

"Why would she lie, Holmes?" asked Watson-now-in-control-of-Shad.

"That depends on what she wishes to conceal and how important it is for her to conceal it."

2

I put down the cruiser in Bailey at the end of a pedestrian thoroughfare between Boots and the Allure Laboratories Building known as Romangate Passage. As two figures, a man and a woman, approached the cruiser, I noted my partner frowning and nodding to himself. "Something troubling you?"

"Could have been a ferret," he quacked.

"What could have been a ferret?" I asked.

"The ghost in my flat last night, Jaggs. What do I know from ferrets and weasels? Could have been a ferret."

I thought for a moment. "This is quite a way from Colleton Crescent."

"Yeah. I wonder how long it takes to walk to the crescent through all these passages beneath the streets."

"Do they reach that far?" I asked.

He faced me. "Sure. There's that abandoned underground amusement park near South Street—Watchamacallitland—connected to the passages," he quacked. "That's almost to Southgate. The woman who lives in the flat below mine said the cliffs beneath the crescent are rumored to be riddled with old smugglers tunnels. Perhaps they connect."

"Would they need to if your visitor was truly a ghost?"

"He wasn't a ghost. Ghosts don't leave foot prints. There are little flour tracks all over the place."

A tap on the driver's side window interrupted the conversation. I turned to see a slender woman with step-cut red hair and a modest amount of freckles wearing crisp white coveralls and a blue hardhat mounted with a torch. Her eyes were narrowed, her lips pressed into a thin line. She gave every appearance of being rather harried.

Standing beside her was a strange fellow who seemed to be a rather aggressive-looking albino. His eyes were hidden behind dark goggles, his facial skin almost translucent and pinkish blue where it wasn't covered with silky white hair. The fellow sported a full moustache and beard. His coveralls were black and made from some kind of fleece. In addition, he was smiling and holding a very large hunting rifle across his chest. As Watson took the ring from Celebrity Lookalikes concerning his new download, I opened the cruiser's doors and showed my identity card to the young woman. "DI Jaggers and DS Shad, Devon ABCD." I climbed out of the cruiser. "Are you Ms. Kelland?"

She stared dumbly at both of us for a moment, her frustration morphing into bewilderment. "Yes I am," she answered. "Pardon me for mentioning it, but are you the two detectives doing the Sherlock Holmes and Dr. Watson impressions?"

"We are who we are, madam."

"I only ask, inspector, because this is a serious matter. I won't tolerate any foolishness."

"You may find comfort in sharing the majority opinion in that regard." I nodded toward her armed companion. "Ernest Hemingway's ghost, perchance?"

"No need for impertinence, inspector," she said coolly.

I cocked my head toward Shad—or Watson. "My partner will wait only another ten seconds for you to provide me with a satisfactory answer to my impertinent question before ringing for an Armed Response Team."

Her face reddened. "Don't be absurd." She nodded toward the man in black, "Mr. Graves is an exterminator."

"Pleased to meet you," said Mr. Graves with a wide grin that displayed quite prominently his flawless white teeth against his horribly red gums. I glanced at my partner curious as to whom would respond with what.

After giving me a slightly pained look in return, Shad looked past me to Ms. Kelland and began quacking. "Exterminator is the word worrying us, lady. Who is it that Mr. Graves proposes to exterminate?"

She stared at my partner, an expression of confusion on her face. "He doesn't do a very good Nigel Bruce, does he?"

"He has his moments. Meanwhile, could you address Sergeant Shad's question?"

"Oh, Mort has nothing lethal in that weapon, inspector. Just somnidarts. You know: knock-out juice in case we run into something we need to subdue."

I felt my eyebrows arise. "Is that likely?"

She frowned. "Precautionary, inspector. Better to be safe than sorry."

Her body language indicated a rather high degree of deception. I would have put her on a polygraph but she would have crisped every perishing circuit in the bloody thing. "Please be honest with us, Ms. Kelland. We know there is no construction in the area of Paris Street. What happened at the Paris Street entrance?"

She looked around, noting surveillance cameras and the occasional passerby. "It may have been vandalism," she answered, her voice lowered almost to a whisper. "Possibly something more sinister."

"Are you talking terrorism? Should we bring in MI5?"

"No!" she protested, her hands out in front of her. "Please. There has been a partial collapse in the Paris Street passage, that's all we know for certain. Only one of several collapses in the combined passages in recent months. No one killed or injured. No demands have been made; no notices to the media. Hence, there is no *conclusive* evidence of terrorism."

"Strange spin on that word *conclusive*," quacked Watson.

"If you had such evidence, Ms. Kelland, what then?" I asked.

"Inspector, if we report a terrorist incident," Graves joined in, "it would take us another bloody six months to get started on this safety inspection." He nodded thoughtfully to himself. "Curious when red tape and paperwork hold more frightening terrors than bombers."

"There are terrors and there are terrors," said Watson in his excellent Nigel Bruce voice. Watson got out of the cruiser. With my wireless implant I closed the doors and put the vehicle up in hover park as the old fellow walked over to Engineer Kelland. "Have you reported any of this to the police?" he asked her.

"We are presently doing all we can to keep our disasters out of the media, Dr. Watson." Her eyebrows went up. "Sorry. Sgt. Shad."

"Pay it no mind, my dear." Then he suddenly quacked, "Keeping out of the media has become something of a need of ours, too."

"I shouldn't wonder," she said, one eyebrow quizzically arched.

"About the something that may need subduing?" I urged.

Her voice lowered noticeably. "This is not for public consumption."

"We are as the Sphinx—" began Watson.

"—Who must eventually file a report with Heavitree," I hastily completed.

She frowned and mentally cornered herself into answering. "There have been things beneath the streets. Over the centuries everything from rats as big as Rottweilers and snakes as big as fire hoses have been reported down there. Mostly discounted, of course. Henriettaland, the underground amusement park corporation from the Twenty-one thirties, claimed all of the animals from their zoological exhibits were accounted for when they went bankrupt and vacated the tunnels they constructed, but reports of Moby Gator still find their way into office memos."

"Moby Gator?" repeated Shad with a wak-wak-wak guffaw.

"I thought the park was based on England's Civil War," I said. "Where do alligators enter the equation?"

"Perhaps Oliver Cromwell kept one for a pet," quacked Shad.

"There is nothing funny about this," said Ms. Kelland rather sharply. To Watson, she said, "I would add I find your Donald Duck impressions quite juvenile."

"Pardon?" said Watson-as-Watson.

I turned to her. "Forgive us our little amusements, my dear. Please, do continue."

"Make jokes if you wish, gentlemen, but Moby Gator is reported to be dead white, six meters long, and with the remains of a spear gun caught in a set of great yellow teeth."

"Have you actually seen this creature in the passages?" I asked.

"I haven't seen him myself, no. The last reported sighting was a few years ago. I have heard his roar, however." She shuddered. "I've seen rats," she added, "but to be honest nothing bigger than a large cat."

"By 'large cat' are you referring to a tabby or a tiger class feline?" Watson inquired somewhat alarmed.

Ms. Kelland smiled. "Tabby sized, sergeant. Large enough to frighten me, nevertheless. I've heard some strange growls and hisses on the other side of the amusement park passages toward the old Watergate. I've failed to catch much more than glimpses of the things who issued them, however. I saw enough, though, to keep Mort Graves and his dart gun close by when I'm beneath the streets."

While I pondered the prospect of meeting a slavering pack of rats and terrorists in a confined space in the dark, Ms. Kelland said, "There has been plenty of evidence on guides and workers in the passages: Bites, broken bones from being attacked or startled, one bloke a few years ago had his knee wounded. He saw his attacker and he swore it was Moby Gator."

"That fellow was possessed of a special sight, however," added Mr. Graves with a gesture suggesting the fellow with the skinned knee might have had more than a passing acquaintance with granulated mood enhancers.

"About Mr. Mogridge?" I urged.

"Sorry?" she asked.

"The ferret bio?"

"Of course." Kelland nodded toward the southwest. "Some of my associates have him cornered near a blocked passage beneath Mermaid Court. That's just past one of the abandoned Henriettaland passages this side of Western Way inside the south corner of the walled city."

"Did you wish to charge him with anything? Trespass or vandalism, perhaps?"

"Mr. Holmes . . ." She closed her eyes, took a breath, and opened her eyes. "Inspector Jaggers, the ferret requested

ABCD involvement. We didn't. All we want is for the ferret to be removed so we may continue with our safety evaluation. There are archeological, business, and city development concerns in the balance all of which are at a standstill until this matter is resolved."

"Mermaid Court," muttered Watson with his Watson voice. "That's a bloody good jog from here. Isn't there an entrance to the amusement park passages near the White Hart Hotel? That's much nearer Western Way than is Romangate. I could swear it was pointed out to me on a tour."

"Yes, Dr. Watson is it now?" She looked at me. "I find his voice switching silliness quite distracting."

"It's a software glitch, Ms. Kelland," I explained. "It does rather interrupt one's train of thought, though, I agree. About the entrance near the White Hart?"

"Coombe Street. That's the original Henriettaland main entrance. There was a collapse in the passage there a few nights ago. I'm afraid it's blocked."

"More vandalism?" I suggested.

"The fire brigade think it may have been a gas explosion. The electrical for all the passages went out, as well."

"So, that's why we're going to the same place by another route?" Watson quacked, his eyes wide.

"And in the dark," added Mr. Graves with a ghastly grin. "Might finally get my chance at the great white gator, eh?" He brandished his weapon in the air.

"Easy Ahab," cautioned Ms. Kelland with a bit of a smile. "Nothing to concern us," she continued as she faced Watson. "Those passages really haven't been maintained over the decades. It may have been a simple collapse."

Something was bothering me. "Aren't the Henriettaland passages made from transcompressed matter?" I asked.

"Yes."

"How could it collapse, then? That's heavy duty ceramic. They make hardened bomb shelters and reactor containment buildings out of TCM glass. We will have evolved into an entirely new species before that stuff degrades and Devon is hardly in an earthquake zone."

"I have no idea, inspector. These are all questions I'll be in a better position to answer once you have removed the ferret and we can conduct our inspection." Ms. Kelland turned and called over to a fellow standing at the corner of the Allure Building. He was dressed in a pale blue security uniform. Judging by the closed eyelash logo on his coveralls he was an employee of Allure Laboratories, Ltd. Allure produce a very successful line of cosmetics for women, men, human bios, amdroids, and finish paints for mechs. Val was especially fond of their men's cologne; thought it smelled like catnip.

The man from Allure was medium height, brown and blue, and groomed to recruiting poster perfection. His name was Thomas ("Call me Tom") Avery. As he led us between the bits-and-bobs shops in Romangate Passage, I listened as Avery, Kelland, and Graves exchanged views on the future of Exeter's underground.

There was some talk of putting in a tube system beneath the city, Exeter being the only major metropolis in all of England that hadn't installed one. That was opposed by some on Council who wanted to reopen Henriettaland. The recently discovered drains dating back to the Roman occupation had the academic community eager to attack the underground armed with trowels, computers, and cameras. How to do any of these and not damage the medieval passages—the currently accessible as well as the unrestored—was a knotty problem no one had managed to unravel. Before anything could be approached, everything underground had to be made safe. Before that could occur, there were studies that needed to be conducted. Before the studies could proceed there was a troublesome ferret and his concerns that needed to be addressed. Enter the intrepid duo from Artificial Beings Crimes. We fell in behind Mr. Avery as he took a left into a dark doorway and led the way into the building, I noticed Mr. Graves had slung his weapon and was aiming something small and red at Watson and myself, all the time grinning at us with those horrible red gums.

"What's he doing now?" I discreetly asked Ms. Kelland.

She turned. "Mort's a dedicated Holmes and Watson spotter, gentlemen. There are three chapters in Exeter alone.

You'll probably be all over the net by nightfall. I'm afraid you've made his day."

"He's certainly made Superintendent Matheson's," Shad quacked darkly.

3

Once inside the building, Mr. Avery left us. Ms. Kelland and Mr. Graves functioned as makeshift tour guides as we donned the hard hats they supplied from a locked cabinet and then descended a concrete staircase through a barred doorway into the claustrophobic world of Exeter's Medieval public works. With torches on our hard hats illuminated, Ms. Kelland led, I followed, Watson was behind me, and friend Graves and his blunderbuss brought up the rear. I had heard much of the passages' history before on aboveground tours, but it is quite different in the dark among the echoing steps and silence below street level, the weight of the entire city pressing down on one.

Ms. Kelland: "The passageways were begun in the late Fourteenth Century. They were built to make repairing and expanding the leaky lead pipes of the water system easier. During the Civil War, however, the Parliamentarian forces holding the city regarded the passages a threat and had them blocked where they breached the defensive walls. Later, when Royalist forces took the city and held it against the Parliamentarians, more passages were blocked. A few years after the war, the system was restored and water flowed again. A cholera outbreak in the mid Nineteenth Century made necessary an entirely new water system, though. Much of the lead piping was salvaged, the passageways abandoned, and for the most part forgotten. During the Second World War parts of the passages were used as air raid shelters. After that war, the remaining bits became a tourist attraction."

"Who came?" nervously quacked Shad from behind me. "A previously unrecognized pool of troglodytes and agoraphobics?"

Ms. Kelland stopped and turned around. "In a small way, Sgt. Shad, the Underground Passages are Exeter's very own time machine," she said.

"Right," remarked the ever open-minded Guy Shad.

"Do you have one?" she called back to Mr. Graves.

"Always," Graves answered amiably. In a moment we heard the ignition and smelled the sulphur of an old-fashioned match being struck.

Ms. Kelland turned out her hard-hat and hand torches. "Turn off your torches, gentlemen. Please." We did so and were soon plunged into a profound darkness eased only by the feeble flame of the lone candle held by Mr. Graves. He held it above his head casting his face in shadow. "Listen. Look and listen," said Ms. Kelland quietly.

The shadows were deep, the silences deeper. I expected to hear at least a little traffic noise from above but could not. I could hear water dripping somewhere, a foot shift against stone, my own heartbeat. "See the tiers of cut stone in the walls, the vaulting. Everything you can see is exactly as it was in the Fourteenth Century."

I looked and with the light from the candle at such an angle, the relief was distinctive. The flickering of the candle made the stones seem alive. It took very little imagination to see workmen during the Restoration grumbling on their way to remove the rubble and repair the piping beneath the city. "This is how those workmen saw things as they went to repair the pipes." She reached out and touched one of the stones. "There's no other place in England quite like this. Touching the past, Sgt. Shad, that's the attraction."

"You are a romantic, Ms. Kelland," said my partner as Dr. Watson.

She glanced back at him, let her hand fall to her side, and turned on her torch. "Perhaps. But I believe that's why Henriettaland failed. The real passages, in their own unique way, are romantic. Transcompressed pseudo-Heavitreestone-lined passages made wide for open-car electric trains with illuminated mechanical Parliamentarians in lobster-tailed helmets swinging plastic swords and jumping from crevasses going 'boo' at passersby are not romantic. Did you know that the original tour plans called for a beheading of King Charles at the end?"

"Came up short, did he?" Shad inquired.

"What caused the corporation to forego such a valuable theatrical dénouement?" I asked hastily.

She smiled with just a touch of irony. "Since the original beheading took place in London in the open air before the Banqueting House of Whitehall Palace, it was felt executing King Charles in Exeter in an underground chamber beneath McDonald's lacked a certain authenticity."

"It wasn't just that," said Graves. "The current monarch's father has Stuart blood in him. Twice-hourly beheadings of one of his ancestors was thought possibly insensitive—even disloyal. The city's motto, you know."

"Semper Fidelis," quacked Shad. "I saw it on the Guildhall beneath the city's bit of heraldic art." He held up his hand anticipating Graves's addendum. "I am also aware that Exeter had the motto three centuries before the United States Marine Corps. The city missed out on a terrific merchandising tie-in, though, didn't it?"

"Sorry?"

"Considering the location," Watson added.

"Merchandising tie-in?" asked Graves.

"Certainly. Beneath McDonald's? Your headsman, just before swinging his blade, asks the king, 'You want fries with that?' Would've made a fortune. Haw." Shad was amusing himself no end, chuckling gleefully until Mr. Graves turned on his hard hat torch and cycled the bolt on his rifle. "What are you about, sir?" demanded Watson, somewhat alarmed.

"Fancied I spied something that needed shooting, sergeant. I may have been mistaken. Were you about to make another remark?"

"My mind is an absolute blank," he quacked in response. My partner turned about and looked at me with very wide eyes.

"Turn on your torch, Shad," I said, "and let's find out what's troubling Mr. Mogridge, shall we? And perhaps you should keep your conversation to a minimum until we can get your patch reinstalled."

He nodded emphatically. I turned around, nodded at Ms. Kelland, and illuminated my own torch as I sent a wireless to Shad to check on Graves at ABCD. He replied he had already done so.

"No previous. Comes from a long line of rat catchers. Holds a master of arts from Berkley in California. English major."

"Always good to see an English major gainfully employed," I responded.

As Ms. Kelland turned sharply to the right into a narrower course with a lower base, she informed us this particular passage ran beneath High Street. Several concerns were teasing the back of my head, not the least of which was the distance. If we took no turns at all, it would be well over a kilometer from the entrance by the time we reached the opposite side of Henriettaland. If needed, help would be a long time coming.

4

High Street passage, Ms. Kelland informed us, was one of the newer Underground Passages, having been constructed and extended in the Fifteenth and Sixteenth Centuries. Later it had been deepened to lessen the gradient and restorations over the centuries had made the passage safe down to where the streets from the ancient city gates came together: High with Fore and North with South. The water thus conveyed had once supplied an elaborate fountain at the crossing, the fountain having been demolished in the late Eighteenth Century.

"The Henriettaland people convinced the Council to allow them to tie into the Underground Passages at this point," said Ms. Kelland, "This allowed clientele from the Passages access to the amusement park and *vice-versa,* in order to benefit the bottom lines of both attractions. After touring the park, those who arrived *via* the Underground Passages would exit on Coombe Street and be shuttled back to Paris Street. I gather the backers of Henriettaland were very convincing that a Civil War attraction based in Exeter would rival Camelot and Legoland. Exeter was the last city to fall to Cromwell, you know. When Exeter surrendered, the war was over."

"Why was the park named Henriettaland?" I inquired.

"It was named after Charles's infant daughter Princess Henrietta Anne, who was born in Exeter twenty months before the surrender. Unfortunate name choice, though. Most of the patrons who arrived came with children expecting a cartoon theme park."

"Sorry?" I inquired.

"Henrietta Hen," she answered. I looked inquiringly at my partner.

"Henrietta Hen played Miss Prissy," replied Shad. "She was the object of Foghorn Leghorn's affections."

"I see. Expecting Miss Prissy, Foghorn Leghorn, and Henry Hawk, a bit of a shock then to find oneself in the midst of a robotic civil war."

"With much realism in special effects," she said. "The park was nicknamed Tomatojuiceland: Severed limbs, arterial squirting, that sort of stuff."

Ms. Kelland held out a hand and followed it through a passage toward the left. As I made the turn and walked down a ramp I could see what she meant about the amusement park passages. They were taller than the medieval passages by fifty centimeters and wider by at least three meters. The walls were made of transcompressed stone, which was a ceramic made from the material that had been removed to construct the passage. The glass was colored and textured to resemble Heavitreestone, but it just didn't look old. Marks on the floor showed where the cushioned wheels of cars passed as the train was guided along its path by a magnetic strip set in the cement floor.

The train cars were gone. We walked the length of the modest "Great Conduit Station," named for the demolished fountain above, to where it widened more and increased in height. There was an abandoned booth there for collecting admission for the Underground Passages, another for the amusement park, and signs directing those who had completed the tour but wished not to do the passages to another train which returned them to Coombe Street Station. Ms. Kelland pointed up and Watson and I both followed with our hat torches. Above where the train once passed was an arch. Carved into it was a quotation of Oliver Cromwell's: "I tell you we will cut off his head with the crown upon it."

"Charming," said Watson as Watson.

I lowered my gaze and was quite startled to see a very realistic robotic headsman glaring at me through the eyeholes of his black mask. Whatever implement he was supposed to be holding in his powerful metal hands was missing, as was the subject of the exercise on the chopping block. The look in the headsman's eyes was sufficient to give anyone pause.

"Ms. Kelland," said Watson, "I cannot see how this amusement park failed. It is so discerningly done and *so* educational for the children."

"Your irony aside, Dr. Watson, what killed off Henriettaland, in addition to low attendance and abominable marketing, was the Parliamentary Reform Act of 2132 emancipating advanced artificial intelligence. Most of the mechanicals in the park were AI operated."

"They weren't robotic?" I asked.

"No. AIs initially were the less expensive investment."

"After Emancipation, the wages, labor, health and safety costs sank it," added Mr. Graves.

The direct car return route was blocked with rubbish, hence we walked through the three sieges of Exeter in reverse order, occupations of Parliamentarians and Royalists, back to Parliamentarians. Dust covered cannons, muskets, battlements, artfully posed corpses interspersed with tableaus of a grim Oliver Cromwell and his New Model Army marching into the city while the Royalists—lighted match cords swinging—marched out, Princess Henrietta Anne's baptism at St. Peters, her birth, a jubilant King Charles after his forces defeated the Earl of Essex at Lostwithiel, and the final tableau—which was the first of the tour for those entering at Coombe Street—of the Royalist members of the Exeter Chamber resigning as that narrowly divided body first voted the city into the ranks of the Parliamentarians. The name of one of the resigning members, John Colleton, piqued my interest.

"Ms. Kelland," I asked, "would this John Colleton be related somehow to Colleton Crescent?"

"Yes. The Colleton family used to own most of the land above the Quay cliffs. John Colleton, however, left the city after the surrender, I believe. Mort?"

Mr. Graves nodded. "When the Royalists wrested control of the city from the Parliamentarians, Colleton and the others who had resigned took back control of the Chamber. When the Parliamentarians regained control, however, John Colleton emigrated to Barbados and became a planter. When the monarchy was restored, though, he went to the Carolinas on a charter granted by Charles II where he went on to become the father of North American slavery."

"There's an item to spruce up the old *curriculum vitae*," remarked Watson.

"May we cleave to the matter at hand?" I prompted. "Mr. Mogridge?"

"This way just past the turn to the entrance," said Ms. Kelland. "Watch your step. We haven't yet cleared the debris from the collapse."

Past the Colleton resignation tableau was another train station. This one, however, had the remains of a train, the open-topped cars all heaped with rubble that mostly resembled red sandstone. More sandstone rubble was between the cars and the side of the passage burying the cars and all of whatever engine once pulled the thing. The wheels were missing from all the cars we could see. A genuine rat streaked from a corner to safety in the rubble before Graves could get off a shot.

There was another arch and another quotation. King Charles I, however, was a bit more windy than his executioner. "Your king is both your cause, your quarrel and your captain. The foe is in sight. The best encouragement I can give you is this, that come life or death, your king will bear you company and ever keep this field, this place and this day's service in his grateful remembrances."

After the king's pep talk to his captains was a rubble-choked passage presumably going to the entrance on Coombe Street. The rubble in this case was composed of shattered pieces of transcompressed glass and very ordinary looking dirt. A closer look at the minute bits of the shattered glass looked very much like the results of high velocity explosives. Watson and I exchanged glances. We'd both had some training in bomb disposal and had noticed the same thing. I looked back at the red sandstone rubble. Something familiar about it.

"This way, inspector," said Ms. Kelland. I picked up a smallish lump of the sandstone, put it in my pocket, and turned to see Ms. Kelland and her armed assistant standing on the west side of the collapsed entrance next to what looked like a large utility closet. The metal door was open. From the cracked and bent edge of the door as well as tool marks, it was obvious the door had been forced. When Shad and I looked in we saw the back of the closet was missing. The opening had been made by chipping through the transcompressed glass. Beyond it, the lights of hard hats just visible in the distance, was another passage, its scalloped sides made from purplish transcompressed ceramic. Watson and I exchanged another set of glances. We'd seen interior walls like this on our first case together out at Houndtor Down. That scalloped surface was the signature of a large passage made by a small diameter boring tool called a Magic Mole manufactured by the Whack-A-Hole Corporation of Burbank, California.

"Who made this passage?" I asked.

"Before my time," said Ms. Kelland. "My predecessor speculated that the Henriettaland people might have toyed with clandestinely expanding their operation. Bit of a riddle, though, if so." She pointed at the scalloped wall surface. "This tunnel was made with boring equipment, the kind for putting in pipes and drains."

"We recognized the work of a Magic Mole," Watson said to her. "What's the riddle?"

"The year Henriettaland closed, the Magic Mole hadn't yet been developed and made commercially available."

"Where does the passage go?" I asked.

"We've mapped it as far as Mermaid Court," answered Ms. Kelland. "Up to that point all the maps agree. Past that, things are somewhat confused."

"Either a passage is there or it isn't," quacked Shad.

"An issue that we will clarify just as soon as you get that ferret out of there. The passage was filled with that rubble you saw piled in the station. We've been clearing it out in preparation for the survey. The university archeologists are anxious to get to what may be part of an old Roman sewer system we discovered. Before we can continue, however—"

"—The ferret," I completed. I walked around Graves to look once more at the opening chipped into the back of the closet, playing the light from my torch on the edge of the remaining transcompressed surface. It was flat on the Henriettaland side of the opening, typical of large scale transcompression construction. The scalloped surfaces on the opposite side of the opening came within millimeters of the flat surface. Before it had been chipped away, the partition must have been thin enough to allow light to pass.

It may even have been thin enough to act as a window. I examined the edges more closely.

Conchoidal fractures leave curved rib marks which are, almost without exception, concave in the direction from which the fracturing force is applied. Whoever had chipped through the back of that closet had done so from the mystery passage side, not the Henriettaland side. I took the lump of red sandstone from my pocket, looked at it for a few seconds, then held it up to Watson. "What do you make of that, Watson?"

He took the specimen in hand. "It's part of a broken pucket made of red sandstone." He handed it back to me.

"I thought the waste leftovers from transcompression boring were made of purple glass such as those we found out at Hound Tor."

"The Mole can leave the puckets in any form the operator wants." He studied upon that for a moment and looked at me. "What's this got to do with the ferret thing?"

"My Sherlock Holmes patch has an itch," I said. "This entire matter may be more involved than has been represented." I stood and followed the exterminator toward the trapped ferret.

5

Thirty meters past the opening in the back of the Henriettaland closet, the passage was blocked with more red sandstone. Shining my torch above the rubble, however, I could make out that the passageway went beyond the obstruction and then appeared to fork. Two human naturals, a human bio, and a mech—all four clad in white Underground Passages coveralls and hard hats—had the subject, Rodney Mogridge, trapped in a rubble pile against the solid right-hand wall of the passage. The mech watched the top of the rubble, the human bio the right side, and the human nats the left and bottom. The ones on the sides held Stunspray wands in their right hands and all four carried Flashnet guns in their left hands.

"Seems a bit tense," Watson observed.

"Is all this necessary?" I asked Ms. Kelland.

She nodded emphatically. "The police wouldn't do anything. We've been trying to catch this fellow for months. Now we've got him."

"I would like to speak with Mr. Mogridge, if I might. Could you have everyone put away their weapons and step back please?"

Kelland and her entire crew, including Graves, assumed expressions indicating their shared opinion that I had cracked the barmpot. They didn't move and continued standing motionless with Flashnet guns and Stunspray wands at the ready. Quite blasé, Watson strode through the armed semicircle and squatted down before the mound of broken stone. "I say there, Mogridge? Dr. John Watson here."

It was silent in the passage for a moment, the silence at last broken by a voice that sounded remarkably like mid Twentieth Century actor Peter Lorre. "Pleased to meet you, doctor, despite the inordinate length of time it took for you to respond. Is Mr. Sherlock Holmes with you?"

"Indeed he is, sir. Now, what's all this then?"

"Mr. Holmes," called that strange Viennese accented voice. "May I speak with you directly?"

Quite an astonishing variety of peculiar looks from Kelland and company as I made my way to the rubble pile. I squatted next to Watson and said to a shadowy place between several stones. "I'm not really Sherlock Holmes, you know."

"No shite, Sherlock," said the voice with a tone of weary sarcasm. A face emerged from the shadows: the bandit-masked eyes of an adult black footed ferret. The eyes were black, he had tiny teddy bear ears, thin black whiskers, and a good coating of what appeared to be flour still on his nose and burnt-honey fur. The garment the ferret was wearing appeared to be a faded red tunic cinched partway down with a thin black leather tie. The image of a capricorn was centered in the garment's front.

"You're the one who broke into my flat," said Watson. "You're no ghost."

"And you are no doctor."

Watson's liability-shy program had no difficulty whatever with that question. "No. I am not a medical doctor. Why is your bio marker masked?"

"Have you ever tried sneaking past guards playing cymbals and whistling 'The Stars and Stripes Forever?'"

Watson's eyebrows went up. "Can't say that I have."

"Neither has he had the occasion," I added. "Ms. Kelland said you wanted to report a crime. It was rather vague. Burglaries? A murder? Why did you ask to speak with ABCD? And what's all this about a bomb?"

Mogridge seemed to sag as he exhaled with an exhausted sigh. "I was desperate, obviously." He held a forefoot against his face. "My god, man, I'm juggling so many bloody balls I've lost track how many are up in the air. If I stopped long enough to scratch my own I'd be crushed in the bloody avalanche."

"Do you need a doctor?" asked Watson. "A real one," he added hastily.

The ferret thought about it for a moment. "Yes and no."

"That brings everything sharply into focus," I said. "In either case, Artificial Beings Crimes can't help."

The ferret glanced between us at Ms. Kelland and her crew. "Can you get them to step back a little and lower those weapons?" Mogridge asked me.

I turned and saw a heavyset fellow with a chin like a cement block. "Could you give us a bit of room please?" I asked.

"Not bloody likely, mate," said the fellow with as adamant an expression as I have ever seen on a human nat.

"Your name?" I asked attempting to sound officious.

"Jim Tolley. Now aim a flippin' ear trumpet this way, Sherlock. We been pissin' around after that half-pint blagger for months. First, he was lost and couldn't find his family. Then his mum was sick. Then there was the Longbrook Treasure. He'd cut us in for a percentage if we'd let him go."

"Don't forget your Spotted Dick," reminded the mech.

Tolley nodded. "That's right, sunshine. When he wasn't talking stock options or threatening us with this old German unexploded bomb he said he found, he was in my vittles snagging me bloody dessert. Either you walk that wrung-out rat topside or we Flashnet him and that whole rubble pile along with him, then bugger-all we can do about the wankstain gettin' crushed. We mean to have him."

I glanced at Ms. Kelland. She returned my look with one as resolute as Mr. Tolley's. Looking back at Mr. Mogridge I could tell that the ferret was about at the end of his thread. Tired, shivering slightly, he appeared close to nervous collapse. "For an accused blag-artist, Mr. Mogridge, you seem to have little to say."

"For a detective, Mr. Holmes, you seem to have sodding few answers."

"You know," Shad quacked, "I'm beginning to appreciate Mr. Tolley's take on the situation."

"Terrible Donald Duck impression," said the ferret. "Can you do better with a Goofy?" he asked Shad.

"I see what you mean," I said to Shad. Looking at Mogridge I said, "You being here in this passage at first glance would seem to be trespassing, at least. Unless you can tell me otherwise or leave on your own, I'll have to allow Mr. Tolley and his colleagues to remove you."

"I know about a murder," said the ferret quietly. His demeanor seemed deceptive, but I discounted it not being acquainted with what an honest ferret's demeanor resembled.

"An artificial being, old weasel?" asked Watson. "Victim or murderer, makes no difference to us."

The ferret held out his little paws. "Who can say?"

"Is this something you should bring to the attention of the police?" I suggested.

"It was a very old murder." The ferret shrugged slightly. His eyes widened and seemed to focus as his brain seemed to grasp a bit of reality. "The burglaries, though. Some of them were committed by artificial beings: human bios, amdroids, mechs. Some of the victims were ABs, too."

"How many burglaries are we talking about?" I asked.

"Must be thousands," answered Mogridge as he looked about. "Perhaps even tens of thousands."

I asked the ferret, "How do you know of these break-ins, Mr. Mogridge? Are you involved?"

"I want a deal," he answered with a conspiratorial sneer. "I'll flip on the others, but I want to walk."

I was about to inform Mr. Mogridge that all such deal making needed to take place between himself, the constabulary, and the crown prosecutor. Before I could do that, however, I detected an additional marker from a receiver beacon—someone not present in the passage. Mogridge noted it, as well, for he perked up his ears.

Suddenly there was a substantial *woomf* sound from the opposite end of the passage that very much resembled a muffled explosion or mine cave-in. As my ears popped and a haze of rock dust filled the passage, Ms. Kelland and her crew looked in the direction of the noise which was all Mogridge needed to streak out of the rubble pile and through a shadowy opening in the scalloped wall that hadn't been there the instant before. Without hesitation Watson sprang up and followed and once again I leaped after my faithful companion into the void.

The opening shut silently behind me. An instant later the entire passage was illuminated by a variety of lights, a few of them resembling the street lights the city had recently replaced. The walls were scalloped purple glass. Standing behind me was a mech at least twenty centimeters taller than Watson. He had a strictly functional metallic exterior partially covered by a faded red jerkin matching Mogridge's complete with Capricorn. The dual optical sensors, speakers, audio and olfactory pickups were unsuccessfully arranged to give the machine a benign expression. The effect was actually rather malevolent.

"You fool! You bungling idiot!" shouted Mogridge at the mech. "Why did you let these two in? They are coppers, you moron! You circuit-fried scrap pile, you walking jumble sale, you bloated animated junkyard! Nitwit! Brainless tin dustbin! You have the intellect of a VIC-20 filled with dead midges!"

"It was either let them pass, Rodney, or crush them with the door," explained the mech patiently. He had a slight accent I couldn't quite place. He tilted his head toward Watson. "His legs left on the other side of the secret door might show the Underground Passages crew where the door is, don't you think?"

"Thanks for sparing me, old wing nut," quacked Shad.

"My name is Arif," responded the mech.

"Never mind the sodding niceties!" the ferret squeaked, wildly waving its forelegs in the air. "Do you realize how long I've been out there? The UP people had me cornered, you oaf! In another minute I would have been fried or turned into jam! I called you hours ago, imbecile! Now all the bloody wheels are coming off! We are riding on axel pins and smoking floorboards, Arif! What took you so bloody long?"

"Captain Bound," answered the mech. "He can no longer sit in front of the screens and has taken to his bed. I had to carry him. Molly needed me to watch the screens until she got the captain settled."

All of the anger seemed to drain from the ferret in a great rush. He stood there, limp. "I don't know what to do," said Mogridge. "I simply don't know what to do."

Arif faced Watson. "I heard them in the passage refer to you as 'doctor'. Are you indeed a medical doctor?"

"No. Sorry."

"Then there seems little hope," said the mech.

The ferret pulled himself up from the passage floor by sheer will, faced the mech, and placed a gentle forefoot upon the mech's left knee-joint. "We can't give up, Arif. While there's life there's hope."

"One diminishes, Rodney," responded the mech, "hence the other." Arif bent over, lifted Mogridge up with his left hand, and placed the weary ferret upon his left shoulder. "Mr. Holmes, Dr. Watson," he said, "best you come with us. If you become lost in this maze, you could starve to death before anyone found you." He then turned and walked toward what my inner compass believed to be west. Once I heard the sound of rock moving against rock and looked back in disbelief. The passage from which we had just emerged was now a blank wall.

While we walked I took Arif's Mechanical Being Identification Number (MBIN) and ran it through Heavitree. Arif-126699 was one of the Destroyer series of slave mechs produced for Desert Lion in the mid Twenty-one hundreds. Destroyers were designed to be economical to-the-death soldiers and assassins used by a variety of related but sometimes opposing groups. When all Modified Engram Based Intelligence Technology (MEBIT) beings were emancipated by having their choices restored, however, criminal and terrorist organizations, of course, did not voluntarily comply. This was expected and for which World Human Engram Watch (WHEW) was more-or-less prepared. For much of Asia, the Middle East, and parts of Russia and New Jersey the choice restoring patch download was delivered by satellite wireless broadcast. Once mentally freed, most of the Destroyers revolted against their masters often utilizing the means and methods their masters had taught them. Nasty bit of work that.

In any event, Arif had no previous in British jurisdiction. It was Shad who pointed out to me the second thing of note: Arif was missing most of his right hand.

My Sherlock Holmes patch began to itch. "Shad," I said out loud, "can you get a signal to the Sky Rover?"

"I'm no longer allowed to drive—My Watson bumble factor, you know," he said petulantly.

"I am quite concerned about your mental clarity, Watson. However, I am quite a bit more concerned about remote operation of a cruiser in city rush hour traffic for the first time. I assessed the alternatives and determined letting you remote pilot the Sky Rover was the lesser of two outrageously unacceptable risks."

"Thank you, old trout . . . I think." He waved a hand in dismissal. "Place your mind at rest, Holmes. Of course I can bring it right along. Why do we need the cruiser?"

"A hunch, old fellow. Just a hunch."

6

Quite disturbing to have lived in Exeter for all these years and have no idea of the extent of this secret tunnel network mere meters below street level. It was a warren of passages of assorted vintages ranging from Roman times to the present with varied constructions including cut Heavitree stone without mortar, cut stone and mortar, carved sandstone, corrugated metal tubing, concrete block, timber upright and crossbeam, poured reinforced concrete, as well as transcompressed matter. Whatever fantasy I had about being able to find my way back again was evaporated by Arif closing certain passages and diverting others by means of carefully balanced masonry doors and portions of tunnel making the whole of it a constantly changing maze. Luckily the Sky Rover was equipped with GPS.

Shortly after beginning this subterranean odyssey I called Ms. Kelland's mobile using my own wireless to inform her that Watson and I were hot on Mogridge's trail, it was safe for her and her crew to proceed with the survey, and, no, I couldn't explain what had happened to us.

At a bend in one passage, Arif stopped abruptly, turned, and asked Watson and myself to close up the distance between us and himself. As soon as we did so, a slab of opaque glass dropped down behind us, blocking the passage. When I looked to Arif I noticed a second slab had dropped down in front of him. The rumble of the falling slabs caused Mogridge to stir slightly, his eyes opened, noted his surroundings, then he fell back into his exhausted slumber upon Arif's shoulder.

Suddenly came a woman's voice saying, "Who goes there?"

"Sigmund Freud, Steven Forrest, and two prospective recruits," answered Arif.

Watson and I exchanged glances, then the slab in front of the mech lifted. Instead of the turn in the passage to the left that was there before the slab fell, there was now a straight passage into what looked like a room with walls made from red sandstone blocks. "Advance, Sigmund, and please bring good news."

Arif with Mogridge on his shoulder stepped into the room and Watson and I followed. Inside the room, the ceiling was vaulted in a single Roman arch also made from red sandstone, the walls about six or seven meters on a side. Light was provided by two ancient neon screw-in lamps dangling from the overhead arch and from a bank of a dozen or so vintage computer monitors against the far wall. Painted in big faded red letters on the adjoining wall were some lines:

> Until the rightful monarch send to Captain Bound,
> To his officers and watchmen all —
> Stand ye down—
> Keep this passage sealed and show match and blade and pike
> To city watch and soldier, friend and foe alike,
> Let no one though the passage in or out of town
> Upon the honor, blood, and soul of Captain Bound.
> —*Semper Fidelis*

"Not exactly Tennyson," commented Watson from behind me.

Beside an old wooden desk in front of the screens stood a human bio, a female who was too old to guess at her age, either bio or imprint. She was wearing a patched Harris tweed jacket over what appeared to be a faded red jerkin, the tail of the capricorn visible partially emerged from beneath her left lapel. Her pants were so patched the original fabric had probably been forgotten. Held properly in a stiff-armed two handed grip she had what appeared to be a rather modern Police Special H970 MultiTaser aimed directly at me.

"I say, madam," began Watson, "could you lower that instrument, please. I hear one can fry eggs with one of those things."

"Sperms, too," she assured him. Watson unconsciously put Nigel Bruce's knees together.

"Should we raise our hands?" I asked.

"Not necessary," she answered. "If you feel lucky, try something." She motioned us away from the passage door. When we had complied she reached back to the computer array and tapped an old fashioned keyboard. The slab closed behind us, additional rumbling beyond the walls signifying the reconfiguration of the passages we had traveled thus far, no doubt.

Rodney Mogridge groggily stirred, sat upright on Arif's shoulder, glanced at the woman with the MultiTaser, and sadly shook his head. In turn, her expression changed from determined to quite grim. She nodded at us. "What about them?"

The ferret quickly explained how we had become attached to their getaway, and how the "doctor" in Dr. Watson was strictly for entertainment purposes. This was why, when he had ransacked Watson's flat at Colleton Crescent the night before, he had been unable to locate a medical diagnostic scanner.

"Did you think I kept the thing in the flour tin, you filthy vermin," demanded Watson, as always spreading oil on troubled waters.

"I tripped over something and knocked it over," explained the ferret. "My apologies."

"If I might interrupt," I said with nods to Mogridge and the woman heavy with Taser, "I am Detective Inspector Jaggers, Devon ABCD. My partner is Detective Sergeant Shad. And you are?"

"Molly Dotting," answered the woman.

"If you could explain the situation, Ms. Dotting, perhaps Sgt. Shad and I could offer a suggestion."

She gave me a look that said without words something quite rude. Eventually she came forth with a request. "First, inspector, explain why two police detectives are fancied up like you blokes."

I glanced back at Watson. His hardhat had been replaced by his homburg. I turned back, removed my own hardhat, and donned my deerstalker. "A joke gone awry, I fear, madam. Nothing more sinister."

She cocked her head toward the computer screens. "You two been on the telly quite a bit the past few weeks. Seven blogs and three Holmes and Watson spotting chat rooms, not to mention the media coverage and the movie channels running the old Rathbone and Bruce vids. I just finished watching *The Woman In Green*."

"Remarkable when you consider how hard we've been trying to avoid just that sort of notice," remarked Watson. "Your predicament?" he prompted.

She wiggled the Taser and arched her eyebrows toward Arif. "No weapons showed on the scan," said the big mech. Rodney Mogridge climbed down to the floor and skittered off through a door to the left of the desk. Ms. Dotting lowered her MultiTaser to the desk, but kept it within easy reach.

"Our watch commander, Captain Bound, is quite ill," she said. "The diagnose-it-yourself sites are split between flu, heart failure, and allergies. We don't know what's wrong so we don't know what to do to treat it."

"Why doesn't he go in hospital?" I inquired.

She looked at me as though preparing to explain things to a child. "Captain Bound cannot leave his post until properly relieved." She held up a hand to forestall my next question. "He cannot be relieved except by a blood relative descended by the original Captain Bound." She let her hand drop slowly to the desk.

"Well," said Watson, "he's in a pip of a union."

"It's too complicated to explain," she said. "We simply need to find out what's causing his illness and then try and figure out what to do about it."

"What did the captain say about my suggestion?" asked Arif.

"Kidnapping a doctor and bringing him down here?" She shook her head. "You know what we'd have to do if the bloke didn't agree to join the watch." She gave a dismissive wave of her hand. "Captain refused."

Then Shad quacked out a suggestion: "Jaggs, what about flying a micro in here to do a scan—"

"What's that?" Molly Dotting demanded, the MultiTaser back in her hands.

"Please," I said. "No cause for alarm, Ms. Dotting. My partner suggested bringing in one of the forensic instruments from our cruiser. It can do a scan on your commander."

"Micro?" she wanted to know.

"Yes, it's a lipstick-sized vehicle capable of taking a human imprint we use for getting into tight places. Its scanning function is similar to the instrument diagnosticians use."

"You cannot leave," she stated flatly.

"No problem," quacked Shad. "Just guide me and rearrange the route as I fly the thing and I can bring it in by remote."

"I told the captain about you two," interrupted Mogridge. He was standing in the doorway through which he had exited. "If you join the watch he wishes to see you. If you do not join," the ferret shrugged and held out its tiny paws, "he begs your forgiveness."

"Forgiveness?" I glanced at Arif. "What's he mean? Forgiveness for what?"

"If you don't join, inspector, you must be either imprisoned or put to death."

My eyebrows arched sufficiently to disturb the bill on my deerstalker as I asked Molly Dotting, "A trifle medieval, isn't it?"

"It hasn't been necessary to execute anyone for well over two centuries," she assured me.

"Well," quacked Shad, "what's the job pay?"

"Eight shillings sixpence a week, payable in foodstuffs and lodging."

"I guess it's been awhile since you guys had a raise."

"Sixteen thirty-nine," she answered. She glanced at me. "Regrettable your partner was so quick to remain on Rodney's trail. Why does he do these terrible Donald Duck impressions?"

"That's the Aflak duck," Shad corrected with the voice of Lawrence Olivier playing Marcus Licinius Crassus.

Apparently that time he heard the change. He absentmindedly leaned against the big mech shaking his head as though it might somehow resolve his software glitches.

Arif patted Shad's shoulder with his good hand. "It is a very quick death, if the headsman's strike is true. We have the axe from the headsman mech at Great Conduit Station. The blade is aluminum and rather dull, but I imagine it will do the trick with enough force behind it."

"Remarkably incentive recruitment program, old chap," said Watson now with Nigel Bruce's voice. "Police work is where you find it, I suppose. Where do I sign for The Watch?"

Arif looked at me. Shad's and my engrams were on file back at Heavitree, hence the threat of death was not as dire as it appeared. It would leave us missing a few hours, however; hours that would have to be investigated in order to determine what had happened to us. One could only wonder to what lengths ABCD would have to go to arrive even upon the same continent as the truth. Ah, me. Discretion, valor, and whatnot. "I am pleased to join with my companion in entering the watch rolls. What do we do?"

What we did was swear allegiance to Captain Bound, his officers, and the fellow members of The Watch. Molly Dotting administered the oaths. In addition to serving Bound and keeping faith with the others of The Watch, we pledged our honor, our lives, and our souls to keep anyone from utilizing a particular passage. Betraying any part of The Watch's mission, it was made clear, was punishable by death. Apparently the news of the official abolishment of the death penalty in the mid Twentieth Century had yet to reach these fellows. Since it seemed paramount to becoming a useful member of The Watch, I asked which passage it was that needed such protection.

Molly pointed toward those lines we had seen inscribed upon the wall. "That is the passage."

"It's a wall," countered Watson.

Molly Dotting went to the wall, bent to her left, and touched certain stones up, across, and down to her right tracing out a perfect Roman arch. "That's the passage." She placed both hands upon the sandstone filling the arch. "This is the door."

"How thick is that door, my dear?" asked Watson.

"Twenty paces," she said.

"Eh? Paces? That's what, fifteen meters?" Watson chuckled. "Well, I don't imagine anyone will sneak past us in the night, wot?" He laughed.

"As you well know," I said to Watson, "modern boring equipment can turn that blockage into a motorway in a matter of minutes." Facing Mogridge then facing Dotting and Arif it became obvious what had been the reason behind all of the collapses in the Underground Passages and Henriettaland. We were smack in the middle of a cell of urban terrorists bent on keeping any and everyone away from this particular wall. I nodded toward it. "How old is that arch?" I asked Molly Dotting.

"It dates back to the Third Century. It was put in as a storm drain discharging into the river when the new and larger defensive walls were built enclosing the original Roman fort and the town that had grown around it."

I knew several Exeter historians and antiquarians who would go into paroxysms of ecstasy simply at the thought of excavating this old Roman work and its surroundings. That left at least one question unanswered. I read again the writing on the wall:

Until the rightful monarch send to Captain Bound,

To his officers and watchmen all —Stand ye down—

Keep this passage sealed and show match and blade and pike

To city watch and soldier, friend and foe alike,

Let no one though the passage in or out of town

Upon the honor, blood, and soul of Captain Bound.

—Semper Fidelis

Rightful monarch . . . match and blade and pike. The wages were from the Seventeenth Century. "This refers to the Civil War, doesn't it? Five hundred years ago?"

"Yes," answered Molly Dotting. "When the Parliamentarians held Exeter and the Royalist forces besieged the city, members of The Watch faithful to the crown led a small number of Royalists into the city through this long abandoned and forgotten drain. What those men did tipped the scales and gave King Charles the city. When the king heard of the valor of Captain Bound's watch, he was moved to personally visit the post when he came to the city for his daughter's birth. It was upon meeting Captain Bound he took the captain's oath to keep that passage secret and safe for the Royalists in case it was needed in the future."

"What happened when the Parliamentarians took back the city?" I asked.

Molly Dotting's expression became troubled. "They discovered the drain and sent in a company to demand the surrender of The Watch. It was refused. After losing quite a number of soldiers to Bound and his watchmen who refused to surrender, General Fairfax ordered his men to starve out or kill all Bound's men. Gawen Bound had The Watch build a five foot thick wall filling the opening of the drain. Fairfax's boys eventually filled the rest of the drain inside the wall as well as filling in or burying all the openings outside the wall."

"Fairfax buried them alive," I said. It took a moment or two in order to digest that. "Obviously they survived."

"The original Captain Bound had prepared in case the Parliamentarians somehow regained control of the city. Many of the extra rooms here were carved out and filled with arms and provisions during that period, as well as a sufficient number of airshafts. Once buried, though, the Watch was for all intents forgotten—another bad memory left over from a bad war. Eventually they tunneled out, disguised the new entrances with secret doors, and clandestinely rejoined their families, still serving The Watch in its mission by shifts."

"Now, let me understand this," I said, not quite believing what I thought I understood. "The Watch has been here for the past five hundred years, guarding this wall, waiting for new orders from the king?"

"From the rightful monarch," she corrected.

"This is preposterous," protested Watson. "I've never heard such twaddle. Are you telling me no one has even tried getting through to the monarch with a request for new orders? "

"According to our unit history, said Mogridge, "the mail from this post lined royal dustbins from the Restoration until they ran out of Stuarts."

"The Watch notifications weren't even getting past the secretarys' secretaries," said Molly Dotting.

"That fellow Graves told us the current monarch has Stuart blood in him," I added.

"He also has a phalanx of secretaries to send back stock replies to fan and crank mail," said Mogridge. "We keep getting thanked warmly for our support."

"Again, I say twaddle," declared Watson.

"Twaddle which we are sworn to continue," I softly reminded him, discreetly drawing my thumb across my throat.

"No need to be graphic, old fellow."

"I apologize. Watson, while I go and visit with the good captain, be a good fellow and work with Ms. Dotting to see if you can bring in one of our micros."

"Captain Bound," urged the ferret. He held a paw out toward the door to the left of the desk. I went ahead of him into the dark passage.

The word "unbelievable" brushed my thoughts almost as often as the word "bizarre." If we were to believe what we were being told, not only had this particular unit of the constabulary stood its watch since the time of Charles I, it had done it in secret and while living among the everyday citizenry of Exeter. M5 and the CIA should be able to keep secrets so well. A monarch's order and a watch captain's oath to obey it fantastically manifesting itself down the centuries until it eventually snared Shad and myself. And now we were in it proper: The Watch. Perhaps donning the red tunic might aid us in getting to the bottom of this peculiar situation and possibly get medical help for this mysterious Captain Bound.

7

There was a sharp turn to the right in the passage which then opened upon another chamber perhaps half the size of the watch room. The walls were filled with shelves of books save two places: The center of the wall to my right which was filled by an old-fashioned flat-screen telly, and the center of the wall to my left which was filled by the head of an even more old-fashioned canopied bed complete with bed curtains. Next to the bed was a chair and a nightstand with a shaded lamp on the opposite side. Upon the bed beneath a gray and blue coverlet was an old man, human natural, who looked every bit the part of the grandfather, played by C. Aubrey Smith, in the 1936 version of *Little Lord Fauntleroy*. He had bushy white brows, a shock of white hair brushed straight back, strong chin, and a white mustache that served as the parting waves before the prow of his magnificent nose. He turned from the book he was reading and peered at me from beneath those hedgerow brows over his gold-rimmed reading spectacles. The eyebrows ascended. "By Jupiter, it looks as though the jig is up, Mogridge," he said jokingly to the ferret. "It's Sherlock Holmes."

I smiled at his allusion to the old Basil Rathbone vids. "It is an honor to at last meet the Earl of Doringcourt," I responded.

The bushy eyebrows climbed even higher on his forehead. "By gad, sir, I say you are as entertaining in person as on the telly."

"This is Detective Inspector Jaggers of Devon ABCD," said Mogridge.

The old man waved a dismissive hand at the ferret. "Of course. Of course I know who this is. Sherlock Holmes in his present incarnation, wot?" He faced me. "How is your partner, Sgt. Shad, getting along without his feathers? Is the Watson role all he hoped it would be?"

I took another quick glance at the telly screen. Captain Bound was very well informed. I shrugged and said, "We've both found Watson to be quite a bit more than we had expected."

He lowered his head back upon his pillows, his face suddenly drained of color. "Dear me." He nodded once. "Watch out for that chief constable, inspector," he said. "CC Crowe is a bad egg in my opinion. He certainly has no use for you bios—especially you chaps in ABC." His eyes opened and he looked around the room. "Where is Shad?"

"At present, captain, he is working with your Molly Dotting trying to get a diagnostic instrument down from our cruiser in order to find out what's ailing you."

"A micro?" he asked.

"Why, yes."

"Shad escaped death out at Hangingstone Hill imprinted in one of those things, didn't he?" Before I could answer he said, "I've followed all your adventures, inspector, since you caught the Mayfair Mangler when you were with Scotland Yard."

"That was over sixty years ago." I thought for a moment. "My first big case."

"You two seem to be getting on," remarked the ferret with just a touch of sarcasm. "Do you need me for anything else?" he asked the captain.

"No, Rodney. Go and get some rest. You have done all you can do. On your way out, please ask Dr. Watson to come in when he has finished." He turned to me as Mogridge exited. "This is excellent. I haven't had this much fun in decades." He held his hand out toward the chair next to his bed. "How thoughtless of me. Please have a seat, sir, and tell me all about your career."

As I sat down I said, "I'd much rather talk about what brought Shad and me here."

"No secret to my illness, inspector. It's my heart. Found out about that fifteen, eighteen years ago when my grandson James took over for me here. I went in hospital and the doctors there had a look. Heart attack, they said. It's simply acting up again." I opened my mouth to speak and he interrupted with a gaze that fixed me to the spot. "You have no idea, Inspector Jaggers, how many times I have had to answer what you were about to ask."

"Which was?" I inquired.

"The Civil War was done with centuries ago. Why not leave it all, go home, and take care of myself? If not that, why don't I copy into a bio and have it take over the watch?" He reached out a hand and grabbed my knee giving it a feeble shake. "My boy, have you read the lines painted on the watch room wall?"

"I have."

"My great-great-great grandfather, Capt. Hugh Bound, wrote those lines and did the lettering himself. He had sons who felt little in the way of obligation to the charge King Charlie gave the first Capt. Bound. His boys wanted something called rap-and-roll, to follow the Beagles, consume mood altering substances, and examine their navels. However, the king of England personally put the safety of that entrance to Exeter into the hands of Captain Gawen Bound and swore him upon his honor and the honor of all his descendents to keep the passage safe for the crown until relieved by the rightful monarch. Gawen Bound didn't swear to keep it safe until he got tired of the task, or he got old or sick, or there didn't seem to be any point, or until he could get someone else to stand in for him. 'Until the rightful monarch send to Captain Bound, To his officers and watchmen all —Stand ye down—' That's how long Bound's watch is, young man. You know what *semper fidelis* means, don't you?"

"Always faithful," I answered.

"*Always*," he said. "The word means for all time; *forever*." He gave my knee one final shake and released it. "No more of this nonsense, lad. Leave me be for now. I'll see Sgt. Shad when he's gotten in his gadget." He turned his book over upon his lap, keeping his place, settled back, and closed his eyes. His color was very pale, his skin glistening. The book was a well-worn volume of Victor Hugo's *The Count of Monte Cristo*.

As I reentered the dark passage following the mech, I noticed another door. It was dark inside. "What's in there?" I asked Arif.

He reached in, climbed up on a post, and tripped a switch turning on a light panel salvaged from someplace. It was The Watch's armory and contained everything from half pikes to bayonets and matchlocks to plasma guns. Mounted on the wall at the back was a very large, very black headsman's axe.

♠

With Molly Dotting's aid, Watson managed to thread a micro through pipes, airshafts, and passages until it reached the watch room. Once he had it hovering beside him, it took only moments and Watson disappeared into the captain's bedroom. He was in there for over an hour while Molly Dotting watched the screens, Mogridge sat staring at the captain's door, and Arif stood motionless against a wall after plugging himself into an orange extension cord. When Watson returned he was talking like his old self: a duck. "Man, I thought *I* knew movies. Bound even knows the name of the guy who directed the 1943 *I walked with a Zombie.*"

"Those books and that telly are his windows to the world, old man," I said. "What did the scan show?"

He sat rather heavily into a chair next to the screens. "It's his heart, Jaggs. An ejection fraction in the very low teens. Clogs, leaks, murmurs, irregular heartbeats. The captain's pump is barely hanging on by a cockle. Blood pressure redlined on the low end. The scanner thinks it might be affecting his liver."

"How long, do you think?" asked Mogridge.

"I don't know. The scanner we use only estimates the other side of time-of-death. My non-medical opinion though is that the clock is ticking."

8

Under Arif's watchful video pickup, we ate in The Watch mess, a chamber northwest of the watch room reached by reconfiguring a few passages. We were served by Cook, a damaged Rent-A-Mech who looked very much like Walter, the mech Val and I pay to cook and clean at home. Unlike Walter Cogg, however, Cook's head was partially crushed. The fellow could remember neither his name nor anything called Rent-A-Mech. Whatever other limitations it might have caused, the damage made it unable for Cook to communicate by anything other than sign language. Neither could he access his recipes, if the fare at that establishment was any evidence. On the menu that day was hellishly salty boiled beef, mustard, and cabbage that possibly could have been left over from the Battle of Trafalgar. On the other hand it might have been influenced by Cook's other duty: The Watch laundry. Whether he washed their uniforms and bed covers in the cabbage broth or cooked their meals in the wash tub I could not determine; that it was one or the other was decided. Cook is the one who issued Watson and myself our faded red capricorn shirts. Cook had been salvaged, along with most of the cast off computer and industrial control equipment in the post, by the captain's grandson, James Bound. This second mention of a grandson teased at my head.

While in the mess I noticed what looked like a Victorian accountant's desk. Upon it was a very thick, very large leather-bound volume. Six similar but rather shabbier volumes were on the shelf above the desk. "What might those be?" I asked Arif.

"That is where Rodney keeps our pay records and the inventory of goods and services commandeered by The Watch."

Watson nodded to himself. "Holmes, there's something about a weasel doing accounting that seems terribly apt."

"Indeed." I glanced at Arif. "Do the contents of those volumes include by any chance the thousands of robberies to which Rodney Mogridge referred?" I asked.

"Yes," answered the mech, "although I believe they are technically confiscations and commandeerings."

Watson got up from the table and went to the accountant's desk. He simply looked at the open page. "There," he said. "I haven't been robbed at all, Holmes. I've been commandeered." He bent over and looked more closely. "I thought so: the weasel *did* make off with my Weetabix." He turned to the beginning of the volume and glanced at the first page. "Good lord, Holmes, this is dated One January, Two thousand." He slowly looked up at the volumes upon the shelf. From the look on Watson's face, I had no doubt that the dates went all of the way back to at least Sixteen forty-six.

"So, Arif," I said to our keeper, "The Watch is responsible for all of the ghost sightings around the Quay and in Colleton Crescent?"

"Only some," said the mech. "Imagination and retelling added a few. The Watch carved a network of passages all along the Quay through Colleton Crescent up to Holloway Street and west along Commercial Way almost to Frog Street. There are passages all under the southwest end of the walled city this side of Henriettaland. Often members of The Watch have other lives to live in the city—rearing families, attending school, holding down employment, shopping for food and clothing. Sometimes they are seen appearing and disappearing into walks or walls and are mistaken for something supernatural."

"Who did the work on the passages?" asked Watson. "The secret doors and tunnel switches—all of it seems rather sophisticated and modern."

"Watchmen with electrical, construction, and engineering skills over the past three centuries helped reconfigure the passages and secure the entrances. The captain's grandson did much of the recent industrial control and computer work."

"What about the murder Rodney mentioned?" Shad quacked as his Nigel Bruce resumed its seat at the table.

"The only murder I know . . ." The mech paused and seemed to revise what he was going to say. Possibly a retired slave soldier for a terrorist organization would know of any number of murders. "This particular murder," continued Arif, "was a fellow named Poenius Postumius."

"Odd name," said Watson. "Slavic?" he asked.

"Italian," answered Arif. "He was the prefect of the Second Legion *Augustus* which was stationed here and built the original fort. Poenius Postumius was murdered by the legion's centurions, probably with the full knowledge of the unit's tribunes, the whole thing done in secret and represented as a suicide."

"Rodney did say it was a very old murder," I said to Watson. I faced Arif, "What was the motive, fellow?" I asked with more than a bit of irony. "To investigate this murder properly, we must know the motive."

"The motive was to save face and avenge the honor of the Second Augustus," said the mech. "It was during the revolt of Boudicca, Queen of the Iceni, in the First Century. Boudicca's huge army was chewing up and spitting out settlements and Roman units like sunflower seeds and getting stronger with every victory. After the Ninth Legion was crushed by her army, it looked as though nothing could stop her. Gaius Suetonius Paulinus was governor then and he was determined to make a stand, engage the rebels, and defeat them. He had the Fourteenth and Twentieth legions, less than ten thousand men, against Boudicca's two hundred thousand or more. The governor sent here to the Second Legion to join him for the battle. The new legate had yet to report for duty, which left the prefect in charge. The prefect, Poenius Postumius, looked at the odds and decided at twenty-to-one the smart money was on Boudicca. He refused the order and kept the Second here safe in the fort. Suetonius won a great victory over Boudicca nevertheless and broke the revolt. The Fourteenth and Twentieth legions were greatly honored for their parts in the battle."

"And the Second received the white feather," I remarked. "That was fifteen hundred years before the Civil

War. How does that incident figure in the lore of The Watch."

"As far as Suetonius was concerned, Poenius Postumius paid for his cowardice by falling on his sword. Those centurions who assisted Poenius up onto his sword, however, never again wanted to suffer such dishonor. They would be the first to follow orders, serve the standard, and die if necessary to protect the legion's honor. They adopted a secret creed which each legionary was sworn to follow regardless of consequence. They passed down the creed to the city watch and to every soldier in this part of England."

"Semper Fidelis," I said to myself. "The city and The Watch took the motto from the legion, as did the Devon militia that became the Devonshire Regiment, later the Devonshire and Dorset."

"Honor, Holmes," said Watson. "Insane, ridiculous, blind stupid, absolutely magnificent honor. Five hundred years ago, King Charles told Captain Bound to plug that hole and allow no one through until properly relieved." He sat back in his chair and looked at me. "We aren't going to be able simply to pick up this old man and hustle him off to hospital, are we?"

"Not and leave his post without a Bound commanding, old fellow. To do so would destroy him, as well as a few important intangibles." I drummed my fingers on the table, glanced up at Arif, and back at Watson. "We'll simply have to think of something else."

When we returned to the watch room, Molly Dotting had been relieved by a fellow known only as Crazy. He was fairly short, somewhat plump, and his thinning black hair was combed back with what appeared to be an amount of gel far too generous for the number of hairs it supported. He had a tiny little black waxed moustache with tips twisted up into a miniature handlebar. The face was very familiar to me and I ran his image through Heavitree to make certain. A ninety-seven percent facial ID match: he was escaped French murderer Anton Vavasour convicted nine years earlier for killing four members of a Paris crime family allegedly responsible for the death of Vavasour's favorite nephew. Crazy was working on the rather eccentric computer system.

"Come with me," said Arif to Watson and myself. "Time to acquaint you with your post." As Arif ostensibly gave us a tour of the passages for which we'd be responsible, I sent the information on Vavasour to Watson by wireless. His return:

"Interesting. I ran Molly Dotting. Former mental patient at Tangents in Reading—"

"Forgive me for listening in," Arif interrupted out loud, "but I was originally configured with wideband reception capabilities that I cannot disable. One can never tell an enemy's transmission frequency, you see."

"Handy in the terrorism trade, no doubt," said Watson with a slightly offended tone.

"It has its uses, doctor. The upshot is, gentlemen, if you are within range, I cannot help but pick up your wireless transmissions. I thought you should know."

"Quite right," I said. "Sooner would have been even better."

He stopped and faced us. "I should mention, as well, we don't ask questions about a watchman's past before, during, or after swearing to The Watch. When a person pledges to keep the passage safe until the rightful monarch orders us to stand down, we take the person at his word—even you two."

"Recklessly generous of you, old rust bucket," offered Watson.

"Not at all, doctor. We have your word of honor and that of Mr. Holmes. Honor is important to us. It's been unnecessary to shave anyone for betraying their word for almost two centuries." He bent over toward Watson to emphasize his point. "Nevertheless, we keep the axe sharp."

"Arif, could you answer a question for me?" I asked.

He straightened and turned toward me. "I would have to hear it before I would know."

"Quite. The captain mentioned to me a grandson, James, who temporarily took his place some years back. Is James still living?"

"James Bound is alive and in prison in Exeter serving a five-year sentence for computer fraud."

"I see. Has the captain any other children or grandchildren, siblings—anyone else qualified to command The Watch?"

"Captain Bound had an older brother named Peter. He lost a finger, I gather, and it eventually became infected. He died shortly thereafter. The captain's only child, Hugh, stood the watch for a few years during which he fathered two sons, William and James. Soon after the birth of James, though, Hugh divorced his wife and moved to London with a massage therapist leaving his wife with the boys. Hugh eventually committed suicide. Hugh's eldest son, William, grew to became rather famous as BBC 227 game show host Billy Bonds."

"*Date A Dream*," I said. "My wife used to watch it every weekday until she died and became a cat. I don't recall seeing the show for some years. Where is Billy Bonds now?"

Arif seemed to freeze for a second, then said, "He retired to his estate in Tregassack Road north of Longrock, Cornwall and became something of a recluse."

"Perfect. What if we ask him to fill in for the captain for a few days?" asked Watson. "For his grandfather's sake? It seems not a great deal to ask."

"Rodney and I did just that, gentlemen, five months ago." He held up his mangled and mostly missing right hand. "We also learned Billy Bonds owns an elephant gun." He lowered the injured hand. "From what he said during our brief encounter, I gather William blames his grandfather for his father's suicide and for everything else bad that has befallen him."

"I say, old tank," Watson said to Arif, "I think I saw a right hand assembly compatible with your model back there on one of the figures in Henriettaland. I believe I can repair your hand."

"You said you are not a doctor."

"I am not. In another life, however, I did bomb squad training. That takes a certain aptitude at electrical and mechanical tinkering."

"Really." Arif was silent for a moment. "With what sort of bombs have you worked, doctor?" he asked at last.

While they discussed mechanical health issues and blowing the hell out of things, my Sherlock Holmes patch began itching. To paraphrase Conan Doyle, when all the possible routes have been blocked, the one filled with the least amount of rubbish is the most promising way to go. "Arif," I interrupted, "it is necessary for me to make a wireless call. I have no objection if you listen in, but please do not interrupt."

"I cannot swear to that unless I know who and about what you are calling."

"Fair enough. I'm calling His Majesty's Prison Exeter up there in New North Road to see if Prisoner James Bound is eligible for work release. I think I may have found him employment in the community."

9

After removing my capricorn shirt, I'd left Watson to keep an eye on things underground and perhaps prepare to tinker on Arif's hand. After being escorted by Crazy, I emerged from a secret entrance which opened next to the loo and changing rooms in the rear of a boutique located in one of the historical warehouses built into the red sandstone cliffs overlooking the Quay. The establishment, "Betty Bumps," exclusively handled sequin-festooned fashions for pregnant "under-twenties," hence I drew a few looks and a muttered "perv" or two on my way out. A bit red-faced, I brought the cruiser down and took it to the prison campus in New North. A peculiar bit of architecture, that. Built in 2115, it reflected several incompatible approaches to prison reform: punishment, penitence, rehabilitation, education, job training, psychotherapy, indifference, and a loving family environment. It looked like the aftermath of a collision between Queen's College, Disney's Fantasyland castle, Little House on the Prairie, and Devil's Island.

I went through the security checks and levels, and had a sit-down with their community employment counselor, a Ms. Tangerine Cox. I could only imagine the fun HMP Exeter's inmates had with Ms. Cox's name. She was a pleasant enough person in her very late fifties who very much reminded me of a picture I'd once seen of Eleanor Roosevelt. She said I reminded her of a very bad man in an old flik she'd seen about a masked bandito in old California called Sore-O. In any event, Captain Bound's grandson had less than two years to do on his sentence and was indeed eligible for work release, the only difficulty being in finding a non-criminal firm with a computer related position willing to employ a fellow convicted of computer fraud. I assured her The Watch had just such a position.

She wanted to know what The Watch was.

"An Exeter city police sub department," I said.

"I've never heard of it."

"Not well known," I answered, truthfully. "Very old, though. A lot of secret activities. They've lately had some difficulty filling positions."

"Oh?"

"Yes. James would be doing four twenty-four hour shifts a week." Sometimes I'm astounded by my own ability to keep a straight face.

"That's ruddy barbaric," she said. "No wonder it has difficulty in filling its posts."

"I admit, their union hasn't had a new contract in some time," I offered. "Room, board, and uniforms are supplied by the organization, however."

"It is HMP policy that new work release applicants be chaperoned by a prison officer for the first few days of outside employment for purposes of checking out the work environment as well as keeping an eye on the new employee to see how he takes to the situation."

"Oh?" Crikey, I thought. "I'm not certain how that would play—all of The Watch's secret work, you understand."

Her eyebrows rose skeptically as she said, "If this unit is willing to admit a convicted felon into its ranks, I feel certain it will be willing to risk admitting a prison officer with a spotless record." Her logic, regrettably, was flawless.

Without an idea on how to discourage the addition of a chaperone, she assigned me Prison Officer Mimba Stormer, a female of Jamaican extraction in her late thirties who, when she arrived in Ms. Cox's office, reminded me a bit of Queen Latifah in the musical *Chicago*. Queen Latifah, however, was rather petite compared to PO Stormer. She looked like she could take a couple of telephone poles and do a good job of knitting rolls of rebar into antisubmarine nets.

"Now," said Eleanor Roosevelt with a ghastly wrinkled grin and a fist full of papers, "All you need do is have James sign the agreement where I've indicated. Deposit the signed documents with the gate commander. He'll assign someone to out-process James. I'll give him a ring to let him know you're coming. Good luck."

There was a courtyard to cross and I wagered the entire future of my ploy on being honest with PO Stormer about the situation. We had to stop half of the way across the yard to allow me to finish and to allow her face to go through several levels of disbelief, wonder, amazement, and much more disbelief.

"If it's the way you say, inspector, they're as mad as a box o' bedbugs," she said. "You actually got the front office to go along with this?"

"I had a case not long ago," I said, recalling Ms. Lolita Doll, "where the subject had been let out of this very institution on work release to her partner in crime."

"Frankie Statten," she said, nodding. "I know the case. So you tellin' me this bunch hasn't stolen any more than Frankie Statten."

I thought on that for a bit. "Well, technically, as an arm of the city police—"

"Yeah. Confiscation. You better roll up your trouser leg, mon," she said scornfully, "I see a tide of very nasty stuff comin' in and it gettin' deeper by the second."

"I've told you the situation," I said at last. "Do you have another suggestion?"

She grinned widely. "You mean beside all of you bein' put on a couch and talked to by a professional man?"

"Beside that."

She stared at me a moment, looked down and stared at the brick walk for a moment longer, then back at me. "Let's talk to James."

Mimba Stormer sat across the table from James. I sat on the end with my back toward the door. "No," he said flatly. Then he added, "I wouldn't lift a flippin' finger to help that barking old fool guard his damned hole in the ground. The Watch," he said scornfully. "Hole-In-The-Wall Gang is what they ought to be called—no! Hole-In-The-Head Gang." He looked at PO Stormer. "Did this barmcake explain to you what The Watch is?"

"He did," she answered.

"You're kidding me. How could they approve work release for this?" he demanded. "They're all bloody barking."

Her full lips pulled back into a smile. "The inspector told me his version, James. Why don't you explain your version."

"Bloody hell, I'm going to do just that!"

And he did, without interruption from either PO Stormer or myself. His own introduction to The Watch at the age of ten, how cool it seemed to run around the passages, play with ancient weapons, and have this great secret no one else in the country could know. Then to work on the computer systems. His computer mentor was mentally challenged program engineer Miles Hintworthy, late of al-Jazira Disney in Saudi Arabia and Henriettaland in Exeter. James assisted Hintworthy by searching dustbins and jumble sales in the city for discarded computer equipment and parts, and doing the same at various industrial sites, including the closed down Henriettaland. He collected up and repaired servos, electrically controlled valves, hydraulic motors, masonry cutting and drilling equipment, parts, instrumentation, and such. By the time he was fourteen he was running security for The Watch. When he was fifteen, his grandfather had his heart attack. James was made Captain of The Watch while old Gawen Bond went in hospital. Three years later, when James was eighteen, his brother William dropped by to inform Gawen and James Bound that Gawen's son and James's father, Hugh, had taken a gun and blown out his brains in London the day before.

"It was all Gramps's fault," James said to PO Stormer. "My dad was consumed with guilt, Billy said. Guilt because of that damned hole in the ground, Captain Bound, and all that rubbish. If Gramps dies in that hole, the old fool brought it on himself. King Charles," he sneered. "He was a bloody awful king. The arsewipe brought in England's enemies to fight against Parliament. The only one worse was Cromwell and the bloody Puritan Taliban. That pair was a bloody treat for old Blighty. The whole lot were off with the mixer. I'd rather sit here, PO Stormer, and whistle 'Barbara Ellen' than help that old man destroy anyone else with this bloody nonsense."

Very heavy silence in that room as we all sat there frozen. The montage was finally broken by PO Stormer nodding her massive head while giving James Bound a very knowing smile. "You poor boy. What a hard life you got. And all because an old man wants to uphold the honor of your family."

"You don't understand, PO Stormer," he began, but she leaned on the table with her elbows. It was like the Matterhorn leaning on a table: it got one's attention.

"I tell you something, James Bound: I come to work here every day, open doors, close doors, fill out paperwork, escort fools like you from one place to another, and watch visitors come in. I see their faces. Most visitors hoping their fathers, brothers, mothers, sisters, sons, or daughters somehow going get turned around in here and stop hurtin' themselves, stop hurtin' their families, stop hurtin' their town, stop shamin' everyone." She leaned back. "Yeah, mon, and I see you fools in the yard and in dorms hangin' 'round, playin' the angles, waitin' for release so you can go out, get a little ganja, find a little trouble, and start all over, all the time feelin' like it's somebody else's fault. Boy, you ever read the police report on your papa's suicide?"

"No. My brother told me—"

"Billy Bonds," she said scornfully. "What he know, James? For years he make a game out of fixin' up Mr. Right with Ms. Right, object matrimony. He been married and divorced four times himself, boy, and right now he livin' all alone—No kids, no pets, no friends, no one holdin' down the other side of his bed."

PO Stormer studied James for a second then pulled the hipcomp from her holster and held it out to him. In her hand it looked like a postage stamp. "You a big computer hacker man, boy. You know what this is. I make it easy on you. I give you the codes, you call up you papa's police report at the Yard in London town, see what really happened."

He looked over his folded arms, down at the tiny computer, regarding it as though it might bite him. "I can't do that, PO Stormer. Those records are confidential. I'd get in trouble and they'd increase my time." He looked at me for confirmation.

"To me it just looks like you're stalling, James," I said. "If it was me, I'd at least be curious."

He sucked his upper lip in and pressed on it with his lower lip as he contemplated PO Stormer's hipcomp along with her offer. A terrible choice, really: let go of a really painful but comfortable resentment in exchange for another roll of reality's dice which are prone to come up losers. His fingers actually trembled as he picked up the instrument. With PO Stormer's help, he was soon into the Metro confidential files and at last the file of Hugh Bond, suicide. He read in silence for a little over fifteen minutes. Every second of that time he was under Mimba Stormer's unwavering gaze. When he was done he closed out the document and handed the hipcomp back to her. "Thanks," he said to her.

She took the instrument from his hand and replaced it into its holster, all the while with a very confident look upon her face. It didn't take Sherlock Holmes to deduce that she had long ago read the file of James's father. James looked at me, shrugged, and shook his head.

"They have a picture of me Dad in there—before he died. Don't know his face at all. Billy and me were four and three when he left. Wasn't long after that me mum dumped us on Gramps and Granny May." He shook his head. "Dad, the old bugger, was in a pub. Got in a fight over money and killed a man with a gun." He shook his head. "What's the old bugger doing carrying a gun?" He looked at me. "When he saw what he done, he turned the gun on himself. Billy had this story about how Grandpa drove our dad off, because of The Watch, and how . . ." He unfolded his arms, leaned his elbows on the table, and rested his face in his hands. "Blimey," he concluded.

Stormer and I exchanged looks. "So," I said to James, "we can count on you to take your grandfather's place as captain of The Watch while we take the old man to hospital?"

He frowned and looked at me and then PO Stormer. "This isn't a real job, you know. I don't know how those papers got approved, but The Watch hasn't met a payroll since Cromwell's time."

"When times are hard, some institutions fall behind," said Mimba Stormer. "It's your grandfather, James. He needs your help."

"PO Stormer, they steal food, clothing, power, internet service, cable—"

"City employees in an official capacity," said PO Stormer, "do not steal. They confiscate. They commandeer."

I looked at her with new eyes. "PO Stormer, forgive me for saying so, but you are going to fit right in," I said.

"I don't know about that," said James Bound. "The Watch is sworn to use all possible means including killing to keep anyone from going through that passage. You know what's going on, don't you? It's been on the telly for weeks."

"What?" Stormer and I asked together.

"In a couple days the city council along with the Underground Passages people and the Early Sites Restoration bunch is going to begin unblocking that drain from the Henriettaland end."

"I thought they were held up by a safety survey?" I protested.

"According to a news release from the Underground Passages people, a couple of blokes who looked like Sherlock Holmes and Dr. Watson cleared the way for the safety survey, mate. The survey for that section is done and they're bringing in the lads with the jackhammers and picks. To do the jobs we'll be swearing to do, we may have to cripple up or kill a few chaps."

"That would not be good," said PO Stormer.

"I agree," said James Bound, "but for five hundred years that's been part of the job."

10

It was a somber trio that entered Watson's flat on the third floor of Number 5, Colleton Crescent. I had arranged with Arif to reenter The Watch passages that way mainly to avoid being observed. A masonry panel behind the refrigerator in Watson's kitchen sunk in approximately a meter, allowing us to enter. It was a squeeze but PO Stormer made it. From there it was a succession of steep brick staircases going down and down—passing a succession of other closed masonry doors—until we were in an illuminated corridor cut through red sandstone. Mogridge met us there, administered the oath to PO Stormer, and led us back to the watch room after calling to Crazy that he had visitors. He listed all of our names, all with the initials S.F. This time I was identified as Sam Fiddle. SF. *Semper Fidelis.* Not a particularly difficult code to break, but well steeped in tradition.

Once in the watch room, James went in to talk with his grandfather. A few minutes later he, Arif, Mimba, and Molly emerged with Gawen balanced on an ancient litter. Before he left, the captain addressed us in a steely whisper. "Do your duty and serve your new captain with courage and honor. Semper fidelis."

We repeated the motto that was so much more than a motto, the old captain leveled a gaze at me, and then the litter bearers left carrying Gawen Bound, Rodney Mogridge following closely behind. Passages configured for a quick exit, they carried Capt. Bound to a waiting ambulance in Quay Hill, the ambulance attendants somewhat surprised to see the party emerge apparently from a solid wall. I was in the watch room with Crazy observing the ambulance attendants pack up old Gawen and hustle him off to Royal Devon when Crazy said, "You know who I am, don't you, inspector?"

I glanced at him and back at the departing ambulance. "I do."

"What are you planning?" he asked me.

I let out a breath that felt as though I had been holding it all day. "I haven't thought much past relieving Captain Bound and getting him to hospital." I thought a moment and reached a decision. "Right now, Mr. Vavasour, I plan on fulfilling my oath as a member of The Watch." I did a quick scan of all the live screens. A sinking feeling crept into my heart. "Where is Watson?"

"He told me he had some important errands to run."

"Bloody hell. And you let him *out?* All by himself? Are you *crazy?*"

He lifted a hand, "As a matter of fact—"

I did a quick wireless check. The cruiser was gone. "What errands?" I asked.

Crazy turned a switch and one of the screens changed to show a tunnel illuminated by torches and stand lights. Ms. Kelland and her crew, Mort Graves standing guard, were escorting a pick, trowel, and bucket wielding company of about five hard-hatted academicians. I recognized Prof. Ian Bilderson of Exeter University. He held the archeology chair there. "Is that at the other end of the drain block?" I asked.

"Yes. Fortunately they'll be going at it one stone at a time rather than using boring equipment." He glanced at me. "Still, it won't take very long. The stones in that seal were put together with hot mortar—quicklime mixed with rock dust, bits of brick—what they used back then. Not like modern mortar that glues rocks together. This stuff you can pick out with your fingernail. They'll be at this side of the watch room wall in a few days—maybe four days if they cherish, clean, sketch, scan, and record each rock as it comes out. Your Dr. Watson said he thought he might be able to arrange a delay."

I issued an expression quite unfit for the printed page. The thought of Shad in his brain-scrambled Nigel Bruce suit loose on the city arranging who knows what with both constabulary and media salivating in expectation of us causing an embarrassment had my blood running at about 4.2 Kelvin.

"You don't look well, inspector."

"Really?" I giggled just a trifle giddily. "Did my partner happen to say anything about those errands he mentioned? Anything at all?"

"Sorry, inspector. He wanted to keep it a surprise. He sounded like a duck, but that's all he said. I suppose we'll have to wait and see."

I giggled again. I couldn't seem to stop. "That's life with Guy Shad, Mr. Vavasour: One long never-ending Christmas morning."

Crazy looked somewhat wistful. "I've never had anyone say anything that nice about me."

I didn't bother to clear up that particular misunderstanding. In a few minutes more Captain James, PO Stormer, Arif, and Molly returned. Rodney had accompanied the ambulance after agreeing at the insistence of the paramedics to ride in a new medical waste bag with nothing but the tip of his nose sticking out. Captain James stood silently watching the screen showing the activity at the other end of the blocked drain. He glanced down at a couple of switches then said to Crazy, "Is the Albert Place tunnel switch down?"

"For over a year," Molly and Crazy said at the same time.

"The movable tunnel seems jammed," continued Molly. "The hydraulic motor is working and there aren't any leaks to the pistons."

"We didn't want to force it," said Crazy, "for fear of cracking or shattering the tube. But we can't figure out what's sticking."

James nodded, rubbed his chin, and turned to face us. "I think I know what it is. Nothing we can do until after they leave the passages

. They don't seem as though they'll get very far today. They're all taking pictures, making measurements, and I think possibly preparing to tunnel straight up to the surface to bring in more equipment." He glanced back at the screen. "Won't take them too long to uncover the tracks and hydraulics once they begin cutting through walls. We take it easy until tonight."

"Then what do we do?" I asked.

"We'll see about repairing that switch and making that drain vanish," he said with a bit of a smile. He motioned for Mimba Stormer to follow him and they went into Gawen's bed chamber. Cook followed with a faded red tunic for James and a new scarlet tunic—freshly made—for Mimba.

♠

I had nothing better to do after notifying Val I wouldn't be home that night, except wait for Watson to reappear. Hence, after another ghastly dining experience in the mess—some kind of mortified animal flesh creamed on bits of toast—I accepted Crazy's invitation to watch vids in his quarters, a smallish room off the main corridor to Henriettaland. On DTV 9997 we found *The Life of Brian* followed by *The Time Machine* with Rod Taylor. We laughed uproariously at the first. As good members of The Watch, during the second, members of the underground in good standing as we were, we cheered for the Morlocks.

Afterward, we talked a bit. Crazy had come to Britain fleeing from both the Paris Police and the Sommer crime family organization. I speculated that it must have taken a great deal of courage for a single man to go up against the Sommer Family. "I understand they have several judges and police officials in their pockets," I said.

"Yes. The honest magistrates in Paris hold their annual meeting in a *pissoir*. There was not a prayer my nephew's killers would be apprehended." He looked at me with glistening eyes. "It was a mistake, you know: killing my nephew. Bad address, mistaken identification, something. A week after the killing a fellow came by my music store and said someone who won't be named was most regretful about Degare's unfortunate 'accident.' If I would agree to shut up about it and quit putting it in front of the news cameras at every opportunity, I might find a very large sum of tax-free currency on my doorstep some day. If I didn't, I might instead find myself splattered all over my steps."

"Subtle," I offered.

Anton shrugged. "He was the first one I killed. I'm something of a pianist, you know. Thugs are always surprised at how strong my hands are. The information I got from him before he died led me to the two men who did the

239

actual shooting. Surprising the amount of information one can get just by exhibiting a length of piano wire."

"That's what I've always said," I remarked, a bit of dryness in my throat.

"The information I obtained from them led me to Gosse Sommer, the old man himself. Gosse was the one who gave the order."

"Anton," I said, "telling me this is probably not very wise. Although what you did and where you did it are outside my purview, I can still be called as a witness by the Paris court. I'd have to go."

"It doesn't matter," he said. "For six years I have been in The Watch occupied by keeping people who don't know it's there from walking through a solid wall. Seems silly when I put it like that." He looked at me. "All that time I've known Captain Bound—Gawen Bound. Maybe he's bonkers. Maybe we're all barking mad. But he's spent his life and his health doing what he thinks is right. Inside his heart he is calm. Notice that about him?"

"I did."

"Inside his heart he is the sanest man I know." Anton nodded in the general direction of the upcoming excavations. "However this ends, if I'm still alive, I'm on my way back to Paris to turn myself in to the authorities."

"Why?"

"It is the right thing to do."

"Not if it is still a rigged game."

"Perhaps my case can draw media attention to that very fact," said Anton. "Wouldn't that be worthwhile?"

I regarded the funny little man. "Perhaps you are not so crazy after all, Crazy."

The knowledge of a wireless call came into my head. *"Holmes, old man!"* It was Watson.

"Where are you, Watson. What have you done?"

"Not over the wireless, old trout. Can't trust where those pesky microwaves go, wot?" He chuckled.

"Watson—"

"Don't have all night, dear boy. Just wanted to let you know some friends of mine will be coming down the parking lot air shaft at the Southgate end of Western Way

tomorrow before work. Be a good fellow and let Arif know, will you? They'll need an escort."

"He already knows," I informed him.

"Of course. How right you are, Holmes. Hi, Arif."

"Greetings, doctor," came the transmission from the ever listening Arif.

"In any event," continued Watson, *"my friends ought to delay things until I can finish my other errand. Call you tomorrow."*

"Watson? What other errand? Watson?" He was gone. I called and my transmission was blocked. I looked and Arif was standing in Crazy's doorway.

"What is Watson going to do, inspector?" the mech asked.

"I'd give worlds to know," I said somewhat frantically. "If they were only aware, nations would tremble at the possibilities." I looked about in a bit of a frenzy as I projected a future trying to make a living as a night watchman in Aberstwyth, or somesuch.

"The diggers and UP people are leaving the passage," said Arif pointing at one of the screens. "Work must be over. Captain James needs us to help him fix the switch."

11

A long, difficult, exhausting night. It began by utilizing a parallel tunnel to get behind the newly installed surveillance cameras and introduce image loops to disguise what we were doing. Then we removed the cameras. Whoever was observing would see nothing but unchanging passage walls until we were finished. Then came the hard part. The movable part of the tunnel, perhaps six meters northeast of the nearest end of the drain, was as clever a bit of masonry work as I'd ever seen. It looked like any other section of passage, but it was a segmented assembly of reinforced concrete tubes lined inside with stone matching the walls of the passage. Captain James checked out all of the transmitters, receivers, power receptors, and hydraulics and everything was working just fine. At last he had all of us climb upon the end of a long steel lever and jack up the drain end of the segmented assembly. Mimba Stormer added her bulk and practically drove the whole thing through the top of Quay Hill.

It took only a glance to see what was wrong. There were sliding masonry plates in the floor beneath which were casters made from Henriettaland train wheels. The casters moved in the grooves beneath the plates and the rubber tread on one of the casters had somehow gotten chewed to pieces, altering the careful balance of the tunnel segment, jamming it in place. James had brought another wheel with him, and in a matter of half an hour that end of the blocked Roman drain had transformed into a gentle curve in the passage to the northwest with no sign of any Roman drain having been there ever. Those fellows from the university must have been looking at a different spot.

There was another Roman drain that looked vaguely similar, although there was no switch there and very little plugging the drain. We relocated the wireless surveillance cameras there, stacked a bit of loose rubble in the drain,

242

rattled the cameras a bit to make static, detached the loops, and returned by way of Henriettaland. All they could tell from anything less than closely observing the surveillance recordings was that somehow a mysterious force had come and made much of the stuff blocking the Roman drain they were excavating simply disappear. A few hours of confusion, perhaps. Between GPS, measuring tapes, maps, and Ms. Kelland it wouldn't take a very long time for them to figure out the ruse and then what to do about it. An additional day or two, perhaps. Captain James, one-by-one, examined and tested all of the movable parts of the incredibly complex tunnel systems until I lost count of them. My amazement at what had been accomplished over the centuries by a few dedicated rubbish heap raiders eventually gave way to weariness. I was stumbling by the time we finished.

After a quick shower in a narrow ice cold facility The Watch called the frigidarium, I went to bed on a plank of a cot in the tiny room I shared with the missing Watson. I was too tired to wonder where he had gone, what he was up to, or what was going to happen.

That night I dreamed once again of being murdered, screaming myself awake. Once my heart stopped thumping I stumbled into the mess to get some brewed tea from Cook. The liquid in the cup I received was hot and dark but tasted less like PG Tips and more like old boiled socks leavened with used kitty litter. I thought about asking where The Watch obtained its water and tea, but declined. I really didn't want to know.

There was no one in Gawen Bound's bedroom, Capt. James did his sleeping in an alcove off one of the secret passages behind the monitors. I went into the room, took a book from the many on the shelves, sat on a chair, turned on an ancient floor lamp, and spent the remainder of the night reading the Nineteen thirty-eight edition of <u>A Handbook On Hanging</u>, by British executioner Charles Duff. Its subtitle revealed much: "Being a short introduction to the fine art of Execution, and containing much useful information on Neck-breaking, Throttling, Strangling, Asphyxiation, Decapitation and Electrocution; as well as Data and Wrinkles for Hangmen, an account of the late Mr. Berry's method of Killing and his working list of Drops; to which is added a

Hangman's Ready Reckoner and certain other items of interest."

It took my mind off my nightmare.

The next morning I found out why Gawen Bound had become such a movie buff. When you're sitting in a hole in the ground for five hundred years waiting for something to happen, there is prayer, meditation, rebuilding pieces of the sham passages, carving new rooms, stealing parts and provisions, and feeding off the fare provided by the world's television outlets. There was a martial arts flik called something like *Leaping Dragon, Squatting Tiger* that interested me not at all. On one of the sets in the watch room, however, they were watching an ancient Brian Donlevy grayscale vid titled *Wake Island,* a Watch favorite. It was about a very few U.S. Marines (*Semper Fidelis,* you know) in WWII defending a tiny atoll against a great many Japanese Imperial soldiers, sailors, and airmen. The Marines were, in fact, defeated quite soundly. I suppose this was peculiarly uplifting to some of my colleagues, but not to me.

I wasn't concerned about being overrun by the enemy—not being quite certain who *they* were in any event. My main unease centered around the possibility of all of us eventually being stunned, flashnetted, and dragged out into the light of media ridicule followed soon after with reserved rooms in the loopyloo. Superintendent Matheson would probably throw himself from the top of Heavitree Tower—after first tossing Shad and myself. Worse than that would be The Watch failing to keep the passage sealed until that letter finally arrived from the rightful monarch: *Sorry about the late notice, chaps. Trot on home and thanks awfully for your service.*

Worst of all would be that old man in the hospital whose ancestor, the first Captain Bound, had sworn the honors, blood, and souls of himself and his descendents in perpetuity to an institution that forgot all about him and his post when Charles I's head went into the basket.

And where was Shad? I tried several times to raise him and the cruiser with my wireless, but neither answered. Another vid began, this one in color: the 1953 version of *Invaders From Mars*. An amusing period piece with aliens

244

from outer space with zippers running up their backsides. Funny rather than frightening, which is why the bone shattering scream from Molly Dotting on my left rather astonished me. Then I saw what she was seeing on her screen: dozens of large, hideously deformed rats coming at us through the Southgate passage. I was close to hysterical myself when I noticed false eyelashes on one of the rats, blush on another. They were Shad's friends from the Allure Laboratories. The rats congregated before the identification camera and the closest rat, a large black thing with patchy fur and a hideous red growth on its back, looked into the camera and said, "Hi, dears. Salotta Festation and company here. Our friend Guy said you could use help from a non lethal plague."

Molly pointed a shaking finger. "That rat is wearing blue eye shadow and carrying a purse."

I nodded. "Lipstick, too." I looked at Molly. "I think I see at least a part of what my partner had in mind. Rather clever, too. Let his friends in." I smiled. "It should work."

12

The rat bios were employed at Allure Laboratories. Animals for research purposes had been forbidden in the UK for better than a century. Just as the prohibitions against fox hunting did not apply to fox bios, however, the prohibition against use of lab rats did not apply to lab rat bios. Now, who would want to copy into a rat and have possible carcinogens injected or rubbed into one? "It's a marvelous retirement position, dearie," said Priscilla Naseby, the rodent with the large red growth. "The wages help out ever so much, and I still feel better in my rat than in that old body of mine. I stay in my rat all the time now."

"Don't forget all the benefits," added Bianca Crowley, a brown rat with great blue running sores on her hips and highlighted coifed hair. "We get all the free cosmetic samples we want."

"Oh, I know," said Priscilla. "Forty percent off on all Allure catalog gift items. What savings."

A three-legged white rat covered with big pink tumors and gold metallic lip gloss lumbered over. Her name was Millary. "I got a programmable makeover console for my grandniece for a song. Ever so sheik. Pick the look she wants, stick in her head, and out she pops, hair, makeup, designer contacts, tattoos freshened up, perforations polished, the works."

"Sounds like a deal," I offered warily.

"Oh, it is, dearie. It is," insisted Millary. "My man Myron—he's me hubby—getting much better about it now. Ain't blown chunk at dinner for weeks."

"Especially now you eats with a fork," Bianca qualified.

"Sorry to rush," interrupted Priscilla. "We have to be at work after lunch." She looked to the others. "Girls, shall we get to business?" She looked at Captain James. "Guy said he thought the Great Conduit end of Henriettaland would be a good place for a toxic waste contamination."

James gave them his full attention. They all had either purses or little backpacks. Priscilla showed the contents of her purse to Captain James. She had a half-liter of Karo Syrup. Hillary and the others opened their packs and purses. As soon as James saw the plastic envelopes of chartreuse neon hair sprinkles glowing in the dark, he grinned. "Ladies," he said to the assembly of research specialists, "I think you have bought us some more time."

While the passages were still deserted, we ran a dribble of chartreuse and red neon sprinkles mixed with syrup down a Henriettaland passage from the end of High Street to the train station where we had a glowing puddle of the stuff. "Chances are it leaked down from an old abandoned toxic waste dump," offered Captain James as he examined the work. With the lights out the puddle's light emissions cast that part of the passage in an eerie green glow. "Highly radioactive, no doubt," he concluded.

"If there're any doubts, dearie," said Priscilla, "We'll take care of that."

She stretched out at the edge of the puddle on her right side, her nose in the puddle, her hideous red growth toward our expected visitors. She coughed a little, then I was quite startled myself as Bianca began crawling up my pants leg, her face covered in glowing syrup. It should work. The rats arranged themselves in the headsman's end of Henriettaland to await the archeologists and we returned to the watch room to observe the fun.

As entertaining as it promised to be, I had been concerned for the safety of Shad's friends. I still remembered those UP workers with their Stunsprays and Flashnets, not to mention Mort Graves and his artillery. I needn't have worried, however. One look at that puddle with Priscilla and her friends suffering several kinds of agonizing hideous death throes around it, and archeologists, rat catchers, and engineers alike were on their way out at high speed all of the way to Romangate. We had everything cleaned up by the time the brigade of HazMat mechs arrived. Since they couldn't find anything dangerous, they assumed their instructions had been corrupted and began surveying the entirety of the Underground Passages and Henriettaland both, which promised to take up at least the remainder of the day. I do believe they found a slight radon problem down by Saint Peters.

That evening, after the HazMat mechs had departed, Crazy spied Watson in Henriettaland at Great Conduit Station with some tools removing the right hand from the motionless headsman. He already had the skin off and was working on the mounting screws. Arif went out to bring him in. While we were waiting for their return, we at last heard from Rodney about Gawen Bound's condition. He'd had a heart attack, he would recover, but he'd need an operation and a minimum of another six days in hospital before they could begin thinking of sending him home or to a minimum care facility. James Bound only had another two and a half days before he had to report back to HMP Exeter.

In the watch room Mimba Stormer called Tangerine Cox to feel her out on James getting an extension on his shift. While she was on her mobile, she looked at me and shook her head. In sixty hours James needed to report back to prison. She closed her mobile and put it away as an alarm on her PDA sounded. She took out her unit, cleared the alarm, and showed me the screen. The instrument's sniffer had detected MX-81, a very powerful kind of plastic explosive. "This alarm been going off since we in the tunnels. I haven't been able to locate the source."

"Might be something wrong with your hipcomp," I suggested.

"Maybe. Molly says you have a micro down here. Mind giving me a crosscheck?"

"Not at all." I remotely flew the micro in from my room. I'd never operated a micro by remote before so the chemical residue test took a good deal longer than it should have. In the end, though, it came up with the same results: positive presence of MX-81. The screens changed and I looked up. Watson's face was in front of the security camera. Arif was behind him. "Silly Fisher and Sheik Faruq here," said Watson. "Prepare operating theater number one. The doctor is in the house."

We observed the operation in the mess. Arif sat at one of the tables, his right hand and forearm stretched out in front of Watson. By then Rodney had returned. Along with him, Molly, Crazy, and Cook watched as did PO Stormer and Captain James. It was surprisingly delicate work replacing the mech's hand. It wasn't as complicated as a human hand, but nonetheless required disconnecting and reconnecting hundreds of sensors, switches, and miniature motorized pistons with an assortment of chip arrays and power transformers. My partner looked and sounded like Nigel Bruce, but there was not a whit of bumble about his performance. Once he was done, Arif brought up his arm, flexed his fingers, and declared, "Now I am a man of many more parts."

A small round of applause went around the room which Cook mistook for a machine gun attack. Took us twenty minutes to coax him out from under a table. Once we calmed down Cook, Mimba showed me her hipcomp. She had muted the alarm but the screen read a strong positive for MX-81. It was very close. We were silently wondering what to do about it when the problem took care of itself. "Doctor," said Arif, "I thank you for restoring my hand. There is one more procedure I need and I believe you are the man for the job."

Watson was quite flattered. "Well," he said, "of course I'll do what I can. Frozen joint? Need a bulb replaced? Body piercing? Right now I feel I could cure a stormy day."

"This." Arif stood and with his new right hand removed his jerkin revealing a chest somewhat scarred from an ineptly controlled screwdriver. Arif took a screwdriver from Watson's tool assortment and with his new right hand popped six screws on a large formed plate that covered his chest and most of his abdomen. He then replaced the screwdriver on the table. Taking the edges of the plate in both hands, he removed it. There, among the usual batteries, hydraulic reservoirs, motors, and sealed circuit blocks inside his torso were pack after pack of 250 mg paper-wrapped blocks of MX-81 plastic explosive. He placed the chest plate on the table, removed one of the blocks with his new hand, and held it up for us to see.

"Are they real?" asked Watson.

"Yes. I was packed full of these when I received my freedom and left the service of the organization that had planned on using me to kill a lot of people. There were eighty-five blocks when I left. I had already been smuggled into England. I had no papers and no wish to fall into the hands of the security people and be mother boarded. However, even if I could arrange false papers, there was no way I could pass sniff tests for explosives. Such things are always a risk. I was homeless for quite awhile until Captain Gawen recruited me. Since then, these explosives have been what I've been using to collapse or destabilize portions of the passages to discourage interest in Henriettaland and the underground."

"How powerful are they?" asked Mimba.

"A half of a block is what I used to take down the Coombe Street entrance," he said. "That collapsed five meters of tunnel and shattered another eight." He nodded at the little paper-covered brick. "Quite powerful." He put that block down on the table and removed eleven more blocks, placing them next to the first. "Those are all I have left that I can remove without help. They are not wired in. There are eighteen others still in me, some of which are actually wired in, some appear to be wired in but aren't, and others may have various triggers and other devices designed to kill anyone attempting to disarm me. Doctor, I'd like you to remove the remaining explosives."

"Mother Machree!" quoth the doctor.

A dozen years earlier, then Patrolman Guy Shad had spent a brief time with the NYPD Bomb Squad learning mostly that he didn't want to end swept up and dumped into an ash tray. Then he had been blown up for real out at Hangingstone Hill. "Tends to make one goosey," the duck once said. He looked at me. "What do you think, Jaggs?"

"You are the doctor, old fellow. What do *you* think?"

He bent over, stuck his head almost inside Arif's chest for a closer look, then stood up. To Arif he said, "You've gotten along this far with the stuff."

"I have an automatic detonation circuit that's been necessary for me to constantly override ever since Emancipation. It functions as a dead man's switch. If I run

250

out of power, get killed, or sleep too soundly, it detonates me. It's rather a drain."

"I should say," agreed Watson. My partner frowned, took another peek inside Arif, tugged at his moustache, and shrugged. "I'll give it a go, if you want, Arif. Bear in mind, my engrams are copied back to Heavitree Tower. If I get blown up, all I'll get stuck with is a hefty bill from Celebrity Lookalikes for this meat suit. Are you copied anywhere?"

"No, doctor."

Watson looked at me. "We could copy him into one of the mechs if we could get him to the cruiser."

"No, doctor," said Arif. "If someone should attempt to copy my engrams, my internal sensors would detect it and detonate my entire remaining load of explosives—A security measure I cannot override."

"Important safety tip," said Watson, his face draining. "Yes. I see. Then, do you still want me to try? Constabulary demolitions experts would know more. They'd be better trained, more up-to-date, and much better at it."

"They would use scanners and certain tools that would also trigger my payload, doctor. Even if they should be successful, they'd take me away from my post. There are a few terrorism charges they'd need to sort out."

"Or," interjected PO Stormer, "they might take him out to their boom yard and detonate him themselves."

"Is that legal?" I asked.

"Arif used to work for a terrorist organization, he is in England illegally, he's working illegally, he has already used a succession of explosive events to obstruct legitimate functions of government—one of our current definitions of terrorism—and he's a mech."

Rodney got up on the table, stood, and faced Watson. "No cops."

Watson thought on it for a moment, then waved his hand at the explosives on the table and said to PO Stormer. "If you would, please, have Cook melt these in a pot then mix them with baking soda—a tablespoon or so per brick. Once it cools you can use it for modeling clay."

She gathered them up and got Cook to provide her with a plastic bag into which she put them. Watson gathered up his tools and said to Arif, "Gather up your chest plate, young fellow m'lad. If we trigger off four and a half kilos of MX-81 here in the mess, no one will ever have to worry about keeping that drain blocked ever again because it will be in Basingstoke. Where can we go so that if we do light up, no one else will get harmed?"

"The zoo," said Rodney. "The Henriettaland zoo is directly under that old parking tower scheduled for demolition in Smythen Street."

"Will we have time enough to rescue Moby Gator?" asked Crazy.

"Moby Gator is real?" I asked incredulously.

Crazy nodded toward Captain James. "Captain Gawen told me James built Moby from robbie parts and costume pieces from Henriettaland. It was motorized and would snap its jaws, wave its feet about, slip along the passages, and roar. Moby hasn't worked for years, though. We keep him hidden in the monkey house."

Captain James shook his head. "There's no point cranking Moby up again," he said. "We're long past the time a whitewashed swamp dragon with rubber teeth can help us." He looked at me. "What about going to the media?"

"No," I pleaded. "Not the media. Great jumping Jupiter, my boy! Anything but the bloody media!"

Watson put his hand on my arm. "Steady there, Holmes." He looked at Captain James. "Forgive him, captain. Holmes has been under a bit of a strain. About going to the reporters, I may be wrong, but I find it hard to believe that stealing all that has been commandeered by The Watch, all the ghost scares, not to mention tossing bombs about beneath the streets of Exeter will find a sympathetic ear outside the local anarchist chapter." He looked at PO Stormer.

"He's right, child," she said to Captain James. "They'd eat your grandfather alive. You might want to think a little about the pinch media exposure would put us in, too: you and me."

"I don't know what to do," he protested.

"We could blow up more passages," offered Arif. "That seems to discourage them."

Watson turned from Mogridge, looked at his patient, and gave his moustache a quick stroke with a forefinger. "I say, old bucket, you use a self-generated focused signal to detonate the explosives you plant, correct?"

"Yes."

"Do you have any other means of triggering the stuff?"

"Not voluntarily. The leadership of al-Sa'ah had been wiped out several times by careless bomb making and handling of explosives. That's why the new leadership changed to MX-81. It's remarkably stable and requires a sustained amplitude modulated FM signal of a certain combination of frequencies to detonate. It lowered work related deaths by almost eighty percent."

"I suppose the manufacturers used al-Sa'ah's safety record in their adverts," Watson speculated facetiously.

Arif began chuckling, then burst out laughing. When all of us had finished laughing, Arif gazed at Watson for a moment, then nodded. "No point in talking about bombing with MX-81 unless the trigger is still around to detonate the stuff. Let's go to the zoo, doctor. We can pick up this discussion if we return."

I was all prepared to cheer on my partner from the safety of the watch room. Watson turned to me and said, "Be a good fellow and bring a couple of torches, would you Holmes? I'll need a steady hand."

13

So, there we were: east of the monkey house in the center of a dark, scrap-littered promenade. Arif was stretched out face up on a row of dustbins we'd put together for a makeshift operating table. Watson was tinkering inside the mech's chest cavity while I played the beams from two torches on his work area. Rodney was observing from his perch upon my right shoulder while the micro hovered inside the cavity giving Watson an assist peeking at things in difficult places.

"Holmes," said Watson without looking up, "you do have bomb disposal experience, correct?"

"Just a familiarization course I took back when I was a constable," I answered. "A very long time ago."

"They had gunpowder back then, did they?" inquired the ferret.

Ignoring Rodney's comment, I continued. "All I learned, old fellow, was not to touch anything, get everyone out of the area, and call the bomb disposal chaps. You actually served with a bomb squad, didn't you?"

Watson shrugged. "Less than a year. Hardly enough time to get my name on my locker much less learn all the tricks. It seemed romantic until I realized the number of my coworkers who had names like Lefty, Stumpy, Wheels, Gimp, and Twitchy. I learned a lot, but MX-81 hadn't even been invented yet." He stood up and rested his wrists on the edge of the mech's chest cavity. "Of the eighteen remaining blocks, thirteen aren't wired in. However, they are all glued to the other five making a plate of the stuff. It is flexible to a degree. Using the micro I can see in back of it. I can't be certain, but I believe there are wires running through the entire pack."

"You're saying cutting away some of the packs may not be feasible," I said.

"Correct."

"What about the five that are plugged in?" I asked.

"This is ridiculous," accused Rodney. "Neither of you imbeciles knows the first thing about disarming a bomb."

"Do you?" I asked testily.

"I'm not the one representing myself as competent to do this work, you bumbling idiot. Why don't you remove his AI chip? I could take it to a safe place, then when you clumsy morons blow yourselves to pieces, Arif's imprint won't be harmed."

"Disconnecting my AI chip will automatically trigger a detonation," said Arif. "I know you are concerned for me, Rodney, but we are making the best of inadequate training, experience, and resources."

"What would you have me do, Arif?" demanded the ferret.

The mech ran through several possible responses for a second or two. "Pray," he answered at last. Good advice.

"To whom?" demanded Rodney.

"Whomever is listening," answered Arif, which was a remarkably wise answer.

I looked at Watson. I do believe the old fellow was perspiring although the temperature was a bit on the brisk side. "Watson," I said.

"What is it, Holmes?"

"About the blocks that are wired?"

He nodded. "Yes. They all contain chips and all are wired to plug-in connectors."

"So, it is designed to make disarming possible."

"That would be my guess, old man. As near as I can tell using the camera in the micro, it looks as if the wiring on only one connector goes into actual circuitry. The others don't appear to go anywhere. I can get at the wires from the block to the plug and can see them with the micro. Three wires: Black, white, and green."

"Don't cut the green one," cautioned Arif.

"Why is that?" I asked him.

"Green is the favorite color of Hootan Eftekhari. He is the one who modified me for my ultimate mission. Possibly cutting the wire would be regarded as disrespectful to him. Therefore the cutting would need to be punished."

"Boom," said Watson.

"Exactly," confirmed Arif.

"Nonsense," said Rodney. "Those psychotic killers get off on the murder, don't they? Cutting the green wire would be like flipping the switch to another glorious carnage."

"Again: boom," said Watson. "So, we are agreed: We don't cut the green wire."

I held up a hand. "Unless that's exactly what Mr. Eftekhari wants us to think just before we blow ourselves to bits. Was he a devious fellow, Arif?

The mech turned his head and looked at me.

"Sorry," I said. "Stupid question. In case you needed to be disarmed, what instructions were you given?"

"I was never sent on a mission and had no such instructions. I overheard other mechs get instructions, though. If they needed to disarm for any reason they were to call up and run Protocol 622."

"Have you ever tried it?" I asked.

"Of course not. 622 is the *Hijrah*, the end of the Age of Ignorance, the beginning of the Muslim calendar."

We seemed to be at a standstill. Every choice had multiple interpretations pointing to both "safe" and "see you in Paradise." Yet I could think of any number of situations in which disarming a slave bomber would be necessary. As ignorant of computers and electronics as I was, even I knew enough to unplug a toaster before working on it. If one needed to alter or copy the mech's programming or change the nature of the explosive package, sanity dictated an easily accessible, quick disarming feature. And, I reminded myself, the designers of this particular package would love nothing more than to have those attempting to disarm their soldier standing around the bomb for a long time trying to figure out just what to do. I ran Hootan Eftekhari through Heavitree and got nothing except that the fellow had managed to blow himself and his bomb factory to pieces a little under four years ago—Not encouraging news concerning Mr. Eftekhari's contributions to bomb-design.

Just then the knowledge of a wireless call came into my mind. I opened it and it was Superintendant. Matheson. *"I say, Jaggers, where are you and Shad on this Mogridge matter?"*

"Ah, we still have a few things left to tidy up, sir."

From the operating platform Arif gave off a deep booming laugh.

"What was that?"

"We're right in the middle of some questioning, sir. I fear one of the participants found your question a bit droll."

Arif boomed out with another laugh. "Forgive me, inspector," he whispered. "I fear my situation has made me a bit giddy."

"Nothing to forgive—"

"Jaggers," interrupted Matheson, *"Never mind that. I've gotten a call from this Kelland woman and she's fit to chuck a wobbly over how long it's taking you with this Mogridge matter and something about radio active rats. Can Mogridge's concerns be addressed away from the passages?"*

"Sir, there are certain—" Watson dropped a screwdriver and everyone but Arif instinctively jumped back, Mogridge flying off my shoulder. In a few seconds I managed to begin breathing once again. The ferret handed the tool to Arif. "There are certain delicacies, sir, that need to be taken into consideration." I leaned my hand against a Coade Stone mermaid convinced I was about to have a cardiac event. I didn't even move it after I looked and realized I was being supported by the aquatic maiden's ample left mammary gland.

"Well, Jaggers, I received a discreet little word from a friend over at BBC. It seems that Ms. Kelland and the lads in Underground Passages sound ripe for a bit of a story— the kind of story Chief Constable Crowe could use to further discredit Artificial Beings Crimes. We don't want all this to blow up in our faces, do we."

"Decidedly not, superintendant."

Matheson ended the call. His words made me think, however.

If one builds a single purpose bomb and blows it up, its disarming procedures can be made as complicated or impossible as one wants. Slave mech bombers were multipurpose weapons, however. They were walking guided missiles that could be recalled or redirected. This made for a complication.

Take your typical young university student with the brain of a baboon drunk on history, religion, or some such who wants to give all for the cause whatever it is. Long on enthusiasm and short on practical skills, the fellow leading a cell of slave mechs would have to be able to change payloads in the mechs as needed. In the Metropolitan Police Museum in London was an exhibit I'd seen showing how slave mechs had been used in the 2091 anthrax attack in Knightsbridge and again in the 2117 Sarin attack in Soho. Later investigations in both inquiries showed original missions scrapped and payloads changed in the field by expendable controllers—those same university baboons.

Protocol 622. Blow up in our faces. Simplicity, speed, safety.

I looked up at Watson. "I think we all need to take a break, old fellow. Stretch your back. It might help clear your mind."

He nodded. "By Jove, I think it might, Holmes." He straightened, took his hands from Arif's chest, placed them at the small of his back, and began stretching. "By the by, while I was away, I managed to get that program patch sorted out. They had a fellow at Celebrity Lookalikes who whipped up something that eliminated the bumble factor altogether."

"You were in London?"

"Indeed. Now I do my own Dr. Watson."

"A distinct improvement," I said, frowning as I wondered what in bloody hell else he had been doing in London. Then, as inspiration struck me, I put aside my concerns about Watson's doings, quickly reached into Arif's chest, grabbed the deck of glued together blocks of MX-81, yanked them free, and Bob's your uncle.

I stood, holding the explosives in my hands, eyes closed, waiting for my possible reincarnation back in the Heavitree mainframe. After a few moments, I risked opening my eyes and looked at the others. The only one who didn't have his mouth hanging open was Arif, but only because he didn't have a mouth.

"Great Caesar's ghost!" whispered Watson.

"Age of Ignorance," I explained. "Don't let the mech know when you're disarming it."

Rodney looked around, held a tiny paw to his forehead, and looked at our surroundings. "We're already dead. We just haven't realized it yet. The lights! It's all growing dim. We're inhabiting this ghostly plane between life and the afterlife, doomed forever to wander—"

"Hand me that screwdriver, will you old bucket?" Watson asked Arif.

The mech reached up and handed the requested tool to Watson who began buttoning up Arif's chest. "That fellow over there is Sherlock Holmes," said Watson. "He has one of the greatest deductive minds in the world."

The ferret looked at me for a moment, cocked his head to one side, still looking at me.

"Yes," I responded to his unanswered question, "I possibly could have been in error."

"But he wasn't, of course," said Watson. "The fellow is Sherlock Holmes, old weasel, master—"

"Doctor," interrupted Arif as he sat up. "I just got a hot line from Molly: The university and UP crews are in the High Street passage along with a squad of HazMat mechs and they're coming to look for their Roman drain. Something else: Molly says less than a minute after entered they jammed all our surveillance screens."

"I'll scout," said Rodney, apparently back from the dead.

"She wants Watson to go as far as he can toward the Great Conduit Station. It still looks as though they have to come through there. As soon as you hear them, doctor, warn the watch room and trip the passage switch at the end of High Street. After that, Molly will guide your return. Mr. Holmes, Captain James wants you back at the watch room." Arif stood and took the package of MX-81 out of my hands.

"What are you going to do with that?" I demanded.

"If necessary, a little here, a little there. Delay. Just in case." He faced Watson. "Thank you ever so much for disarming me."

"Not at all, old bucket. Not at all," he said looking quite troubled.

14

Captain James, Molly, Crazy, and Mimba Stormer were in the watch room when I arrived after using the code name Sang Froid. Most of the screens were black. Those that weren't were filled with static. PO Stormer looked quite concerned.

"What is it?" I asked.

"Captain James is determined to keep them out of the passage," she said to me. "By any means," she added pointedly. She shook her head. "We cannot be a part of this—not if it gets into killing."

I looked at James. His eyes were actually glistening. "James, what are you going to do?"

"I've been thinking very hard on that, Mr. Holmes—Jaggers, whatever. That first Captain Bound, what was his idea of honor back in that July of Sixteen forty-four when the king gave him his orders and he swore to carry them out. 'You can rely on the Bound family,' is what he meant. That's what my grandfather thinks he meant. I do too. You can rely on the Bound family and The Watch. Always faithful. *Always.*"

Mimba looked at me pleadingly and all I could do was hold out my hands and shrug. I hadn't the heart to tell her what Arif was doing. "I'm sure the captain knows best," I offered.

Captain James looked quizzically at me then motioned to Crazy. The pair of them bent to the task of restoring the computer system.

Having ones engrams copied and in a safe place lessens the fear of death considerably. It didn't do much, however, to lessen my scruples against risking the lives of others. Trying to talk James out of what he had sworn to do, especially after my speech at the prison talking him into swearing to do it, was a tangle I was spared by the computers suddenly coming back up and Watson appearing in the entrance security monitor wild-eyed, hands waving, and quacking, "Sodding Fidelis! The redcoats are coming! The redcoats are coming!"

We watched on the monitors as Ms. Kelland, her crew, and the blokes from the university shook their GPS units at each other as they argued about what had happened to Henriettaland. Shad, Crazy, and I manned the computer array.

"I am afraid your American antecedents have gotten the better of you, old duck," I said to Shad.

"What do you mean?"

"'The redcoats are coming?'" I quoted.

"An honorable cry if there ever was one," he insisted.

I poked his red jerkin. "We *are* the redcoats, old fellow."

"Mon Dieu," said Crazy, pointing at the High Street monitor. "What is that?"

Two men wearing Underground Passages hardhats and coveralls were carrying something rather heavy toward the end of the passage where Henriettaland had vanished. It looked like a very tall silver cup of about thirty centimeters diameter on its side with large yellow handles opposite the open end and a heavy red body carrying the logo of the Whack-A-Hole Corporation. I nodded at Crazy and he was already on the Whack-A-Hole site.

"It's new," he said. "It's just for cutting through . . . everything: dirt, rock, metal, wood, bone."

"What about power requirements?" asked Watson. "The Magic Mole was nuke powered. The equipment was very bulky."

Crazy slowly shook his head. "Runs off of electricity. Two hundred and twelve volts. You can plug it in next to your teapot. They call it the Wonder Worm."

They brought the tool to the end of the passage where, to proceed ahead, one would have to enter an unrestored segment. However, all of them remembered a left turn at the end of which was once a rather wide opening to Henriettaland. Everyone near the thing put on hearing protection.

261

"Omigod," said Watson. I looked where he was looking. It was the Great Conduit Station camera facing the other side of the wall which the UP people were planning to Wonder Worm their way through. In the shadows waiting for them, a large bundle of MX-81 in his new hand, stood the ever faithful Arif. I said something that need not be repeated here, pushed back my chair, and ran to the mess. Cook was there mixing something brown with something green, no Captain James and no PO Stormer. I ran back through the watch room into Gawen Bound's bedroom. Stormer was sitting in the chair next to the floor light and James was leaning against one of the bookshelves. He looked up at me.

"Captain, it's time to flash Arif to stand down. He's got enough explosives at Great Conduit to put a crater in that intersection the size of a St. James Park and he's going to use them."

They both sprang into action and beat me out the door to the watch room. Arif was still standing, motionless, while on the other side of the wall the Wonder Worm gang was giving their new toy a couple of test cranks. James was shouting into a mike for Arif to return to the watch room. Someone in an army uniform, a brigadier, with an entourage of four or five torch-wielding aides came up behind Ms. Kelland and got her attention. We were treated to her jaw falling open to see the army there. She had the boys on the worm shut down the contraption. The brigadier—looked a bit like Jack Hawkins in the original *Lawrence of Arabia*—he handed Ms. Kelland what looked like a very official letter. Her jaw dropped father.

"Well," said Watson impatiently. "It's about time."

I looked at him. "It's about time for what?"

He looked at me, quite a smug expression on his face. "The notice from the king ordering The Watch to stand down. That was the errand I was on yesterday. Got in touch with His Majesty's secretary, explained things, and he said he'd take care of it. Took his bloody time."

"What do you mean . . . how?" I was at a loss.

One of his eyebrows arose. "Don't you ever read any of the Holmes and Watson sites?"

I shook my head.

"Dear me, Holmes, you absolutely astound me. If you'd even glanced at any of those sites you'd know that His Majesty, under the screen name Reggie, is a big fan."

While I was digesting that, Captain James relayed the information to Arif. The big mech tucked the plate of explosives beneath his left arm, tripped the switch, and opened the passage to all the surprised faces, official and otherwise. "Watchman Arif," he introduced himself to them all. To the brigadier he said, "Sir, I understand you have a letter for my captain."

The general looked at what Arif had beneath his arm and without changing expression held out his other hand and said, "Trade you, sir."

Arif handed the brigadier the explosives and took the very fancy envelope from him. "Come this way," he said to the general and his aides. "Bring the MX-81 and we'll be pleased to deactivate it for you." When he reached the security passage to the watch room, Arif introduced himself with the code name Semper Fidelis who was bringing a messenger from the rightful monarch.

The actual message was for Captain James's eyes only and we are not allowed to reproduce it here. One of many reasons was that His Majesty also wished to keep this matter out of the media, which is what he told Gawen Bound in hospital at Royal Devon when he visited him there. The Monarch went incognito, or as incognito as a ninety-piece brass band can go. I never heard what was said during that visit, but I suspect His Majesty wanted to hear the tale from Gawen Bound himself. There was also the continuing difficulty with Parliament His Majesty needed to mind.

Parliament's political parties, you see, look upon handing out places on the Honors list as one of their prerogatives and unruffled feathers are not future problems. It was still legal for the monarch to knight subjects on his own, however, and this was a special case. The knighthood for Gawen Bound was made hereditary though his descendents who had stood the watch. Upon his grandfather's death, James would become Sir James Bound. When James realized that, he wondered what shame he would bring to the title should it come to him while still in prison. PO Stormer pointed out to him, as they left on their way back to New North Street, that bigger titles than his have put in their time behind prison walls. What's even better, she added, James gets to keep his head.

Watson and I arranged with the original division of Interpol to take Anton into custody. In addition, we had a watch-and-report unit assigned to him to chaperone the security care exhibited in Paris for their prisoner. They were to observe and report on the progress and conclusion of the justice received by Anton with a colony of eager reporters visibly watching every little step.

Arif was considered not legally "born" until emancipation, which meant that he was "born" in England. The paper wizards waved a wand or three and he was a citizen. He and Molly Dotting were hired by Underground Passages as tour guides to all of the passages, as well as instructors to their operation and maintenance crews. There would be a job there waiting for Captain James once he was also emancipated. It looked as though all of the passages would be opened for tourism: old plumbing, Civil War park, archeological digs, and the newest and likely most popular draw, the quarters and secret passages of The Watch. Exeter City Council expected the renewed system to be even bigger than Hogwarts Moscow.

After turning the account books over to the city, Rodney Mogridge went into retirement along with Gawen. When Sir Gawen Bound, Captain, Exeter City Watch (Ret.) took a small cottage in Dawlish Warren, Rodney stayed with the old man to care for him. The stories that did eventually make it into the media were tales of honor, redemption, historical significance, courage, and faithfulness. Almost everyone in the city had a new regard for their motto: *Semper Fidelis*.

One final footnote: A few days after the conclusion of the Mogridge matter, the waters quiet out at Heavitree Tower as Shad and I made plans to go to London in order to exchange his Watson suit for his replacement duck, there was a slight ripple in the pool of Devon law enforcement. Our John Dillinger lookalike boss, Detective Superintendant Matheson, called us into his office. As we stood in front of his portrait of the Biograph Theater he informed us that the monarch had affixed his signatures to letters placed in Shad's and my files expressing His Majesty's gratitude concerning the handling of the "*Semper Fidelis* matter."

"Why on earth didn't you inform me of His Majesty's involvement?" asked Matheson. "This will be deucedly good publicity for ABCD. The story of Gawen Bound and his descendents, the mystery of it, the story of the city's motto, the murder of Poenius Postumius, the lineage of the motto *semper fidelis,* James Bound out of the nick just in time to save his grandfather, the King of England knighting Captain Bound—the involvement of Artificial Beings Crimes a shade bit more than a footnote. What a story it will make." He looked at us, his eyebrows ascendant. "What's going on? Why do you two look as though you just found half a worm?"

"Sir, I think we'd best limit ABCD involvement in the matter to the ferret. Rodney Mogridge was successfully removed from the passages, his concerns resolved. Enquiry closed."

Matheson's gaze darted back and forth between Watson and myself. "What about the rest? Captain Bound, the king, The Watch, all of it?" He looked at Watson. "Surely you agree."

"I'm afraid not, superintendant," responded Watson. "On this I must agree with Holmes." He glanced at me.

I looked at Matheson. "Sorry to disappoint, sir. But, you see, through his intervention His Majesty has essentially legitimized everything The Watch has done since 1646 making The Watch a now retired branch of the city police and the watchmen former employees of Exeter Council. Remember the careful records kept by Mogridge and his predecessors?"

"Yes. I don't quite understand your attitude, Jaggers. The discovery of those volumes alone demand a bit of credit in our column, don't you agree?"

"No sir. And I think you'll want to have done with this enquiry yourself, all forgotten and far, far away when the Exeter City Council is served papers and gets presented its bills for damages, commandeered goods, and back wages for the past half millennium."

"Uh," said the superintendant, his Dillinger face moving rapidly from bewilderment to horror. "Uh," he repeated more quietly.

"Well said, sir," said Watson clapping his hands. "Well said."

♠

THE SHERIFF'S TALE

-1-

"O frabjous day! Callooh! Callay!" I chortled. That morning I had Lewis Carroll in mind. The Exeter day was warmish, sky clear, gentle breezes, and in just a few hours Dr. John Watson the meat suit was to meet his ignominious end. I was as giddy as a child awaiting the arrival of Saint Nick. A strange thing for Sherlock Holmes to celebrate I grant you. But since I wasn't really Sherlock Holmes and Dr. Watson was neither a doctor nor Watson, I felt entitled to my joy.

Shad had been notified his replacement duck bio had been delivered to Celebrity Lookalikes in London and it was time to turn in his Nigel Bruce. Superintendent Matheson had given us special leave to go to Lookalikes that day to lay the good doctor to rest. I was well pleased that the twin Jabberwocks of Superintendant Matheson and Chief Constable Crowe would soon be off my back about the entire Holmes and Watson embarrassment. That bumbling, half-witted, glitch-ridden Dr. Watson suit was to be out of my life for good. Snicker-snack! The bloody joke was done.

It wasn't all hugs from Dad, though. Losing my Sherlock Holmes software patch would be hard. I rather enjoyed the fictional sleuth's attitude and way of getting results. However, my wife Val wanted her old broken down ex-Metro detective back. Even amdroid cats don't really care much for change. Move her litter box a centimeter in any direction and it's all tail twitching and stony silence. The love of my life, nevertheless. Hence in the end it would be well worth parting with Holmes to ameliorate the heat we were getting from the media and Middlemoor as well as

267

bring peace to the home front. What could possibly go wrong on a day of such rich potential?

It began with the flipping cruiser being missing. I left my front door expecting to find the ABCD Sky Rover hover parked there. I called it down with my wireless and nothing arrived. I glanced up and where the effing vehicle should have been was more of that dreadful blue sky. There was no way the cruiser could have been stolen, straight away deduced my Sherlock patch. Hence, it had to have been remotely recalled. If Heavitree had recalled it, I should have been notified. I had not been so notified.

I was heatedly engaged in calling Heavitree Tower when a dark shape arrived overhead. I looked up and it was the Sky Rover. As it settled in Waverly Avenue I could see at least two manifestations of Shad through the windscreen. The Nigel Bruce bio made up as Dr. Watson was out cold in the rear stasis bed that should have been occupied by the large walking mech. The large walking mech on the other hand was in the driver's seat, the orange-peel shaped smoked lens down covering its sensor array.

The window on the driver's side opened and the head of the mech faced me and quacked, "Jaggs! We got a job guarding movie stars at the London Video Festival!" I cut my call to Heavitree. His mention of movie stars had thrown a bit of a spanner into my more than justified irritation. I went to the driver's side and said, "What's this about movie stars?"

"It's the London VidFest, Jaggs. It's been going on for a week and still has a couple weeks to go. The planning committee putting it on thought it would be cute to have bios resembling famous movie greats as guards at the festival. So they've been running security with law enforcement officers in replacement bios who look like historical movie personalities. There are law enforcement officers from all over Europe working in shifts. Matheson got Basil Rathbone and Nigel Bruce as Holmes and Watson assigned to today's shift. He even said a few complimentary words about salvaging at least something from the Holmes-Watson fiasco."

"Cute?" I repeated.

"C'mon, Jaggs. It's a little exploitive, perhaps. Degrading even. But do you have any idea who is going to be there?" He pointed a metallic finger toward the instrument panel readout. I leaned back so I could see. Displayed on the screen was an impressive list of current vid celebrities. Imogene Pigeon, Burk Stuller, and Lara Poona were a few names I recognized. I knew little of the modern cinema—

—*Emmy Tay!* Callooh and bloody Callay! O still my thumping heart.

Emmy Tay was the female lead in *Serpentina*, the fantasy martial arts blockbuster released the previous year which had been one of the very few modern fliks I'd found worth watching. It was every bit as exciting and sensual as the classic *Ultraviolet*, and Emmy Tay was Milla Jojovitch reincarnate—which may even have been the case, bio replacements being what they are. An absolute raven-haired vision in skin-tight lavender laser-vinyl. I perused further.

Harvard Oakes, the great director who had done *Alien's Eleven*, would be there. Jeremy Fennelworth and Lisha Tung from *Black Leather Bible,* Carlotta Wayne from *Hondo, Jr.* —so many. As much as I hated to admit it, the assignment looked like a rattling good time. Still, there was something that needed a bit of sorting.

I looked sternly at Shad in his mech. "You volunteered us for this assignment, didn't you? And then you talked Matheson into assigning us. Moreover you hijacked the Sky Rover from my parking spot and performed an unauthorized imprint swap with an additional unauthorized use of an ABCD mech, all without my knowledge. Tell me Shad: Is there some reason you didn't clear any of this with me first?"

"Sure. You would've said no," Shad answered.

His logic was impeccable. I provided an obligatory moment of hesitation, then relented. "It may not be so bad," I said. "But what about the appointment with Celebrity Lookalikes?"

"I moved it to this evening. We work our shift, meet the stars, then run on down to London, dump Watson, and pick up our new suits."

"Eh? What's this about new suits?"

"Remember? You said when Nigel Bruce goes back on the rack I could pick any two celebrity lookalike characters I liked, we'd copy into them and do a night on the town. I sort of fancied myself as Charlie Chan and you as Number One Son."

I vaguely recalled making such an offer once in an attempt at cheering up Shad. He had been so unhappy at losing his position as the insurance duck as well as his Watson joke flopping I had to do something to snap him out of his emotional slump. Leave it to Shad to take things literally. Still, winding up as Number One Son was not the worst thing that could happen to me. Being in London at night was.

Chilled fingers clutched my heart at the prospect of being there. In an instant that whole nightmare in Trafalgar Square coiled around my mind, from knives to dying in a pool of my own blood, while Shad prattled on about celebrity-couple lookalikes: Nero Wolf and Archie, Cagney and Lacy, Hercule Poirot and Capt. Hastings, the Cisco Kid and Pancho.

"If you get in the cruiser you can read the guest list without straining your neck," the mech urged. "We report at nine-thirty. If we get there early enough maybe we can peek around some before our shift."

I rubbed my eyes and lowered my hand to my side. "A practical matter, Shad. How are we going to do our Holmes and Watson thing with brain-sprung Nigel back there drooling away in a stasis bed?"

"I thought on that. What if I bring Watson out of stasis once we get to the fest and I stay in the mech, too."

"Run your imprint in both suits simultaneously?"

"Yeah. That way I can watch myself. I think I can get the mech through the door as Gort the cop robot from *The Day The Earth Stood Still*. With the shade lens down it kinda looks like Gort, doesn't it?"

"Klaatu barada nikto."

"Well said, Jaggs."

"All joking aside, Shad, you're planning on running two imprints of yourself concurrently? What about the sync difficulties? They never sort out properly."

"That Watson software is so corrupt, Jaggs, I'm not sure I'll even recognize myself. I decided against syncing at the end. Once we get inside we put Watson at something uncomplicated like taking a nap and you and I go and meet the stars."

"As Sherlock Holmes and his associate Dr. Gort the interstellar robotic cop and executioner?" I inquired facetiously.

"I didn't say it was a great plan," he said with just a hint of petulance. "After that I skip synch resolution between Gort and Watson. Once we have Watson at Celebrity Lookalikes and I get my new duck I'll just have Watson wiped."

I walked to the passenger side, climbed into the seat, and touched the close-door. As it descended into place and sealed, I asked, "How did you find out about this invitation to ABCD officers?"

"Didn't you check your Email?"

"Never."

"How very primeval of you, old toothpick. Well, I'll have you know we—Sherlock Holmes and Dr. Watson—were personally invited. The industry heard enough about us that we were personally recommended by vid producer Carlton Zane. He dropped me a note himself."

"Who? Recommended? For what?" I asked suspiciously.

"He's an independent doing a vid on the festival. I'm not familiar with his stuff, but we might even be in his new vid. I gather we are rather special—Holmes and Watson, that is. When he's ready for us we're to drop by his digs at the Videoke II exhibition."

I smiled. "An old pro such as yourself having his head turned by a little on-screen face time?"

"Pardon me for not being thrilled at losing my television career, winding up here in West Hicksville, getting blown to pieces by some nutball, and all at a tenth of the income I was getting selling that insurance corporation." He wriggled uncomfortably for a moment, then swiveled his head until he was facing at me. "It bothers you, doesn't it: being in London at night? When I mentioned it you went paler than Casper."

I waved a dismissive hand at him. "A bit of unresolved post traumatic stress, old wing nut. Pay it no mind."

"A bit, huh? You went pale enough to give me lens flare." He paused a moment then asked, "Never convicted those guys, did they?"

I took a breath and let it out. That "bit of stress" was a rather large and restless elephant sitting in the middle of my existence. Not thinking of it all the time was a constant effort. It eventually made it impossible for me to work at Metro, which is really why I was let go. Detectives who are afraid of the city in which they work aren't much use. "No," I answered at last. "No convictions. The yobs all alibied each other. Obvious cases of mistaken identity to a man." It was getting time to change the subject. "Shad, how do you find inhabiting the large walking mech? This is your first time, I believe."

"It's all right except I feel like I need to pee all the time. When I looked I didn't have anything with which to make my bladder gladder. Where's the drain on this thing?"

"It's a peculiarity of the walking mech's software. I never use that device myself. Damned distracting."

"You sure it's crankcase isn't overfilled?" he asked.

"It doesn't have a crankcase," I assured him. "It's strictly a software glitch and the problem's been resolved in later models. Meanwhile, simply keep your knees together."

Shad brought up the vehicle into the traffic corridor, faced us East, turned on the green flashing lights, and practically firewalled us toward the main vector to Taunton. "Think about movie stars," he advised.

Good advice even coming from an animated pressure cooker.

2

The first thing one learns about the London Video Festival is that it isn't held in London. For the past sixteen years it had been held in the vast ornate Leighton Buzzard Pavilion in Hemel Hempstead northwest of London, which placed security at the festival under jurisdiction of the Hertfordshire Constabulary, Western Area. The second thing one learns about the London Video Festival is that it is not a festival, in that it is not a time set aside for feasting and celebration. It is, instead, strictly business: Showcasing product for publicity, placement, and profit. The last thing we learned about our roles at the do was that we were not among those favored few assigned to the screening complexes where the stars, directors, and other famous personages would be gathering to watch the three hundred or so vids up for awards and mentions. Those choice assignments had been filled up weeks before. However, thanks to the special request of little known director Carlton Zane—the git—Shad and I were stuck with the unit providing security for the Vid Franchise Hall, an exhibition area approximately the size of two rugby fields far away from the screenings.

The Vid Franchise Hall was divided up into stalls, minitheaters, concourses, malls, courts, and suitable places for inserting one's name in blank fields and electrically transferring vast sums of currency. Essentially we were guarding the demo equipment, rerun, and old flik park. On the whole, traffic was light at that time of day.

On one demo screen I did catch a glimpse of Emmy Tay in her debut flik, a western released the previous decade, *Samurai Schoolmarm.* In it she was an absolute vision in skin tight gingham. Other than that it was to be little more than a shoplifting patrol. "Next time I should read the fine print," as Shad put it resignedly.

After getting our instructions from Groucho Marx—a detective superintendant with Cumbria ABCD named Potts, Shad Gort, Shad Watson, and I patrolled among the stalls and view areas with half a dozen or more other officers who resembled classic movie greats such as Humphrey Bogart, Bette Davis, Charlton Heston, David Niven, and Helen Mirren. Actually, it had its moments. Gort and I managed to assist Broderick Crawford in detaining a light fingered fellow who was taking a personal discount on microvids by dropping handfuls of the tiny disks without purchase into his drawers. We all stood by rather uncomfortably as Shad Watson reached into the culprit's drawers down among the fellow's naughty bits and retrieved the merchandise. Once the goods were secured and the poor fellow was led away holding a fridgebag to his crotch, Broderick Crawford could only say, "Ten-four."

After having Watson wash up a bit in the lavatory, we saw a Charles Boyer, which was an early model fallen officer replacement model bio once used by the *Police Nationale*. This fellow was a detective constable with Lyon ABCD. At a midday luncheon and briefing, Groucho Potts teamed us up with a new addition to our highly temporary force. Rather amusing when I saw Shad's reaction, both as Gort and as Dr. Watson. Shad was absolutely stunned at seeing a meat suit resembling his great acting hero Lawrence Olivier. The fellow, named Louis Graziano, turned out to be a prison officer at Belmarsh in London, the final resting place for several of the more intense clients of mine when I had been with Metro. While I was busy recalling my London years with mixed feelings, both Shads were doing their best to pump Graziano on where he had gotten the Olivier bio. Prison Officer Graziano was somewhat taken aback since both Shads, as Gort and Dr. Watson, were quacking at him with the same voice.

"The missus got the suit from A Star Is Born in Reading," he said at last. "They let celebrity and monster bios, don't they. They obtained the Olivier suit from a production company doing a remake of *The Prince and the Showgirl*. You know, with Marilyn Monroe?"

"We know," I and the two Shads answered in unison.

"Anyways, I seen the papers on this suit. This here is a bio grown direct from Olivier's own DNA. Must be something wrong with it, though."

"Why do you say that?" I asked.

"See, accordin' to the director it don't make a bit of difference whose imprint was put in this Larry, the meat suit simply refused to participate in making the movie. They said he had some rather hard things to say about *The Prince and the Showgirl*, too. Got into the media. Finally the producer had had it, wiped this bio, put him up for sale, and Star got him for a song. A history of resistin' the imprint, though, put Star Is Born's lawyers in a bit of a dribble—who knows what barmy Olivier might do next—so Larry was discounted again. The missus got him for under four hundred after the rebate, and it turns out guardin' gits in the nick is just his cuppa."

"Where's your nat?" asked Watson Shad.

"In bits and pieces all over bloody Thamesmead, sad to say. I wasn't a bad-looking chap meself, but was caught up in that attempted breakout from Belmarsh four years ago. Bleeders used a floor fan and a bag of wheat flour in a closet next to the residence guard headquarters. Once the air was thick with dust, they tossed a spark into it. Explosion killed the lot of 'em and serves 'em right, too. Took out the guardroom wall, though, and I was on the other side. Nothin' left of me but engrams."

We all related to that and nodded in sympathy.

"You have to make do, don't you, the pittance we get paid. Anyways, Star Is Born lets its vintage celebrity meat suits go for a couple hundred bob when they've become ill, worn out, injured, or program corrupted. All of the chains do it." Graziano pointed at Shad Watson. "Chances are you could pick up your Nigel Bruce there for a couple quid if you like. I hear that model's software is a bit on the iffy."

"I think not," responded Shad Gort and Shad Watson.

"Too much of a good thing, you know," I added.

We continued on our rounds, with Shad Gort searching for vid promos in which the producer's stars might be wooing the yokels.

There were some old vids on new micro disk releases in several places in the exhibition hall. Once we picked up a schedule, we hit them one at a time. The classic stars were long dead, of course, and the more recent ones now reduced to shilling old fliks were a rum lot. Terrible to see what time and a dissolute lifestyle had done for Studley Turkle. The Spencer Tracy and Katherine Hepburn bios running the Fabulous Forties Fest stall looked terrific, but were sadly lacking with their impressions. In between interruptions steering his other self out of trouble, Shad Gort never got tired of walking next to Lawrence Olivier, but kept reminding him, "Please, don't speak." Graziano didn't seem to mind.

We did see Dirk Placer and Bini Stole from the neopunk war thriller *Jenkins' Other Ear*. After that we saw the Pintata sisters promoting their MVD release of the science-fiction horror flik, *Flubber's Revenge*. There were several others whose names and productions I didn't feel obligated to remember. Just after two in the afternoon Graziano received a call for us to go to the Videoke II exhibit. It was located near the center of the great hall. As the garish large red and gold Videoke II banner came into view, Prison Officer Graziano said, "Never got a taste for recreations needin' stasis beds. I hear that Videoke can put you into any vid you want."

"I once did Hamlet as you," said Gort Shad. "Couldn't remember my lines."

"Videoke's been about for a while," I said. "It enables the viewer to enter a popular motion picture as one of the characters and play along seeing everything as it was in the original motion picture, in three dimensions, and from that character's point-of-view."

"Ah," said Shad Watson nodding to himself. "The genre that made Bill Cable a star."

"Who?" asked Graziano.

"Bill Cable," I answered. "He played the part of Johnny Boz in the classic detective vid *Basic Instinct*."

"Now that flik I know," he said. "Don't recall offhand the character of Johnny Boz."

"In the opening of the flik, Boz was the first of Sharon Stone's victims," explained Shad Gort.

"Oh," said our new acquaintance. After reflecting for a moment upon why this bit part would have been a

276

sufficiently desirable Videoke choice to propel a minor actor to stardom, his eyebrows ratcheted up and he said, *"Oh!"*

"This is Videoke II, though," I said. "I'm not familiar with it."

"Astounding, Holmes," said Watson. "Something you don't know? Absolutely astounding. The mech there and I know all about it."

Shad Gort walked up to an clear plastic oval door and pointed to the placard posted there. It announced a sample preview of Videoke II, the recently released, *The Adventures of Robin Hood* based on the 1938 Technicolor film with Errol Flynn and Olivia de Havilland, as well as my personal look alike, Basil Rathbone. It was produced and adapted for Videoke II, according to the advert, by Carlton Zane.

"Holmes," said Watson, "isn't that the fellow who wanted us at the show?"

"Yes, old man." I looked to Officer Graziano. "Where do we report?"

"Detective Inspector Jaggers," exclaimed a voice from behind me. I turned and saw a balding round-faced fellow clad in tan shirt tucked into tan jodhpurs tucked into gleaming brown riding boots. No riding crop. He reached out his hand. "Carlton Zane. Very pleased to meet you." We shook and his grip was like holding a fist full of dead sardines. We released and he turned toward Shad Watson. "And this is the good Dr. Watson, of course." He held out his hand.

Instead of taking the proffered hand, Watson said in his Nigel Bruce voice, "I say, Holmes, the fellow is tricked out like an early Cecil B. DeMille."

"Ready when you are, Mr. DeMille," quacked Shad Gort, which earned him a pained glance from Mr. Zane.

"Never heard that one before," said the director to Gort as he withdrew his ignored hand, his lips pulled back in a sour grin. "And you are?" he asked.

"Detective Sergeant Guy Shad, ABCD Devon Office. I was the one you contacted about coming here."

Zane's face assumed an expression of confusion. He gently cocked his head toward Shad Watson. "I thought . . . well, that you were in the Watson suit."

"I am," the mech answered. "I'm in both."

"Aflak!" suddenly quacked Watson.

Zane's eyebrows climbed almost to his absent hairline. "I see." He seemed to shake it out of his head and faced me. "Irrelevant. I principally wanted to see you, inspector, to invite you to perform the Basil Rathbone part in a demonstration of my new Videoke II release, *The Adventures of Robin Hood.*"

"I'm afraid I have other duties to perform, Mr. Zane," I responded.

"Oh, sorry inspector," interrupted Prison Officer Graziano. "Superintendent Potts sent us to Mr. Zane's exhibition. He's given his permission. Hearts and minds, public relations, and all that."

"Really." A few curious sorts began gathering. On the side of the viewing booth was an enormous holoposter of Basil Rathbone and Errol Flynn sword fighting on a set of castle steps. Mr. Zane and I were standing in front of the moving image while an increasing number spectators compared me to the holo-Basil Rathbone.

"You can see why I wanted you, inspector," said Zane.

"Slightly," I answered. "Very well. I'm willing to participate if you could indulge me a moment."

"Of course."

"Could you tell me the difference between original Videoke and Videoke II?"

"Be happy to, inspector. The new platform is ever so much more sophisticated. The old system had a fixed script with which one played along to the best of one's ability. If you forgot your lines, stumbled, or something else you looked the fool. Videoke II has what has been termed a floating reality. That means the script is constantly affected by the choices and actions of the characters. There are only so many roles, but the user can fill any of them, or there can be more than one user."

"With all of them able to affect the script," said Gort. "I've done a bit of reading on Videoke II," he explained.

"You're correct, but the players can only affect the script within certain limits. Must remain within period—

can't have you going after Robin Hood with an armed stealth drone, could we?"

"This is more like a game then," I said. "With Videoke II The Sheriff of Nottingham could conceivably capture and execute Robin Hood. Is that what you're saying?"

Carlton Zane nodded. "That is quite possible. Now, if you'll be so kind, we'll want you to sign a release granting Videoke II permission to use this performance in our adverts."

I was about to refuse—what if I came across as a fool? That would hardly do. Before I could refuse, Shad in his Gort suit interrupted with, "Of course he'll sign your release. This is all in good fun, right?"

"Excellent," said Zane, a genuine smile on his face.

"But I go with him," added Shad Gort.

After a stunned moment, Mr. Zane said, "I'm sorry, Mr. Shad, there are no Twelfth Century roles available for mechanicals."

"I'm young, but I wasn't hatched yesterday. I'm not a mechanical, pal; I'm an imprint and my imprint can fill any character image you have in data, right? Original Videoke can do that."

"Of course," said Zane hesitantly. "I misspoke. Simply hadn't planned on filling more than the Rathbone role."

"I can be Errol Flynn," Shad offered magnanimously. "Always thought I'd make a magnificent Robin Hood."

"Sorry. That role has already been taken. There are roles open, however. We can find something."

Watching them negotiate, an uncomfortable feeling crept up the back of my neck. I couldn't pin down a cause for it immediately. Then I recalled the vid release schedule we'd picked up. I patted down my pockets until I found it. There was no *The Adventures of Robin Hood* on the schedule. The Videoke II exhibition scheduled for that time slot was *El Cid* featuring Charlton Heston and Sophia Loren.

"The schedule says you're supposed to be running the Videoke II release of *El Cid* today," I said to Zane.

"Minor software problems bollixed up the release," explained Zane apologetically. "We had to substitute *Robin Hood* for the festival. Shall we begin?"

I smiled brightly. "Ready when you are, Mr. DeMille."

3

Inside the Videoke II compound, in a brightly lit rear stasis chamber containing a large monitor above a programming station as well as five new black-and-chrome stasis beds—four of them empty—I inquired of Mr. Zane where the other performers in his game play were. "Excepting this fellow, all of them are online," was all he said, then left to introduce his production to those filling the enclosure's mini theater while a technician in black who resembled a healthy John Carradine hooked me into one of the beds. When he was done, he said to me in a deep rumbling voice, "It will be a few minutes while Mr. Zane introduces the game to the prospective licensees." He gestured vaguely toward the programming console. "The alarm will sound when we're about to begin." He looked at Shad Gort. "Depending on the character you decide upon, sir, we may need you rather soon." To Shad Watson he cautioned, "Don't touch anything." He then exited, exhibit left.

Alone with the two Shads, I asked Gort, "What role did you pick?"

"I haven't settled on one. Friar Tuck and King Richard are open, but Tuck would be going over to the other side and Richard doesn't come in until the finish. Bess is open, but I'm not up to kissing Much the Miller's Son. The sheriff is open—"

"I thought I was the sheriff."

"Nonsense," said Shad Nigel in Watson mode. "I'm surprised at you, Holmes. Basil Rathbone played Sir Guy Gisbourne—"

"And Guy Gisbourne *was* the sheriff," I insisted.

"I beg to differ with you, old trout," said Watson. "In the flik, Gisbourne was the fellow who ran Nottinghamshire for Prince John. John was the Earl of Nottingham, you know."

"Really."

"Yes. Let's see. The sheriff was played by that terribly amusing fellow—"

"—Melville Cooper," completed Shad Gort.

"Are you certain, Shad?" I addressed that inquiry to Gort but both of them answered.

"Yes. Of course." Added Watson, "Perhaps that Sherlock Holmes patch is fuddling *your* head, eh Holmes? Getting a touch of seniorphasia?" He chuckled to himself then became fascinated by a pulled thread in his left sleeve.

Doubting Shad's cinematic knowledge was tantamount to questioning Sir Isaac Newton's expertise on the subject of the *malus domestica*. But I must have seen *The Adventures of Robin Hood* two dozen times over the ninety plus years of my imprint yet came out of all those experiences believing that Basil Rathbone played the sheriff. "I can't imagine how I made such a blunder."

"It was a fairly common mistake back in the Twentieth Century, and even now," interjected Shad Gort. "The film needs a villain of a certain caliber to go against Robin, but the screenwriters made such an ineffectual buffoon out of Cooper's character, they pretty much had to use the character of Sir Guy to perform the functions of sheriff. He walked, talked, schemed, fought, lead, and died like the sheriff, so folks who never paid super close attention naturally assumed he was the sheriff."

I sighed. "I feel like such a dunderhead. How could I have made such a mistake?"

"My very words," chimed in Watson.

The mech sent an unnoticed glare in Watson's direction then faced me. "Look, Jaggs, don't worry about what was in the movie. This is Videoke II. Write your own script."

"What do you mean?"

"Apply for the job of sheriff, put Robin in the nick, hang him, become king, wed Lady Marian, settle down and raise a police force, whatever. As I understand it, you can't control everything, but you can control your own character. The other characters have to react to a degree according to what your character does."

While I pondered hanging Robin Hood, the alarm beeped quietly and I could hear the beginning of the lively Erich Korngold score. On the monitor facing the stasis beds appeared the Warner Brothers logo with medieval trimmings against a parchment-looking background. Shad Gort held up its right hand, pointed a finger toward the heavens, and said in Rex Harrison's voice, "By Jove, I think I've got it! I know which role to play." He turned toward me and quacked, "First I have to find out if this is even possible."

I could feel myself going under. "How will I know you?" I called.

"You'll know me," came his confident quack into my mind. Then I thought he said, "Guard this room with your life, Watson."

As Watson began gently snoring, I heard the violins play as an illuminated page from a book appeared for the purpose of backgrounding those who didn't know that while off killing people in the Crusades, King Richard left his friend Longchamp (spelled Longchamps in the vid) in charge of the kingdom rather than Prince John (the treacherous). Resenting this treatment, John planned to seize the throne for himself.

Drums, trumpets sounding a fanfare, and some liveried chap on horseback informs us and the village crowd that a funny thing happened on King Richard's way back from the Holy Land: Richard had been nabbed by Duke Leopold of Austria and tossed in the nick. More news when it happens.

—Just then I recalled the fellow in the other stasis bed. He was much older than I remembered, but I was sure it was Peter Steerman: vid pioneer, avid gamer, and the inventor of Videoke. I wondered which role Mr. Steerman had chosen for himself. Given all the choices available, it had to be Robin Hood. With his reputation as a gamer, I felt I could count on Robin of Locksley putting up quite a scrap. This is going to be terrific fun, I thought.

♠

"And how are the dear Saxons taking the news, Sir Guy," Claude Rains as the villainous Prince John asked me. We were in a huge hall built of stone, which seemed real to the touch. My view from the great window was of castle battlements, guards walking their posts, the green of a Nottinghamshire evening beyond. There was also my own reflection. I looked bloody marvelous in mail, black surcoat emblazoned with a great golden griffin, and a satiny blue cape over my shoulders. Basil looked to be about ten years younger than my bio, too, with dark brown hair and a natty little goatee.

I turned to face his highness and the set was complete, in that there were no cameras or production personnel. It was, in fact, a virtual reality setting. This was Nottingham Castle, Guy of Gisbourne's stronghold. *My* stronghold. Seated amongst candles, a silver service, and a plate of fruit, Prince John was at the table plucking the seeds from what appeared to be a pomegranate with the point of a dagger. One can only wonder why, since once you have divested a pomegranate of its seeds nothing edible remains.

I quickly ran my plan through Sir Guy's head. Ever since my first time watching *The Adventures of Robin Hood,* there had been changes I'd wanted to make. To be perfectly honest, the historical Richard the Lionheart was a terrible monarch, even by the undemanding standards of the period. His stooge, Longchamp, Bishop of Ely, had been bleeding the English population white, extorting huge sums of money to support Richard's armies in the Holy Land. Seizing the throne from Richard and eliminating Richard's terrorist supporters in Sherwood always struck me as eminently sensible goals. The steps taken to achieve those goals, however, had always been frightfully inept. It was high time proper law enforcement and administration came to Nottingham and to England.

"They're even more worried than Longchamps, Your Highness," I responded in answer to Prince John's question.

"They'll be more than worried when I get through squeezing the fat out of their pampered hides," said Prince John.

"I'm astonished they have any fat left after the financial hiding Longchamps gave them, Your Highness." I leaned forward conspiratorially and lowered my voice suitably. "I've been considering some minor amendments to improve your plans."

"Oh?" John's eyebrows arched. "Really."

I seated myself in a courtly manner in the chair opposite him. "With Richard imprisoned in Austria, and Longchamps out of the way, Your Highness, you are in unique position to make a number of very profitable changes."

"First among them," emphasized the prince, "that I ascend to the throne."

"After the proper preparations, of course," I insisted.

"Preparations?" he repeated, his eyebrows climbing ever higher. He placed the disemboweled pomegranate on his plate. "What do you have in mind, Sir Guy?"

"As we discussed earlier, Your Highness, you are to appoint me to collect your taxes."

He nodded. "Go on."

I began going through my checklist. "First, it would be ever so much more efficient performing my tax collection duties in this shire if I was also the high sheriff of Nottingham."

Prince John smiled slyly. "There is a sheriff—"

"—Who is a man with no name to speak of," I interrupted. "Forgive me, Your Highness, but the man is a bungling coward and buffoon. Should that not be sufficient motivation to sack him, he owes his office and therefore his allegiance to your brother, Richard."

The prince gave the table top a worrisome look. "I rely upon him to enforce my laws in Nottingham."

"Aside from his loyalties, Your Highness, what sort of job has he done?" I asked. "Is Robin Hood hanging from a gibbet? Are you rich?"

"Neither." The Prince nodded. "You make your point well, Sir Guy."

"Make me Sheriff of Nottingham, Your Highness, and you will avert a coming disaster."

The prince was still reluctant. "It is a very low occupation," his highness cautioned.

"Enforcing the new laws you will make, Your Highness, will be both my pleasure and my honor."

"Really, Sir Guy. Will it be so much pleasure for you to whip the backs and apply hot irons to the heels of those Saxon dogs until you've shucked them free of every last farthing?"

"Such exertions are hardly necessary, Your Highness. The people of this shire and all across England will willingly pay your taxes and bless you for them."

Prince John reached out his hand, took the silver ewer of wine, raised its lid, glanced in and studied the contents. The answer to my peculiar behavior not found within, he replace the container on the table and studied me for a moment. "Explain."

"Certainly Your Highness. At present Richard's taxes are twenty schillings on every fee and a quarter of the income on clergy and laity. You are going to repeal the tax on property altogether and lower the tax on income from a quarter to a twelfth."

The prince glanced at the ewer of wine once more, frowned, and faced me. "Why on earth would I do such a foolish thing? I want more money out of the filthy swine, not less."

"I'm sure Your Highness understands that the heavier the burden of taxes, the less of their own monies the merchants and peasants have to invest in their own pursuits."

"What concern of mine is that?" demanded Prince John.

"Their main pursuit, my prince, is the same as your own: money. If left to their own devices, they would take their additional funds and put them to things that would earn them even more money. At present, thanks to Richard's hungry pocketbook, everyone is poor. Every bit of revenue must be wheedled, tricked, confiscated in goods, or whipped out of the people—quite labor intensive collection practices I might add." I leaned back in my chair. "Allow the people to make themselves wealthy, Your Highness. Your smaller part of their much greater incomes will be double and double again what you are getting now."

I had to explain it to him again, as well as show him a few examples in figures, but at long last the prince finally understood that a twelfth of a prosperous something is greater than a quarter of a poor nothing. "There remains one thing that bothers me about your scheme, Sir Guy," said the prince. "Should I do as you request, and if things transpire as you suggest, the people—all of them—would be growing wealthier, fatter, happier. If they aren't starving, trodden down, and covered in filth what presumptions might they take upon themselves? How might they regard me?"

"For one, they won't join Robin Hood, Your Highness. Moreover, they will love you and make you their monarch."

That put him into deep thought. He nodded to himself several times, then rubbed his bearded chin, shrugged, and said to me, "I know it's foolish, but there is something still vexing me, Sir Guy. Where is the fear, the tears, the cries of anguish, the respect?"

I picked up the ewer of wine and poured wine for us both. As we lifted our goblets, I gave him a toast that explained the terrible sacrifice I was asking of him. "Becoming a good, beloved, and powerful monarch of a prosperous realm is the price you pay, Your Highness, for riches beyond the dreams of avarice."

4

Thence followed a series of vignettes that in the original flik showed Gisbourne's men taking money and goods from the people for taxes, with a bit of torture and enslavement thrown in for good measure. The policy changes ordered by Prince John in our Videoke II production, though, resulted in a quite different set of snippets.

There was a wealthy butcher handing over a leather pouch bulging with coin, blessing the commander of the tax collectors for the lower rate, for the convenience of cash payment at his own door rather than having to ride all of the way into the village, and for not having to fill out a lot of nonsense forms.

That was followed by Sir Guy's overseer, paying the increased wages of his farm workers, being informed all slaves in England had been freed upon orders of Prince John to help ease the climbing cost of labor. In both vignettes were villainous armed tax collectors who had taken to doing without arms or armor, downing tankards of free ale gifted them by the prosperous owners of a string of Nottinghamshire taverns. Weeping into their beverages, they bemoaned the bygone days of good King Richard when a truly corrupt and brutal official was feared as well as adequately bribed.

Wailed one fellow: "Oi can't get no respect!"

An additional new vignette was of a strange black troubadour clad in lime green with a buff leather waistcoat and green peaked cap topped with a reddish feather. He stood in the village green, a bow and quiver of arrows slung upon his back, his nimble fingers playing a lute.

Hear my tale of good Prince John,
Went to court with his brother gone,
Made English life both rich and good,
A-a-a-a-nd

Maketh a jerk of Robin Hood.

The fellow's lyric scanned not well at all, but the villagers enthusiastically applauded the verse and tapped their toes. The troubadour sang in a quite familiar voice. I frowned until I managed to squeeze from my imprint's memory whose voice it was: Mel Blanc. It was Mel Blanc doing the venerable animated cartoon character, Daffy Duck. Now the troubadour's yellow bill made a bit more sense. As Shad said, I'd know him when I saw him. No one in the crowd appeared to notice they were witnessing a cartoon duck singing in English and playing a lute. Considering it was Twelfth Century England, one would expect at least a witch burning or two. Videoke II, though: everyone adjusted to the character.

The next verse began with, "Poor Robin once had a bucket. . ." The remainder of the verse is not necessary to the furtherance of this tale, except to say it reflected unfavorably on the thief of Sherwood's manhood as well as his relations with his parents and certain barnyard animals. I wasn't terribly familiar with the law of the period, assuming whatever the monarch said goes. I wondered if Shad's plan was of the Tombstone ilk: to get Robin Hood to come to town in person and call Shad out, as it were. A quick-draw duel with bows and arrows in front of the Crystal Palace Pub ought to be diverting. Of course Shad's plan might be simply to have Sir Robin of Locksley sue him for liable and wear out the fellow's finances and patience with endless appeals.

Since Much the Miller's Son had been profitably occupied guiding wealthy weekend hunters at ten schillings a head, thanks to the new tax schedule as well other changes in Sherwood, there was no opportunity for Robin Hood to save Much from Sir Guy's men for killing the king's deer. (Much had another commitment, but promised Robin that they'd "have lunch.") Sir Guy and his men, therefore, weren't chased out of the Sherwood. They were, instead, gainfully employed enforcing contracts, gathering the tax monies, and prosecuting the few malcontents who insisted upon being criminals no matter how prosperous things became.

Meanwhile, back at the castle, recently installed regent Prince John was throwing a feast at Sir Guy's digs to celebrate John's coming coronation and to honor the presence of Lady Marian, Richard's ward, played by Olivia de Havilland. With her brocaded gown, black cape and head scarf, and that little gold cap thingy upon her head, she was absolutely lovely. It was an effort to keep my vision from going into soft focus every time my gaze turned in her direction. In the original vid, Sir Guy was supposed to be in love with Lady Marian, unrequited as it turned out. But what hath Videoke II wrought? Lady Marian spent her time at the feast leaning across Prince John, making eyes at me, and saying things most complimentary about the changes in England's taxation and law enforcement policies. She also admired the striking red and gold surcoat I had worn for the occasion.

"This old thing," I said deprecatingly.

"It makes you look very manly, Sir Guy," said she.

The prince looked at me and smirked. "Perhaps, Sir Guy, the pair of you should find a quiet nook in which to, eh . . . discuss fashions." The Prince's tongue in cheek suggestion was accentuated by a romantic tune being played upon a lute.

Lady Marian held her hand before her mouth and blushed.

I giggled.

I was halfway drawn to an indiscretion when I realized the music being played in the background was the old Hoagy Carmichael tune, "As Time Goes By." I looked above and beyond the feasting knights to where the musicians were playing their instruments and was not surprised to see Allan-a-Duck on lute. I couldn't imagine how Shad had managed that. Although Allan-a-Dale had a place in the print versions of the Robin Hood legend, the only troubadour in the Errol Flynn movie was Will Scarlet. Nevertheless, backed up by his band, Daffy began singing with the voice of Dooley Wilson.

He was cut short as Prince John arose and the great hall quieted. As soon as it was sufficiently silent, his highness said a few words acknowledging the loyalty of the assembled knights in his try for the crown. He was just about to announce what we had decided to do about Leopold of Austria's imprisonment of Richard, when a pounding came from the great doors. Someone commanded, "Open the door!" the background music began a swashbuckler riff, and the guards pulled open the doors to reveal Robin Hood, a dead deer across his shoulders, easily knocking aside with deer butt and antlers the two most inept pikemen in all the realm both of whom had been charged with guarding the door.

The great Errol Flynn as Robin Hood strode manfully into the hall, his deadly longbow clutched in his right hand, the animal still across his shoulders. He paused as soldiers crossed their pikes blocking his way.

"Who is this . . . this . . ." sputtered Prince John.

A computer-generated fellow with a big key dangling from his neck and only one line came to a halt in front of the prince and announced, "Sir Robin of Locksley, Your Highness."

"Let him approach," commanded the prince.

The pikes parted and Robin swaggered across the floor until he stood before his highness's table. From a security standpoint, it was barking-nutter insanity. Here is the sworn enemy of Prince John, mastermind of the Richardist terrorists, reputedly the deadliest archer in all of England, in possession of his weapons, and with a hundred or more pounds of who knows what stuffing a deerskin across his shoulders. All that and we allow him to come within a few feet of the person we were all sworn to protect. For an extra little sweet, the prince was unarmed. One could only hope that Peter Steerman would stick to the old script. He did, for awhile.

"Greetings, Your Highness," said the thief. "You know you should really teach Gisbourne hospitality. I no sooner enter his castle doors there with a piece of meat than his starving servants try and snatch it from me."

A chord on a lute sounded and a familiar voice from behind me sang to Robin,

"Gisbourne is rubber, thou craven knave. You are glue,
Yea, thy words bounceth off he and sticketh to you."

The assembly laughed uproariously at this—all but Robin of Sherwood. He pointed with his left hand at Daffy

Duck. "Allan! I know you! How did you get here, ungrateful Allan-a-Dale."

"The friendly skies," answered the duck.

"How you treat me. For shame," admonished the outlaw. "Did I not come to your aid when your future bride was taken by her cruel father to wed that scoundrel of a knight? Did I not rescue her, bring her to you, and stand with you when you two were wed? Is this how you repay me?"

And Allan-a-Duck answered with a strum of his lute and a verse:

♠

I had a love, which now is lost,
Her name was Barbra Ellen,
She had a beard and hands like frost,
And her feet were smellin'.

♠

Once the laughter subsided, the troubadour doffed his cap and bowed to Sir Robin. "I fear sirrah, that instead of my fiancé Ellen, you brought me the knight instead. I'm simply not a knight person."

In the midst of the raucous laughter, a bit wild-eyed with what he perceived to be Allan's mocking betrayal, Robin heaved the deer carcass from his shoulders over his head and onto the table in front of Prince John.

"Now what is this?" inquired his highness.

"I'll have you know," said Robin, "that I myself have killed a royal deer." He faced me, his eyes narrowing. "I believe that crime is punishable by death."

"An obvious case of attempted suicide by cop," offered the itinerant lute player.

"On the contrary, Sir Robin," I responded. "That used to be the penalty for killing a king's deer during the reign of Richard the Insensitive. Since Prince John became regent, that law has been removed from the books. Even if there were such a law, you would still be innocent of that crime. There are no longer any royal deer. I'm afraid you may have absconded, though, with someone else's property."

The scoundrel of Sherwood frowned and looked at the prince, who was carving a bit of mutton from the joint on his plate. He glanced up at Robin. "I'm afraid it's true, Sir Robin. All the king's deer have been sold. We rid ourselves of that holding, at a handsome price I might add, to a wealthy freedman named Sainsbury. I believe he intends opening shops all over England to sell venison and other surplus foodstuffs. Your difficulty is with this Sainsbury fellow, not with me."

"Sainsbury's got that meat going for two schillings sixpence a pound," said Allan-a-Duck with a smirk, "so bring your purse."

"Perhaps he could turn the carcass into Sainsbury's Lost and Found," I suggested, turning to Robin. "The fellow might even award you a small fee for harvesting his venison for him, although I fear that you failed to dress your kill. The meat may already be spoiled."

Sir Robin of Locksley then gave me a look that chilled me to my very marrow. My automatic reaction was an old, familiar fear and it tied my tongue proper. It was not Peter Steerman playing Robin Hood. Whoever was playing that part, though, was familiar. Deadly familiar.

"Is there something else?" Asked Prince John of the rogue. The regent turned to Lady Marian and said, "I fear the poor dolt expects to be seated."

She held a handkerchief before her face and said within the midst of a titter, "He isn't even properly attired."

Robin moved his glare from me to Prince John. "What of your brother, King Richard, Your Highness? What have you done about Leopold's demand for ransom?"

"I was just about to make an announcement concerning that very thing when you rudely interrupted us to boast about dispatching this poor woodland creature. Thank you for reminding me." Prince John stood and looked around at his assembled nobles, knights, and the lone detractor. "As you know, my brother Richard is a prisoner of Leopold of Austria. From Leopold I have recently received a ransom demand of one hundred and fifty thousand gold marks."

In response were gasps and grumblings in the hall at the brass of the Austrian duke. Good Prince John raised his hands for silence and the hall quieted.

"I responded," continued the prince, "by complimenting Leopold on his excellent wit—"

"Wit, Your Highness?" demanded an offended Robin.

"Yes. Wit. I mean the fellow wants money from us so that we might *pay* for the return of Richard as well as the return of all the poverty and strife that would follow him to England like so many mice after a bit of cheese. I call that a fine joke."

The guests at the feast dutifully laughed at the prince's words. "Poor Leopold," said the regent with mock compassion, the great hall quieting again. "Can you imagine what it must be like to be Richard's jailer? One's blood simply curdles at the thought: endless boasting, that crushingly monotonous poetry, not to mention his dreadful singing."

"A terrible fate, indeed, Your Highness," I agreed.

Prince John smiled at Robin. "Hence, I made Leopold a counter offer."

"What might that be, Your Highness?" Robin inquired.

The prince turned and nodded to me. I smiled and nodded back. We had discussed the royal response to Leopold's demands in some detail. Prince John faced Robin. "We have offered to take Richard off Leopold's hands if the duke will pay the crown of England *three* hundred thousand gold marks . . . what was that phrase, Sir Guy?"

"Cash in advance, Your Highness."

He thanked me with a gesture of his head and faced the outlaw. "Three hundred thousand gold marks, cash-in-advance."

The assembly—save Robin—applauded the prince's wise decision. The less of King Richard the better. Prince John had offered to regard all debts paid if Leopold would keep Richard *and* kidnap queen mother Eleanor, as well. The duke was having none of that. Crone and whelp giving voice together in his dungeon like a pair of rusty hinges would have driven poor Leopold out of his castle altogether. The duke, however, was still mulling over what to do about Richard and *our* ransom demands.

Sir Robin of Locksley then said something quite rude. Actually he said several rude things in a row, making Lady Marian blush as well as Allan-a-Duck, hard as it was to

294

see blushing upon a cartoon mallard. I recognized the phrasing, however. I could only hope that Robin's use of those particular expletives was coincidental.

Prince John bid us all return to our eating. His royal highness resumed his own seat and returned to his mutton. The audience was concluded.

Robin simply stood there with his teeth in his mouth, the veins on his forehead protruding like purple noodles. I turned to my right and Allan-a-Duck was sitting in the place occupied by the nameless sheriff in the original version of the flik. The old sheriff had been sacked, however, leaving the chair open.

"I say, troubadour, how ever did you get Allan-a-Dale into the production?" I asked him.

"Perfectly simple, sirrah," said Daffy grandly. "I've been following the development of Videoke II through the trades for years. Lots of little known features. Once I had a bit of time with the game control, I put in a print version upgrade. Hoo hoo hoo!"

"That explains Allan-a-Dale being here, but why as Daffy Duck?"

"They're both Warner Brothers compatible so the image was on file. Besides, how else would you be certain it's me?"

"I concede the point, but clarify something for me. Why would a Robin Hood production have an image on file for Daffy Duck?"

"Daffy once played the outlaw of Sherwood in *Robin Hood Daffy*. The golden age of comedy," responded a wistful duck. He leaned over and whispered to me, "You did notice the Errol Flynn Robin is about to pop his cork."

"He is rather tense," I agreed glancing at Sir Robin. The fellow's face was contorted with such a fierce mixture of hatred and frustration I feared his nat would go into a stasis bed stroke. "I'd rather not arrest him, though," I said to the duck. "Aside from the potential shoplifting charge, we have nothing on the fellow. Besides, in trying to capture him the sheriff's men and all these knights together couldn't accomplish anything except get themselves killed. I'd prefer some venue in which my boys have a better chance of capturing the rogue."

"The archery tournament."

"Yes—"

"You *will* attend to me!" screamed Sir Robin at the room. The room hushed. He had his bow in hand, an arrow nocked, the bowstring drawn back to his shoulder, the razor-sharp point of the arrow aimed at my heart.

"You notice that arrow is black," observed Allan-a-Duck as he nimbly jumped upon the table.

"Indeed," answered I nervously. "Rather ominous, wouldn't you say?"

Before Robin could let fly, Shad flew at him and grabbed the shaft of the arrow right behind the head. Robin stumbled back releasing the shaft. Duck and arrow took a wobbly flight up over the table and into a betassled golden wall hanging. I stood and addressed the fellow.

"You are becoming quite ill-mannered, Sir Robin. I would ask you to go now before you embarrass yourself further."

"The matter of the king's deer has not yet been satisfactorily resolved!" the thief protested.

There were two rather competent looking helmeted fellows, one on either side of Locksley, both of whom were looking at me, palms outstretched, and pleading with their eyes. Not at all certain what they had in mind, I nodded at them.

Thence ensued a series of moves that rather surprised us all, but no more than Robin Hood himself. The fellow on Sir Robin's left relieved the thief of his bow and sword while the fellow on his right relieved him of his dagger and quiver while at the same time coshing him with a rather big club. Both men then deposited the weapons they had collected to confederates standing close by, flipped Robin over, picked up the thief of Sherwood by his shoulders and the seat of his tights, and ran him out of the hall, the entire assembly close upon their heels. At the castle entrance, they stopped, heaved Robin through it into the dust and horse muffins, tossed his weapons after him, and had the guards close the doors to the cheers of Prince John's guests. I motioned for the two men to approach me. To my astonishment they were both weeping.

"Gaad bless ya, Mac," said the first with a distinctly American accent as he fell to his knees before me, kissing my hand.

The second fell to his knees and began slobbering over my other hand. "Tanks, sheriff. We been itchin' to do dat since Nineteen thirty-eight."

"But you're walk-ons, right? Extras? Computer generated images?"

The one on my left arched his eyebrows and said in hurt tones, "Yeah, but dat don't mean we ain't got feelin's."

5

Once we obtained a ladder and had a servant retrieve Shad from the tapestry, I bid good night to Lady Marian and the prince, then repaired to my quarters for a word with Allan-a-Duck, receiving several sly grins and knowing glances from my servants along the way. Once in my quarters, after plucking out broken and bent feathers, Allan-a-Duck began jumping up and down upon my bed. "Calm down, lad," I said to him. "I need for you to explain a few things to me."

On his last bounce, he landed with a flutter softly upon his posterior. "What's up, doc?" he inquired, crossing his legs and batting suddenly longish eyelashes at me.

There was a heavy writing desk with a single candle upon it which appeared bright enough to illuminate the entire chamber. I pulled an oaken chair from before it and seated myself. In the vid there are no scenes which take place in Sir Guy of Gisbourne's apartments. Therefore, the room's furnishings were from my own imagination. Aside from the huge canopied bed, the rest was disappointingly Spartan. No carpets, no chests overflowing with gold, not even a change of armor. Mounted upon the wall to my right in a gilded frame and done in the style of Boris Vallejo, however, was a lavish painting of a voluptuous Golden Tonkinese cat seated upon a turquoise cushion and wearing the slightest suggestion of a veil across her lower face. It was Val.

"Hubba hubba," remarked the duck accompanied by a remarkable set of eyebrow calisthenics.

"How much do you know about Videoke II?" I asked him.

"Just what was in the trades and on the spoiler sites," he answered, turning away from the painting. "What do you want to know?"

"First, is it possible to have a private conversation, removed from the audience?"

"No." He faced a wall to my left, waved, and said, "Hi, folks!" He faced me. "Everything that happens during the course of the story can be seen by the viewers. All of the filled roles can see all of the scenes that correspond to scenes in the original vid—like those vignettes of your boys doing their tax collecting—but completely new scenes can only be observed by those in them. When you and I are in a scene like this, no one in the story but us can see or hear what we're saying."

"We're on continuous synch with our bodies in stasis, right?"

"Yes, and before you ask, no we can't utilize our wireless packages. Out of period."

"Is there no way to communicate from where we are now to the outside—outside of the Videoke II reality?"

"Just directly to the audience. They can't communicate with us, however. What's up?"

I gestured with my head toward the blank wall that had come to be the audience in my mind. "Shad, there is more to this thing than an entertainment."

"Like what?"

"Take notice of the following, old lute-plucker: First, you and I were specifically invited to come here supposedly because we had been such a smash as Holmes and Watson."

"Okay."

"Next, we meet up with a prison officer who is employed at Belmarsh, which houses a number of very old Category A prisoners who owe their residency there to my years as a murder cop in Metro."

He rubbed his bill with a finger. "Go on."

"Next, Shad, there is Cecil B. DeMille: Carlton Zane, the alleged producer and director of this epic. He totally ignores Watson and goes to great lengths to get me to play the Guy of Gisbourne role, which has absolutely nothing to do with Sherlock Holmes—the original justification for our presence, as you will recall."

"Hoo hoo," said Daffy, signifying deep thought. "The plot thickens."

"Zane's last name is an anagram for a fellow I put away for murder . . . it had to be twenty-four years ago. Karl Enza. Vicious fellow. Didn't look a thing like Cecil B.

DeMille, but was almost a perv on wearing riding boots until we got him in the nick."

"Which, coincidentally, made him a Category A prisoner in Belmarsh," added Shad.

I nodded. "Yes. If I recall correctly, Enza has been out a few months."

"So, what's he up to?" asked the duck. "Is he Robin Hood?"

"No. For awhile I thought it was that old cove in one of the stasis beds when I went under."

Daffy nodded. "Wasn't that Pete Steerman, the inventor of Videoke?"

"I believe it was, Shad. What's more I don't believe he's participating at all in our little drama as one of the characters."

"He was definitely in stasis. If he isn't in the vid, what?"

"Our friend Robin Hood, Shad. He looks and sounds like Errol Flynn, but the look in his eyes, the way he reacts to having his plans thwarted, his gestures, temper, the pattern of veins across his forehead, not to mention his language, all remind me of a quite nasty fellow I once tossed in the nick named Red Toddy Cole."

"The Kensington Butcher," said Shad softly.

I nodded. "Fourteen killings of which we know," I added.

Allan-a-Duck frowned for a moment then looked at me. "The guy's got to be near seventy years old."

"Seventy-three, Shad, and full of cancer. I put him in Belmarsh thirty-two years ago—"

"—Belmarsh again," interrupted Shad. He looked puzzled for a moment, held out his wings, and said, "So, what's going on? What's he trying to do? Make you look bad?"

"That's certainly a part of it, but I think there's more. I believe Toddy has figured out a way around the engram tattoo block all prisoners get to prevent a prisoner's imprint from escaping confinement through electrical routes. Somehow, when this drama is finished and we return to our old selves, I believe an old cancer-ridden killer in a Belmarsh recreational stasis bed is going to come up an imprint short."

"Breakout," Shad said to himself. "Think he's figured out a way to wind up in Mr. Steerman's nat?"

"Or in my own bio, old duck. As you know, Robin kills Guy of Gisbourne in the drama's big action finish."

"Why would he need two meat suits in stasis? In case he errs, a spare?"

"Possibly. He couldn't have depended solely on us showing up today."

Daffy looked slyly at me. "Do you think Watson is watching?"

I glanced at the blank wall, shrugged, and shook my head. "Wasn't he snoring when I went under?"

"We could do a Tinkerbell," he suggested cryptically.

"Eh?"

"You know. You say to the audience if you want Tinkerbell to live, clap harder. Might wake up Watson."

"I don't believe Tinkerbell is at any risk in Nottingham."

"No, but someone sure is," he said hopping off the bed and walking to the blank wall. "If you want the Sheriff of Nottingham to kill Robin Hood, clap your hands!" He raised his arms and jumped. "Clap harder! *Clap harder!*"

Nothing.

"Put it up, lad. You're embarrassing yourself. No one is going to cheer on the Sheriff of Nottingham to execute Robin Hood. That would go against the entire grain of Western civilization. And even if they did clap and Watson did wake up and did appreciate our predicament, what on earth might he do about it?"

Allan-a-Duck turned from the blank wall, his shoulders slumped. "One trembles at the possibilities," he admitted. He looked up at me. "So, we cut to the archery tournament?"

"Yes. We cut to the archery tournament," I agreed. "Perhaps we can end this thing in a scene or two and then get some answers."

Red Toddy Cole in a healthy younger meat suit and loose upon an unsuspecting population to commit his grisly killings again was neither something I wanted to see nor have a part in bringing to fruition. He had to be stopped. To do that, however, it appeared that Sir Guy of Gisbourne,

301

Sheriff of Nottingham, would have to do something he had been unable to do no matter how many times he'd tried since the mid Twentieth Century: He'd have to kill Robin Hood.

Allan-a-Duck went off on an errand and left me alone. There in my quarters, I pondered. The archery tournament, with its prize of a golden arrow presented by Lady Marian, was an appeal to Sir Robin's twin weaknesses: pride and lust. Robin always fell for it, but I had my doubts that Red Toddy Cole would. Toddy was a clever killer, his signature being a lack of repetition. The only pattern common to all of his scenes of crime was practically nothing forensically useful. Early on the higher ups in Metro decided the Kensington Butcher had to be a scenes of crime officer, police officer, or private detective, all of which turned out to be untrue.

A single two-by-five millimeter spatter of blood upon a wall, that tiny droplet incongruent with the shapes of the victim's substantially larger contribution, was how we eventually put the nab on Toddy. Seems the killer had given himself a slight cut in the tip of his left ring finger while he concentrated on butchering his latest victim. He hadn't noticed. Once we identified blood at the scene that didn't belong to the vic, DNA pointed to Toddy Cole, a hardware engineer for Peach Computers, who also was as it happened very well read in forensic evidence. It came out in the trial my singularly plodding unimaginative approach, personally examining and measuring every spatter of blood at every scene—hundreds and hundreds of thousands of them—was what eventually led to Cole's arrest.

When I came down from the witness box, everyone in court heard Cole whisper to his barrister: "No one on *earth* has that much patience!"

Toddy misunderstood. It wasn't patience. Instead it was a white-hot searing abhorrence of this killer that I somehow needed to channel into some mundane task simply to keep my sanity. So I studied endless one-to-one images of blood spatter until I found the droplet that put away Red Toddy. It got me the George medal, but more importantly, it got me Red Toddy Cole in the nick. And now, had I guessed correctly, Toddy was Robin Hood. He had come on like the old Errol Flynn Robin—bold, brash, and deadly—but in the end had allowed himself to be tossed from the castle door as though he were a penniless vagabond rudely ejected from a pub for lack of payment.

I glanced at the blank wall wishing there was some way to find out what *they* knew. I had a bad feeling about the whole thing. Toddy used to design and build computers. I could barely use my wife's Ding Dong Dell to put in a search or call into Heavitree Tower. In my universe Toddy had evaded detection and capture for more than two years. Now I was in his universe and really wasn't up on the rules.

"You can't *all* be confederates of Toddy Cole," I said to the wall. But, I said to myself, they could all be gone by now. How much trouble would it have been to have the theater screen malfunction, apologize, and empty the theater. That would leave Toddy and his three friends a free hand to wait until the game ran out, diddle with the sync unit, then collect Toddy's engrams and put them into an unoccupied bio. It would probably be mine. Red Toddy knew enough about police language, science, and procedure to take my place. What a platform from which to launch his new series of killings. Before that, though, he'd also have to wipe out Shad Gort and Shad Watson—

—My mouth went dry as I thought of something else: If Red Toddy Cole was going to relocate his hideous efforts to Exeter, he'd also have to get rid of Val. It seemed my only hope was to get Robin Hood to the gibbet and this time do a proper job of it.

6

The tournament the next morning began with trumpets, knights mounted upon horses parading around the jousting grounds surrounded by hundreds of computer generated commoners cheering before the marquees within which were seated Prince John and his guests, which included the Lady Marian and myself. Lady Marian was seated on the prince's right, I was seated at the prince's left, and to my left was Daffy Duck, who turned to me and said, "I hope our little golden hook will catch the fish."

"You hope?" posed Prince John, speaking across me.

"Oh, it will, if he's here," the duck assured his highness.

"If he's not," said Prince John, "we'll stick your head upon the target and shoot at that."

Allan-a-Duck gave out with a predictable hoo-hoo-hoo which the Prince surprisingly took within his stride. I gave Shad a look that had every particle of confusion I possessed in its expression. "Someone had to deliver the sheriff's lines, Jaggs," he explained quietly. "I mean, you had Melville Cooper sacked."

"Upon your suggestion, ducky, I might add. Would I be rash in thinking this means Daffy Duck is now heading security at the tournament?"

"Brother did I talk fast. I was appointed consultant to the captain of guards this very morning. And why not? I'm an experienced police officer and detective, hoo hoo hoo."

"And you sing filthy songs, play the lute, and occasionally get your bill shot off by Elmer Fudd. Are your men sure of their orders?"

"Actually, I wanted to talk to you about that. Last night I began wondering if any of Toddy's chums in Belmarsh might be among the merry men. I thought it might be a good idea to know who is computer generated and who isn't."

"How?"

"Oh, I still remember some of the cheat codes from the Videoke II spoiler sites. Anyway, there are a bunch of the merry men in the crowd right now—they're pretty easy to spot—but none of them are filled roles."

"They're all computer generated?" I asked.

"That's what I'm saying. Even Tuck, Little John, and Will Scarlet. They're using their own names and aren't in disguises. I talked to a couple of them and I don't think Robin Hood has any men, merry or otherwise."

"He's alone?" I asked.

"Toddy Cole's confederates all appear to be outside the game. I also checked his highness and Maid Marian. You, me, and Toddy boy appear to be the only players. Everyone else is computer generated."

I rested my chin upon my fist. "Shad, one cannot say too often, I have a bad feeling about this."

The duck looked out upon the field and pointed. "My boys are stationed all around the field. I put those two who pitched Robin out the front door in charge."

"They talk as if this were a trap," said Lady Marian to the Prince.

"Indeed it is, my dear," said his highness. "We're hoping to draw in that rude fellow who marred your arrival at Nottingham Castle, clap him in irons, and put him on trial for murder."

"Dear me," said the maid. "Who has he killed?"

"Why . . . I'm afraid I don't know." Prince John frowned for a moment then looked at me. "Sir Guy?"

"He'll kill someone before the day is over," I said.

"Now, Sir Guy, how can you possibly know what will happen in the future?" the Lady Marian asked.

"I have it on the very best authority, my lady." I held a hand out toward the duck.

Shad thought a moment then said, "Richard's astrologer has been out of work ever since he failed to predict the king's kidnapping. I got him to do a reading for me at a bargain rate."

"Well done, duck," I said to him.

"You never want to say 'well done' to a duck," he cautioned.

It was announced that the champions of Sir Guy and the knights would shoot an elimination round, the winning team to meet all comers. As they loosed their arrows, Shad was hunched down in thought, a bit of cartoon smoke rising from his head. "What is it, Shad?" I asked.

"Well, right about now in the original vid is when Robin and his gang lieutenants arrive on the field: Little John, Friar Tuck, and Will Scarlet."

"You said those three are already here."

"Yeah. I did." He stood and glanced at me. "Got to check on something," and before I could ask him what, he was gone. I am so much more confident in playing a game if I know the rules. I suppose Shad was suffering the same discomfort.

The elimination round concluded, the winning team of archers, began competing as individuals: Captain Phillip of Arras, Elwyn the Welshman, and Matt of Sleaford. I vaguely recalled that the person playing Phillip, Captain of Archers in the original vid, was Howard Hill, a championship professional archer who had taught everyone else in the original motion picture how to shoot arrows without looking foolish. In fact it was he—off camera—who had performed the famous shot in which he had split his own arrow. Even if Robin Hood had made that shot, as the story held, what was Toddy's scheme?

Why walk into the camp of the enemy all alone? Why risk the exposure, I asked myself. This taunting behavior was quite consistent with the profile Metro had developed on Toddy Cole. How close could he come to getting caught and still escape for the single purpose of showing up the authorities. Robin Hood and Toddy actually did have much in common. Robin Hood however was doing his deeds in service to that maniac and royal nutter, King Richard. Toddy Cole was serving an even darker demon: his own twisted mind.

I looked around for a likely tree from which to hang the scoundrel straight away. Little point in wasting expensive court time on a pointless trial. If that was indeed Red Toddy Cole's imprint on Errol Flynn, the sooner Flynn's neck was stretched and Cole's imprint shunted back into Belmarsh the better. The longer this went on, the more chance Toddy had of turning the tables on us.

I was distracted by Lady Marian leaning across Prince John to say complimentary things to me—lovely woman, Olivia de Havilland—

"Matt of Sleaford, out!" called the official refereeing the contest. "Elwyn the Welshman, out!"

"Ah!" exclaimed Prince John. "The tall tinker."

I did not urge Robin's immediate arrest as did Gisbourne in the original vid. Instead I said, "I think we shall wait on taking him, Your Highness. I'm curious as to how the match will finish."

"I'm having the men move in," said Daffy. I turned and saw that he was back.

"Finish your errand, ducky?"

"Yeah. There's a fourth and fifth filled roles in this production, Jaggs."

"Really. You, me, Toddy, and?"

"I don't know who they are. I'm guessing it's your boy Enza and the prison officer or maybe that creepy technician. In any event, one of them is coming as King Richard."

I held a finger in front of my lips. "Keep your voice down. Richard doesn't come into the story until much later. Are you certain?"

The tall tinker loosed his shaft and it hit the center of the target to the cheers of the crowd. Prince John issued a compliment and asked if Lady Marian had ever before seen the fellow. While she answered, Shad gave me a string of numbers and a code phrase which I repeated. Suddenly fixed over my vision appeared a semi-transparent map showing all of the players in the game and their locations: Shad and I in the marquee, Toddy out in the field, and the mysterious fourth and fifth players out on the village road moving toward us at the jousting field. There was a cursor I could move. Over my spot and Shad's it showed our character names. Over Toddy's spot appeared "Robin Hood." Over the third spot appeared "Follower #1." Over the fourth spot appeared "King Richard."

The captain of archers loosed his shaft, and the official called it, "Tie! You will be allowed another flight."

"Target's a deal too close," said the tinker to the official. "Can we have it removed to a fit distance for men to shoot at?"

The official looked at Phillip of Arras and the captain of archers nodded his agreement. "You know," said Shad, "Howard Hill had not a single line in that entire movie. I always suspected he had a voice like Goofy."

"Another twenty paces!" shouted the official.

The lackeys in the red hoods picked up the target and ran it another twenty paces down the field. Prince John said to me, "If your archer captain wins at that distance, I'll give you a thousand gold marks for him."

I nodded. "Thank you, Your Highness. Perhaps he can use the funds to find a suitable voice coach. Have you heard news of Richard?"

"Not a whisper, Sir Guy. I fear that Duke Leopold thought our offer less than amusing." His eyebrows arched. "Have you heard something?" King Richard's spot on the village road moved across Prince John's nose.

"A bit more than a whisper, Your Highness." I turned to Shad. "How do I get this dratted map out of my field of vision. It's quite disconcerting."

He gave me the cheat code and my vision cleared in time to see Phillip of Arras loose his shaft toward the target. it struck dead center. I faced the cartoon stand-in for Melville Cooper. "You were about to say?"

"I'm not a betting duck. However," in a louder voice he continued, "Why he can't win now. No living man could beat that shot. I'll wager my broken yo-yo and piece of blue bottle glass on Phillip of Arras."

The tinker nocked an arrow and pulled it back to the strains of mounting tension music. He loosed it and we all cut to the target to show Phillip's arrow being split by the tinker's.

"He split Phillips arrow!" called someone, presumably the official. "The tinker wins! He wins."

"Instant playback!" shouted Daffy. "Bad call! Bring that cross-eyed umpire over here!"

The referee—wide-eyed and mouth gaping—was dragged by a hefty pair of guards before Prince John. His highness faced me, and said, "You dispute the call, Sir Guy?"

"I do, Your Highness. If you will permit me?"

The prince gestured with his hand toward the official who had made so errant a call. "Fellow," I said, "you called that the tinker won, did you not?"

"I did, my lord. The tinker's shot fair split Captain Phillip's arrow."

"I still do not see, my good man, how this constitutes a win. Did not both arrows strike the target in the exact same place with neither closer to the center than the other?"

The official thought upon that for a moment, and then nodded. "Aye, you are correct, Sir Guy. It was a tie." He turned and faced the field. "It is a tie!" he called to the crowd. Turning toward the remaining contestants, he called, "You will be allowed another flight."

Then, in a really fine voice reminiscent of Gregory Peck's, Phillip of Arras, captain of archers, said, "Perhaps we could have the target moved back a wee bit further. Say another *forty* paces."

The official looked at the tinker, who was looking just a bit wild-eyed. The tinker paused, then nodded at the official.

The official pointed down the field. "Another forty paces!" he called.

It was the tinker's turn to shoot first, but he bowed and said to Phillip, "After you."

The captain of archers smirked at the tinker, bowed toward me, then nocked an arrow, pulled the shaft to his ear, and let fly. The arrow struck the target dead center. The crowd erupted in cheers.

The previous pair of shots had been programmed into the scene by the original vid. This new wrinkle was made up out of the give-and-take between my imagination, Shad's, and Red Toddy Cole's. It also had a bit to do with Toddy's skill level as an archer *versus* Howard Hill's.

The tinker took his place, nocked an arrow, pulled the shaft back almost to his ear, and let fly. The arrow flew so quickly its flight could not be followed by eye. All could see, however, that it did not strike any part of the target. Then came a cry and all eyes turned to see Little John downrange at the right side of the field standing with an arrow stuck in his arse. He teetered a moment, then fell upon his face.

"Excellent choice," observed the duck. "Landing on his other side would have been a genuine tragedy."

"You were right, Sir Guy!" said Lady Marian. "He did kill someone."

"Phillip of Arras wins!" called the official. "He wins!"

The cheering crowd hoisted the captain of archers to their shoulders and carried him to the royal marquee, depositing him before Prince John, Lady Marian, and myself. Prince John stood and said, "I pronounce you champion archer of England. And from the gracious hand of Lady Marian you'll receive your reward."

A page liveried in blue and holding a matching blue pillow with a golden arrow upon it knelt before Lady Marian. As she took the prize to pass it onto Phillip, I turned to Shad. "We'd best get our business with the loser sorted out before Richard arrives."

Daffy drew his thumb—I never realized ducks had thumbs—across his throat. I nodded my agreement and we repaired to the field where several burly guards, including my two Americans, were holding the tinker prisoner. "To the nearest tree," I called to them and they began hustling Robin Hood off to the edge of the field opposite the royal marquee where stood several suitably sturdy oaks.

"Somebody bring a rope!" called Allan-a-Duck. Several hands bearing coils of rope went up in the air. I hoped we wouldn't have to have another contest to see which hangman got the honor of stringing up Sir Robin of Locksley.

Never to worry. By the time we arrived at the tree, someone had already thrown a noosed coil over a sturdy branch and was eagerly gripping the tugging end. One fellow was tying Robin's hands behind him while a second put the noose around the outlaw's neck. During all of this the subject of the exercise put up no resistance. Instead he stood, awaiting his elevation, a tiny smirk upon his lips.

Once all preparations had been completed, silence. All that could be heard was the continuing celebration from across the field as all rejoiced at Phillip of Arras's long awaited victory, not to mention Howard Hill's.

"He's smirking," said Allan-a-Duck to me. "King Richard could be riding a rocket and not get here in time to save him."

Robin Hood's smirk vanished. "Richard?" he said with a frown. "What's he doing here at this point in the tale?"

"He's not here quite yet, Sir Robin," said I. "You did not expect him and his followers? Your friends Enza and Graziano?"

The outlaw fell silent, but his face was in a frown, the smirk barely a fleeting memory. "Pull him up, Sir Guy?" called the hangman. The cry was picked up by the other guards.

"Hang him! Hang him! Hang him!"

Bleeding hell, all I could think of was that pack of yobs in Trafalgar Square, their knives out, all of them shouting, *"Kill him! Kill him! Kill the bloody copper!"*

"Jaggs?" I felt someone shaking my arm. I looked and it was the duck. "If we're going to do something, we'd better get to it. Richard and his boys just came on the field."

In the distance I could see Ian Hunter as King Richard followed by several knights in Crusader garb riding up to the royal marquee. Before they could pull up their steeds, however, one of the knights pointed in our direction and shouted to the king. Richard had his mount change direction and spurred it along, his knights accompanying him. When they reached our side of the field, the king pulled up his mount, noted the position Robin was in, then looked at me and said, "Heavens, Holmes! Whatever do you have in mind?"

I felt my jaw drop. "Watson?" I said at last.

"Of course, dear fellow. Here to save the day, wot?"

"Just a little late," interjected Allan-a-Duck. He looked suspiciously at the nameless knight who had pointed us out to the king. "And who might you be, sirrah?"

"My, look who it is! I loved you as Dorlock Homes in *Deduce, you say*. What a treat!"

"And your companion is?" urged the duck.

"Forgive my thoughtlessness," said King Watson. "Sherlock Holmes and Daffy, I would like to introduce you to Sir Peter of Steerman, the inventor of this entertainment."

"Pleased to meet you," I said.

"Likewise," muttered the duck. He pointed at Robin Hood. "You have any idea who this is?"

"Certainly," answered Peter Steerman. "That's renowned murderer Red Toddy Cole. What are you intending to do with that dreadful rope?"

"We had thoughts of pinching off the electronic escape of Red Toddy from Belmarsh by the application of a bit of oxygen depletion."

"Admirable goal, Holmes," said King Watson, "but your method is faulty." He bowed his head toward Steerman.

"Thank you, Your Highness," said Steerman. To us he said, "Killing Robin Hood actually releases Toddy Cole's engrams to imprint on any nat or bio in the system still in stasis."

"That's why Robin made killing him so easy," I observed for my own benefit.

Steerman climbed down from his steed and walked over to the outlaw in the noose. "Cole worked on the plans for some time, I gather. Once he'd invented the hardware to circumvent the tattoo block, he wanted to have a confederate take his plans and build the necessary equipment outside Belmarsh. Before that could be arranged, though, I unwittingly aided him in his attempt by inventing Videoke II. Along about the same time he heard of you and your partner putting on a Sherlock Holmes and Doctor Watson charade out there in Exeter. He wanted so much to involve you. I gather he harbors a bit of resentment there."

"A tad," I agreed.

"Well, by then Karl Enza had been released, Prison Officer Graziano had been bribed, and all that was necessary was to get you to the VidFest. Lewis Parson, the stasis technician, was another recently released inmate from Belmarsh. Terrible things he used to do to persons in stasis."

I looked at Robin Hood, and asked Mr. Steerman, "What do you suggest we do with him?"

"Order your men to lock him in your dungeon and throw away the key, I suppose."

I looked at my men. "You heard him."

Slightly let down at the hanging being called off, my men pulled the loose end of the noose from the tree and led Robin Hood by his neck off to the dungeon.

"What now?" asked Allan-a-Duck.

Peter Steerman looked toward King Richard. The king chuckled and said, "Holmes, you astound me. At times I wonder how you ever got this reputation as a great detective. Everyone knows what happens now."

"What?" I demanded.

"The End," he said.

7

Upon awakening in the stasis bed, I heard the Korngold score playing, opened my eyes, and saw the playing cast list for the production, amended by the addition of the game players' names. I looked to my left and Shad Gort was coming out of it and checking the credits to see if his name was mentioned. It was. Midway down the list it showed that the role of Allan-a-Dale had been played by Gort. He humphed and did a quick check with Belmarsh. Prisoner Toddy Cole was in his own head and back in prison hospital. I felt something within me ease up and relax.

On my right Shad Watson was chuckling to himself, repeating "The End." On the other side of Watson Peter Steerman was sitting up and entering notes into a handheld. "Inspector Jaggers," he said after a moment, "you have given me a terrific idea for an entire new game platform. I mean, you turned Prince John into a great monarch and England into a prosperous nation all without altering the little tyrant's motives a whit." He shook his head. "When I think of the applications—the fall of Carthage, the Inquisition, the Great Depression, the invention of bubble-wrap—" He looked at me. "I'm going to call it Historioke. Who says you can't change the past?"

"Excellent, Mr. Steerman, I said. "There are any number of persons I know who'd like another crack at Cromwell. What I'd like to know, however, is how you and Watson managed to get into the game and save the day. Where are Enza and Graziano? Also, that technician who looked like John Carradine. He had to have been in on it."

"I don't know," Mr. Steerman responded looking to his left. "Dr. Watson?"

Watson chuckled again. "Those three boys are now in the custody of our colleagues of the Hertfordshire Constabulary, Holmes. You see, the audience began clapping and raising such a din—"

"Tinkerbell," said Gort wondrously.

"Yes, by gad, where was I?" floundered Watson. "Oh, everyone in the audience shouting for the sheriff to kill Robin Hood. I don't mind saying it was a bit of a surprise."

"I can imagine," I said. "Please go on."

"I looked at the monitor but before I could see what was happening, those three blokes came running in here to escape from the audience." He shook his aging gray head in wonder, then shrugged. "So I captured them, turned them over to Hertfordshire Constabulary, brought Mr. Steerman out of stasis, and asked him what we should do. He knew all about Toddy Cole's escape plans. After he removed a couple of cards from the program console that Enza had forced him to install, he said that the one thing we must do is not let Robin Hood die. We went into stasis, entered the game, and the rest is Historioke, wot?" He chuckled again.

"Well done, Watson," I said, "but how did you manage to overcome those three men?"

Watson reached into the right pocket of his jacket and pulled out an ugly black handgun that looked to be an old .38 Police Special. "Everyone forgets that Dr. Watson is the one with the gun."

"My god!" I cried. "How did you get that in here? Where did you get it?"

He waved it my direction and I ducked as good as I could while still in a stasis bed. "I picked it up at that Fabulous Forties Fliks exhibit," he said. "You know, that dreadful Tracy and Hepburn couple?"

"Yes," I said warily, trying to figure out how to get the gun from him without getting anyone injured or killed.

"They have boxes of these things over there." He turned the weapon until it was pointed at his own face, opened his mouth and put the barrel inside it.

"No!" we all cried.

Watson bit off the end of the barrel and began chewing. "Licorice, you know." He looked across me at himself in the walking mech. "I'm really surprised at you, my boy." He dangled the shortened candy pistol in the air. "How could you ever forget Tracy and Hepburn in *Adam's Rib?"* He took another bite of his weapon and chewed contentedly.

♠

That evening, at the walnut paneled and softly illuminated Celebrity Lookalikes facility in Bond Street, Shad and I were both surprised at how sad we were to see the Nigel Bruce bio wiped. Watson had, in the end, saved the day. Melancholy as we were, I didn't think Shad would insist on his night on the town. He insisted, nonetheless. Because of all the positive attention the Watson bio had drawn to Celebrity Lookalikes—After the news of Toddy Cole's foiled escape, Lookalikes had to hire a firm to handle the publicity—the manager, a Uriah Heepish bit of a fellow, Mr. Manfred Coates, insisted on forgiving the remaining amount Shad owed on the Bruce, which was a considerable sum. When Mr. Coates heard about our detective couple's night on the town, he magnanimously threw in the evening's hire on any two meat suits on the premises. Astoundingly generous gesture. He also had a bit of news for me. When they wiped Watson they did a software analysis and found that the Sherlock Holmes patch in Watson had been faulty. It had never been transmitted to my bio receiver, hence there was no need to uninstall it from me.

Shad proffered the theory that I had been channeling the real Sherlock Holmes through spiritual means. I had a different theory. After the trauma of getting so brutally murdered in London and how it had affected me, perhaps I was now, at last, getting back my abilities as a detective. "But whatever am I going to tell Val?" I asked Shad, still in the large mech. "When I return, she expects her Harry to be there and Sherlock Holmes to be gone. How can I tell her Sherlock was never there in the first place?"

Gort rubbed his chin with his right forefinger, the titanium-on-titanium friction producing a sound that made the sound of fingernails scratching on slate more beautiful than a Mozart serenade. "I say lose the tweed hunting jacket, the meerschaum bubble pipe, the deerstalker cap and you'll be okay. Did you ever get that violin?"

"I think I can still cancel the order."

"Shrewd move." He swiveled his head until he was looking once again at the Nigel Bruce suit. "We did have a few interesting times as Holmes and Watson."

"It had its moments," I agreed.

"Gentlemen, Mr. Shad's replacement bio is ready for viewing," said Mr. Coates as he bowed and rubbed his hand together. We went to a curtained viewing port, Coates pulled the curtain aside, and we looked. It was a mallard duck, the old Guy Shad in every respect, "and without the load of birdshot in his butt," my partner observed.

Mr. Coates smiled, rubbed his hands together once again, and asked Shad, "Have you decided upon the bios for your night on the town, sir?"

"Yes," he said.

"Who did you pick?" I asked him. "I'd like to see you as Nero Wolf sniffing an orchid."

"It's a surprise," he said.

"Isn't it always," I muttered to myself.

When I awakened in the stasis bed, got up and looked at myself in one of the mirror walls, I was a bit confused. I was big, fortyish, with a massively well-developed musculature. I was wearing a glossy full-length black leather overcoat over a deep purple suit with matching shirt and necktie. I looked down and the shoes matched the suit. My skin was the color of coffee with one cream, excellent teeth when I grinned, wraparound sunglasses, a glossy black leather cap on my hairless pate, and a thin black moustache with a smidgen of chin scraggle. I removed the glasses and stared myself in the eyes, searching for a name.

"Avery Brooks," I said at last, more than a little disappointed. I was Hawk of Spenser and Hawk, and I had always been somewhat disappointed in the *Spenser For Hire* vids. In the old Robert B. Parker mystery books, Spenser and Hawk were a deadly combination who did what needed to be done, vanquished their opponents—often terminally—and did so cleanly with grit, wit, and intelligence.

The Spenser series of vids too often played their heroes for laughs, the bad guys catching them unaware in situations that would never fool the print duo.

I saw Robert Urich as Spenser stand next to me on my right, also looking in the mirror. "Cheer up," he said. "I got the Spenser and Hawk print book upgrades."

"I didn't think Avery Brooks was this well developed," I commented, flexing a bicep and restraining it just in time from splitting that beautiful overcoat.

I replaced the glasses and gave Spenser a good silent look.

He gave his left shoulder a tiny shrug and cocked his head to one side. "Thought I'd like to do a little sightseeing. I've never seen Trafalgar Square at night. I checked with Metro and, you know, your old crowd still hangs there."

"Do tell."

"I thought if we went over there to take in the sights, we might run into a familiar face or two."

"By run into a face or two," I said, "you mean that figuratively."

"We can do that, too."

Spenser reached over and handed me a fistful of quite real-looking stage money. "And this?" I asked.

"Carry these with the ends sticking out of your pockets"

"A-hah."

"A-hah?" Spenser repeated.

"I hear you say it sometime, gumshoe. Figure it mean something profound." I waved the stage money at him. "This be lookin' just a tad like revenge."

He shrugged and gave me an innocent little boy look. "We're merely a couple of wealthy American sightseers in town to look over the mother country."

"Mother," I repeated.

"Certainly no one can object if, when attacked by a bunch of ruffians, we defend ourselves." He raised an eyebrow. "It's good you have someone smart like me to explain things to you."

"It an honor to be associated with a master sleuth," I said. "Tell me something, Spenser, one thug to another."

"Certainly."

"What about, '"Vengeance is mine,"' sayeth the Lord'?"

"I always considered that a very selfish attitude."

"Indubitably. But rules be rules."

"You think so? I always considered them kind of like guidelines, but if you'd rather not—

318

"Not so fast, you hazel-eyed devil. Already gave it a think." I pursed my lips as I chose my words. "See it like this: we not getting medieval on a bunch of thugs as much as we restoring balance to karma."

Spenser nodded. "That's right. We're not looking for a fight; we're seekers of sights bringing spirituality to a troubled land. What a wonderful rapport we're having."

"You get full collision and liability coverage on these karma suits, maharishi?" I asked him.

"Uh-huh. Coates threw that in, too."

"Good man, that Coates. Does he understand that what happens in London stays in London?"

"Discretion is his middle name."

"Hard going through school with a funny name."

"I don't know, Hawk. Manny Discretion Coates has a certain ring to it."

I took a deep breath, acknowledged the remaining pockets of fear within me, then exhaled. It was going to be an interesting outing. "So, shall we see if Admiral Nelson is still up there on his column?"

"Let's do," said Spenser.

"Metro said there were eight of them?"

"At least."

"That make the odds about even."

"Hawk, you ever wonder how odds could be even?"

"Not even once."

He opened the door for me, I went through, and the pair of us walked south toward Piccadilly singing "A Foggy Day (In London Town)."

♠

MURDER IN PARLIAMENT STREET

-1-

"Cold and windy, dreary and damp," muttered Detective Superintendant Marvin Matheson. "No wonder Guy Fawkes chose November in which to kill King James and blow up bloody Parliament."

It was a day after that particular celebration, but apparently superintendent was still celebrating. No knock-knock jokes which meant he was really down the pipe this time. Matheson was standing behind his desk, his hands clasped behind his back, head hung forward, eyes looking up through a frown and his office window at the gloom of the latest weather front. Superintendent's early model police replacement meat suit strongly resembled a historical American gangster named John Dillinger. I for one never wished to see John Dillinger depressed. Media ridicule of that model meat suit, in combination with his wife's insistence he keep it, lost Matheson his position as Assistant Chief Constable of Greater Manchester. He was eventually deposed in Artificial Beings Crimes Division of Interpol as a lowly detective superintendent running ABCD's Devon office in Exeter. Never quite let go of that.

"You wanted to see me, superintendent?" I said brightly.

He slowly turned his face toward me. "Jaggers."

"Yes sir."

He turned and looked down at his desk. Twice he tapped on a few papers with the tip of a stylus. "It has been pointed out to me, Inspector Jaggers, you and Shad deserve a day off principally in recognition of your work on the Hound Tor and Hangingstone Rat inquiries. That recommendation, incidentally, came directly from Middlemoor." He smiled sadly. "I heartily concur."

That took me back a step. It was uncommon at best to have any mention at all of ABCD issue from the rarified climes of the chief constable's office. Well known to us all, ever since a particular award ceremony, Raymond Crowe, chief constable of the Devon & Cornwall Constabulary, had been rather frosty on the subject of artificial beings, particularly on amdroids in law enforcement. Perhaps we were coming up in the world. "Good news, sir."

Matheson almost maintained his sad smile. "Nice spot of media buzz on both cases, Jaggers. Shad and you have the rest of the day and this evening off. Pass on the word to Shad, if you would be so kind."

"Thank you, sir, I will. Doesn't that leave the office a bit shorthanded? Towson called in sick."

"Stay on call, but Parker should be able to handle anything that comes up." He gave himself a moment of silence thinking upon DC Ralph Parker, incontinent flea-infested gorilla. His sad gaze elevated until it rested upon me. "So, Jaggers, how is Shad settling into his replacement duck suit?"

"Well enough, sir. There are a few glitches, but he looks and sounds like his old self."

"A bit embarrassing him renting that Watson meat suit from Celebrity Lookalikes after his duck caught it at Hangingstone."

"That was a Nigel Bruce suit, sir, made up to look like Dr. Watson."

Matheson shook his head and looked again at the gloomy sky. "Damned silly. You looking like Basil Rathbone and Shad doing his Watson. Damned silly. The chief constable put a bug in my shell-like when he heard about it, I can tell you."

"Remarkable amount of cooperation we received from the public, though, sir, as Holmes and Watson, not to mention Buckingham Palace. CC Crowe, in addition, appears to have forgiven us with this suggestion of a day off."

Matheson looked confused for a moment then sloughed it off. "True. Mercurial man, the chief constable." He turned and faced me. "I find it hard to tell with a duck,

Jaggers, but at times Shad seems rather depressed. Still recovering from the Hangingstone thing?"

"I don't believe it's Post Traumatic Stress Syndrome, sir. As you know better than anyone else, no one ends in ABCD by choice. Being a star on the telly must have been very exciting for him."

"He didn't find getting blown to pieces exciting?"

"I hardly think he regards that as a job perk."

"I suppose not." He shook his head. "Those adverts Shad was in: You suppose there's anything to that insurance?" He waved a hand at me to fend off my uninformed answer to his idle question. "All rubbish now they've gone to that slimy little yob of a lizard for a mascot, isn't it. In any event, some time off will do Shad and you both some good. AB Emancipation Week, you know. I may take the missus out tonight myself." He sat down, opened a file, and said without looking up, "Try and enjoy yourself, Jaggers. Hate to waste a perfectly good gesture."

It *was* going to be a good night out. I called Val with the news and she suggested a double date with Shad and Nadine. I put it to my partner and Shad decided to shake off his mood and agreed to go with us to a showing of *The Adventures of Robin Hood* at Exeter's Picture House. Aside from our own contributions to the Robin Hood saga, part of the film's appeal to the AB community was the strong resemblance of Dr. Hitchins, the current Archbishop of Canterbury, to the actor Eugene Pallette who played Friar Tuck. The archbishop was a very outspoken—dare I say rabid—opponent not only of AB rights but of AB existence, which is why Eugene Pallette always drew some good natured booing from the ABs in the audience every time he appeared on screen.

Shad and his date shared a seat. Val, of course, watched from my lap while I scratched her ears. I had disabled my wireless interface, the theater was darkening, the new stadium seating was packed with just about every kind of artificial being in town, bio and mech, amdroid and android, as well as the occasional human natural. The flik had barely begun when Shad's head went back, shook, and faced me, his bill dropping open. I sighed glumly knowing

322

either it was a call from Heavitree Tower or Shad was suffering a massive stroke. Either way the evening's entertainment was concluded.

"It's Parker," Shad quacked.

"Told you to disable your wireless."

"Exeter cops have a dead bio, Jaggs. Parker says it's on Parliament Street and he can't fit. What's he mean he can't fit?"

"It means he's too big to fit in the street," I answered curtly as evil Prince John and the sheriff conversed up on the screen. "Call in the cruiser and run up the mechs." I bent over and said to Val, "I'm terribly sorry, dear, but we have a call."

"Harry," Val purred, "Nadine and I can make it home on our own. You two go and take your call."

"We'll be fine," Nadine mewed to Shad. "Take care."

I stood and put Val down on the seat as Shad hopped off their seat and followed me out into the aisle at a brisk waddle.

Outside the sky was dark, the wind coming up from the Exe dank and chilly. Tarp fields protecting the unfinished new apartment construction across Bartholomew from the theater cast the street in a powder blue glow. I turned up my collar against the chill, but only a bit to conserve the charge.

"Cruiser's on the way, Jaggs. Parker says he's running his command post out of Broadgate."

"Shad, do you still have that can of flea spray we picked up from the chemist's last time we worked with Parker? I can't afford to bring an infestation home with me again. Val is terribly sensitive."

"That can's gone," said the duck with a smirk, which is not easily done with a bill. "I mixed the flea spray in the can with deodorant, had the mix put in a cut glass atomizer I got at Boots, gift wrapped it, and gave it to Parker during that fireworks show yesterday."

I frowned. "Guy Fawkes Day."

"Whatever. I told Parker it was cologne. Eau Le Monk, all the rage among the simian set, and Merry Fawkesmas. He was quite moved."

"Guy Fawkes attempted blowing up Parliament, Shad. We don't usually give presents on Guy Fawkes Day."

"I imagine that depends on your opinion of Parliament. Parker is, however, using the spray."

"You are a devious duck."

"Thanks. Now, if we can only get Parker to make it to a loo before he a takes a dump there will be peace in our time." He looked up in the direction of the Pennsylvania—St. Thomas Corridor, the traffic in the air vector sparse at this time of night. "Here's our ride."

The cruiser, an issue gray and electric-green Sky Rover Metropolitan, descended in front of us, its green strobe array flashing, its doors rotating up as the wheels touched down on Bartholomew. Shad flew into the driver side and I entered the passenger side, checking the mechs in back on my way in. Parker could've used a mech to work his crime scene, but he numbered copying among his many phobias and there was simply no point in arguing with him about it. Green readouts on the bed panels showed mechs operational, charged, internal laboratories stocked and ready, our engrams as of this morning copied into the Heavitree mainframe.

Doors closed and as the cruiser ascended toward the corridor Shad said, "Do you Brits have a weird spelling for parliament?"

"Why?"

"I entered it twice, but this heap's GPS doesn't have a listing in Exeter for any Parliament Street."

I looked at the GPS readout. "You spelled it correctly. Parliament isn't on the cruiser response GPS. Put the cruiser down on High Street in front of the Guildhall."

"A secret street and Parker can't fit in it?"

"No secret but neither Parker nor a cruiser can fit. You'll see why."

He waited a moment for a further explanation. When none came, he said, "Be mysterious."

Grumpily Shad guided the cruiser through the Cathedral Vector Roundabout. No sooner were we through it, the cruiser dropped from the corridor and headed toward the illuminated columned gingerbread of the medieval Exeter Guildhall immediately below us, still the oldest working municipal building in Britain. High Street, though, was choked with bright lights, news vehicles, and a crowd. The media were in force.

"Is the king visiting?" asked Shad.

"Not to my knowledge." I looked around. "Change of plan," I said seeing a place nearby where we could put down unobserved. "Behind the Guildhall, Market Square in the shopping center. Put us down just beyond that small church." I reached forward and flicked off the switch for the light array. The entire block of buildings, of which the Guildhall was only one, was a warren of little streets, shops, and walks which had been turned entirely over to foot traffic and enterprise. The lot of it was called the Guildhall Shopping Centre. At this time of night, the shops were closed and the walkways mostly deserted.

Shad changed course slightly and nodded toward the square and the tiny ancient church constructed from local red stone. "Isn't that church St. Pancreas?"

"St. *Pancras*, not pancreas." I saw the duck laughing silently. "As you well know," I added, dreading my partner's delight once he found out the block opposite the High Street end of Parliament Street had another old church called St. Petrocks.

After Shad settled the cruiser down next to the small stone church, I had us both copy into the micros. With them I hoped Shad and I could get to the scene without drawing attention.

Once copied into the lipstick-sized vehicles, our usual meat suits in stasis, we flew from the vehicle and Shad put the cruiser up in hover park. At an altitude of approximately two meters we flew around the west end of the tiny church into a shop-lined walkway that led to the north end of Trickhay Street walk. We streaked south between the furniture stores, gadget emporiums, wireless shops, restaurants, tea shops, and AB boutiques passing only a lone bipedal dustmech with attached dustbin. He was attempting to scrape what appeared to be a flattened wad of chewing gum from the pavement.

"Bloody AB Emancipation Week, me tin arse," the dustmech muttered. "Doin' the same bloody thing and payin' bloody taxes for the privilege is all it is. Bloody wankers in bloody Parliament, tossers the lot—"

We turned right when we came to Waterbeer Street walk, leaving the unhappy mech and his soliloquy on unrequited expectation behind. After only a few meters we came to a police constable standing by himself in the dark. His hands were clasped behind his back, his stocky form fairly filling the hundred centimeter-wide entrance of a long narrow walk between two buildings. Partly obscured by his shoulder on the right-hand wall of the walkway was a regulation size traffic sign that read: Parliament St.

"I can see why Parker can't work the scene," transmitted Shad out of the cop's hearing. *"He'd need a shoehorn to get in there."*

"It's even narrower at the High Street end," I responded. *"Imagine Parker dropping a load as he tried to wriggle his way into the crime scene in front of all those cameras. That would've been a proper cock-up. Turn on your lights, Shad, go on external audio, and let's log in with the constable."*

We were both hovering in the dark in front of the fellow's face. When we turned on our lights I'm afraid we startled the poor chap. He jumped, bellowed, screamed, and swung his arms about.

"Detective Inspector Harrington Jaggers and Detective Sergeant Guy Shad, Devon ABCD," I quickly introduced us.

The constable froze for an instant, let out a breath, then bent over to pick up his helmet, muttering about bloody pips, the noun modified by an additional Middle English adjective or two. Some words simply never go out of fashion.

"Police Constable Styles," he introduced himself as he stood, a rather peeved expression on his face. Styles was a big ruddy-looking chap in his late twenties, sandy-haired and attempting rather fruitlessly to raise a moustache. After brushing off his helmet, he replaced it upon his head, smoothed his yellow anorak, adopted a stiff military posture, and said, "Now then. You're the Interpollys."

"Detectives Artificial Beings Crimes Division of Interpol, Devon Office, actually," Shad said using his Laurence Olivier playing Marcus Licinius Crassus voice. Quite intimidating, even coming from an illuminated flying lipstick.

"No offense there, detective," said the officer stiffly. "But, you two bits pop out the dark all sudden like a couple eyeballs from bleedin' Hell. Not half taken aback I was."

"Our apologies, Styles," I said. "We were trying to avoid the media tumult at the High Street end. Do we log in with you?"

"Sergeant Dunn, sir." He gestured with his head toward the walkway he was guarding. "Sergeant's at the other end. He sort of expected you to report there."

"Indeed. Are you chaps responsible for all the media attention? On High Street it looks like the resurrection and marriage of Princess Di and Elvis."

The corners of Styles's mouth turned down as he shook his head. "Don't understand it. Nowt there but a dead bird."

"It was reported to us that the deceased is a bio," I said.

He shook his head and turned down the corners of his mouth. "Can't prove it by me, inspector. Looks like any other old sky rat to me." He grinned. "No shortage of pigeons in Exeter, is there," he said with an attempt at jocularity that faded rather rapidly as neither of the pips hovering before him reacted. The corners of his mouth resumed their downward turn.

"If the victim is a bio," said Shad, still as Marcus Licinius Crassus, "it probably carries a human imprint, Styles. It may be a murder victim."

The police constable shrugged his wide shoulders, his face devoid of expression. "Not paid to worry about bios," he said. "Your job, now, isn't it. No offense, detective, but the bloke couldn't of thought much of hisself getting copied into a pigeon suit. Might as well've copied into a toad or a flippin' dung beetle, right? Besides, amdroids all got real bodies tucked away in stasis somewheres, don't they?"

"Some do," began Shad coolly.

"Thank you PC Styles." Outside of Styles's hearing, I transmitted to Shad, *"Stop turning your crank and follow me."*

"The bozo," Shad muttered as we swooped into the dark narrow passage, the walls on either side made of poured

composite glass, smooth but tinted to look like brick. The only illumination came from the lights on High Street.

As we reached midway in the walk, my light picked up a small still figure on the left near the northeast wall. We descended until we were next to it. The corpse was indeed a pigeon. The bird was lying on its right side on the cracked gray paving, his head toward High Street, his dark pink toes curled up, landing gear retracted in death. The bird's feathers were disheveled particularly on the side against the pavement. There were a few spatter marks near the corpse that could have been blood. I went to audio. "Shad?"

"Yeah?"

"Be a good fellow and notify Sergeant Dunn of our presence. Ask him to make available whoever it was who reported finding this body over at DC Parker's command post. Also, explain we're shorthanded and ask Dunn to keep his men on duty until we clear the scene."

"You got it."

As Shad streaked toward High Street, I played my lights down the length of the bird, measured it's dimensions and calculated its weight. It was a common Rock Dove model, bluish-gray wings, no wing bands but white coloring along the wings' leading edges. It had a partial white ring around its neck, open in the front, and its breast was a warmer hue than the rest of him. The bird's head coloring was darker, but not iridescent toward the neck as you see with so many pigeons. As the general run of pigeons go, this one was neither handsome nor unique. It was almost as though this model had been chosen for its dullness—its ability to blend into a background.

I checked my instruments and picked up the fading marker beacon of a bio receiver. This was how one bio could always identify another as a bio, which meant the one who discovered the body was likely an amdroid or human bio. I opened the mech's neural reader and checked the pigeon's imprint and recall bank. Both zeroed out. Unless the occupant had been on continuous sync with a neural net or a body in stasis, the memory information was lost to wherever such energies go after life can no longer sustain them.

"We're logged in, Jaggs," transmitted Shad as he returned. "I don't get it. That Dunn seemed really irritated we didn't come in from High Street. There're two mechs out there from the Forensic Medical Examiner. Dunn says he'll send them in to haul off the vic once we're done. There was a newshound out there who says you know him."

"Fidelis?" I asked.

"That's the one. Sniffs out tips for BBC 228? I know him from Rougemont Gardens."

"I've thrown him a bone on occasion. What does Fido have to say about the news frenzy out on High Street?"

"He was told to be there and to be heavy with camera. Worthwhile story alert."

"Any idea what the story concerned?"

"I got the definite feeling everyone out there is expecting to catch someone official with his pants down."

"Really." I thought on that for a second then shrugged. "Shad, scan the vic, get a liver temp, DNA, and ID while I set up a prang and fly the grid. Analyze this spatter here, as well."

While Shad got to work, I pulled away and up until I hovered approximately ten meters away from the corpse toward the shopping center end of the walk. Because of the narrowness of Parliament Street I couldn't both get a good view and a solid fixed wall position upon which to mount the Vader prang. I attached one end of a high-tension poly web to one building wall about four meters up, stretched the web across the street, and attached it to the opposite wall. Mounting the prang in the center of the web, I remotely activated it. Once it settled down it began making a three-dimensional wideband record of the scene and I began a grid search of the entire space between the walls.

The walkway was unobstructed relatively clean concrete, it's condition making the paving more than fifty years old. Save for the images of a couple of false doors imbedded in the glass below and images of a couple of false windows and exhaust ports four stories above, the building walls were simply two solid featureless slabs of poured glass: Modern, secure, low maintenance. When I got to the High Street end I looked out at the crowd. Although the curiosity seekers had thinned somewhat, the media reporters were just as thick as before and not moving. Nothing to see at that end; no one issuing statements. The tip they had gotten must have been made of solid gold—or that's the way they were regarding it. I returned to the grid.

I noticed a small whitish feather stuck on the southwest wall approximately three meters up from the corpse. I closed on the site and hovered across from it. UV light showed a variety of organic materials such as bird waste, skin cells, and a small amount of medium-velocity blood spatter. It surrounded the feather in a vertically elongated impact pattern. In normal light there were a few microscopic red fibers scattered through the lower right portion of the pattern. I took images of the site, retrieved samples of the fiber evidence, took DNAs from the skin cells, feather, and blood, then measured the impact pattern to compare with the corpse's particulars to calculate impact angle, force, and trajectory.

"Jaggs," said Shad, "The spatter on the walk is medium-velocity blood matching the vic's. Pattern is the result of ground impact on already present surface blood. The vic's wound is on the side against the ground. Scan shows several broken bones on the bird's right side: Two in the right wing, five ribs on the right side of the breast. Wing and rib bones broke the skin. Dead about four hours."

"Around Five this evening, then." I transmitted my data. "Does this match your DNA?"

A pause. "It's a match," answered Shad. "What do you have?"

"Blood, a feather, and some additional material. It appears that the deceased was propelled against the southwest wall from below—perhaps someone throwing the body up against the wall. It bounced, the trajectory arced up and the body landed next to the opposite wall. Evidence would indicate that the vic was already dead."

"Kids playing handball with a dead bird?"

"Only one wall impact. Do you have the area surveillance camera locations yet?"

"Working."

"ID?"

"No name yet, Jaggs, but Bio Registry says this is one of a super flock of eight thousand basically identical pigeons purchased from London Industrial Biotronics four

330

years ago by a private security firm headquartered in Slough called Pureledge, Ltd."

I descended toward Shad and the corpse. "Are you telling me that bird is a private dick?"

"Rent-a-cop. Pureledge hires out to keep real pigeons off of buildings, monuments, and out of the ground transit stations. Remember the old movie, *To Catch a Thief?*"

"Certainly. Hitchcock film. Cary Grant and Grace Kelly." I fought manfully for the date, but had to relent. "Released in the Nineteen sixties, yes?"

"Fifty-five," corrected Shad.

"Set a pigeon to catch a pigeon."

"Jaggs, I'm going through Pureledge's site right now. Pureledge has an office here in Exeter on Castle Street. It runs three wings of three hundred and twenty birds per wing." Shad paused for a moment. "*Ledge marshals* is what they're called."

"Shad, did you get any fiber trace off the body?"

"Red fiber. Only one thread visible, the rest microscopic. All of the fibers are centered on the same impact point that broke all these bones. You have red fiber up there?"

"All microscopic. The impact pattern on the wall shows the bulk of the fiber trace considerably off center, though. Between that and the blood spatter, when the bird hit this wall his bones had already been broken and the body already bleeding. What's your guess on the fibers?"

"It was wrapped around whatever killed this bird."

"Shad, do these ledge marshals maintain continuous sync while on duty?"

"Their site doesn't say and no one right now is answering the phone. Jaggs, did you know this was how they were keeping pigeons from nesting on building ledges?"

"I noticed a dozen years ago or so in London when they took down the pigeon netting from several of the buildings there. I never thought to question why. Pigeons still seemed the same. Fewer of them, perhaps. Buildings and walks were remarkably cleaner. Get in touch with Pureledge Exeter and have them check vitals on their stasis beds. What's on the other sides of these walls? A computer establishment on the northeast side, right?"

"Dell Bio & Mech. It's an AB tech gift shop. In the building on the opposite side is Madame Fifi's Feather, Scale, and Fur. She's an amdroid stylist."

"The vic was killed elsewhere, Shad. Why dump the body on Parliament?"

"Say, Jaggs, how come this—it's not even wide enough to call an alley—how come this particular crack between two buildings is called a street?"

"I'll have you know, Shad, Exeter's Parliament Street holds the record as the narrowest street in the world. As it was explained to me on a tour when I first came to the city, it had to do with some act of Parliament in the Nineteenth Century. The burghers on the city council took exception to the act, but really couldn't do anything in retaliation except deliver an insult to the body that passed it. Hence they named the narrowest thoroughfare in the city Parliament Street. Rather silly, really."

"Not at all," objected Shad. "I mean, here we are centuries later and Exeter *still* has a Parliament Street. That is vendetta-grade grudge." Shad's mech nodded. "This town is really beginning to grow on me," he said as he streaked off toward High to release the scene to the FMEs. Despairing for Shad's value system, I ascended to the roof, flew grids on each, but found no cameras, latents, trace, impressions, feathers, scales, nor fur.

I had just completed my examination when I was joined by Shad's micro coming over the High Street edge. "Someone at Pureledge finally answered the phone," he announced. "ID on the imprint is a six-month Pureledge rookie named Darcy Flanagan, eighty-seven, resides in a flat at Seventeen Hoopern Street. He began his shift at three this afternoon and he and his flight leader belong to 712 Squadron. The Seven-Twelve patrols the Cathedral Church of St. Peter."

"Flight leader? Squadron?"

"That's what they call them. The fellow on the phone said the scuttlebutt in the ready room at Castle Field is that Jerry got young Darcy."

"Jerry? What is he talking about? Germans?"

"'Hop in the old crate and tally ho! Chocks away!' Jaggs, it was like talking to Fowler in *Chicken Run*."

Fowler, the aged and absurdly militaristic dotty rooster in the old Nick Park animated feature—voice done by Benjamin Whitrow—seemed to think he was in the Royal Air Force rather than a chicken yard. Every AI, and particularly every amdroid, knew the classic *Chicken Run* almost by rote. Decades ago the beheading-of-Edwina scene on the telly and bio blogs in combination with the U.S. Supreme Court's decision in Grant *v.* Hudder helped put the AI Rights Act in Britain over the top. "What did he mean, 'young Darcy'? You said the fellow was eighty-seven."

"Average age of 'the lads' is ninety-three," countered Shad.

"I see."

"Ledge marshals maintain continuous sync between bodies and bios, which would be good for us except they checked what they call their barracks. Darcy Flanagan the human natural is dead."

"Poor fellow. Did they say how?"

"Sudden massive heart attack according to the stasis bed readout. Too severe for the bed to maintain him and he was past revival by the time their medical mech reached him. Pureledge has a lot of really old pensioners as ledge marshals. They make a little cash and for a few hours a day they get to fly, serve a useful purpose, and feel young and pain free, according to the fellow on the phone, a Mr. James Duggan. Duggan says six to eight of the old coves cack out in the barrack racks every year, another seven or eight onliners at their homes."

"Hard done by Flanagan's demise, was he?"

"The poor guy could hardly butter his crumpet. Jaggs, the stasis bed recorded Flanagan's death at eight minutes to five this evening. The pigeon bio died eleven seconds later. Unless Flanagan managed to bust up his own pigeon suit like that, it's murder. That means media." The duck tossed his next question around in his head a bit before reluctantly asking it. "What do we do about Parker?"

I thought on that. "To be perfectly candid, Shad, I'm not terribly sanguine about having our end of the enquiry represented by an incontinent gorilla with self-esteem issues."

His micro swung around and looked deeply into the shadows. "Man, I can't believe I've come down to this. When I was the spokescritter for that insurance company, I used to have *staff,* bill polish, ermine feather extensions, my own dressing room. You should've seen my apartment in New York, Jaggs. I had a *fountain* in my living room. Ledge marshals! Gorilla poop!"

"Those, Shad, are the challenging, exciting, ever-changing facets of a fulfilling career in ABCD law enforcement."

He dropped a heavy sigh and shook all over. "Sorry about the whining. About Parker, the division doesn't need any more bad air. Do we go to Matheson and take over the case?"

I pushed Shad's suggestion around in my mind for a moment. Neither Shad nor I were there to hurt other cops, especially those who, like us, had been flushed down into ABCD due to mishap, misunderstanding, or murder. I'd already put a smudge on Parker's record by refusing to work with him. The whole Parliament Street case was looking, however, like a giant slapstick aimed directly at ABCD Devon's collective posterior.

"Back to the cruiser, Shad, copy into our own suits, and secure our evidence. Then we report to the command post and see where things go from there."

2

In the cruiser, copied into our own skins, Shad gave the Sky Rover instructions to come up on Broadgate by a circuitous route. By swinging out over Queen Street, heading southeast, and doubling back over St. Peters Cathedral, we might lessen our chances of attracting notice.

Shad faced me. "What if Parker cut back on the bananas? Less in, less out."

"Been tried. The fellow is addicted. He has them squirreled away everywhere. A few months before you came to the Devon office, Shad, Parker and I were assigned to represent ABCD at an award ceremony at the Royal Diana Devon & Cornwall Force Museum theater."

"Handing out attaboys to the local blue?"

"Yes, although we call the medals *gongs*. A very solemn occasion officiated by Chief Constable Crowe. In attendance were two Members of Parliament, the Earl of Devon, and Her Royal Highness Princess Mehitabel. Matheson and I took Parker's bananas away, dehydrated him, and tried to keep an eye on him. Nevertheless, he managed to tuck away a bunch or two before the ceremony."

"Naw. He didn't," said Shad.

"Oh, indeed he did, ducky. What's more, Parker didn't even notice he'd done it. Nothing quite like a fellow dropping his load before royalty right in the middle of bleeding 'God Save The King'."

"Make the news, did it?"

"Shad, Matheson's office was showered with media thank you notes and fruit baskets.

"What'd the superintendent say when you all got back to the tower?"

"He called us into his office, pointed at his telly, and stared at Parker, his finger trembling. Matheson's face went bright red and he did a respectable impression of a beached

335

cod. Then he waved us out of his office, came up behind us, and slammed the door."

"British reserve, wot, wot, Jaggers old sock?" he said using his Fowler voice.

"Frightening, actually. The superintendent really does bear a striking resemblance to John Dillinger. I half expected to be perforated by a Tommy gun. He ordered Parker into therapy."

"To potty train him?" asked Shad.

"That's what it amounted to." I looked down through my window. The red air-vehicle warning lights above the crenellated spires crowning the Norman towers of St. Peters glowed softly on and off below. "He went faithfully twice each week and Matheson received in return a lot of cleaning bills and the therapist's conclusion that gorillas—gorilla bios, in any event—cannot be trained in that regard. There are no internal warning signs noticeable to the gorilla, so the gorilla simply delivers wherever it is whenever a shipment comes in."

"Like the old joke," observed Shad.

"Yes. Wherever he wants."

Shad glanced down through his side window. "Oh boy. Hey, Jaggs? We're over Broadgate. I don't see the ABCD van." He placed the cruiser in stationary hover.

He banked the cruiser my way and I looked down. Opposite Dell and Madame Fifi's side of High Street was St. Petrocks. Between the block upon which that church stood and the block opposite the Guildhall was Broadgate: a short, wide, shop-festooned thoroughfare connecting High Street and Cathedral Yard. Parked in Broadgate were three tellynet media vans, a blogosphere pool mobile, a Devon Forensic Medical Examiner's van, and a constabulary electric, presumably Sgt. Dunn's. There were no vehicles of any kind belonging to ABCD and no ABCD personnel I recognized, not even a furtive mountain gorilla in the shadows stealthily evacuating his bowels.

"Bugger," I remarked.

Shad's comment was earthier but equally apt.

There was nothing to do but head to Heavitree Consolidated Police Administration Tower in which the constabulary's Exeter Station, Devon ABCD Interpol, and the Devon Magistrate's Court were headquartered. As the cruiser came down from the St. James—Heavitree Air Vector Corridor, Shad brought us in over St. Luke's College and Heavitree Hospital as we circled down to the sky dock on top of the tower. As we approached we could see that the media had already gathered far below at street level entrance. Up on the roof by himself someone very large, dark, hairy, and dejected was skulking next to the landing target. It was Detective Constable Parker. After coming in and docking in our assigned slot, we got out of the cruiser and walked across the target to the fellow.

As we approached Parker, Shad said to him in his Fowler voice, "I say, old hairball, the ruddy bloomin' corpus is in the middle of flippin' Parliament Street. Don't Heavitree Tower strike you as rather inconvenient for a local command post, wot, wot?"

Upon witnessing Shad's passive-aggressive performance, Parker's massive shoulders sagged even farther as his incredibly ugly head hung down, his knuckles dragging against the rooftop.

"Terribly sorry, Inspector Jaggers," he said, his voice rumbling eloquently in posh Oxford-educated tones. The urgency of his current predicament appeared to have frightened off his occasional ape-of-the-people Estuary affectation. "I had the van on Broadgate, sir, but the tellies, bloggies, and shutter rats were everywhere waiting for me! Peering in the windows, underfoot, poking in their heads, all of them on geek hunts, and, good lord, the *questions*. Cameras . . . all aimed at the van. It was like they were waiting for me to . . . you know."

"Yes," I responded. "I know."

"I didn't want to let down the side again, inspector. I couldn't've fit in that narrow passage in any event. Wouldn't the tellies love seeing me try, though. That's why I asked for someone else to work the scene. I'm so grateful to you and Sergeant Shad."

"You did the right thing, Parker," I said.

"You see why I had to get out of there, don't you?" The gorilla was motionless for a split second, then grew a bit wild-eyed. He suddenly grunted loudly, smacked his fist against the edge of the concrete landing target, cracking it. Suddenly Parker began turning about in a tiny circle, waving his heavily muscled arms above his head.

"Steady," I cautioned as I backed away almost stumbling over Shad who had managed to get behind me.

Parker stopped, lowered his arms, and slumped. "Sorry. But will no one in this bloody city ever forget that damned awards ceremony?" He thumped his chest angrily with his fists. Seeing that he startled me again and caused Shad to take wing, he said "Sorry. Terribly sorry, sir. Sorry sergeant." He was even more crestfallen.

Shad settled further away from the gorilla. "Keep cool, Ralph. Okay?"

"Yes. Sorry."

"What seems to be the trouble, Parker?" I prompted.

He sadly shook his head, his gaze somewhere around my feet. "It all began at Royal Diane. Before that ceremony I was just another cop bio trying to make a place for himself in ABCD. After that ceremony I was a world-wide joke. There were tourists here last summer from Kazakhstan, inspector. *From Kazakhstan!* Their children had these bloody little animated stuffed gorilla toys! They sing 'God Save The King' and then poop little licorice sweeties! I simply can't bear it!"

"I never got my own action figure," muttered the duck sullenly.

Parker held out his massive hands. "Princess Mehitabel has forgiven me. I wrote her soon after . . ."

"After the goods were delivered," completed still sullen Shad.

"Her Highness's secretary wrote me a few weeks ago. He wrote—well, his letter said that Princess Mehitabel understands completely, stuff happens and not to worry myself over it. Water under the bridge." He let out his breath with what appeared to be his remaining resolve and looked up at me. "Inspector, should I tell the superintendent I can't handle the Parliament Street enquiry? If I lead this case, the media'll make a laughingstock of all of us."

Shad and I glanced at each other for a beat, the duck shut his eyes, shrugged, and nodded once at me. I faced the gorilla. "Detective Constable Parker, you have an enquiry to run and I suggest you run it. Shad and I have worked the

338

scene and we're prepared to brief you on the evidence and the progress of the investigation. We will also back you up however we can. Leading this case will give you much needed experience. I expect you to make the most of it."

There was a touch of panic in Parker's expression. "It's not just a dead pigeon, is it, sir?"

"It's murder," said Shad. "Murder most fowl," he added with a straight face.

"Shall we get on with the briefing." I suggested.

"Yes, inspector." Parker looked up at me with sad yellowish eyes. "What ever shall I do about the media?"

"Later we'll need to prepare something. Right now we need to know how you wish us to proceed."

Parker stared at me for two seconds, then frowned, reared back until he was at his full height, puffed out his chest, and bellowed, "Very well!" He thumped his chest with both fists several times, and bellowed, "Very well, then! We'll grasp the nettle, shall we? On to Room Nine fourteen!" On his knuckles and feet he scooted toward the access door, nearly ripped it off its hinges, and all thirty-five stone of him disappeared down into the stairwell, his parting cry of, "Jam tomorrow!" echoing from below.

Something of stunned silence descended upon the roof. I glanced at my partner. "What happened to his accent?" asked Shad.

I shook my head. "For some reason he's returned to Received Pronunciation. I believe he only adopted Estuary to fit in, which he really never did."

"I hate it when that happens."

"Oxford graduate, you know."

"I'll be a monkey's uncle."

I hoisted an eyebrow in Shad's direction. "Murder most fowl?"

The mallard nodded. *"Murder Most Foul,* directed by George Pollock starring Margaret Rutherford, Nineteen sixty-four." Looking sideways at me, he said, "Foul, fowl, dead pigeon—get it? Huh? Huh?"

"Yes, yes. I quite get it," I acknowledged painfully. "Thank you."

"Any time. Give any thought to how we're going to work this case with Parker running it? I mean, he gave you the perfect out. Why didn't you take it?"

"As I recall, Shad, you nodded at me."

"That's because I'm a big marshmallow. You're a tough old ex-London Metro murder cop and our leader. We depend upon you to keep us out of silly predicaments."

I frowned deeply. "Shad, surely you see if Parker quits this case because he's frightened of the media—"

"—Among other things," interrupted Shad.

"For any reason. Parker's not stupid. He's just—"

"Six cashews crazier than a Nutter Bar."

"Shad, if he doesn't lead this case and win doing it, he'll be useless in the future both to ABCD and himself. We cannot stand by and watch that happen."

"I suppose not." Shad examined my face for a moment cocking his head to one side. "There's something else, though, isn't there?"

My gaze rested momentarily on the distant ground vehicle lights circling the St. Sidwell Roundabout west of the tower. "This insane degree of media attention over what appears to be a less-than-interesting case. Add to that the timing."

Shad nodded. "You and I suddenly get the evening off, Towson's out sick, Parker's holding the fort all by his lonesome."

I nodded. "The one detective who because of his copy phobia and size couldn't possibly fit into the scene of the crime, the one detective who with each public bowel movement brings into question the seriousness of amdroids being in law enforcement at all, he's the one who catches the case."

"I checked the tower call log, Jaggs. Your newshound buddy Fido got the call to come to Parliament Street a good fifteen minutes before the Exeter cops notified ABCD."

"Record on the call?"

"Throwaway mobile. Do you think that's what the killer wants: ABCD to fall on its pratt and to look ridiculous in doing so?"

"Or someone using the occasion created by the killer. One question that remains to be answered is at whom this exercise has been aimed: Parker or ABCD."

Shad cackled out a wak-wak-wak laugh. "If it's Parker, that makes Nigel Towson our prime suspect."

Despite an involuntary smile, I shook my head. "DS Towson may be dogging it, but he's the grandfather of by-the-book cops. Former Royal Canadian Mounted Police, you know."

"Yeah." Shad shuddered. "I heard about that grizzly attack in the Yukon. Lucky his head was found by that RCMP tracking unit and they could copy his engrams into one of their bloodhound bios."

"Yes. And as soon as he finished copying, he continued tracking down the killer he'd been after. Got his man, too. A lesser cop would've gone after the bear."

"The media should hear some of these stories—how the cops in ABCD got here—rather than focusing on Parker's poop and all this silliness," Shad declared.

"Wouldn't that be a treat. The media have programmed this city to expect ABCD to fall on its face and have a big laugh every time we do. Our success with the Hound Tor case, though, and getting blown up out on the moor stepped on their laugh lines rather severely. They seem grimly determined to get back to the giggles, however. That is why we must succeed in this enquiry, Shad. We must succeed, look magnificently competent in doing so, *and* with Parker in charge."

The duck leveled a gaze at me. "And we are going to bring this to pass how?"

I looked down my Basil Rathbone nose at him and arched an eyebrow. "I have brushed in the broad outlines of the concept, dear boy. Your job is to fill in the details." I pointed at the open door to downstairs. "Shall we brief our lead on his murder case?"

"Oh, let's do." Shad waddled toward the door muttering gloomily about computer-generated lizards, penthouses, Waterford Crystal birdbaths, action figures, and outrageous fortune.

3

Room Nine fourteen looked like every other interrogation room in every police station in every country in the world: featureless pale beige walls, white light panel above a plain white plastic table flanked by two sets of composite wood stools on opposite sides, audio-visual recording controls in a black enameled wall panel next to the desk. The only way Nine fourteen differed from other interrogation rooms was that it was en suite, or as Shad would have it, the room had an attached crapper. I sat on a stool at the table, Shad squatted upon the table, and Parker sat in the loo with the room's door open—undignified, perhaps, but with olfactory compensations.

Through the open door Shad briefed Parker on the scene of the crime, the position and condition of Darcy Flanagan's bio, and the impact and trace evidence. "Flanagan was killed elsewhere and dumped at the scene," said Parker.

"Shad and I concur."

"Security cameras in the area?"

I looked at Shad. He shook his head. "Nothing yet," he said to the toilet door. "I've downloaded the area traffic surveillance records for this evening into the Heavitree mainframe as well as the private security recordings. The tech mechs are just getting started on them."

The toilet flushed, however Parker failed to emerge. Nothing but silence for a long uncomfortable stretch.

"Parker?" I called at last.

"Sorry, sir. I was just thinking. What if Flanagan's body was carefully inserted into Parliament Street for a purpose?"

"What purpose?"

"A political statement."

Shad and I exchanged glances. "Dead bird in an alley—vote for Arthur Q. Schnebble?" cracked Shad.

"Hear me out, sergeant," said Parker. "The deceased is a bio, isn't he? We're right in the middle of AB Emancipation Week, right? E-Week marks the Parliamentary Reform Act of 2132 which maintains suffrage for the human engram imprint, even onto mechanical or non-human bios, and it extends suffrage to artificially created intelligences otherwise qualifying as independent intelligent beings. See?"

Shad and I exchanged additional confused glances.

"It's symbolic, sir," continued Parker. "See, if Flanagan was purposefully dumped on Parliament Street, it may well hearken back to the original reform act that led to that little passage being named after Parliament. A possibility?"

Mallards don't have eyebrows, but I swear Shad's went up. "Parker, I bet you could tell me what the original act of Parliament was that lead to the naming of Parliament Street."

"Yes, sergeant. It was the Reform Act of 1832. The act changed a number of laws in Britain, Scotland, Ireland, and Wales regarding representation in Parliament, but the main thing it did was to increase the number of males who could vote by approximately thirty percent."

"Fair to say it extended suffrage to the less worthy?" Shad inquired.

"That was certainly how the Exeter city fathers regarded it at the time. As we are all aware, that's how the archbishop and the rest of the anti AB crowd today currently regard the Act of 2132."

I pondered that in silence for a moment. I glanced at Shad. He was looking at the tabletop. Once he had concluded shaking out his feathers from his head to his tail, he looked at me and said, "Well, gang, this nothing case fairly reeks with significant coincidence."

"If DC Parker is correct in his facts," I cautioned.

"He is. Checked it all out on *Ferdie's Freepaedia*," Shad explained. "Parker—" he began but stopped short. "Autopsy report coming in," he said, his eyes focused at an invisible point between the toilet door and myself. "Flanagan's human meat suit likely died as a result of a heart attack induced by the violent death of his pigeon bio. Death

343

in the pigeon bio was caused by a broken rib through the heart as the result of blunt force trauma, the weapon being circular, approximately seven centimeters in diameter, convex in shape, fabric enclosed, flexible—"

"Shad," I interrupted, "doesn't that sound like one of those old beanbag loads for a what-do-you-call-it?"

A brief pause as Shad consulted Ferdie's, then he said, "Gas gun. They were miscreant-safe weapons for use in riot control. The 37mm gas gun fired a seven-point-five centimeter fabric covered flexible-baton filled with a hundred and fifty grams of lead shot."

"Sounds like one of those could do a dandy job of mangling a pigeon," said Parker.

Shad faced the toilet. "They're antiques, Parker. We've got Greasefoot, Flashnet, and Stunspray now. Gas guns haven't been used anywhere for anything in over a century."

Before I could suggest Parker put in a search for gas guns in Devon, he mentioned it himself. "Research will keep me out of public view," he offered contritely as a wistful note came into his voice. "That's what I used to do, you know. Research."

Shad looked at me and held out his wings questioningly as the voice from the loo fell silent.

"Parker was once a police historian," I explained. "Oxford, wasn't it, Parker?"

"Yes," he replied gloomily. "'Bliss was it in that dawn to be alive, But to be young was very heaven!'"

I glanced at Shad.

"Wordsworth," Shad muttered back at me. Facing the door to the toilet he began to ask a question—probably concerning just how a police historian in Oxford wound up as a gorilla bio—when another call came in on Shad's interface. "Tox screen on Flanagan." He stood and faced me, nonexistent eyebrows arched. "Alcohol. In Flanagan's blood. Enough to pickle a pigeon."

We all thought on that for a moment. It was a case wrinkle with which none of knew what to do just then. Shad's tail resumed twitching, signifying another incoming call.

"The person who reported finding the body, Parker," I said, "did he or she ever show?"

"Yes. Sharissa Thule. She's a thirty-one year old woman—human natural—from Dawlish. She was in the city shopping and visiting relatives and was on her way from the Guildhall Shopping Centre to have tea at the Milkmaid on Catherine. She found the body on Parliament and reported it to a constable."

"Why would a nat report a dead bird to the police unless she knew it was a bio?" I asked.

"She could tell it was a bio. I gather Ms. Thule carries a marker detector."

"Really. Why?"

"The way she put it, sir, 'I want to know whether to pet a cute little doggie on the head or send the bloody pervert packing.' A bit anti-amdroid. Said something about a wolfhound in Lympstone two summers ago. The creature rubbed against her leg rather passionately. Turned out to be an amdroid."

Shad's tail stopped twitching, he spread his wings, and faced me, his bill hanging open. He froze that way for almost a minute, and then said, "They want me back!"

"Sorry?"

"They want me back!" He lowered his wings and began pacing rapidly in a circle. "That was my New York agent. Barton Stanky? The duck stockholders somehow regained control of the insurance conglomerate over the lizard faction—I don't know the details, but Barton baby says the corporation stock has been diving for the bottom ever since their advertising firm dumped the duck! The clients have been demanding the return of the duck! Aa-flak!" he cried "Aa-flak! They want me back!"

4

"I swear, Val, I have the karma of Tantalus," I said later at home as I poked at the shepherd's pie Val had Walter prepare for me. Walter, the mech who did our cooking and housework, had even made spotted dick for dessert, but I could only pick at it.

"I finally get a partner I can work with—that I like—and bleeding Madison Avenue wants to make Shad a flipping billionaire clowning around and falling on his pratt to sell insurance."

"How nice for Guy. He was so unhappy to be let go," she said, her aqua eyes focused on mine. She sat across from me on the table, her tail wrapped around her legs. "Aren't you happy for him?"

"Oh," I let out my breath and turned my scowl toward my dinner. "Of course I am, dear. I am being quite selfish."

"Just a tad."

I took a breath, let it out, and tried a bit of pie. "This is rather good, isn't it?"

"Yes. Walter said he was trying a new recipe."

"Excellent." I leaned back in my chair, took a sip of tea, replaced the cup on the table, and smiled at her. "I suppose if I got a call from Metro to go back to London the sonic boom of my run back to the Yard would uproot half the trees in southern England. Thank you for being patient with me, dear."

"Cats are nothing if not patient, Harry."

"I'll miss Shad, though. He saved my life in that stable out at Hound Tor Hunts. We've talked old films for hours, and he tells the most outlandish stories. His rather disrespectful comments of certain political and police personalities from time-to-time have kept me in stitches, not to mention his terrible puns. Did I tell you—"

"Murder most fowl," she interrupted.

"Yes. Sorry. I forget at times." Val walked the length of the table and seated herself next to my left shoulder. "Looks as though this might be my last case with Shad," I said to her.

"If that's so, Harry, make it a good one."

"Of course. We'll make it a good one—if we can. Parker's career, ABCD's existence, may well depend upon it."

"What's on for tomorrow?"

"Parker will be tracking down antique beanbag guns while Shad and I question Flanagan's coworkers. We'll see if we can piece together Darcy Flanagan's movements prior to his demise."

"Do you know yet what to do about Ralph Parker leading the case? I'll never forget the horror of that ceremony at the Royal Diane Museum when I saw it on the telly."

"Many of us have been having rather fearsome flashbacks this evening on that account. After we briefed Parker, I prepared and read a brief statement to the reporters and took no questions. They didn't like that at all. Hardly any of the questions they tried to ask were about the murder."

"About Ralph?" she asked.

I nodded. "Sooner or later, Parker is going to have to face the media if he's going to lead this case."

"Ralph must be so worried."

"A concern shared by a small but anxious legion at ABCD, my dear."

The next morning constables from the Exeter Station brought in only a single coworker of Darcy Flanagan's, a pigeon bio named Tommy Shay. He was a deep-gray bird with gleaming white wing bands, a blued-gunmetal colored hood that came down to his shoulders, white beak, and deep pink feet—a much more handsome model than that flown by the deceased. Shay was a flight lieutenant and the commander of Puss-in-Boots Flight, the late Darcy Flanagan's unit. The remaining two members of Puss-in-Boots, flying officers Jock Munro and Art Krauthammer, were in hospice at Royal Devon & Exeter Hospital where Pureledge kept Munro and Krauthammer's stasis beds. Both were in their late nineties and bedridden, hence unavailable until they came on duty at three in the afternoon, should they live so long.

Flt. Lt. Shay was brought in wearing his pigeon suit, which for him was a permanent arrangement. It seems that the year before, ninety-seven year old Tommy Shay cacked out on his barracks stasis bed at Castle Street while his engrams were still on patrol at St. Peters. "When that happens," Shay said from his perch on a stool at the interrogation table, "Pureledge lets their old time employees live out their lives wearing wings, if they like. Those who take to it permanent even get a new bio once the old pigeon goes toes up."

"Generous of the company," I said.

The pigeon shrugged. "Pigeon bios is cheap when you get 'em by the thousand. Builds good will with the lads, though."

"And for you?" I asked.

"A pigeon on this side o' the dirt's better'n worms on t' other, the way I looks at it," he answered philosophically.

Shad squatted on the end of the table as I leaned my elbows on it. "What can you tell us about Darcy Flanagan?" Shad asked the pigeon.

"Not much, sergeant. See, the RPAF is kind like the old French Foreign Legion. You get a job, training, equipment, burial expenses, and no questions."

"RPAF?" asked Shad.

"Royal Pigeon Air Force," answered Shay.

"Is that actually connected to the British military?"

Shay shook his head at the duck. "No, guv. Haw! The RPAF is just somethin' the original lads dreamed up to make the job a bit more fun. Long as we keep Jerry off the ledges, company don't mind."

"Tell us what you can about Darcy," I said.

"Darcy joined the Seven-Twelve middle of June. He was issued one of them old-line model pigeon suits. We calls 'em 'Hurricanes.'"

"I noticed," I said, "that your bio is much better looking than Flanagan's."

"Better performin' too. This here is a Spitfire," said Shay, opening and closing his wings, turning about, giving Shad and me a good look. "We calls 'em Spits. Great improvement over the Hurricane, detective. Better speed, climb and dive rates, higher ceiling, more maneuverable, can take a whale more punishment, too. I rammed me a couple o' pushy ravens settin' up house on a turret on the cathedral south tower in this suit back in March. Tangled toes with the buggers, I did, 'til they got discouraged and headed for the countryside. Never mussed a feather of me own." He looked at Shad. "Raven's bigger'n a pigeon," he explained.

"Do tell," Shad responded. "About Flanagan?" he urged.

"Oh. Well, Castle Field was short o' Spits when young Darcy joined Seven-twelve. Still is." He faced me. "I do believe Artie Krauthammer got the last Spit."

"Darcy?" I reminded him.

"Right. So when Darcy shows at flight school I looks at that old Hurricane bag 'o feathers and says I to Squadron Leader Haverill, 'Les,' I says to him, 'you can't send the kid up in a crate like that!'"

I glanced at Shad. He appeared to be gnawing on the edge of his own wing.

"Squadron leader says Flanagan flies the Hurricane 'til the new Spits come in. 'Make do,' says he."

"Well, Tommy," I said as I faced Shay, "How did he do?"

"Oh, he took to flying well enough. Loved it so, he did. Inspector, you take dim eyes, sore knees, bad back, weak heart, a scarred liver, and no wind, leave that all behind and put on wings—even one 'o them Hurricanes—and all you wants is to get up in the sky—" Shay interrupted himself, looked down lost in thought for a moment, then he faced me. "On patrol though sometimes he'd lag behind. Hurricanes just can't keep up with Spits. We'd get to diving on Jerry, chasing him 'round the towers . . . well, sometimes Darcy wouldn't quite be on time. Tried to keep down the speed, but in the heat of the chase—"

"Tally ho," said Shad.

"Exactly."

"See, Puss-in-Boots Flight patrols the south side of St. Peters. I ain't unfair in sayin' we're hard done by with just the one flight. Wolf Flight has the north cathedral patrol which is just that side o' the church. Red Riding Hood Flight only has Mol's, St. Martins, and them other old shops on Cathedral Close. Cinderella Flight's only got east end 'o Cathedral Yard, the Royal Clarence and a couple shops. On the cathedral's south side, though, Puss-in-Boots's got half the cathedral plus the Cloisters, plus the Diocesan House, and plus the Bishop's bleedin' Palace."

"And Flanagan couldn't keep up," I urged.

"What I thought I done was make a problem into a virtue, inspector. After a few days I put him on lone patrol flying the Diocesan House and the Bishop's Palace. Just surveillance, mind. While me, Jock, and Art buzzed Jerry off the rest, Darcy would patrol his part and send up the balloon if he saw Jerry heading his way. We'd come running and the four of us would roust the Hun and chase 'em off."

"So for most of the shift—ah, patrol—you wouldn't see Flanagan at all," said Shad.

The pigeon nodded. "True enough, but he'd radio in every so often when he'd see Jerry or to check in. It was just until Darcy got his Spit." The bird thought for a moment. "It worked good for a few weeks. Darcy would put in a call and the rest o' the lads'd come a-runnin'. Kept the ledges pristine, we did." Shay fell silent, shook his head. "Then Darcy stopped calling in for help. He could do it on his own. When I'd check, the ledges were clean so I left well enough alone."

"And yesterday?" I asked.

"Patrol started at three, our flight was posted and Darcy peeled off for the palace. We got two calls from Darcy that first hour. Both times he said he'd taken care of Jerry on his own. We got no more calls. It were busy on the south side. Besides Jerrys there was dole bums and pige freaks—other pigeon bios. They had us fagged so it wasn't 'til a bit before five I radioed Darcy, see how he was makin' out. I got no answer and ordered the flight onto Darcy's patrol area. He wasn't there. We split up and searched all over for him but couldn't find a feather. Can't see how he wound up on Parliament Street. That's way out of our patrol area."

"Did Flanagan drink?" asked Shad.

"Darcy's Irish so he has to put away his jar, right?" Shay said scornfully. He glanced at me, then faced Shad as he adopted a completely phony uncaring demeanor, standing slouched upon his stool. "Wouldn't know about Darcy drinkin', sergeant. Surely wouldn't. Don't socialize with the lads off duty. Wouldn't be none o' my concern anyways, would it."

"On duty," I said. "Did he drink on duty?"

"Do I look like a stool pigeon to you?" he demanded.

Shad was back to chewing on his wing. I found a sudden need to rub my eyes. "Flanagan's autopsy," gasped Shad, "it showed that he'd been drinking quite a bit before he was killed."

"A wee touch o' the dew, eh?"

"He was pissed," I insisted.

Tommy Shay raised his right wing. "God's honest truth, detective, I never seen young Darcy take a drink on or off duty."

"So, the last time you saw him was at the beginning of the patrol, three in the afternoon, and the last time you heard from him was before four."

"Yes."

"What kind of transmission range you birds have?" asked Shad.

"About twenty-five kilometers before there's a noticeable drop in signal strength."

"That narrows it down," he said sarcastically.

Shay looked from Shad to me. "What's he mean?"

"Hell, man." I held out my hands. "Flanagan could've been in bloody Exmouth for those two transmissions for all you knew."

Although Tommy Shay felt bad about young Darcy, we got nothing more useful out of him. We detained him, however, until we had a chance to brief Parker.

After delivering our report through the open toilet door in Room Nine fourteen our aromatic leader said, "There are nine gas guns currently registered in England. The Manchester Worker's Museum has one, the Imperial War Museum in London has one, the British Museum has two, all four inoperable according to museum curators. The police force museum in Bristol has two, one of them possibly operable. The Royal Diane Museum here in Exeter has one, functional according to the curator. Of the remaining two, Morton Geller, an antique weapons dealer in Leeds, has one. Mr. Geller believes that with the investment of just a few hundred quid the gas gun he has in inventory might be made operable, although he hasn't a clue where to obtain ammunition for it. The remaining gas gun belongs to the Office of the Bishop of Exeter."

"Whoa!" said Shad, looking at me. I faced the door to the WC.

"Parker, what about that last?"

"The lord bishop, Dr. Reginald Koch. His secretary will get back to us about the gun. Apparently they cannot locate it. No one recalls seeing it ever and the last record of its existence is a century old." Parker punctuated his finding by flushing the toilet.

Shad looked at me. "That might even be a clue."

While Parker continued his investigations and sorting through the surveillance videos, Shad and I arranged with Flight Leader Tommy Shay, 712 Squadron Leader Patricia Kwela—a.k.a. "Mother Goose—and Pureledge Exeter Manager Lucinda Martini for Shad and me to go undercover that evening as ledge marshals, Puss-in-Boots Flight, Seven-Twelve Squadron, Royal Pigeon Air Force.

5

Since we were new to the service, Shad and I had to arrive at Pureledge two hours early for flight training. Shad put the cruiser down on High Street at Castle, we climbed out, then he sent it back to Heavitree Tower. Castle Street there is a wide park-like thoroughfare given over to foot traffic, mercilessly hard stainless steel benches from another age, the occasional tree, and the obligatory busker or three. That afternoon, despite the chill, entertainment was provided by a kangaroo bio singing "Charlie Is My Darling" with a Scottish accent to the accompaniment of a banjo played by a Joey bio located in the 'roo's pouch. Shad actually coded a fiver into the creditron in the open banjo case at the 'roo's feet.

"Tough business," he explained as he waddled up past Musgrave Row toward the rounded white south-facing side of the Pureledge building. Castle went up the left side of Pureledge, a narrower street named Little Castle went up the right. The pigeon chasing company's building was the southernmost of the buildings bounded by the two Castle streets and on the south by the doglegged joining of Musgrave Row and Bailey. The building itself was a five-story Neo-Georgian structure with multi-paned double-hung windows above and larger display windows at street level the panes of which displayed graphics mostly of Exeter's various buildings and monuments, pristine and pigeon free. A lone "before" graphic showed a beer stone statue of some king, lord, or martyr from the west facade at St. Peters Cathedral, a furtive-looking pigeon behind the statue's right shoulder guarding a huge black nest that extended behind the statue's head and to its left shoulder. Pigeon waste coated the statue's shoulders and folded arms. At the bottom of the poster was printed, "Don't let this happen to you."

The windows set in the Mansard roof were open and a group of about forty pigeons exited one of the windows on the left and took a westerly heading. There was something strange about how they were flying. "Shad?"

"I see it. Don't know what it is." He glanced back at me. "It's like they're doing a continuous stadium wave in all different directions with their wings but I can't follow it with my eyes. Weird." He waddled the semicircle to the Castle Street entrance and entered.

The receptionist was a rather attractive human nat in her early thirties named Naomi Foon, according to her illuminated plastic desking accessory. She appeared quite normal in lavender pantaloon and vest business attire, spiked black hair with lavender tips, and matching lavender communications array plugged into her right ear. In fact everything about the sales floor of Pureledge was traditional: liquid crystal walnut paneling, virtual gaslight, plush red algae carpeting, hand-painted ties on the sales agents, and the reek of preserved Albion.

Receptionist Foon took our names and looked over her desk down at Shad. "I don't believe we've ever before had a ducky as one of our flyers." She batted her feather extended eyelashes and flashed Shad a smile.

"I'm already in a low paying job and I thought I'd explore some of the other options available in poverty," he said.

She nodded vacantly. "We once had a wildebeest bio."

"Why would a wildebeest want to be a pigeon?" I asked.

"He was a very old wildebeest," she explained. Her lavender streaked eyebrows went up. "Not that I'm implying either of you gentlemen are very old." She looked at me. "I would say, Mr. Jaggers, that you look very young to be one of our flyers. How old are you, if you don't mind me asking."

"The bio was grown forty-five; I've had it twelve years. The engrams are . . ." I had to think for a moment. "The engrams are ninety-three."

"You look just like Sherlock Holmes—you know, in the old telly flicks? That actor, Basir Redbone?"

"Hadn't noticed it myself."

She looked at Shad. "I would say you are a young-looking duck."

"Ducks never show their age until they find themselves plucked, glazed, and surrounded by chopsticks," responded Shad curtly. "Where do we go?"

"Second floor," she answered. "Good hunting, fellows."

As we went to the elevator, I asked Shad, "Are you looking for a fight or has that fellow from the Chinese restaurant been lurking around your flat again?"

"Sorry there, Holmes. Things on my mind."

"Things theatrical?"

We entered the elevator, the doors formed and hardened, and Shad barked "Two" at the control panel. He looked up at me as the car elevated. "I guess I'm a little torn between work here and going back to doing commercials."

"Ever since that lizard bumped you out of your advert slot and you wound up in ABCD you've been unhappy, Shad. Now they want you back. I'd think you'd be quite pleased."

The car stopped and the doors softened and faded. Shad didn't move. "I know. But, I've had a ball working with you, Jaggs. I kind of like Exeter. There's Nadine, of course. Hell, Jaggs, you saved my life out at Hangingstone."

"I'll not be happy to see you go, Shad, although I will enjoy seeing you on the telly again. You're the only television star I've ever known. Val is very happy for you. So am I."

"Well, it's been a sincere privilege to work with someone who looks so much like Basir Redbone, wak, wak, w—"

Shad was staring straight ahead, his countenance frozen. I turned to look at what had captured his attention. We stepped out into the room. The second floor looked like a military officer's club from the mid Twentieth Century, leather-covered overstuffed chairs, dim lights, a piano mech who played itself, and dozens of posters on the walls and ceiling of fighter aircraft of World War II, with several of the Hurricane but mostly of the Spitfire fighter: Spits diving, climbing, turning, shooting, on floats, and on wheels. The piano mech was playing "The White Cliffs of Dover" and accompanying itself with a familiar sounding female voice. I glanced at Shad and he said, "Vera Lynn" in answer to my unasked question.

"How do you know it's Vera Lynn?"

"I recognize her from the end of *Dr. Strangelove* when she sang 'We'll Meet Again.'"

"Ah, yes. With the nuclear mushroom clouds going up. Nineteen sixty-six?"

"'Sixty-four," he corrected. "Get a load of this room, Jaggs. I feel like Errol Flynn in *Dawn Patrol*." He nodded his head toward a strange-looking mech who was approaching us silently on soft rubber wheels. She was wearing a starched white dress, white cap, and a short midnight blue cape. The mech's right eye looked human. The left eye glowed green resembling a night scope with a variety of interchangeable lenses and filters. Instead of fingers her hands bristled with sensors, various tools such as a rubber hammer, tongue depressor, and things that poked, stuck, cut, sewed, cleansed, taped, and perhaps knitted for all I could tell. The most formidable of these instruments was a sensor that resembled a huge rubber finger.

"I'm Nurse Florence," she announced in a raspy voice. As she came to a halt, her big rubber finger thrust up toward a poster of a ME 109 going down in flames.

"I'm just a little duck," whimpered Shad to sister in a tiny voice.

The big rubber finger retracted and was replaced by a smaller, but still fearsome, digit. "Follow me," she commanded.

"Chocks away, lad," I said to Shad. As we followed Sister Florence to the examination rooms, the piano mech struck up the Glenn Miller version of "Little Brown Jug."

After our stasis bed physicals, about which the less said the better, we were escorted to a third floor room which housed approximately eighty triple bunk stasis beds about half filled, with old men, old women, old bios, and at least one very rusty mech. "Two-sixty-four Squadron," whispered our escort, a tech mech named Watkins. "Them's the blokes you chaps'll relieve once you get in the air." In the 712 area, along with a woman in her seventies named Mathilda, Shad and I copied into our Hurricane pigeon suits. Watkins ran the three of us and eight other "chicks" directly to the roof where we met Hell's pigeon.

"You lot will never make it."

Flight Sergeant Ponsonby marched up and down our file of eleven ledge marshal trainees, his gray, black, and white Spit feathers glossed back, his pink toes gleaming with some sort of gloss, and something resembling a chopstick thrust beneath his left wing. He alternated his growling and barking with the following: "You lot come creepin' up on me roof from hospital, from the flippin' dole queue, from bloomin' Bide-A-Wee Nursin' Home, or hidin' out from old bill or the missus happy as you please, all fired up to singe Jerry's tail feathers for Pureledge's tenner, and not a bleedin' clue how to get in the bleedin' air. Just look at you feather bags. I might as well be talkin' to a stack of flippin' flapjacks—"

And so on. Once flight sergeant was finished with his set piece, he bellowed, "Staff!" and two pigeons emerged marching from in back of us. Through a series of shouts, bellows, shoves, and curses they herded us over to a skylight. Standing upon the edge of the raised casement looking down upon us was a one-legged, one-eyed pigeon Spit with one droopy wing. The missing undercarriage limb had been replaced by a red plastic peg leg. The missing eye was covered by a black patch held in place by a thin black elastic band.

"I am Squadron Leader Leslie Haverill, ground commander of Castle Field," he said in a calm voice. "I, Flight Sergeant Ponsonby, and the staff personnel at Castle Field welcome you to RPAF, Exeter. I know you'll do well here, become part of our rich tradition, and be credits to the Royal Pigeon Air Force."

Squadron Leader Haverill then read us *Kings Regulations* pertaining to private investigators, guards, watch officers, and ledge marshals. Curiously enough, besides chasing pigeons and other fowl off ledges, unlike detectives from the Artificial Beings Crimes Division, ledge marshals were actually allowed to detain suspects and make arrests. In cases of pigeon and other fowl bios carrying human imprints, those trespassing on private, company, corporate, or government property protected by Pureledge were subject to arrest using whatever force necessary to subdue said arrestee. Miscreants thus detained were then to be turned over to the Devon & Cornwall Constabulary, Exeter Police Station. There was, in addition, a robust course in beak-to-toe combat during which Staff Foster—a Spit pigeon wearing a tiny set of prescription goggles—mentioned that all those staffing ground and flight schools had been killed in action. That is, their suits reclining in stasis had cacked out. Like Tommy Shay, they had opted to remain in wings.

"What happened to the squadron leader's Spit?" asked Shad when we were on break.

"Terrible thing, lad," answered Sgt. Foster shaking his head, his voice lowered. "A year ago squadron leader used to command 331 of the First, covering Rougemont Castle down to High and southwest to Iron Bridge. Out on the rooftops, towers, and ledges, lads: That's where Jerry is; that's where we expect the attack." He shook his head sadly. "Danger's all around, lads, everywhere. See, back then we had a brand new pilot officer assigned to Seven-twelve, lad by name of Kumar. He took to that Spit like he was born to it. Once off the tower and he was airborne. A natural flyer. Only with us a few days, though. Disappeared, he did. They only found a feather or two over by the Royal Clarence. Must've took on a falcon or hawk. Snapped him up quick as an eye blink, his parts parceled out 'mongst Henry and the other hawk chicks in the nest I imagine. Heart of an eagle, young Kumar, but he had the body of a pigeon and the judgment of a scone. You find a hawk or falcon squattin' in your patrol area, flyer, you call it in. Special Unit goes after the big ones."

"Haverill?" prompted Shad.

"Don't be impatient, lad." He regarded Shad down the length of his beak. "Let's see, then. Squadron Leader Haverill in his pigeon suit was cuttin' through 712's stasis beds when Kumar went down. Kumar he slams awake all stressed from bein' turned into hawk vittles. Wildebeest bio, he was. Sprung right off that bed he did, hit the ceiling, and landed on Haverill all four hoofs a-runnin' at the same time. Tore up squadron leader proper." Foster faced me. "Took poor Kumar in his wildebeest suit that night and run him straight off to the wigpicker works, bleedin Happy Valley, they did. Still there, poor lad." He returned his goggled gaze to Shad. "Pieced squadron leader together but his flyin' days was done. Took him out of the air and made him ground commander."

"Why the prescription goggles, staff?" asked Shad, nodding toward flight's set. "Aren't all Spit bios genetically coded for good eyesight?"

"Well, lad, that were a cock-up of me own. I joined back when each squadron did it's own flight training. About eight years ago it was. They sent me straight into the Nine-nine-four patrol area south o' the Guildhall. Only an hour or so in the air, lad, then we was on break. I put down on a windowsill by the Catacombs. Nice little stair climb o' houses called Napier Terrace. I was recitin' the wing flap changes—" He lowered his voice as though passing on official secrets. "The changes was brand new back then. Your flight leader'll fill you in. I was number five in the flight and it were one, two, three, four, five, six—a flap on me own number, see— then two, one, four, three, six, five—up flap—then two, four, one . . . or was that two, one, five—bugger it. Been so long I forget. Anyway, I was recitin' the changes out loud when next thing I know Jerry hits me with poison gas."

"Sorry?" I said.

"Poison gas, lad—bug spray according' to the tox screen they did on me in hospital. Blinds me and knocked me colder'n January lager, as we say in the RPAF. Next I know I'm in hospital. Findin' out what happened to me upset my nat in stasis so, Billy Foster the natural man cacked out." He held out his wings. "Company's gift." He lowered his wings. "Had to get specs, though, 'cause the poison fried me corneas. Can't see much with 'em but can't see a bleedin' thing without."

When Staff Foster marched off to abrade some trainee's ego, I turned to Shad. "We need to know if the scenes of crime officers ever found Kumar's pigeon bio, exactly where the SOCOs found those feathers, and what they did with them. We also need a detailed map of the squadron patrol areas in Exeter. I'm very curious who was living in Napier Terrace eight years ago when Staff Foster caught it."

Shad's pigeon suit looked at me for a beat then nodded. "Fitness reports and other pigeon injuries and deaths?"

"Absolutely. Get details, location, and date of each incident. We need police reports and lists of every employee, guest, and residence in each area as well as traffic and private surveillance video archives. Stasis bed consequences, too."

"You think our boy has been busy before?"

"Seems likely."

"Awright, you lot! Don't be late for parade!" bellowed Staff Foster. "To the tower, lads. Let's see if those new feathers fly or bounce!"

6

Part of the package in all ledge marshal bios is a flight program that does most of the work involved in knowing how to fly. On the roof the eleven of us were run up little ramps to the top of a tower and kicked off into the air until, instead of landing crumpled up at the foot of the tower, we flew down under our own power. I did it in three tries but it took Shad five.

"Ducks don't fly the same as pigeons," he explained. "I finally had to disable my duck program before I could work these pigeon wings."

We flew circuits around the building, higher and higher, almost to the level of the air vectors, then circled back down. It was the most wonderful sensation I have ever experienced. Even in one of their old Hurricanes, the strength, the freedom, the thrill, combined with the incredible degree of control, the excitement was such I was certain DI Harrington Jaggers below was grinning in his stasis bed.

One final ground parade and caution from Sqn. Ldr. Haverill prohibiting flight formations and synchronous wing flapping: "Lads, our function is to keep the ledges of our clients clean and to do so in a natural-appearing manner. No one objects to pigeons. They are natural; they are beautiful. What our clients object to is filth. However, if we eliminate the filth but fly fighter and bomber formations, we no longer look natural. Instead, we look threatening. Flapping wings in unison, I would add, does not look natural. Report to your commands."

Flight Sergeant Ponsonby and his two staffs barked us down to the ready room on the Fifth Floor where Shad, Mathilda, and I joined Puss-in-Boots Flight as the Seven-twelve Squadron of the Third Wing prepared to relieve Two-fourteen of the Second. We had a few minutes and Tommy

Shay, Jock Munro, and Artie Krauthammer explained to the three of us what they called "the changes."

"Years ago we used to flap in unison. Took great pride in it, we did," said Shay. "The legs downstairs," *legs* appeared to be a term of derision, "The legs says they got complaints, so no more synchronous flappin'. Well, we still takes pride in our flyin', so we flies changes. Got it from the bell ringers what do change ringing. Now we up to full strength, we got six birds in the flight. We can do it proper." And then Tommy explained the mysteries of the 'Blue Line,' otherwise known as 'Plain Bob Minor.' Tommy was Puss-in-Boots One, Jock was Two, Artie was Three, I was four, Shad was Five, and Mathilda was Six. After going from One to Six in order, the variations began, 214365, then 241635, 426153, and so on. "I'll call 'em out 'til you get the hang of it. You flap down on your first number, raise on your next, then down on the next. I'll time my call to start once I see where Wolf Flight is in the pattern. You'll pick it up soon enough. Any questions?"

"It doesn't look natural," said Shad.

"No, it don't," said Flt. Lt. Shay. "But the legs don't know why it don't."

A buzzer buzzed and a red light began flashing. Shay lead the way out of the ready room into an area ringed with open windows. There were hundreds of the Third Wing milling about. The forty or so "old wings" of the Seven-twelve introduced themselves to the five new "chicks" assigned to the squadron, stating first name then flight, as in "Percival, Wicked Stepmother," and "Jenkins, Tom Thumb." They all made Shad, Mathilda, and I feel quite welcome. On the sill of the southernmost facing window, a handsome Spit pigeon stood and called the Seven-twelve to attention. Other Spits on other windowsills addressed their squadrons. As we fell silent, a second Spit pigeon took the first one's place.

"Mother Goose," Shay whispered to us in the flight.

"I am Squadron Leader Patricia Kwela, commanding officer of Seven-twelve," the pigeon said with a slight accent I couldn't place. "I am notified Seven-twelve has five spankin' new pilot officers this mission. I welcome you. Your flight leaders will give you your orders. Do your most best to follow orders. You do that we look good, keep ledges free of Jerry, go home safe, and all be most dandy. Now we going to have moment of silence for recently departed brother Flying Officer Darcy Flanagan of Puss-in-Boots Flight. I ask you all call down your juju and beg your wing brother Darcy get nothin' but clear skies, soft breezes, cozy dovecotes, and the whole Peanut Mountain."

Someone cooed a whistle and the entire wing fell silent as the piano mech far below softly played "Chariots of Fire." Once that was concluded, the whistle cooed again followed by the buzzer and a green light.

"Chocks away!" bellowed the wing adjutant, the squadrons lined up at their respective windows, and one after another flights flew from the windows. I managed to get Shad to stop laughing long enough not to miss our flight.

♠

As we took up our heading toward the Cathedral, Shad, Mathilda, and I learned to flap changes, and to take a bit of pride in doing so. Learning "the rows," as they were called. "Plain Bob Minor" began:

123456
214365
241635
426153
462513
645231
654321
563412
536142
351624

It went through sixty-two variations, then was repeated from the beginning. As a "four" I could watch the fours ripple though the entire squadron while other numbers rippled in nonparallel directions. Very neat. Once the Seven-twelve was at the Cathedral, Puss-in-Boots and Wolf flights peeled away. Wolf banked left for the north side and Puss-in-Boots banked right for the south where we fell in with the lads we were to relieve—Jimmy Dorsey Flight of 264 Squadron—and did a circuit of the South Cathedral, Cloisters, Diocesan House, and Bishop's Palace. Jimmy One said to Tommy the area had been fairly quiet: only thirteen pigeons and one lone pigeon bio to discourage, and when his flight peeled off to join 264, he called, "Good hunting, chaps. Jimmy One out." Then he called to "Big Band" and Jimmy Dorsey Flight ascended to join Tommy Dorsey Flight and Two-six-four Squadron as it headed back to Castle Field.

I suggested to Tommy that Shad and I take up Flanagan's old patrol area. Since Mathilda was in a Hurricane and couldn't keep up with the Spits, she came with us. The only experienced flyer among the three of us was Shad and Tommy made him our flight leader. We chased a few pigeons off the Bishop's Palace and had a brief encounter with a pigeon bio named McGee on the Diocesan House. McGee was probably the same bio Jimmy Dorsey Flight had run off during their patrol. We chased him off but an hour later had to chase him off again. This time the three of us escorted McGee down to the Quay and showed him the cliffs above the river where the "really in" pigeons lived. Shad issued some formidable audio taken I believe from the second *King Kong* remake: giant gorilla grunts, snorts, thumps, and bellows followed by Arnold Schwarzenegger as the Terminator saying, "Don't come back," which took care of the problem nicely.

We took breaks around Puss-in-Boots patrol area feeder installed by Pureledge on the roof above the cathedral tea room. On the first break, Munro couldn't resist a tired working-for-peanuts reference. After feeding it was off to the loo. Our patrol area's designated bombing area was in the Bishop's Garden, and it took several tries before Shad and I, on the wing, scored bulls eyes on the garden's compost heap. Then it was back to patrol.

On the second break, Artie Krauthammer shared a useful reminiscence or two about Darcy Flanagan. It seemed that, prior to Pureledge, Darcy and Artie had spent much of their lives together in pubs. That continued until they found themselves in failing health, dire legal circumstances, and turning over more than half their pensions for rat poison blends from the offies. I had to explain to Shad that offies were shops, off-license package stores that sold alcohol.

"It was a rum life," said Artie. "Darcy's the one who discovered Pureledge. See, Darcy's old liver couldn't take much more and mine was even worse. 'Another Old Coot Whiskey,' the doc says to me,' and you'll be looking for a bunk down in the Catacombs, me lad.' Darcy and me both swore off but it weren't never an easy oath to keep."

"Why the RPAF?" Shad asked.

"'Pigeons,' Darcy says to me, 'young they are, livers is just fine, and no questions. How much single malt you think it takes to warm up a pigeon?' he asks me. Couple of drops? It's a body weight and metabolism thing, right?"

Shad and I exchanged glances. "Right," we both said facing him.

"Instead of more booze, we went for less body mass. Seemed like an answer to all our prayers. A single bottle could last a couple o' pigeons a month or more. The day we was to show, though, Darcy didn't. He'd spent the night and morning seein' how much scrumpy he could put down and they had him in hospital. By the time he got out I was in my Spit flappin' changes and kind of enjoying having health and a clear head. Wanted to keep it that way. Darcy still had his plan, though. Day he left hospital he was at Castle Street fitted out for wings. All they had left then was Hurricanes. Anyway, Darcy was in the Seven-twelve. I coaxed him to stay off the stuff, and he did for a few weeks. Then I could smell it on him."

"He was drinking on duty?" asked Shad.

"I never saw him. Don't know where he kept his jug," answered Artie. "I wanted to stay sober meself, see. Got into a program: Birds of a Feather. Well, Darcy and I drifted apart. Didn't exchange a word with him except to say hi for weeks. Then yesterday he goes missin' and winds up dead." Artie Krauthammer sadly shook his head. "Poor Darcy."

After the second break Mathilda was missing. Shad and I checked the Bishop's Garden and began running a search grid on the cathedral grounds when we both looked around and noticed she was right behind us. "Sorry, boys. Had to go powder my beak," and then she cackled insanely and began sobbing and singing "Chariots of fire." I dropped back, took a sniff, and Pilot Officer Mathilda was flying a bit too close to the wind.

"Darcy Flanagan was a good man," she declared as Shad fell back, Mathilda flying between us. "Such a dear *urp* poor dearie, dearie poo. Can't believe he's *gone!*" More sobbing. Between us Shad and I guided her to the central peak of a roof, the palace spread out below us. From her babbling monolog, apparently Mathilda knew Darcy from his pub days. Sober old Artie Krauthammer wasn't the only one with whom Darcy had shared his reduced body mass alcohol conservation proposal. She wept, she reminisced, she sang a tune or two, gave a sloppy eulogy for the departed, and sobbed some more. Shad and I were both trying to decide how to get Mathilda to reveal the location of Flanagan's jug when she quieted, thought a moment, then took off. We watched as she glided down toward the palace, landed on the crenellated top of a small octagonal tower, then disappeared between the crenellations. When we joined her we noted a trapdoor set into the roof of the tower and next to it a ceramic jug painted the same dark color as the roof. Set into the base of the jug was a push-button spigot that emptied into the upturned lid of a jar. Mathilda pushed the button with her beak, a dollop of single malt landed in the lid, and she guzzled more than a wee drop or two. I looked at Shad and he was looking along the roof of the Diocesan House to where it joined the Bishop's Palace. I knew he was thinking the same as I: The bishop's gas gun was still unaccounted for.

At eleven that night the Seven Twelve Squadron was relieved by the One-three-two "Big Toon" Squadron. We flew Yosemite Sam Flight around the south cathedral patrol area then climbed to join Mother Goose and the Seven-twelve back to Castle Field all of us cooing the old Vera Lynn song, "We'll Meet Again" as we flapped changes back home, Mathilda's changes flapping to a different ringer.

7

"I am getting considerable pressure from the Chief Constable's office to resolve this dead pigeon matter," declared Superintendant Matheson the next morning. Shad and I were in his office standing in front of his antique mahogany veneer desk. The rest of his office was unadorned save for the image of a gilt-framed painting of the Biograph Theater in Chicago centered in the liquid crystal wall facing the desk. The superintendent's hands were clasped behind his back and DC Parker was behind the image of the Biograph in the superintendent's WC. Between flushes and shouting through the door, Parker did an adequate summary of the progress thus far on the Darcy Flanagan case.

Complete results on pigeon bio deaths and injuries weren't yet in, but what results there were appeared discouraging. Constabulary SOCOs had been called in regarding the Kumar matter, had collected the feathers, but apparently the evidence collected at the scene had been misplaced. The report itself had been scrubbed in the Heavitree Tower computer meltdown that year, the file apparently never having been copied to the archive backup nor forwarded to ABCD. The detectives and SOCOs who worked on the Kumar case were scattered to the winds. They were being tracked down, but with little hope of success.

I could see Matheson was struggling with reconsidering his decision to place Parker in charge of the case. At one point his eyes pleaded as his brows arched, wrinkling his forehead, probably hoping against hope I would insist on taking over. Nevertheless, as Shad would have put it, we continued with the starting line-up. Either we'd pull this lump out of the fire or we'd all be singing the Oscar Meyer wiener anthem.

After concluding the briefing, Matheson turned to his WC and said, "Parker, I rang up DS Towson to hound him about his failure to show at work. Had quite a talk with him." A long uncomfortable pause ensued. "I'm afraid Towson's put in for retirement. Sorry." The superintendent hung his head for a moment, then turned and looked out of his window at the giant mirror-finished icicle advertising the Sport Centre Ski Slope on Gladstone.

"There's something I need to say to all of you." He glanced back at Shad and I then glanced at his toilet door. "I have no one but myself to blame for all this. I went at this job by bits and bobs, always hoping to be called back to Greater Manchester, putting this—what I considered this silliness of AB Crimes—behind me. So many issues I let slide: pay, working conditions, staffing, the entire range of our special problems." He glanced at the toilet door. "At the end of the day, I fear I've failed. I just hope I haven't ruined this office and the entire national and world ABCD offices neck and crop."

He nodded to himself. "AB Crimes is important work because murder is still murder whatever suit carries the imprint. I hope you will all carry on, but I'll understand if anyone wants to bow out." He stood there silently, the gloom in the office so heavy it ought to have posted health warnings. I felt the duck kick my ankle. I looked down at Shad, his nonexistent brows were furrowed, his beak was open, and his wings held out to his sides as he glared at me.

I faced the superintendent. "Well, sir, thank you kindly for the offer, but these are early days. Despite being terribly understaffed and underpaid, and despite the media's current cant on AB Crimes, I've rather gone off the idea of packing it in just yet."

He turned his head and looked at me. "Oh?"

"Parker is doing an admirable job conducting this investigation, sir, we have good leads, excellent detectives to follow up the leads, and it's frankly only a matter of time until we have a suspect. I am confident that the three of us under your leadership will be more than equal to the task. If that's all, sir?"

Matheson nodded, smiled, and nodded again. "Thank you, Jaggers." He studied me for a moment and turned back to his window. "Thank you, gentlemen."

Outside the superintendent's office, the door closed behind the three of us, Shad looked up at me. "You do know you're going to Hell."

I glanced up at Parker and the gorilla nodded sadly. "If lying gets one Hell, inspector, you're done for. I can smell the brimstone."

"Well. Perhaps I'll be offered a position."

While Parker chased down video archives, researched injured and killed pigeon inquiries, and attempted to reconstruct the case work on the Kumar matter, he followed up on the gas guns. I helped him until late afternoon when I was to meet with Dr. Reginald Koch, Bishop of Exeter. Since the lord bishop was something of an anti amdroid fellow, Shad's presence would likely cripple the interview's focus. Hence, Parker had Shad continue service in the RPAF to try to find out more about Flanagan's last patrol.

As I approached the ornate vine-leafed gothic entrance to the palace, I could hear a strange ghostly choir singing high above me. I backed out of the entrance, looked up, and in line high upon the crenellated edge of a decorative battlement above the entrance were the lads—all of Puss-in-Boots Flight including Shad and Mathilda. They were singing Vera Lynn's "When The Lights Go On Again."

I made a rude gesture and pulled the chain. No one answered. Trying the latch, the door opened and inside the palace was a state of barely organized chaos. Carpenters, plasterers, plumbers, glaziers, decorators, architects, contractors, and bishop's minions appeared to be engaged in a shouting and dust generating competition accompanied by power tools of several kinds joined by chipberries playing at top volume several types of music and things that might be music. The choking haze of dust seemed to be settling out on acres of drop cloths while mechs carried stuff from here to there and from there to here.

There was a fellow in dusty livery and I went over to him and waited for a break in the bellowing. He was of medium height, a slender human nat of about forty with black hair, dark gray eyes, and a mouth that looked as though he had been suckled by a lemon. When he noticed me, he smiled, cocked his head to one side, and said, "Yes?"

"I'm Detective Inspector Jaggers here to see Dr. Koch," I yelled and held out my warrant card. "I have an appointment."

His puckered upper lip curled slightly at the sight of my ABCD card. "Artificial Beings," he said as though he had just discovered a decomposed badger in his pudding. "Come this way, inspector. Dr. Koch is expecting you."

I followed him around jack mechs, ladders, scaffolding, and stacks of building materials into a long hall, the walls draped to protect them from construction dust and debris. As I followed my guide, I watched as he brushed off his green and black coat. "Forgive me for not answering the door, inspector, and for not introducing myself. Inexcusable, but you see how things are. My name is Fedders."

"Not at all, Fedders. Making a few changes?"

"It seems endless, inspector. Parts of the palace date back to the Thirteenth Century and I'm afraid the subsequent centuries haven't been kind." He reached a blue glowing tarp field at the end of the hall. Reaching to his vest pocket, Fedders turned off the field, opened the almost black varnish-caked oaken door thus revealed, and leaned his upper body into the room beyond. "Detective Inspector Jaggers, milord."

I couldn't make out a response from within if there was one. The butler stood aside and held the door for me.

"Thank you, Fedders," I said. I entered a study that was all that I imagined a bishop's study should be: book-lined walls, green shaded lights, ornately carved wooden beams, luxuriously stuffed chocolate brown and green leather chairs, and a ceiling mural of one bewhiskered fellow I assumed to be God bestowing upon another bewhiskered fellow who resembled Burt Reynolds a pair of tablets numbered from one to ten. None of this was computer generated or liquid crystal; all quite real. In the midst of this actual and studious piety was the rear-on view of a remarkably overweight fellow in green plaid shorts, purple satin short-sleeved shirt, red-and-green argyle socks, and spiked red-and-yellow golf shoes. As he teetered upon his artery lined legs, he was apparently attempting to knock golf balls with a putter across his solid green carpet into a container that resembled a highball glass.

"A moment, inspector," said the man. His head came up and he was wearing a strange garment upon it that appeared to be a white leather tam with a purple visor and a large purple pom-pom on top. "I finished up an appearance at that three day golf thing at Oak Meadow in Starcross this morning. Abominable weather."

He swung, he hit the ball, the ball rolled straight-and-true across the carpet just where physics sent it: wide of the glass and directly beneath a green leather chair studded with polished brass tacks. The Lord Bishop of Exeter raised a trembling hand gripping his putter above his head, made several gasping and choking noises that to my ear approximated certain Middle English nouns, verbs, and adjectives fighting for expression, then the hand came down. He put the putter handle-first into a large purple bag leaning against a built-in bookcase where the gleaming instrument joined his other implements of improbable relaxation.

"Not as young as I used to be," said the bishop.

"It's going around, milord."

He wiped his fleshy red face with a purple towel. Lowering the towel, he regarded me for a moment, then tossed the towel in the general direction of his golf bag and seated himself in a brown leather chair next to a table that had a drink of some sort requiring a tiny pink umbrella up top and a polished silver tray beneath. He nodded toward another chair and I seated myself in it. He lifted his glass and asked, "Care for something to drink, inspector?"

"No. Thank you."

"Well, you are, aren't you?"

"Sorry, milord?"

"Young as you used to be. At least at some point. Artificial Beings Crimes Division, wot? Everyone in ABCD is a bio or mech, am I right? Never heard of anyone copying into anything older than his natural."

"ABCD is staffed by ABs—artificials. When I used the word *I*, milord, the reference was to my imprint rather than my suit."

"Suit? *Suit?*" His thick white eyebrows arched. "A suit is a jacket, man; Trousers, a waistcoat perhaps. God's truth, man, what you call a suit is a created *body*—what God in his arrogance once thought was *His* domain." The bishop's eyebrows came together into a frown.

Little profit in bandying souls, minds, mortal remains, and afterlifes with someone who was an obvious bigot. He was also a bishop and presumably could quote me under the table regarding my bandying candidates. Putting temptation aside, I said, "I'm inquiring about an antique gas gun registered to your office well over a century ago. We've talked with your secretary and he seems unable to locate it."

"Gas gun? Gas gun? What rot. I own guns. Fowling pieces, wot? Never owned a . . . gas gun, you say?"

"Yes sir."

"What's it for?"

"They were originally used by law enforcement in non-lethal riot control. You might say the one we're looking for now, though, was used as a fowling piece."

"Fowling piece, you say?" His eyebrows went up again as he pointed a finger at me. "Ah, hah! You're talking about that dead pigeon bio on the telly. Ledge marshal chap."

"Yes, milord. He was killed by a gas gun shooting flexible baton."

"Flex—a what?"

"A beanbag."

"Beanbag. Damned silliness if you ask me. Pigeons. Beanbags. If that chap'd stayed in his own skin, he'd still be alive, wot?" The bishop took another drink, placed the glass upon the tray, and faced me. "Jaggers, have you any idea how much it costs churches in this country to keep pigeon filth off sills and ledges? Have any idea at all how it's done?"

"Actually—"

"Cloned pigeon bios, can you believe? All over the sky: Bloody scientific freaks strutting about chasing off real pigeons. Call themselves the bloody Royal Air Force! Ruddy cheek of it. Takes a king's ransom just to keep filth off buildings. Billions we pay across the entire kingdom. You want to see your money grow, sir, sink a few thousand into that Pureledge."

"About—"

"You ever see 'em fly, sir? The pigeon Air Force? See what they do with their wings when they're up in the sky? I pulled a bell rope or two in my time, sir. I know what they're up to."

"About the gas gun, milord."

"Gas gun? Oh." He settled back in his chair, pursed his lips, and raised an eyebrow at me. "Murder weapon, you say?"

"Yes."

"Understand, inspector, my personal possessions are different than things belonging to the bishop's see. I don't own this furniture," he raised a hand, "or any of these books. They all belong to the office." He frowned again, looked at his knees, and looked again at me. "How old was this contraption?"

"It was manufactured in the Twenty-first Century. Your secretary said the last mention in your records is one hundred and forty years old."

"Rubbish. Don't own any guns that old. Wouldn't use them if I did. Unreliable. Something that old belongs in a museum, wot?" He placed his hands upon his knees, leaned forward, and stood. Turning, he went to the writing desk and pushed a button disguised in its surface. His face and hair achieved a bluish-white hue and I realized he was looking at the illuminated side of a virtual video screen. "There's that mention." He studied the screen, his lips silently moving, then moved his fingers about on the desk's surface. "Let's see. There, inspector. Well. What do you make of that? The office owned a Defense Technology 37mm Multi-launcher with folding stock and revolver type motor driven magazine. Here's an image . . ." His eyebrows went up. "Formidable looking device. Fired beanbags, you say."

"Yes, milord."

"Six rounds in three seconds it says. Bloody hell. You could have a Glorious Twelfth shooting party with one of those things—open the shooting season proper." He nodded once. "Let's see. Cathedral groundskeeper then purchased the weapon for pigeon control. Gun was never used." He glanced at me. "Illegal to shoot pigeons then, I suppose."

"As it is now, milord."

"Silly regulation." He looked back at his screen, muttered some numbers, and fingered his desktop. "Ah. There. I was right. A weapon of that make, model, description, and serial number is among the acquisitions of the Royal Diane Devon & Cornwall Force Museum. You know it? Fore Street next to St. Mary Arches?"

"I know it." I got up to look at his screen and verify the bishop's statements. Indeed, the weapon in question resided at the Royal Diane Police Museum. I asked Dr. Koch if I could use his link.

"Feel free, inspector." He nodded and returned to his chair and beverage.

Clerical error. The serial number of the gun belonging to the bishop's office had been entered incorrectly when the gun was donated to the law enforcement museum back when its location had been at Middlemoor at the Police College. Because of Parker's inquiries, the curator at the museum had rechecked the serial number and had made the necessary correction on their site. While I was there, I checked on the bishop's alibi. At the time when Darcy Flanagan was killed, the Bishop of Exeter was indeed in Starcross being entertained by approximately eighty witnesses at the venerable Oak Meadow Golf Club. The soiree had taken place after a blustery day of attempting unsuccessfully to put little white balls into little round holes for the benefit of notorious anti-AB life organization, Natural Pride. The person writing the article was Alicia Pelletier of Starcross, secretary of the local NP chapter.

"Lord Koch, are you a member of Natural Pride?"

"Natural Pride? Heavens, no," he said from his chair. "Don't get me wrong, sir. It's a sound organization doing vital work." He turned in his chair and looked at me. "A view unlikely to be shared by artificial beings I suppose." He turned back, removed the peculiar hat, and placed it on the table next to his drink. "Too controversial, NP. Never do to join in my position. Eight percent of church members in the see are ABs. I have a responsibility." He shook his head. "Human imprints on animals, sir. God never intended kangaroos to play the banjo, sir, nor apes to sing before the royal family."

The Parker reference peaked my interest. The bishop shook his head ruefully, noted his glass was empty, and was about to ring for his butler when the door opened and Fedders appeared with a fresh highball. "Bloody gorillas," he muttered raising the fresh drink to his lips. He glanced back at me. "Conducting your current enquiry I understand."

"Yes, milord."

He turned back, muttering to himself. "How long until the future sees a bloody chipmunk as priest."

I decided to risk a question. "Milord, how would you feel about killing an amdroid."

"Hah! Me, sir? Kill one, sir? I'm a man of God, sir. How do you think I'd feel about murder."

"You consider it murder?"

He looked around again. "My objection to amdroids, inspector, is that in copying into an animal suit, as you put it, I believe the soul is copied in as well. Moving the soul in and out of a body is man's ability, sir, but it is *God's* work. If the only imprint of an individual is in an amdroid, bio, or mech, killing that imprint moves that soul out of the body. Again, sir, I say that is God's work. When men move souls I call it murder. Dread the future, sir. I do." He shook his head and looked down at the tiny pink umbrella in his fresh drink.

"I do," he repeated.

8

That night at home eating dinner—Walter had prepared an excellent pasty—I mentioned to Val my visit with the bishop. "Dr. Koch seemed quite adamant that every time we save an imprint off a dying soul or copy into a mech we're somehow violating God's plan. I'm glad I never had to bother with all of that nonsense."

"You mean religion?"

"Yes. My father thought I should choose for myself. I looked around, experimented some, but in the end decided to leave it all be."

Val lowered the paw she had been licking as she sat on the table and beheld me with those dazzling aqua eyes. "Yet last Christmas Eve," she said, "we went to St. Peters to listen to Christmas carols."

I thought on that, remembering the young male soloist who had moved me to tears with his haunting interpretation of "I Wonder As I Wander." Val had been on my lap.

"There wasn't a thought in my head that night," I said to her. "I was filled with beautiful sounds. Tremendous choir there."

"I remember," she purred as she walked over and sat by my shoulder, leaning against it.

"When that boy sang—you remember the one—when he sang that carol I didn't even hear or understand the words. For a moment I flashed on that terrible night those yobs came at me in London as I crossed Trafalgar Square. The knives, all that blood."

I glanced at Val and her eyes were closed. "When they found me and harvested my engrams I was all the way to Charing Cross Station. I don't remember getting there, but I do remember praying. It wasn't to some bearded gent in a long white nightshirt or even using a name. I asked whatever was out there to get me home to you. When I heard that boy sing, his beautiful voice reverberating from the walls of that ancient cathedral, I was filled with gratitude to still be alive, whatever suit I inhabited. How could that be wrong?"

"Harry," she said, "it doesn't appear to have bothered the entity to whom you prayed." She rubbed her head against my sleeve. "Nor the one to whom I prayed."

We sat like that for the twenty seconds it took for the telephone to ring. I got up, walked into the living room, and said "answer" to the tiny screen on the end table next to the couch. Val liked the screen phone because it was easy for her to ring up and talk with her friends. I didn't like it because any nit with wit enough to punch in our number got a free peek at me. That's why I usually used the old fashioned one in the kitchen. The screen came up and it was Shad. "Hello, old duck."

"Hey, Jaggs. Parker and I have been at the tower all this time trying to crack Lord Bishop Fauntleroy's alibi."

"Find a fissure?"

"Regrettably it's polished titanium. He was definitely at the golf club when Darcy Flanagan was murdered. Something else, though. Do you remember that site write-up on the banquet by one Alicia Pelletier?"

"I do."

"Parker read the whole thing including the mention of those valued Devon Natural Life members who, most regrettably, could not attend that day's festivities at Oak Meadow. Ready for two of those names?"

"Stun me, ducky."

"Sharissa Thule of Dawlish and Raymond Crowe of Exeter."

I stood there, stunned. Half of that duo shouldn't have been a surprise. Two out of three times, the person who finds the body is complicit in the killing. It was the second name, though, that was going to be a problem: Raymond Crowe, Chief Constable of Devon & Cornwall Constabulary. His name answered so many questions it almost outweighed the overwhelming problems.

"Jaggs? I thought that making Crowe our prime suspect would at least be worth a bugger or two. You should've heard what Matheson said." He held a wingtip in front of his bill. *"I quite blushed."*

377

"Send me a cruiser, Shad. I'll be right down."

"He said that, too. Oh, a minor hitch in the murder weapon. The FME is amending his report. It seems that the cause of death wasn't the beanbag."

"Oh?"

"That caused the broken bones and precipitated his nat in stasis to peg it, but doesn't explain how that one rib changed direction eighty degrees from the direction of impact and made it into Flanagan's heart."

"Shad, is it possible that Flanagan was conscious? That he knew his body in stasis was dead?"

"He was on continuous sync with his nat. It's possible."

I rang off and went to the hall to get my coat and hat. "Val," I called. "I have to go out. There's been a possible break in the Flanagan case."

"What is it?" she asked as she came up to me. I reached for the knob.

"I haven't sorted it all out in my mind yet, but our killer might very well be Chief Constable Crowe himself."

"Oh, dear."

I nodded. "Yes. Oh dear, indeed."

The cruiser was waiting for me as I left the house. I climbed in, the vehicle ascended into a clear night sky and turned east, sirens blaring, right-of-way signals interrupting nearby vehicles' GPS controls, my own set of Christmas lights flashing green as the cruiser cut across Pennsylvania-St. Thomas to St. James-Heavitree Corridor. As the cruiser streaked toward the tower the pieces began falling into place: Parliament Street, the evening off for Shad and me, Parker catching the call, the pressure of the chief constable's office to resolve the case, the media there and waiting for Parker to drop it, the missing case file on the Romila Kumar bio disappearance. It wasn't enough to bring charges, though. Finding the rest of our case was going to be the night's likely assignment.

9

Eight the next morning in the superintendent's office, dark circles and baggy eyes all around, including Detective Constable Fatima al-Fasi and Police Constable Duke Milburn both of Exeter CID. They had been the two on call for ABCD requests and had brought in Sharissa Thule just before midnight. Superintendant Matheson asked them to remain pending an additional arrest. Now the sun was up and hurtfully bright.

"I don't quite understand why we still need to be here, superintendent," DC al-Fasi said to Matheson. She was wearing an olive pantsuit with black turtleneck. The first impression she gave was of being young and petit—too much of both for police work. She had bobbed black hair, soft dark eyes, and no obvious makeup. It took awhile to notice the scars and calluses on her hands. She was one of those who worked out by smashing bricks and oak boards. "You have our full cooperation in making arrests," she said. "Simply tell us who you want nicked, hand us the warrant, and we'll bring him in." Milburn nodded, yawned, and nodded again. Middle twenties, brown eyes, buzzed brown hair, square-jawed, and muscular. He was in the usual Exeter blue except instead of a helmet his headgear consisted of a blue watch cap.

Matheson was seated behind his desk. He looked up at his liquid crystal ceiling. Images of little white clouds moved soundlessly across a deep blue sky. Shad and I were in chairs before superintendent's desk, al-Fasi and Milburn seated to our left. Parker occupied his usual seat in the WC. Matheson brought his gaze down until he was looking at DC al-Fasi. "It has taken us awhile to collect enough evidence to obtain an arrest warrant, detective." Milburn was steadily sliding down in his chair, his legs crossed at the ankles, the back of his head in search of rest.

"I apologize, sir," said DC al-Fasi reaching out a hand to awaken her constable.

"Never mind, detective. He'll awaken soon enough." He looked at her. "We have one last task before sending you all out to make this arrest. It will be necessary for you understand the case we've prepared against this individual."

"Why, sir?"

"Unless you understand the evidence, you may be reluctant to carry out the arrest."

She looked a bit impatient. "Reluctant or not, superintendent, we'll do our job," she replied off-handedly as she reached out and jabbed Milburn, barely getting his eyelids to crack open. "Who is the bloke?" she asked in the midst of a barely stifled yawn of her own.

"Chief Constable Crowe."

Milburn almost slid out of his chair. Like a jack-in-the-box he jumped back to an upright seated position. "Blimey," he said. He looked at DC al-Fasi who was looking back with very wide eyes, upraised dark brows, and an open mouth.

She faced Matheson, her eyes still wide, all thoughts of sleep banished. "We'd best see that evidence, then."

Matheson pointed at the wall he was facing. "If you'll turn your chairs about." Except for Shad, we turned our chairs around. Shad simply jumped up on the back of his chair and faced the image of the Biograph Theater. The superintendent said to the toilet door, "Very well, Parker."

The image of the Biograph faded and was replaced by Alicia Pelletier's article on the Oak Meadow Golf Club banquet.

"Chief Constable Crowe was scheduled to be at the special golf tourney in Starcross on the day Flanagan died," said Parker. "Instead he was registered under a false name at the Royal Clarence Hotel. Did you know the Clarence was England's first hotel?"

"The witnesses, Parker," Matheson urged.

The image switched to a security video of two fellows behind a counter facing a bewhiskered fellow in civilian clothes, a large suitcase at his feet.

"Desk clerk and office manager at the Clarence, sir. Chief Crowe and Ms. Thule have been meeting there once or twice a week since last July. The hotel staff pretend they don't recognize him behind that phony beard, but they all know who it is."

"The customer's always right," said Shad.

"Go on, Parker," I urged.

"Yes. Well, they check in, go up to their room, have a wee drop, get naked, put on some erotica, and then—"

"Yes," Matheson said with a pained expression on his face. "As tantalizing as this is—thank you for that mental image, Parker—that is not illegal." He waved a hand toward the image. "Besides, where's the mistress in this shot?"

"On the day Flanagan died, Chief Crowe checked into the Clarence alone. The hotel clerk says the chief appeared to have been drinking rather heavily."

I glanced at DC al-Fasi. We had her attention as well as her constable's. A new image appeared on the wall, that of the Clarence's northeast side. "This is from surveillance taken from St. Martin's across from Dingles Berry Farm store on Catherine," continued Parker. "This was an in-house camera not visible from the street or the hotel. This window is Chief Crowe's room that day." The image centered on a third floor window of the hotel and zoomed in. Despite the blustery cold winds that day, the window to that room was open at the bottom. The curtains weren't completely drawn; a shadowy figure was noticeable between them. Then came Pilot Officer Darcy Flanagan swooping in and thumping into the side of the casement, somehow landing upright on the ledge followed by some severe staggering. Flanagan appeared to be laughing uproariously.

"That bird's pissed," declared Milburn.

"Is there audio on this?" asked al-Fasi.

The sound increased along with a great deal of wind and background noise. When Parker suppressed the background, we could hear Flanagan laughing. He was looking in the window, pointing with his wing. *"Wot's this then!"* we heard him holler, another raucous laugh, then there was a *poomf* sound, and the pigeon was gone. The window quickly closed.

"The surveillance video doesn't cover Martins Lane below where Flanagan landed," said Parker. "The camera that covered Martins Lane had been tampered with." He ran the Dingles Berry Farm video again from when Flanagan pointed with his wing and laughed at the person on the other side of the window. In slow motion we saw a small puff of escaped gas, and Flanagan falling straight back from the window for only a couple of frames, a smeared red object against his right side.

"Sharissa Thule was below the window to collect the corpse and the flexible baton load," said Parker. "We have no video but we do have Sharissa Thule."

The image changed suddenly to the interior of Room 914. On one side of the table were Matheson and I. Shad squatted on the table's end. Seated on the other side was Sharissa Thule.

"Ray was obsessed with bird bios," said Sharissa. *"He was convinced the birds were seeking him out, ridiculing him, trying to do him harm. 'They're out to get me, Shariss,' he'd tell me. This one pigeon bio somehow found out about the trysts Ray and I were having at the Clarence. No matter what room we were in, that bird would be outside the window, marching around, laughing, and calling in to us. It was embarrassing."*

"Go on," prompted my image.

"Ray tried to grab that bird a number of times, but he was just too fast. Smelled of whisky, too. Horrible thing. I said to Ray, why don't we stay someplace else? That'd make sense, wouldn't it? But, no. No bloody amdroid was going to make Ray Crowe give up everything to the damned bios. Ray was once on the Honors List, you know. Then that awards ceremony happened—that gorilla thing?"

"Yes," said Matheson. *"DI Jaggers and I were there. And . . . uh . . . DC Parker."*

She frowned at me, then Shad, then cocked her head toward the loo. Shad and I nodded and she shrugged. *"Well, anyway, you know just what I mean. Getting embarrassed like that knocked Ray off center."* She pointed at her right temple. *"In the head Ray went a bit dotty. Then, after what that bird said . . ."*

"What was that?" Shad's image prodded.

"That bloody rude pigeon said he heard all about us down in the pubs. Ray and me! The whole hotel staff was talking all over the bleeding city!" Sharissa Thule was looking a bit dotty herself. *"All those pigeons, hotel staff, pub*

crawlers, who knew who else was talking? Bloody damned amdroids! I teach third form! What about my reputation?" She looked down and her hands were wringing the life out of a pink tissue. She took a deep breath and released it in a ragged sob. *"He wasn't dead, you know."*

"Who wasn't dead?" Shad's image asked.

"Flanagan. The pigeon bio. When I picked the bird up to put him in the tote he says, "What's all this then?" and he laughed. Sort of choking, but he laughed. I wanted to rush him to hospital, call the medimechs—something. But Ray he was right beside me in a minute. I held the bag out to him and said, 'He's still alive.' Ray looks in the tote and the bird looks Ray right in the eye and says, 'Darcy Flanagan is dead.' Just like that. Darcy Flanagan is dead."

She took another tissue, blew her nose, and slumped forward on her elbows. *"Ray he looks around, makes sure no one's about, reaches into the tote, wraps his big hands around the bird, and squeezes. Not long. Only a little squeeze and the bird was gone."*

The image froze and Parker said, "We talked to the FME and that little squeeze addresses the FME's concern about that rib bone's change in direction; the one that went through Flanagan's heart."

"When Chief Constable Crowe was detective chief superintendent," said Shad, "he and his former spouse Lurella lived in a modest place on Napier Terrace near the catacombs. That was where Pilot Officer Trainee William Foster of Pureledge, Ltd. was hit with insecticide. He still carries the scars of that assault and his natural body expired in stasis as a result of the attack."

"We have the sworn affidavit of Lurella Roberts, eyewitness to the assault against Foster. Years later," continued Parker, "when another pilot officer trainee named Romila Kumar was on break at the Clarence and disappeared, Crowe and a different mistress, one Kati Prien, were upstairs in the hotel having a tryst."

I looked across at Milburn. "We've located the former police records collator, Danielle Mintz, who Chief Crowe ordered to dispose of the Kumar case materials and cook the Heavitree mainframe to eliminate any mention of the case. It was she who dropped Kumar's dead bio into the

Exe. Judging by her description of the weapon, Kumar's bio was killed with the same gas gun that killed Flanagan. She cleaned the weapon and Chief Crowe returned it to the Royal Diane Museum where the curator has the chief on record as a weapons restorer. He has access to whatever he wants whenever he wants it. To get a reduced charge," I concluded, "Ms. Mintz has agreed to testify against the chief."

From deep within the superintendent's WC boomed Parker's dulcet tones, "On foot Sharissa Thule went to Parliament Street and tossed the body up against the southeast wall. She believed it might look like a flying accident. Whoever drove her there either drove between the camera surveillance photons or drove stealth."

Matheson looked at al-Fasi. "And the only vehicles authorized to use image neutralizing software in the county?"

She glanced at Milburn and nodded as she returned Matheson's gaze. "The only vehicles so authorized in the constabulary are the Major Incident Support Team stealth units under Chief Constable Crow's direct command."

The superintendent looked at me. "Getting away with it wasn't enough. He wanted to make a point. It's Artificial Being Emancipation Week and Chief Constable Crowe, valued member of Natural Life, wanted to make a point. He was the one who suggested giving Jaggers and Shad the evening off leaving Parker to catch the Flanagan case. Crowe notified the press to watch out for a really funny story at the High Street end of Parliament, waited fifteen minutes, then had the Exeter Station notify ABCD. The calls were made with a toss phone, but we have the phone records, and soon the phone thanks to Ms. Thule."

DC al-Fasi nodded to herself and looked at Matheson. "Did this Kumar's body die in stasis, as well, superintendent?"

"No. The fellow snapped mentally, crippled another bio, and had to be put in an institution. Poor chap's still there."

"The chief has a lot to answer for," she observed.

"He's a cop. A *chief*," said PC Milburn to DC al-Fasi. "The stink on us'll never go away."

"It might," said Shad as he jumped off the back of his chair and began pacing on the floor at a crisp waddle. "Devon & Cornwall Constabulary, Exeter CID, and ABCD together, brothers and sisters in blue: we go to the chief constable's office in the name of the law and take this crooked cop and murderer down in front of the nation-wide media."

Milburn frowned, thoughts playing across his face. "How you going to get the media in there with us?"

Superintendant Matheson arched his brows innocently and said, "It's just possible, constable, that someone without the permission of either Exeter Station or my office might provide a live feed to the event in HD widescreen." He looked at Shad.

"Complete with EnviroSound and narrated by a celebrity of some note," Shad added.

DC al-Fasi leaned forward and nodded at Shad. "Quite a package you've got there, sergeant. I hear you were the duck in all those telly adverts a couple years ago."

"He will be again, soon," I butted in. "The insurance corporation that was honored to have the duck mascot is bringing him back."

"Never did like that bloomin' lizard," she said. "Always talking like a yob." She looked at me and said, "Heard about you too, Inspector Jaggers. Took down some bad ones in London when you were with Metro." She looked at Matheson. "Superintendent, I hear you practically have to get killed to get in this unit. Everybody here, their natural bodies killed in the line of duty, right?"

"That's correct," he answered.

DC Fatima al-Fasi reached into her pocket and suddenly we could all detect her bio marker beacon. "I had to leave Weymouth, go clean out of Dorset, and do a little truth elongation to get into Exeter CID as a nat. Marker shields cost a bloody fortune at Bio Shack. Been in Exeter CID three years. Heard all the bio jokes, seen too many ABs getting what for and hard done by. I love police work and hate my job. If you'd take me, I'd be honored to serve alongside the likes of you chaps." She smiled really wide. "You blokes go after some really big game."

PC Duke Milburn drummed his fingertips on the arm of his chair. He let out a breath he had apparently been holding. "Well, I guess that just leaves the stink on me. I got no career in the cops after taking town a chief even if I get the bleeding Victoria Cross for it. Do you have to be an AB to be in ABCD?"

Matheson's brows arched. "No. It's not a requirement."

"It's either join the ABCD or hit the road sellin' bleedin' toilet brushes."

"I'll call London and see." Matheson shook his head. "We need to focus, people. Although I hate to discourage such an unexpected upturn in recruitment—I'd be pleased to have both of you—there's just one small matter you two need to get out of the way before climbing down to our rung of law enforcement: The arrest of Chief Constable Raymond Crowe. We aren't allowed to make arrests in ABCD."

Al-Fasi and Milburn stood. "Well, we'd best get cracking then," she said.

"Parker," I called. "We're ready to go."

The toilet flushed, the sink water ran, and Parker emerged drying his hands on about ten paper towels. Both al-Fasi and Milburn froze.

"Hi," said the gorilla.

They muttered something unintelligible in response somehow acknowledging Parker as lead on the enquiry.

"Shad," called Matheson, his face suddenly serious.

The duck turned, "Yes sir?"

"During the arrest, with the feed, try to . . ." He cocked his head gently toward Parker. "You know."

"No sweat, superintendent. It's all been taken care of." He looked at the gorilla. "Right, Parker?"

"All taken care of, sir."

"Really? I mean, *really* taken care of, Shad?"

"Water off a duck's back, boss."

"Indeed. And to think that only hours ago I was contemplating fleeing to the Himalayas disguised as a yak." Matheson reached forward to pick up his phone link. "Well then. I think I'll just ring up a few media fellows and give them each an exclusive anonymous tip about a great big arrest about to go down." He held up a pale green slip of paper. "Shad, this is the feed frequency?"

"Yes sir."

"Good. Good work, Parker," he said. "All of you," he said to Shad and me. To al-Fasi and Milburn he said, "Good hunting at Middlemoor."

The arrest went nearly as planned. Considering the disturbed lethal violence CC Crowe had exhibited on more than one occasion, attempting to resist arrest should have been expected, at least by Shad and myself. We were the most experienced detectives there. Arguably Parker was not prepared either, which didn't matter a whit. Parker *looked* prepared.

When our tiny band reached the second floor of Force Headquarters out at the Police College and entered the chief's outer office, DC al-Fasi simply led us past the chief's secretary and a couple of higher-ups patiently waiting in the outer office for their audiences. Milburn followed al-Fasi, Parker followed Milburn, and Shad followed Parker, his internal camera providing real time action to stations across the planet. I brought up the rear in time to see the chief constable rise from his desk to his full two hundred uniformed centimeters, an old fashioned telephone receiver in his hand, mouthing the word "What?" his attention on Fatima al-Fasi. She was cautioning him as his face began growing a most unhealthful shade of bluish-red.

"Raymond Crowe," said DC al-Fasi in a clear voice, "you are under arrest. You do not have to say anything, but it may harm your defense if you do not mention when questioned something you may later rely on in court—"

"You!" Crowe growled as he saw Parker standing to al-Fasi's right. *"You! Bloody you!"* With one massive hand he pulled his entire telephone free from its old-fashioned cord and threw it at Parker, who caught it in his right hand and just as quickly flung it back, bouncing it off the chief's head. Chief Crowe teetered on his heels for a split second, then dropped behind his desk.

"What did you see, DS Shad?" I asked immediately.

"I saw DC Parker physically assaulted by the suspect and forced to defend himself, inspector," Shad came back as he flew up onto the desk to get a down shot of the chief out colder than January lager, as the lads used to say back in old Puss-in-Boots Flight, wot, wot?

PC Milburn put in a call for paramedics, Shad put in a call for Matheson, and I put in a call for Val.

Three final notes on the Parliament Street enquiry. First, once Raymond Crowe was convicted of premeditated murder, DC Fatima al-Fasi and PC Duke Milburn applied for ABCD Interpol. London sent it up to Baghdad and Baghdad sent it down to London who sent it down to Exeter. The two of them would, in the opinion of Baghdad, be most valuable in ABCD Exeter and were assigned to that office.

Second, Shad decided to stay on. Agent Stanky worked a deal in which Shad would get a share of the residuals in exchange for taking a few weeks off from crime busting and spending that time training his replacement while a clone of his famous duck suit matured. When the first of the new adverts was on the telly all the reviewers said they couldn't tell the difference. Val and I could. There never could be another Guy Shad.

Finally, there was another award ceremony, and among the Devon & Cornwall law enforcement recipients was recently promoted Detective Sergeant Ralph Parker, ABCD Interpol, Exeter. HRH Princess Mehitabel herself insisted on presenting the awards, which had all of us in Matheson's office sweating beanbags—all of us but Shad and Parker. Shad said, "It's been taken care of. During the arrest of CC Crowe, did Parker disgrace himself and the office in front of the camera?"

We had to admit that he had not. Save for a bit of blood dribbled on the chief's carpet by the chief's own head, the carpet was as clean when we accompanied the chief on his stretcher out the tower entrance as when we entered his office. We had thousands of subsequent media camera shots as evidence, many of them showing DC Parker in rather conservative heroic poses.

Neither Shad nor Parker told Matheson what had changed. At the award ceremony in the Royal Diane Museum auditorium the next spring, as Princess Mehitabel pinned the gong—King's Police Medal for Distinguished Service—to

Parker's green sash, I looked down at my green-sashed duck partner and whispered to him, "Give. What did you do to Parker?"

"Madame Fifi's," he whispered back. "The amdroid stylist place on Parliament Street?"

"Yes?"

"Fake fur covered gorilla diapers, Jaggs. The fake fur blends right in with his coat. On special. Check it out. You should see the really cool stuff they have in there for cats, too. Fawkesmas Day comes but once a year."

Gorilla nappies.

I'm afraid the road to the future will be more trying for the lord bishop of Exeter than even he imagines.

♠ ♠ ♠

ACKNOWLEDGMENTS

The author cannot express adequately his gratitude to Dave Adcock, Attractions Development Officer, Economy and Tourism, Exeter City Council and especially the work his staff did in providing me answers concerning Exeter's Underground Passages and matters related to the city of Exeter during the Civil War. I would also like to thank Mary Bray of DAS Publications for steering me along more productive paths.

For both the tour and the information supplied I thank the Underground Passages people (Email: upassages@exeter.gov.uk), and especially Anthony Roach of "Underground Passages Visitor Guide" for their help. I would also like to thank Jannettja Longyear, long time resident of Exeter for her willingness to answer innumerable silly questions regarding everything from local slang to manners and for supplying books and other materials on Exeter. I thank her, as well, for being my sister. Thanks go as well to David Chappell for both leg and camera work, and to my niece Rachael Haynes for supplying a most valuable reference work. I would also like to thank Stanley Schmidt, Editor of *Analog Science Fiction And Fact*, for suggesting this volume (as well as catching numerous errors), and I would especially like to thank the readers of *Analog* for encouraging the writing of these tales through their letters and through their votes awarding two of these stories, "The Good Kill" and "Murder in Parliament Street", the Analytical Laboratory Awards for Best Novella, 2006 and 2007 respectively.

—*Barry B. Longyear*

♠ ♠ ♠